NIGHTSHADE

NIGHTSHADE

STEPHEN LEATHER

ISIS
LARGE PRINT
Oxford

First published in Great Britain 2013
by
Hodder & Stoughton,
An Hachette UK company

Published in Large Print 2013 by ISIS Publishing Ltd.,
7 Centremead, Osney Mead, Oxford OX2 0ES
by arrangement with
Hodder & Stoughton,
an Hachette UK Company

CIP data is available for this title from the British Library

ISBN 978–0–7531–9218–4 (hb)
ISBN 978–0–7531–9219–1 (pb)

Printed and bound in Great Britain by
T. J. International Ltd., Padstow, Cornwall

NIGHTSHADE

Nightingale shivered as he stared at the house. It was a neat semi-detached with a low wall around the garden and a wrought iron gate that opened onto a path leading to the front door. There was no garage, but half of the front lawn had been paved over as a parking space for a five-year-old Hyundai. Beyond the car was a path leading to the rear garden, which was how he planned to get into the house. It was after midnight and the streets were deserted. It was a cloudy night with only occasional glimpses of the moon overhead and the lights were off in pretty much all the houses in the street.

Nightingale eased open the gate, slipped inside and closed it behind him, then walked carefully down the path and around the side of the house. He stopped and peered through the kitchen window until he was sure that there was no one there, then walked to the kitchen door. He tried the handle and wasn't surprised to find that it was locked. He'd brought a makeshift burglary kit with him including tape, a glass cutter and a screwdriver but he didn't want to start breaking glass unless he had no choice.

There was a large glass sliding door that led into the sitting room. The curtains were drawn but there was enough of a gap to see that the room was in darkness. He pulled on a pair of grey surgical gloves, checked the lock at the side of the door and smiled to himself as he took out the screwdriver. It took him only seconds to force the screwdriver into the gap between the door and the wall and pop the lock.

He gently slid the door open, pushed the curtain aside and stepped into the room. He stopped and listened for a full minute, then slowly slid the door closed. There was a sofa and an armchair and a glass and chrome coffee table facing a 42-inch LCD television. He went over to the TV and pressed the back of his hand against the screen. It was cold, so the family had been in bed for some time. In his pocket was a small can of starting fluid that he'd bought from a garage in south London. He'd turned up in his MGB and the mechanic who'd sold him the fluid had assumed that Nightingale was having trouble getting the old car started on the cold mornings and suggested he bring it in for a service. Nightingale said he would have a go himself but that if the problem continued he'd book it in. It was premium starting fluid, which meant that it was sixty per cent diethyl ether, perfect for giving a boost to a reluctant engine, but also a very efficient way of putting someone into a deep sleep.

He tiptoed across the sitting room and into the hallway, listened again and then headed up the stairs, keeping close to the wall to minimise any squeaking

2

boards. When he reached the landing he stopped and listened again. There were four doors. There was one to the rear of the house that he assumed was the little girl's bedroom. The door immediately to his left was open. The bathroom.

He guessed that the bedroom facing the street would be the master bedroom where her parents were sleeping. The door was open slightly and Nightingale tiptoed over to it, breathing shallowly.

He pushed it open. The woman was closest to him, sleeping on her side. Her husband was on his back, snoring softly. Nightingale took a handkerchief from his pocket, twisted the top off the can and soaked the material with the fluid. He tiptoed across the carpet and held the ether-soaked handkerchief under the woman's nose for the best part of a minute, then draped it over her face.

He prepared a second handkerchief and did the same to the husband.

When he was satisfied that they were both unconscious, he tiptoed out of the room and pulled the door closed behind him. His heart was racing and he stood where he was for a full minute, composing himself, before soaking a third handkerchief with ether and pushing open the door to the little girl's bedroom.

She was lying on her back, her blonde hair spreading out across the pillow like a golden halo, breathing slowly and evenly. Nightingale closed the door quietly, wincing as the wood brushed against the carpet. When he turned back to the bed, her eyes were open and she was staring right at him.

"You're Jack Nightingale, aren't you?" she said.

Nightingale said nothing.

"You've come to kill me, haven't you?"

CHAPTER
ONE

Three Weeks Earlier

Jack Nightingale woke up, stretched, and lit a Marlboro. As he lay on his back and blew smoke rings up at his ceiling, he ran through what lay ahead of him that day. He had to explain to a middle-aged woman that the father of her two children had a second family up in Birmingham and that on the nights he told her he was away on business he was actually with them. He had to spend the afternoon in a pub, watching a barmaid who a brewery was convinced was ripping them off to the tune of a grand a week by serving sandwiches she had made herself and not the ones the brewery provided, and in the evening he had to follow an unfaithful wife. Nightingale knew the woman was being unfaithful because he'd already followed her to a hotel where she'd spent two hours in a room with a co-worker. The cuckolded husband had read Nightingale's report but now he wanted photographs. So far as Nightingale was concerned photographs would just be rubbing salt into the wound, but if that's what the client wanted Nightingale was happy enough to provide them — at a price.

He finished the cigarette, stubbed it out in a crystal ashtray on his bedside table and looked at his watch. It was just after eight o'clock. He had set his mobile to silent, so he checked the screen to see if he'd received any calls. He hadn't. He put down the phone and considered lighting another cigarette, but he decided to shave and shower instead. He padded to the bathroom. So far as Nightingale was concerned it was going to be a typical day, business as usual. It was only in the movies that private detectives got involved in car chases and shootouts or met steely-eyed blondes packing heat. Most of Nightingale's work involved following sad, lonely and embittered people on behalf of sad, lonely and embittered clients. But it paid the bills and kept him off the streets. Actually that wasn't true — much of what he did involved being in the street, which is why he favoured comfortable Hush Puppies as his footwear and generally wore a raincoat.

He looked at himself in the bathroom mirror as he shaved. He bared his teeth and wondered how much teeth-whitening would cost. Nightingale was a smoker and coffee-drinker and both addictions played havoc with his enamel.

As he climbed into the shower he had no idea that eight children were going to die that day, nor that their deaths were going to change his life for ever. The man who would kill the children was sitting at his kitchen table cleaning his shotgun as Nightingale rinsed the shampoo from his hair. His name was Jimmy McBride and he was a farmer with a smallholding near

Berwick-upon-Tweed, the most northern town in England.

McBride had made himself a cup of Nescafé and two slices of toast and he kept breaking off from cleaning the shotgun to drink and eat. McBride had a few hundred cattle, a decent number of chickens and almost fifty acres that supplied new potatoes to the Morrisons supermarket chain. McBride lived alone on the farm. He'd never married, and once he'd reached the age of forty he had resigned himself to living a solitary life. He did most of the work on the farm himself, though when the potatoes needed harvesting he bought in a team of Polish contractors. They worked hard, the Poles, and they never complained about the weather or the long hours.

McBride had owned the gun since he was a teenager and used it to keep the rabbit population down. Like most farmers, McBride hated rabbits. They weren't cuddly cartoon characters, they were parasites that needed to be kept under control, and the best way to do that was a blast from a shotgun followed by several hours in a casserole with onions, carrots, served with new potatoes pulled straight from the ground.

There was a box of shotgun shells on the table next to his toast. There had originally been 250 in the box but he'd bought them two years previously and there were only about a hundred left. That would be more than enough. On the chair by his side was the canvas bag he always took with him when he went out rabbit-shooting. It was big enough to hold fifty cartridges, a flask of whisky-laced coffee and a pack of sandwiches.

McBride filled the bag with cartridges, let himself out of his farmhouse, and walked across a ploughed field, whistling softly to himself.

It took him less than half an hour to reach the school. There was a large sign at the entrance that said "Welcome" in a dozen languages. The wrought iron gate was closed but not locked and McBride pushed it open. He already had two cartridges in the breech and as he walked across the playground he snapped the twin barrels into place.

A bald man in a grey suit opened the door that led to the main school offices. The deputy headmaster. Simon Etchells. Etchells frowned as he saw the shotgun in McBride's hands. "Excuse me, can I help you?" he called.

McBride continued to walk across the playground.

"You can't bring a gun onto school premises!" shouted the deputy headmaster. "I really must ask you to leave!"

McBride shot the man in the face without breaking stride. The man fell to the ground, his face and chest a bloody mess. Three pigeons that had been sitting on the roof scattered in a flurry of wings.

He walked into the main school building. The administration offices were to the left, and beyond them was the canteen. McBride turned to the right. There were classrooms leading off both sides of the corridor. There were posters and artwork on the walls, including photographs of all the pupils with their names handwritten underneath, and above the doors in multicoloured capital letters were the names of the teachers.

McBride ignored the first two classrooms. He was humming quietly to himself. Mozart. He seized the handle of the door to his left and opened it slowly. As he stepped into the room the teacher turned to look at him. He frowned and lowered the book he was holding. There were thirty-two boys and girls sitting at tables, sharing textbooks. A few of the children were frowning but most of them were more quizzical than worried.

Grace Campbell was sitting at the table on the left of the room, between a red-haired boy and a plump girl with pigtails. McBride swung the gun up and pulled the trigger. Grace took the full force of the blast in her chest and she fell back as blood sprayed across the wall behind her.

The sound was deafening and the air was thick with acrid, choking cordite, but no one said anything. The children stared open-mouthed at McBride, unable to believe what they'd seen. The teacher, a middle-aged man with a receding hairline and a greying moustache, backed away, his hands up as if hoping to ward off the next shot.

McBride turned on his heel and walked out of the classroom. As he reloaded and headed across the corridor the screams began.

As McBride opened the door to the second classroom, the teacher was standing facing his class and shouting at them to be quiet. The children were talking among themselves but they immediately fell silent when they saw McBride and his shotgun. The teacher held up a hand, palm outward, as if he was a policeman stopping traffic. "You can't come in here," said the teacher firmly, in the voice that he used to keep unruly pupils in order.

McBride brought his gun to bear on a girl sitting by the window. Her name was Ruth Glazebrook and she had arrived at school that day with invitations to her eleventh birthday party. She was only inviting girls because she still thought that boys were yucky and besides, her mother had said that she could only invite six friends because they were going to go to McDonald's and money was tight. McBride pulled the trigger and Ruth's face disintegrated and she slammed against the wall.

The teacher staggered backwards and he tripped over a desk and fell to the floor before scrambling on all fours and hiding behind his desk.

The children sitting at Ruth's table stared at McBride in horror but the rest of the pupils ran to the back of the room. McBride raised the shotgun to his shoulder again, sighted on another girl and pulled the trigger. The girl's name was Emily Smith and she died clutching the invitation that Ruth had given her just minutes earlier. McBride walked out of the classroom, ejecting the two spent cartridges. He slotted in two fresh ones as he walked to the next classroom.

CHAPTER
TWO

Phillippa Pritchard had heard the first shot but it had
been in the playground and she'd assumed that it had
been a car backfiring. The second shot had been closer
but she still hadn't realised what it was until the
screaming had started. The third and fourth shots
followed in quick succession and the thirty-four
children in her class all looked at her fearfully, waiting
to be told what to do. The problem was, Phillippa had
absolutely no idea what to tell them. She had been a
teacher for almost twenty years, but nothing had
prepared her for the sound of gunshots and the
screaming of terrified children.

There was only one way out of the classroom and
that was through the door that led to the corridor.
Phillippa looked at the windows. They led out to the
playing fields at the rear of the school. "Everyone over
to the windows, quickly!" she said. The children looked
at her, too shocked to move. She clapped her hands.
"Come on, this is a fire drill. Let's pretend that the
corridor is filled with smoke and that we have to escape
through the windows." She walked quickly over to the
nearest window. It was the sash type with a catch. She
took a chair from one of the boys and stood on it. She

had to stand on tiptoe to reach the catch and it was stiff but she pushed hard and forced it to the side. She stepped down off the chair and pushed the lower pane up. "Right, come on!" she said, pushing a table close to the window. "Onto the chair and then onto the table and through the window. Come on, quickly!"

She heard a metallic click in the corridor and her stomach lurched as she realised what it was. The shotgun had been reloaded.

"Come on everybody, let's do this as quickly as possible!" shouted Phillippa, fighting to keep the fear out of her voice. The first pupil was on the table, looking nervously out of the window. It was Jacob Gray, a timid boy who had a tendency to blush when spoken to. "Jeremy, jump, go on."

"It's too high, miss," he said, his voice trembling.

"Just do it, Jacob, you're holding everyone up." The door handle turned slowly. Phillippa turned to look at the door, her heart in her mouth. The door opened and she saw the twin barrels of a shotgun followed by a green Wellington boot.

"Miss, I'm scared," said Jacob.

"Just jump, now!" shouted Phillippa.

Phillippa gasped as the middle-aged man stepped into the classroom and raised the shotgun. He was grey-haired and ruddy-cheeked, as if he spent a lot of time outdoors. It was his eyes that chilled Phillippa. They were blank, almost lifeless. There was no tension in the man, no anger, no emotion at all. He just stood in the doorway looking slowly around the room, his finger on the trigger.

12

Phillippa took a step towards the man. She was more terrified than she'd ever been in her whole life but she knew that she had to protect the children. She put up her hands the way she'd try to calm a spooked horse and tried to maintain eye contact. "You need to leave," she said as calmly as she could. "You need to go now. You're frightening the children."

The man didn't look at her. He continued to scan the room, the twin barrels of his shotgun matching his gaze.

"You have to go," said Phillippa, more forcibly this time, but still the man paid her no attention.

Jacob fell through the open window and yelped as he hit the ground outside. Phillippa took a quick look over her shoulder. Two girls were on the table and a third stood on the chair, looking anxiously at the man with the gun. Phillippa made a shooing motion with her hand then turned to look at the gunman.

He had raised his shotgun to his shoulder and Phillippa gasped as she saw his finger tighten on the trigger. He was aiming it at Paul Tomkinson, one of her favourite pupils, always eager to please and one of the first to put up his hand, no matter what the question being asked. She opened her mouth to scream but before the sound could leave her lips there was a deafening bang and the shotgun kicked in his hand. The children screamed and scattered like sheep to the back of the classroom. Phillippa realised that there was a child lying on the ground, what was left of his head touching the wall. Blood and gobs of brain were dripping down the wall.

Phillippa covered her mouth with trembling hands. The two girls on the table threw themselves through the window, screaming.

The man swung the shotgun in Phillippa's direction and her stomach turned liquid. She felt her bladder open and a warm wetness spread around her groin but she was barely aware of it. Her legs began to shake uncontrollably and she mentally began to run through the Lord's Prayer, Our Father, who art in Heaven, and then the shotgun swung away from her and roared again. A girl fell, her chest and face a bloody mess. Phillippa realised it was Brianna Foster, one of the quietest girls in the class, so passive that Phillippa had to constantly keep an eye on her to make sure that she wasn't being bullied.

Brianna lay on the floor like a broken doll as blood pooled around her. The gunman turned back to look at Phillippa and for the first time they had eye contact. He broke the shotgun and ejected the two cartridges. They flew through the air and clattered onto the floor.

The man groped in his haversack with his right hand, slotted in two fresh cartridges and snapped the weapon closed, all the time keeping his eyes fixed on Phillippa. He brought the shotgun up so that it was pointing at her chest and the breath caught in her throat. She was sure that she was going to die there in the classroom, in front of her pupils. Time seemed to freeze and all she could think of was that she would never see her husband again. Her dear darling Clive. She'd kissed him on the cheek when he'd left the house that morning and she'd said that she loved him and it

14

gave her a small feeling of satisfaction that if they were her last words to him then at least he would know that he was loved. For the first time she saw something approaching emotion in his eyes. Not anger, not hatred, not contempt, but something approaching regret. She saw him swallow and then he turned around and walked out of the classroom.

CHAPTER
THREE

The first Armed Response Vehicle pulled up in front of the school with a squeal of brakes. A Firearms Officer piled out of the BMW while the driver unlocked the gun cabinet and pulled out two G36 carbines. Both men were wearing black uniforms and bulletproof vests and had Glock pistols holstered on their hips.

There were more than a hundred pupils gathered in front of the railings. "What the bloody hell are they gawping at?" asked Sergeant Mickey Rawlings, though the question was rhetorical. There were a dozen adults among the crowd, presumably the teachers. Rawlings walked over and raised his hand. "Who's in charge?" he shouted.

A middle-aged man in a tweed jacket with black leather patches on the elbows walked over. "The head is off today and her deputy is . . ." He grimaced and pointed to a body in the playground, about fifty feet away.

"What happened here?" asked Rawlings.

"There's a man in the school with a shotgun. He shot Mr Etchells and he's walking through the school shooting children."

16

"Wait here," said the sergeant, then he raised both hands above his head. "Would you all please move down the road!" he shouted. "I need you to all move well away from the school, now!" No one moved and the sergeant wished that he could do what they did in the movies and fire his gun into the air, but he knew that would be the quickest way off the force. He took a deep breath and shouted at the top of his voice. "Everybody move down the road now!" he yelled. "There's a man in there with a gun and you're all at risk."

A second ARV arrived and squealed to a halt. The teachers started herding the children down the road. The sergeant turned to the teacher next to him. "You're sure it was a shotgun?"

The teacher nodded. An armed policeman ran over from the newly arrived ARV. He was Ricky Gray, a relative newcomer to the unit but an excellent shot and unflappable under pressure. He nodded at Rawlings.

"Any idea how many shots have been fired?" Rawlings asked the teacher.

"Five. Six maybe."

"Was it a double-barrelled shotgun or a pump action?" asked Rawlings.

The teacher frowned. "I'm not sure."

"Did it have two barrels? Or did it just have one?"

The teacher nodded. "Two."

The two ARV drivers hurried over to Rawlings. The driver of Rawlings' car was holding two carbines and he handed one to Rawlings. His name was Vic Rhodes and he'd worked with Rawlings for more than five years.

Four was the minimum for an emergency entry but Rawlings would have been happier with six. As if a fairy godmother was granting him wishes, a third ARV came roaring down the road.

"And what does he look like?" Rawlings asked the teacher.

"Like a farmer. Waterproof coat and green Wellington boots."

"How old?"

"Forty. Fifty maybe. I didn't hang around to get a good look."

Rawlings patted Rhodes on the shoulder. "Call in a sit-rep, Vic," he said, then jogged over to the car. Sergeant Tom Chisholm climbed out of the front passenger seat and nodded at Rawlings. Though he was the same rank as Rawlings he had more experience and he naturally assumed the role of Op Com — operational commander.

"There's another car on the way," said Chisholm. He nodded at the school building. "Heard anything?"

"Five shots. Maybe six. There's one casualty in the playground." Rawlings pointed at the body of the deputy headmaster.

A shot rang out from the school and the policemen flinched. "Make that seven," said the officer who was accompanying Chisholm, twenty-two-year-old Neil Sampson.

"Okay, we're going straight in," said Chisholm. "There are kids at risk, I'm not waiting for a senior officer."

A police van was heading towards them. Sampson handed Chisholm his G36. "Let's get in there," said Chisholm. "If there's a bloody inspector on that bus we'll be out here all day."

The six men ran towards the school entrance, cradling their carbines.

CHAPTER
FOUR

As the armed policemen raced across the playground to the main school building, McBride was walking down the corridor towards the school's gymnasium. In the classroom behind him was another dead girl, shot at point blank range while the rest of the pupils screamed in terror. The double doors leading to the gym were panelled with glass and McBride could see a balding teacher in a dark blue tracksuit peering at him, his hands shading his eyes.

McBride raised his shotgun and the teacher turned and ran away from the doors. McBride stopped, took a long, deep breath, exhaled slowly, and pushed the doors open. Several of the children screamed but most of them just stared at him open-mouthed. The teacher pushed his way through the children to a fire exit. He pushed the metal bar that opened the door and shouted for the pupils to get out.

McBride swept his shotgun from side to side, then settled on a dark-haired boy with girlish features who was standing with his hands over his eyes, peering through his splayed fingers. McBride stepped forward with his left leg, raised the butt to his shoulder, braced himself for the recoil and pulled the trigger.

The boy's white T-shirt burst into a vivid crimson and he fell backwards, his hands still over his face.

CHAPTER
FIVE

Sergeant Chisholm flinched at the gunshot. He turned to look at Rawlings, who was to his left. Chisholm grimaced and pointed straight ahead. They were moving down the corridor, checking the classrooms one by one and making sure that they were clear. They had found two dead girls in a room on the right of the corridor, and another dead girl in a room to the left. They were just about to move into the next room on the left and through the open door they could already see a dead boy sprawled on the floor.

Normal procedure would be to continue checking the rooms as they moved down the corridor, but there was only one gunman and the shot had come from immediately ahead of where they were. The gymnasium. Chisholm pointed straight ahead and Rawlings was already moving. They ran quickly, followed by their four colleagues, guns at the ready.

Their footfalls echoed off the tiled walls as they ran at full pelt but they were still twenty metres from the gymnasium doors when they heard the second shot.

CHAPTER
SIX

The teacher was screaming at the children to get out, standing with his back to McBride with his arms outstretched to the side as if he could shield them with his body. The second boy that McBride had shot in the gym lay twitching on the floor under a basketball hoop. The boy was missing most of his head and the chest was a bloody mess but the legs continued to beat a tattoo on the wooden floor and his right hand was trembling.

"Out, come on, get a move on!" shouted the teacher. The pupils didn't need any urging — they were all terrified, and pushed and shoved as they forced their way through the fire exit.

McBride calmly ejected the two spent cartridges and slotted in two fresh ones. His eyes were stinging from the cordite and his ears were ringing.

He walked over to a wall and slowly sat down. He used his left foot to prise the Wellington boot off his right.

He looked over at the fire exit. Most of the children were gone. The teacher was still standing with his arms outstretched, urging on the stragglers.

The doors to the gymnasium burst open and two men with black carbines appeared, crouching low and swinging their weapons around. One moved to the left and the other to the right, then two more stepped through the doors. All four were dressed in black, with Kevlar body armour and black ceramic helmets.

"Put down the gun or we will shoot!" shouted Chisholm. All four officers had their weapons aimed at McBride. Two more armed officers appeared and all six men fanned out across the gym, their guns trained on McBride's chest.

"It's all right, boys, there's no need for that," said McBride.

"Put the gun down!" yelled the sergeant at the top of his voice. His finger tightened on the trigger of his carbine.

In one smooth motion McBride swung the shotgun around and propped the stock on the floor. He lifted his right foot and slipped his big toe onto the trigger.

CHAPTER
SEVEN

Sergeant Chisholm realised what the man was about to do. He lowered his carbine and began to move forward but he had only taken two steps when the shotgun exploded and the man's head disappeared in a shower of blood and brains that splattered across the climbing bars. The sound was deafening in the combined space and the sergeant's ears were ringing.

Neil Sampson groaned and then threw up, bending double as his chest heaved and vomit splattered over the polished wooden floor.

Sergeant Rawlings went over to the body, picked up the shotgun and broke it open, ejecting the cartridges and placing it back on the ground. "Weapon is clear."

"Let control know what's happened," said Chisholm. "Tell them to send SOCO in."

Sampson dropped down onto his knees and threw up again. The sergeant went over to three officers who were standing around one of the boys that had been shot. Ricky Gray was crying silently as he stared down at the body. The sergeant put a hand on his shoulder. "Back outside, Ricky," he said. "There's nothing more for us to do here."

"Why would anyone kill a kid?"

"Who knows?" said Chisholm. "Come on, outside." Rawlings walked over to the second boy but even from a distance it was obvious that he was stone cold dead.

The officer shook away the sergeant's hand. He was still holding his carbine, his finger inside the trigger guard.

"Stand down, Ricky. Come on."

"Fucking bastard!" The officer turned on his heel and walked across the gym to the dead man. It looked as if he was about to shoot the corpse but instead he drew back his right leg and began to violently kick the body, cursing and swearing with every blow.

Chisholm hurried over and grabbed Ricky's arm. He pulled him away from the body. "Get a fucking grip, will you. That body's got to be post mortemed and there'll be hell to pay if it's black and blue."

"He shot kids. Who the fuck walks around a school shooting kids?"

"Pull yourself together, Ricky. If the top brass see you like this you'll be off the squad."

Ricky nodded and took a deep breath to steady himself. "Okay."

The sergeant released his grip on the officer's arm and jerked a thumb at the door. "Get back to the vehicle and take a chill pill. The day you start making it personal is the day when you go back on the beat. Got it?"

"Got it, sir." He headed out of the door, passing two uniformed officers. One was a superintendent. Chisholm looked down at the body of the shooter and had to fight the urge to kick it. Ricky had been wrong to lose his temper but what he'd said was bang on. What sort of nutter would walk around a school shooting kids?

The superintendent walked up to Chisholm and nodded curtly. "Are you and your men okay?" he asked.

Chisholm appreciated the concern and nodded. "All good. No shots fired."

The superintendent smiled tightly. "Thank heaven for small mercies," he said. "The way the press is just now they'd be trying to make it out that we shot the kids." He grimaced. "This is a mess." He gestured at the shooter's body. Blood was still pooling around it. "Any idea who he is?"

Chisholm shook his head. "Looks like a farmer."

"Did he say anything before he topped himself?"

"Something about it being all right and there was no need for it."

The superintendent frowned. "Need for what?"

"I think he meant there was no need for us to shoot him because he was going to do it himself."

The superintendent sighed. "Why didn't he do that in the first place? Why kill the kids? I'd understand it if he was looking for suicide by cop, but if he was planning to kill himself anyway he could have done us all a favour and thrown himself under a train."

Chisholm scratched his neck. "CID been informed?"

"Yes, but taking their own sweet time, as usual." The superintendent looked at his watch. "SOCO are on their way, too." He looked around the gym, flinching at the bodies of the two children. "My kids are about their age," he said. "Why would anyone do that?"

Chisholm didn't say anything. He knew that the question was rhetorical.

The superintendent noticed the vomit on the floor. "What happened there?"

"Young Neil. I sent him outside."

The superintendent squared his shoulders. "Right, keep this area secure until SOCO get here. I'll be outside, the press'll be over us like a rash."

CHAPTER
EIGHT

On Thursday, three days after the shootings in Berwick, the case came knocking on Jack Nightingale's door. He had his feet up on his desk with a copy of the *Sun* in his lap when Jenny told him there was a client on the way up. Nightingale frowned. "There wasn't anything in the diary."

"There's nothing in the diary except blank pages," said Jenny. "And your only pressing task is the *Sun*'s Sudoku."

"For your information I've finished the Sudoku, I'm on the crossword now. What's his name?"

"He didn't give me his name. He said he'd explain when he got here."

"He could be a nutter."

"Nutters don't tend to phone first," she said.

"Did he say what he wanted?"

"He said it was a case but he wanted to talk to you in person. He sounded all right, Jack. No need to get paranoid."

"Just because I'm paranoid doesn't mean they're not out to get me," he said.

"Who?"

Nightingale grinned. "I was joking," he said. They heard the door to the outer office open. "Frisk him first, though, just to be on the safe side."

Jenny shook her head and went to greet the visitor. Nightingale heard muffled voices, then Jenny showed a middle-aged man in a dark blazer into the room. He was grey-haired, tall and thin, with the bearing of a former soldier. He had a slight limp and had a walking stick in his left hand. He extended his right hand and flashed Nightingale a tight smile. "My name's McBride. Danny McBride."

Nightingale shook the man's hand and waved him to a chair.

"Would you like a tea or a coffee?" asked Jenny. McBride smiled and shook his head and Jenny left the room, closing the door behind her.

"How can I help you, Mr McBride?" asked Nightingale.

"I'm sure you heard about the children who died up in Berwick," he said.

"The ones that were shot by that psycho?" said Nightingale. "Of course."

McBride nodded. "That psycho was my brother. James. Jimmy."

Nightingale frowned. He wasn't sure what to say. "Sorry for your loss?" didn't seem appropriate.

McBride took a deep breath and exhaled slowly. "I want you to find out what happened," he said. "I know what the police think, and I read what was in all the papers. But I want to know the truth, Mr Nightingale. I want to know what happened."

Nightingale ran a hand through his hair and rubbed the back of his neck. "I don't understand what you mean," he said. "The case was closed. Your brother shot the children and then killed himself, didn't he?"

McBride nodded.

"So it was what the police call murder-suicide. An open and shut case."

"I don't think anyone knows the real reason my brother did what he did. I want someone impartial to look into it. Someone who can look into it with an open mind."

"You think the police got it wrong?"

McBride shrugged. "I'm not sure what to think. But he was a quiet man, always kept himself to himself. Spent most of the time working on his farm. But he wasn't a bad man, Mr Nightingale."

"But you believe your brother killed those children?"

"There's no doubt about that, is there? He shot himself in the gym. The school had CCTV and there's footage of him with the gun."

"So what is it you want me to do? Nothing I can find out is going to change things. Those children are dead and your brother killed them."

"I want to know why, Mr Nightingale. My brother loved kids. He was always great with my sons."

Nightingale nodded slowly. "How old are your boys, Mr McBride?"

McBride's eyes hardened a fraction. "Ten and eight," he said quietly.

"They weren't at the school, were they?"

McBride shook his head slowly. "We live in a different town. Alnwick."

"And he was always okay with your children?"

"Of course." He tilted his head on one side and frowned. "What are you suggesting?"

"I'm not suggesting anything. I'm just trying to build a picture of your brother, that's all."

"My brother was great with kids. My boys spent a lot of time on the farm with Jimmy and he never so much as raised his voice to them. Have you got children, Mr Nightingale?"

Nightingale shook his head.

"Kids can try the patience of a saint at times, especially boys. It's only now that I've got kids of my own I realise the hell that Jimmy and I put our parents through. But Jimmy was great with my boys. He loved kids, Mr Nightingale. He sponsored a couple of kids out in Africa and every Christmas he went around the local hospitals and children's homes dressed as Father Christmas, giving out toys."

Nightingale nodded thoughtfully. "So why do you think he did it?"

"I don't know, Mr Nightingale. That's what I want you to find out. I've got money. Jimmy left the farm and everything to me. He had more than a quarter of a million pounds in the bank and it's all mine now. At least it will be when the solicitors have finished whatever it is that they're doing. So I can pay you, Mr Nightingale. Money isn't an issue. I just want to know why Jimmy turned into a serial killer."

"Spree killer," said Nightingale.

"Sorry, what?" McBride frowned in confusion.

"Serial killings happen at different times," explained Nightingale. "When the killings occur at the same time, it's called a spree." He sighed. "Look, Mr McBride, sometimes people just snap. People can do terrible things. Maybe something had pushed your brother over the edge and he just wanted to hit back."

"At children?"

"Maybe kids had been making his life a misery. Maybe they'd been, I don't know, vandalising the farm. Hurting his animals. I don't know."

"I spoke to the local police. Jimmy hadn't reported anything to them. And he would have mentioned it to me."

"Okay, then maybe he just went crazy. People sometimes just lose it. Schizophrenia. Depression."

"Jimmy was a bit depressed, but you find me a farmer who doesn't bitch and moan. It goes with the job. But he wasn't crazy. My brother was definitely not crazy."

As they spoke Nightingale began to recall more details of the case. It had been on the front pages of the tabloid newspapers and led the TV news since it had happened. "What about the devil-worship stuff? The police said they found all sorts of stuff on his computer. Videos of animal sacrifice, end of the world stuff."

"My brother didn't have an internet connection, Mr Nightingale. He used his computer to do the farm accounts and that was it. My kids have been nagging him for months to get online so they could Facebook him but he couldn't be bothered. He doesn't even have a TV on the farm. He's a big reader." McBride forced a smile. "Was a big reader, I mean."

"The police definitely said they found Satanic information on his computer. I remember reading that."

"I'm not arguing with that," said McBride. "I'm just saying it wasn't Jimmy that put it there. And that's why I came to you. I Googled and it said you were a bit of an expert in things like that."

"Things like what?"

"You know. Black magic. Possessions. You've a reputation for working on cases that are a bit out of the ordinary."

"So what do you want me to do, Mr McBride?"

"I want you to find out why he did it. That's all I want. I want to know the real reason he took his shotgun to that school and went on a killing spree. Because it wasn't about devil-worship, I know that for a fact."

"If he was a devil-worshipper he'd hardly advertise the fact, would he? And you must have seen the pictures in the papers. There was a whole Satanic altar thing in his barn. With blood and offerings and all sorts of shit."

McBride nodded. "Sure, I saw the pictures. And I saw the TV coverage, too." He leant forward so his face was just inches from Nightingale's. "But here's the thing. I went to see Jimmy, two days before the killings. I was in that barn with him. And none of that stuff was there then. None of it."

Nightingale frowned and stared at McBride for several seconds without speaking.

"You heard what I said?" said McBride.

"I'm trying to get my head around it," said Nightingale. He reached for his cigarettes. He offered the pack to McBride but he shook his head. Nightingale lit one and stared thoughtfully at McBride as he inhaled the smoke and blew a fairly respectable smoke ring at the ceiling. "So the Satanic stuff was found when?"

"They were around at Jimmy's farm the day of the shootings. Monday."

"And you were there when? Saturday?"

"That's right. Jimmy said one his tractors was playing up and he needed a hand with it. There was no altar there then."

"So you think someone is setting your brother up as a Satanist?"

"That's exactly what I think."

Nightingale flicked his cigarette at the ashtray by his paper but missed by several inches. "But why would anyone do that?"

"That's what I want you to find out, Mr Nightingale."

"Even though you know that your brother did kill those children?"

"There's no doubt that he did. But I want to know why."

Nightingale took another drag on his cigarette. "It won't be cheap, Mr McBride. Berwick isn't my patch and it's going to take time."

"My brother has left everything he had to me and my kids," said McBride. "Money is one thing I don't have to worry about. But I won't be able to rest until I know why Jimmy did what he did."

CHAPTER
NINE

Jenny showed Mr McBride out and then went back into Nightingale's office. He was already back at his Sudoku. She waved the cheque that Mr McBride had given her. "Two thousand pounds on account," she said.

"On account of the fact that his brother is a child-killer," said Nightingale, putting down his paper.

"What do you think?" asked Jenny.

"I think it'll make a change from chasing unfaithful husbands," said Nightingale. "And the whole Satanic thing is interesting."

"Why would a Satanist kill kids with a shotgun? They go in for ritual killings, don't they? Not much in the way of ritual with a 12-bore."

"I'll know better once I've had a look around McBride's barn." He rubbed his chin. "Bit of a drive, Berwick."

"There's a train," she said.

"That'll get me to Berwick, but what do I do then?"

"You can hire a car. Or you could drive up."

"My MGB isn't up for that," he said.

"But my Audi is, is that what you're saying?"

Nightingale grinned. "Vorsprung durch technik," he said.

"I'm not your chauffeur," she said.

"I'll split the driving with you," he said.

"Can't you fly up?"

"To where? Newcastle? I'm still going to have to get a car. Plus I'll have to schlep out to Heathrow. Come on, I'll pay for the petrol and I'll buy you lunch."

"Jack, seriously, it's a six or seven-hour drive. Fourteen hours there and back. It's an overnighter. And someone has to mind the office."

Nightingale nodded. She was right. She usually was. "Can I at least borrow the Audi?"

"If you promise to be careful."

"Cross my heart."

"I'm serious, Jack."

"So am I. We'll do a swap, you can borrow the MGB."

"I'll stick with taxis, thanks. Which you'll pay for. I'll get a hotel fixed up for you. When are you going up?"

"Might as well go tomorrow, strike while the iron's hot. Come on, the office can do without you for one day. The answer machine will be on."

"No can do. I'm at my parents at the weekend."

"Hunting, shooting and fishing?" Jenny's parents owned a huge estate outside Norfolk.

"Eating, walking and napping is what I had planned," said Jenny. "Plus I've a mountain of reading I want to catch up on. I've got Jodi Picoult's new one and I'm dying to get stuck into it."

"Is your Uncle Marcus going to be there?"

"No. Why do you keep asking about him?"

"Do I?"

"Every time I say I'm going home."

"Well, forgive me for expressing an interest in your personal life. Anyway, chick lit trumps a nice drive up to bonnie Scotland, does it?"

"I think you'll find that Berwick is in England," she said. "How long do you think you'll be there?"

"What do you mean?"

"Do you think you'll be back on Saturday? Or Sunday?"

"Doubt I'll be able to get much done on a Saturday," he said. "I'll fly up first thing tomorrow and come back Saturday. Evening maybe."

"I'll book your flights and hotel," she said. "Edinburgh'll probably work best, And I'll arrange a hire car at the airport. I'll get the postcode of the farm so I can get the car people to pre-programme the sat-nav for you."

"I'm not completely helpless," said Nightingale.

"It'll be safer," said Jenny. "That way I won't have to deal with an 'I'm lost' phone call when I'm stuck in to Jodi Picoult."

"Oh ye of little faith."

"I have faith, Jack. Just not in your navigation skills."

CHAPTER
TEN

Nightingale arrived at Heathrow airport at ten o'clock on Friday morning, which gave him more than enough time to check in, pass through security and grab a coffee. As he sat in the café surrounded by suited businessmen tapping away on laptops and BlackBerrys, he phoned Robbie Hoyle. Robbie was one of the few serving officers who'd stayed in touch with him when he'd left the force, but he was more than just a former colleague — he was a friend, and a good one.

Robbie was at his desk when he answered and he told Nightingale that he'd call him right back. Two minutes later Nightingale's phone rang and from the sound of the echo he figured Robbie had moved to the toilets. "I guess I'm still persona non grata," said Nightingale.

Robbie laughed. "Mate, whenever you call you want something so I need to be away from prying ears."

"That's not true. I'm always calling you for a chat. How's Anna?"

"Anna's great."

"The kids?"

"All great. You're coming for dinner week after next, right? Wednesday?"

"Absolutely," said Nightingale. "It's in my diary. I wouldn't miss Anna's cooking for the world. Look mate, I need a favour."

Robbie laughed. "See."

"Okay, I need a favour this time but that's not the only reason I call you."

"Stop digging, Jack, the hole's deep enough as it is. What do you want?"

"Do you have any contacts up in Northumbria? Berwick?"

"What sort of contacts?"

"I'm heading up there as we speak. Remember that farmer who took potshots at schoolkids?"

"Sure. He topped himself before the armed cops got there, right?"

"Yeah, well, the brother's hired me."

"To do what?"

"To find out what happened. He accepts that his brother killed the kids, he just wants to know why." Nightingale realised that a woman in a black suit was looking at him over the top of her spectacles. He covered his mouth with his hand. "Do you know anyone who might be able to give me any pointers?"

"Not off the top of my head, but let me ask around."

Nightingale thanked him, ended the call, and finished his coffee. The flight was full, mainly with businessmen who spent the flight tapping away on BlackBerrys and laptops. Jenny had booked him a window seat and Nightingale spent the hour in the air working on the *Sun*'s Sudoku. He had almost finished it when the plane's wheels touched the runway.

As Nightingale waited in line to collect his rental car, a young girl was being abducted at the other end of the country. Bella Harper was nine years old and she had been wandering around a shopping centre with her mother. Mrs Harper had only taken her eyes off her daughter for a few minutes but it had been long enough. Bella's abductor was a woman and she had enticed Bella out of the store by telling her that her mother had fallen ill and had been taken to a first aid room. Once out of the store the woman was joined by a man, and together they took Bella to a van in the multi-storey car park. It was only as they approached the van that Bella realised something was wrong, but it was too late. The woman pressed a damp cloth over her face and Bella lost consciousness before she was bundled into the back of the van.

As Nightingale started the engine of his rented Vauxhall Insignia, Bella was being driven towards the house where she would spend the next three days. The man driving the van had abducted young girls before and had honed his technique to a fine art. Bella was bound and gagged and lying under a tarpaulin in the back of the van. The house he was taking her to had been well prepared. There was food and clean clothing for the girl, and DVDs to keep her occupied when he wasn't attending to her. And there were large black plastic bags to wrap her in when he'd finished playing with her and a spade to dig the hole in the New Forest where he planned to bury her.

Bella was the fifth child that the man and his girlfriend had abducted. The previous four were all dead and buried. They had never even come close to being caught, and the man doubted that they ever would. It was all about the planning.

As the van drove into the garage and the woman pulled down the door to shield them from prying eyes, Nightingale was driving south to Jimmy McBride's farm. Jenny had been as good as her word — the car rental people had pre-programmed the location into his sat-nav and a female voice that always sounded slightly disapproving directed him to his destination.

He crossed from Scotland into England with no fanfare or change in scenery, and shortly after three o'clock he pulled up at a five-bar gate next to which was a sign that read "Three Hill Farm". There was a grey Peugeot parked next to the barbed wire fence and the driver climbed out. It was McBride's brother, wearing a tweed cap and Barbour jacket. He shook hands with Nightingale and thanked him for coming. He took a set of keys from his coat pocket and unlocked the padlock on the gate. He pushed it open and the two men drove down to the farm buildings. There was a large stone farmhouse with a steeply sloping slate roof, a two-storey corrugated iron barn streaked with red from rusting bolts, and a large white silo with the look of a stubby intercontinental ballistic missile.

McBride parked his Peugeot in front of the farmhouse. Nightingale pulled up next to him and climbed out. "There's no one here?" he asked McBride. A black and white cat was sitting at the front door of the farmhouse and it mewed hopefully at the two men.

"My brother worked the farm on his own," said McBride. "He used contract labour when he needed it but other than that he was here alone."

There were two dull bangs off in the distance and Nightingale flinched. McBride smiled. "Shotgun," he said. "It'll be a farmer taking care of rabbits or crows. You hear them all the time out here."

Nightingale took out his cigarettes and lit one. He offered the pack to McBride but he shook his head. "I gave up, years ago," he said.

"Sorry," said Nightingale. He held up his cigarette. "You don't mind if I do?"

McBride waved his hand dismissively. "They're your lungs," he said.

Nightingale lit his cigarette and put the pack away. "What's going to happen to this place?"

"My brother left it to me in his will," said McBride. "But I'm not a farmer and my kids are too young. My son says he wants to be a farmer but I can't see me hanging on to it for ten years or so." He shrugged. "I guess I'll just have to sell it."

"Your brother made a decent living from the farm?"

McBride smiled ruefully. "You never hear a farmer who isn't complaining," he said. "But he was never short of a bob or two. Once he realised that the EU would pay him not to grow things, he never looked back."

"So he didn't have any money problems?"

McBride shook his head. "He had six figures in the bank," he said.

Nightingale blew smoke up at the leaden sky. "I don't get it," he said. "Your brother seems to have had the life he wanted. Why would he suddenly go off the rails the way he did?"

"If I knew that, I wouldn't have hired you, would I?" said McBride. He pulled a set of keys from his coat pocket. "I'll show you around."

"Let's start with the barn. I'd like to see the altar," said Nightingale.

McBride put the keys back in his pocket and walked over to the barn. Nightingale followed, the wind tugging at his raincoat. McBride pulled open a large metal door. It was on rollers but it was twice his height and he struggled to keep it moving. Nightingale grabbed the handle and helped. Together they pulled it open, revealing a cavernous space with a concrete floor and metal beams overhead from which hung half a dozen fluorescent lights. To the right of the barn were a tractor and a couple of ploughs, and against the wall was a rack of agricultural tools. To the side of the door was a long workbench and beyond it was a run of metal stairs that led up to a metal mezzanine level.

McBride pointed up the stairs. "Up there," he said.

Nightingale stubbed out his cigarette and then went up the stairs slowly, holding onto a metal rail. The stairs were fixed to the metal siding of the barn and they wobbled silently as he made his way up. The altar was at the far end of the mezzanine. Nightingale took out his mobile phone. Jenny had given him the iPhone as a birthday present and he still wasn't quite sure how to work it. He bit down on his lower lip as he tapped at the screen trying to put it into camera mode. "You don't know anything about iPhones do you?" he asked McBride, who had climbed up the stairs to join him.

McBride held out his hand and Nightingale gave it to him. "What are you trying to do?"

"I want to take pictures."

"You want camera mode," said McBride. He tapped the screen a couple of times and handed it back to Nightingale. "Press the camera button thing." Nightingale took several photographs as McBride stood by and watched.

"Why did you come up here on Saturday?" asked Nightingale.

McBride pointed at half a dozen cardboard boxes stacked up against the wall. "He kept his spare parts up here," he said.

Nightingale took more photographs of the altar. The base was a plank of wood across three stacks of six bricks. There were black candles and metal crucibles on the plank. Wax had melted and hardened in rivulets that reached from the plank to the metal floor. Hanging from the wall above the centre of the plank was a goat's skull with twisted horns. To the left of the skull was a bunch of dried herbs hanging from a nail and on its right was a metal pentagram. "And this wasn't here when you came up?"

"I'd hardly have missed it," said McBride.

Nightingale walked up to the altar and took more photographs. There was a red paste in one of the crucibles that might have been dried blood. And a knife with what looked like dried blood on the blade.

46

"Strange that the police didn't take any of this away," said Nightingale. "And it doesn't look as if they took fingerprints."

"They didn't say anything to me about it," said McBride. "First I knew about it was when I saw the photographs in the papers. I drove around and sure enough it was here. But as I said, it wasn't here on the Saturday. Jimmy sent me up to get some parts and the only thing up here was the boxes."

There was a large box of Swan Vesta matches on the altar. Nightingale picked it up and slid it open. There were a dozen or so spent matches among the unlit ones. Nightingale put the box down. All the candles had been used and the altar was covered with melted wax that had hardened. To the left of the altar there was a stack of papers under what appeared to be a lump of coal. Nightingale pulled out the papers and flicked through them. They seemed to be printouts from various Satanic websites.

"What do you think?" asked McBride.

Nightingale rolled the papers up and put them into his raincoat pocket. "It looks like it's been here for a while."

"Well, I can assure you that it wasn't here last Saturday."

"I believe you," said Nightingale. He took more photographs with his phone. "Which means that whoever did it went to a lot of trouble to make it look as if your brother set it up some time ago."

"Does it look like a Satanic altar to you?"

Nightingale leaned over to get a closer look at a pentangle that had been drawn on a sheet of paper in what appeared to be dried blood. "It does, yes. But I'm going to get a professional's opinion."

"A professional?"

"Someone who's a bit more familiar with this."

"I thought you were," said McBride.

"The basics, yes. But I'm going to run it by someone who really knows her stuff."

McBride pointed at the lead crucible in front of Nightingale. "That's blood, isn't it?"

"It might be," said Nightingale. He pulled two plastic evidence bags from his pocket. He put the crucible in one and the knife in the other. "I'll get it checked out." He turned to look at McBride. "Your brother, was he religious?"

"He went to church, but not regularly. Why?"

"Does he have a Bible in the house?"

"I'm not sure? Why?"

"Because if he was a dyed-in-the-wool Satanist he wouldn't have one. Can we have a look around?"

"Not a problem," said McBride. "Are you done here?"

"Just a few more pictures," said Nightingale. He took half a dozen more shots of the altar, then pocketed his phone. "I have to say, it's weird that the police didn't take this away. Or at least rope it off as a crime scene." He shrugged. "Maybe they do things differently up here."

"They've done almost nothing in the way of an investigation so far as I can see," said McBride. "They haven't even spoken to me."

"Are you serious?"

"Well, I went to see them after they took away his computer because they'd smashed in the front door. But they weren't interested in anything I had to say."

"They didn't ask about the altar or what sort of person he was?" McBride shook his head. "Or ask if anything was troubling him?"

"Not a dicky-bird," said McBride. "They couldn't wait to get me out of the station."

Nightingale rubbed the back of his neck. There was clearly something very wrong with the way the Northumbria police were handling the investigation.

They went back down the stairs and out of the barn, then walked around the back of the farmhouse. There was a large, well-tended vegetable garden and beyond it a chicken house the size of a railway carriage. Nightingale winced as the acrid smell of the chickens hit his nostrils. The chickens inside began to cluck and squawk, as if they realised there were strangers around. McBride unlocked the back door of the farmhouse and took Nightingale into the kitchen. There was a large green Aga stove, a weathered pine table and chairs, and an overstuffed armchair next to which was a pile of farming magazines. There was a metal gun cabinet on one wall. The cabinet was open and empty. "How many guns did your brother have?" asked Nightingale.

"Three, I think," said McBride. "He took one to the school and the police took away the other two."

"He never had a problem with his licences?"

"Not that I know of. But they're pretty easy for farmers to get. There are foxes and crows and all sorts of vermin. I wouldn't have a gun in the house, but for Jimmy it was just a tool."

"So they took the guns and the computer. Anything else?"

"The ammunition. But that was about it. I've got a receipt somewhere."

There were two dog bowls by the back door, one half full of water. "He had dogs?"

"Two," said McBride. "I'm taking care of them at the moment."

Nightingale walked out of the kitchen and along a stone-flagged hallway. On the walls were framed water-colours, mainly flowers, that appeared to have been done by an amateur artist.

"Jimmy's study is on the right," said McBride.

The curtains were drawn in the study and Nightingale pulled them open. There was a desk on which there was a printer and two wire baskets full of invoices and paperwork. There was a space where a computer had obviously stood. There were more watercolours on the walls.

"Did your brother paint?" asked Nightingale.

McBride shook his head. "Our mother," he said. "Jimmy hardly changed a thing when our parents passed away. Their bedroom is just the way it was when they lived here, and he sleeps in the same bedroom he slept in as a kid. He's left mine the way it is, too."

"What sort of computer did your brother have?" asked Nightingale.

"I don't know. A Dell, maybe."

"Was it a desktop or a laptop?"

"A desktop. With a monitor and a separate keyboard and a printer. They only left the printer."

Nightingale looked over at the printer. Next to it were half a dozen photographs in frames. Two young boys were in most of the pictures. McBride noticed Nightingale's interest. "My boys," he said. "They worshipped Jimmy. They were like his surrogate kids. That's why what he did made no sense."

Nightingale nodded sympathetically. "Have you asked for it back? The computer?"

"I went to the station but they said that they were working on it."

"Who did you talk to?"

"Some detective. An inspector. Stevenson his name was. To be honest he was a bit short with me, gave me the impression that I was bothering him."

"I'll have a go. He might be more forthcoming with me." He pointed at a Cisco internet router on a table next to a fax machine. "I thought you said he didn't have an internet connection."

"He didn't," said McBride. "It's not plugged in. He couldn't get it to work. The kids got me to buy it for him last birthday so that they could be Facebook friends with him but he couldn't get the hang of it. He kept saying he'd get someone in to connect it, but he never did."

Nightingale went over and peered behind the table. The router wasn't plugged in.

"He still used faxes for business," said McBride. "He didn't even have an email address. I mean, who doesn't have an email address in this day and age?"

Nightingale nodded but didn't reply. Truth be told, Nightingale didn't have an email address either. If he needed to talk to someone he preferred to do it face to face or on the phone. There was a bookcase against one wall and Nightingale went over to it. There were two shelves filled with Reader's Digest condensed books and several hundred romantic novels by writers such as Catherine Cookson and Barbara Cartland.

McBride saw the look of confusion on Nightingale's face at the choice of reading matter. "They were our mum's," he said. "She died ten years ago. Cancer. Our dad died a couple of years later. Jimmy never left home. He ran the farm with Dad and then took it over when he died. The house is pretty much as it was when we were kids here." He laughed ruefully. "Like I said, my bedroom is just as it was. Same wallpaper, same blankets on the bed. Bit of a time warp really."

There was a Bible on one of the lower shelves and Nightingale pulled it out.

"That was our father's," said McBride.

"He was religious?"

"Sure. Church of Scotland. Mum, too. But Dad pretty much gave up on religion after Mum died. It wasn't an easy death and it pretty much destroyed his faith." McBride shrugged. "He didn't even want a Christian funeral service."

"But he kept the Bible?"

McBride nodded. "I guess so. Maybe he forgot it was there."

Nightingale replaced it. "What I don't see is anything that suggests your brother was interested in black magic."

"I never saw anything like that. I suppose he could have hidden them."

"Could we have a look?"

"You mean search the house?"

"If he really was a Satanist then there'd be books or other paraphernalia. It's a complicated business."

McBride looked at his watch. "Okay, let's do it," he said. "But I'll have to call the wife and let her know that I'll be late."

There was a wooden plaque on the wall next to the bookcase and Nightingale walked over to get a better look. There was a pentangle in the middle and below it, a pair of compasses. McBride joined him. "I've never noticed that before," he said. "Is it a witchcraft thing?"

Nightingale shook his head. "It's a Masonic thing." He pointed at a small brass label at the bottom of the plaque. "That's the name of his lodge."

"He never mentioned it."

"It's no big deal — a lot of farmers are Masons. Mainly they're a social and charitable group. A lot of cops used to be Masons but it's fallen out of favour in the last few years." He went over to the desk and put his hand on a drawer, then straightened up and looked at McBride. "With your permission, I'd like to search the house, from top to bottom."

"Looking for what, actually?"

"Anything that suggests your brother really was a Satanist. If he was then there'd be things he wouldn't want anyone else to see."

"The police have been through the house, they searched all the rooms when they took away the computer and the guns."

"Yeah, well, the cops aren't always as thorough as they should be," said Nightingale. "Let's see how I get on."

CHAPTER
ELEVEN

Nightingale spent the best part of four hours searching the farmhouse, from a dusty attic filled with old furniture and long-forgotten clothes and odds and ends, down through all the rooms and ending up in a cold damp basement which contained a fridge-freezer full of pork and lamb, presumably from the farm's stock. But at no point did he find anything that gave a clue to Jimmy McBride's state of mind or suggested that he was in any way interested in Satanism. There was something disconcerting about the bedrooms. The main bedroom with an en-suite bathroom had obviously belonged to the parents — their clothes were still in the wardrobes and there were bottles of make-up and perfume on an old oak dressing table. The bedroom where Danny McBride had slept had posters of rock groups and racing cars on the walls and fishing tackle in one corner, and Nightingale found a collection of dirty magazines at the bottom of a chest of drawers that was still full of underwear, socks and T-shirts.

McBride's own bedroom was a throwback to the fifties, with heavy dark wood furniture and more watercolours on the walls. On a bedside cabinet there was a copy of *Farmer's Weekly*, next to a framed photograph of a middle-aged man wearing thick-framed spectacles and a flat cap, a stocky woman with tightly permed hair and two young boys grinning at the camera. The McBride family.

Nightingale went through every cupboard, every wardrobe, lifted the carpets and checked behind every picture. He checked the toilet cisterns and looked for loose floorboards. He found nothing that suggested McBride was anything other than a hard-working farmer, albeit one with a limited social life.

After he'd finished searching the basement he went upstairs to the kitchen, where the brother was sitting at the table nursing a mug of coffee. He was staring out of the window at the yard and he turned to look at Nightingale. "I made a coffee, do you want one?" he asked.

"I'm okay," said Nightingale, sitting down at the table.

"Find anything?"

Nightingale shook his head. "Nothing," he said. "Not a blind thing. Who's looking after the livestock?"

"I've brought in a contractor from Sunderland," said McBride. "None of the neighbours wanted to help, not after what Jimmy did." He shrugged. "Can't blame them, I suppose."

"You're going to sell it?"

"I'm going to have to," said McBride. "I can't see how me or my family can stay in the area, not after this." He smiled ruefully. "It's not as if I don't understand," he said. "If it had been my kids who had been killed, I'd never forgive anyone connected to the killer. You just can't, can you? Every time you saw them you'd remember what happened, it'd be like rubbing salt into the wound."

"It's a nightmare, I know. In a way your brother has it easy. He's dead, he's out of it."

McBride nodded. "It's my kids I feel sorry for. They're going to carry it with them for the rest of their lives, that their uncle was a mass murderer." He sipped his coffee.

"The policeman who took away your brother's computer. Have you got a number for him?"

"I've got his card, I think." He fished in his wallet and took out a Northumbria Police business card. He gave it to Nightingale. "What's next?"

"I'll try to see this guy and see if I can get the computer back. I'm hoping to get a contact in the police who'll give me some background info. And tomorrow I'll see if I can get a look at the school. I'm heading back to London tomorrow and I'll get a lab to check the blood on the crucible and knife."

"What do you think, Mr Nightingale? You've seen the house, you've seen what's in the barn. What do you think drove my brother to kill those children?"

"I don't know, Mr McBride. I'll have a better idea by tomorrow."

As it turned out, Inspector Colin Stevenson was considerably less forthcoming than Nightingale had hoped. He was a big man with a double chin and a gut that suggested a fondness for beer. He was clearly unhappy at having Nightingale in his office on a Friday afternoon. He sneered at Nightingale's business card and then tossed it onto his desk. The detective's office was a small cubby-hole with a window overlooking the police station's car park. "So why does Mr McBride need a private detective?" he asked.

"There's a few questions about the case that he would like answering," said Nightingale.

"We've been more than happy to communicate with Mr McBride," said the detective. "But to be fair, I don't see that there are any questions that need answering. His brother took his shotgun and killed a teacher and eight children in cold blood and then he turned his gun on himself." He shrugged. "Case closed."

"Mr McBride would like to have his brother's computer returned."

"Why?"

Nightingale frowned. "Why? If the case is closed then it's no longer evidence."

"I'll be the judge of that," said the inspector.

"Well now, that's not strictly true, is it?" said Nightingale. "You're not a judge. You're an investigating officer."

"But I'll be the one who decides when something is no longer evidence." He folded his arms defensively. "That computer is staying where it is."

"Like you said, the case is closed. Why do you need it?"

"The inquest has yet to be heard," said the inspector. "What's on the computer shows the state of his mind."

"Which is?"

The detective smiled thinly. "I'm not a psychiatrist," he said.

Nightingale smiled amiably. "Okay, how about this? It says in the papers that you found evidence of Mr McBride visiting various Satanic websites."

"I can't comment on that."

"You already have. Or someone from your office has. It was all over the papers." Nightingale was finding it hard to keep smiling.

"That may be so, but under the Data Protection Act I can't reveal any details of what might or might not be on his computer."

"But you found Satanic stuff on the computer?"

"I can't comment on that."

"The papers said that McBride had visited various Satanic websites and was researching devil-worship."

The detective shrugged carelessly. "Again, I can't comment on that."

"Someone doesn't appear to have had any problems talking to the press."

"What the papers choose to publish is nothing to do with me," said the detective. He looked at his watch. "I think I've given you more than enough of my time, Mr Nightingale."

"Then I'd better cut to the chase," said Nightingale. "The press have been told that McBride's computer was full of Satanic stuff and that he'd been visiting websites dealing with devil-worship and child sacrifice."

"That's nothing to do with the police," said the inspector flatly, and he looked at his watch again.

"No, but when you put that together with the Satanic altar in the barn, it gives the impression that McBride was some sort of devil-worshipping nutter, doesn't it?"

The inspector put up his hands. "I couldn't possibly comment," he said.

"Here's the thing," said Nightingale. "McBride didn't have an internet connection. He wasn't visiting any websites. He didn't even have access to email."

The inspector's eyes narrowed. "There's a router in the farmhouse. I saw it myself."

"There is indeed. But it's never been connected. His brother bought it for him last year but McBride never got around to having it connected."

The colour seemed to have drained from the policeman's face.

"So you can see why my client's a tad confused," said Nightingale. "There's no internet connection at the farm but you're telling the Press that he was prowling through the web and Googling 'human sacrifice' and downloading all sorts of crap onto his computer, but I think you know as well as I do that didn't happen." Nightingale stood up. "Anyway, I've taken up more than enough of your valuable time."

"I'd be careful, if I were you," said Stevenson.

"Yeah? In what way?"

"Making accusations like you have been, that could come back and bite you in the arse." Nightingale took his cigarettes and slid one between his lips. "You can't smoke in here," said Stevenson.

Nightingale ignored him and walked out of the office. He waited until he was outside the building before lighting a cigarette. As he blew smoke up at the leaden sky, he saw Stevenson looking down at him, a contemptuous sneer on his face. Nightingale smiled up at the detective. "Oh well, can't win them all," Nightingale muttered to himself.

CHAPTER
TWELVE

Jenny had booked Nightingale a room at the Sly Fox, a pub overlooking the North Sea on the outskirts of Berwick. It was a cosy place, with thick walls and small windows to cut down the chill factor of the freezing wind that blew in from the sea. Nightingale's room was comfortably furnished with a large brass bed, a heavy scuffed leather armchair and a massive oak wardrobe with a fox hunt carved into the doors. He tossed his overnight bag onto the bed and phoned Robbie. "Any joy with a Berwick contact?" he asked.

"I'm working on it, mate."

"I'm heading back tomorrow afternoon, be great to see the guy before I go," said Nightingale.

"Seriously, I'm on it," said Robbie. "How's it going?"

"I met a DI today but he's less than helpful."

"What do you expect? No one appreciates strangers on their patch. Especially ones less than forthcoming in the winning friends and influencing people department."

"I've been all sweetness and light," said Nightingale. "He took a computer from McBride's and won't let me have a look at it."

"He won't hand over evidence in a criminal investigation?" said Robbie, his voice loaded with sarcasm. "Well, shame on him."

"There is no investigation, that's the point."

"I'm only winding you up, mate," said Robbie. "Soon as I get a name I'll get back to you."

Nightingale ended the call and went downstairs to the bar. It was an L-shaped room with a roaring fire, the walls dotted with polished horse-brasses and framed paintings of fox hunts. They didn't stock Corona so he ordered a Budweiser. The landlord was the man who'd checked him in, a big bearded Geordie with a tattoo of a mermaid on his right forearm that suggested a previous career in the merchant navy. He gave Nightingale a menu and he ordered fish and chips. The landlord grimaced and he leant across the bar, lowering his voice to a gruff whisper. "I probably shouldn't tell you this, but the chef's off tonight and the missus is cooking. If I were you I'd go for the shepherd's pie or the chicken pasta bake because the chef did them and all she has to do is warm them up." He winked conspiratorially.

Nightingale toasted the landlord with his Budweiser and ordered the shepherd's pie. "So is this England or Scotland?" he asked as he waited to his food to appear from the kitchen.

"You're joking, right?" said the landlord.

"What can I say, I'm from London."

"You don't sound like a southerner."

"I was brought up in Manchester."

"Red or Blue?"

Nightingale chuckled. "United, what else? So joking apart, did we cross the border?"

"The England — Scotland border is a moveable feast," said the landlord. "It's switched back and forth thirteen times over the years. But at the moment you're in Northumberland. Here's hoping it moves back at some point, because between you and me, I'd rather be in Scotland. My kids wouldn't be paying their own university tuition, for a start — that wouldn't be happening if we were counted as Scotland."

"And free prescriptions," said Nightingale. He raised his bottle of Budweiser. "To bonnie old Scotland." He drank and then motioned at the beer pumps. "Get yourself one. Keep me company."

"Don't mind if I do," said the landlord. "I'll take a whisky, if that's okay with you."

"All good," said Nightingale.

The landlord picked up a glass and held it under one of the optics. "You know, this is the Devil's town, truth be told," he said as the whisky sloshed into his glass.

"Say what?"

The landlord grinned. He used his fingers to drop a couple of ice cubes into his whisky. "It's in the Bible. When the Devil was tempting Jesus, trying to get him over to the dark side, he held out a map of the world and told Jesus he could have dominion over everything he could see. But as he held out the map, the Devil had his thumb over Berwick because he wanted to keep it for himself."

"Nice story," said Nightingale.

"There are those around here who say it's more than a story," said the landlord. He raised his glass. "Cheers, anyway."

"Cheers," said Nightingale, and he clinked the neck of his bottle against the landlord's glass.

As the landlord drank he caught sight of the television on the wall. It was tuned to Sky News and a police press conference was about to start. He grabbed the remote and turned up the sound. "Looks like she's still missing," he said.

"Who?"

"Little girl was abducted in Southampton. Some paedo snatched her in a shopping centre."

On the screen a man and a woman were sitting together at a long table. She was in her thirties, hollow-eyed and her blonde hair messy. The man was equally haggard and he was holding the woman's hand tightly.

"That's her parents," said the landlord. "Can you imagine what they're going through?"

"How old's the girl?" asked Nightingale.

"Nine. Mum took her eyes off her for a minute and she was gone."

A uniformed police officer took the seat next to the mother. An assistant chief constable. At the other end of the table was a large man in a dark blue suit with the world-weary eyes of a senior detective.

On a board behind the table were posters featuring the missing girl. In the middle of the poster was a blow-up of her school photograph. She was a little angel with long, curly blonde hair, blue eyes and porcelain skin.

"They should hang them," said the landlord. "Anyone who messes with a kid, hanging's too good for them."

"No arguments here," said Nightingale.

"You got kids?" Nightingale shook his head. "Well, I've got three, two of them are girls. If anyone laid a finger on them I'd swing for them, no question."

The uniformed officer gave a short prepared speech, basically laying out the facts. That nine-year-old Bella Harper had been abducted from a shopping centre in Southampton, possibly by a man and a woman. Witnesses had seen a man and a woman getting into a white van with a girl who might have been Bella. They didn't have a description of the couple or the registration of the van. Then he asked the parents to say a few words. The woman spoke first, or at least tried to. She barely managed a dozen words before she broke down in a flood of tears. Her husband put his arm around her and in a trembling voice appealed for whoever had taken Bella to send her home safe and well. "She's our angel, she's never done a bad thing in her life, she doesn't deserve this. Please, send her home. Please don't hurt her."

"He should use her name," said Nightingale.

"What?"

"He needs to personalise her. He should use her name in every sentence, and he should give more personal information about her. Her pets, her school, what she likes to do. If the guy that has her starts to think of her as a human being and not an object then he's more likely not to kill her." Nightingale realised that heads were starting to turn in his direction and he stopped talking and drank his beer.

"How do you know so much about it?" asked the landlord, putting down his glass.

"I used to be a cop, in another life," said Nightingale. "Down in London."

"And you dealt with stuff like this?"

"Abductions? Yeah, a few."

"How do they normally end?"

"Depends who the abductor is. If it's a family member then there's a good chance they'll find her, but if it's a stranger and they don't find her within twenty-four hours then it's usually bad news." He shrugged and sipped his lager.

The father finished speaking. Tears were running down his face. A telephone number appeared at the bottom of the screen. Nightingale hoped that someone, somewhere, was reaching for a phone with information that would help them find the little girl. But the rational part of his brain knew that such television appeals rarely worked. The police were going through the motions, knowing that they would be criticised if they didn't mount an appeal but knowing that virtually all the calls they received would be false alarms that would tie up valuable police resources.

"I hope to God they find her," said the landlord.

"Amen to that," agreed Nightingale.

"You know it's Friday the thirteenth today?"

"I'd forgotten that," said Nightingale.

"Nothing good happens on Friday the thirteenth. What's the world coming to? Why would anyone take a child?"

"Paedophiles are sick," said Nightingale. "It's their nature. You can't change them, all you can do is keep them away from children. The only safe paedophile is a paedophile behind bars."

"Or dead. They should just put them down, like dogs."

Nightingale nodded but didn't say anything.

"So why are you up here, then?" asked the landlord.

"I'm looking at that school shooting. The farmer who killed the kids."

The landlord frowned. "I thought you weren't a cop any more?"

"I'm a private detective now," said Nightingale.

"And someone is paying you to come up here and investigate?"

Nightingale realised that it probably wouldn't be the smartest move to broadcast who his client was. "Department for Education," he lied. "They want to know if school security was at fault." He held up his empty bottle. "Another, please, and another whisky for yourself."

"Don't mind if I do," said the landlord. He fetched a fresh Budweiser for Nightingale and poured himself another whisky.

"So did you ever run into Jimmy McBride?" asked Nightingale.

"He came in now and then," said the landlord. "Wasn't overly social, you know?" He nodded at a table by the window. "Sat over there on his own when he did come in. He'd drink a couple of pints and read his paper."

"Always on his own?"

The landlord nodded. "I don't remember him ever being with anyone. Don't get me wrong, he wasn't a bad sort — he'd say hello and maybe mention the weather but you'd never find him at the bar chatting with the locals."

"And no sense that he was the sort of guy who'd do what he did?"

"I don't know about that," said the landlord. "But they always say it's the quiet ones, don't they?"

"I'm not sure that's true," said Nightingale. "Usually there are signs. Especially when there's that degree of violence involved. The guy is either a brooder, bottling it all up until he explodes, or he has a temper and has a habit of lashing out."

"McBride wasn't either of those," said the landlord. "He was just a regular guy."

"A regular guy with a shotgun."

"He was a farmer. Every farmer around here has a shotgun or two."

"So when you heard what he'd done, what did you think?"

The landlord scratched his ear. "To be honest, I thought he'd been possessed."

"Possessed?"

"By the Devil. Something made him do it, and the Devil seems like the obvious candidate."

Nightingale couldn't work out if the man was serious or not. Before he could say anything, a stick-thin woman with sharp features appeared with a tray. "Shepherd's pie?" she called, and Nightingale raised his hand.

The woman gave him the tray, scowled at her husband, and went back to the kitchen.

"We've had a bit of a row," explained the landlord. He shrugged. "Women, can't live with them, can't throw them under a bus."

CHAPTER
THIRTEEN

"You know we had witches around here, more witches than almost anywhere in the UK?" said the old man sitting opposite Nightingale. His name was Willie Holiday and he was a retired farmworker, well into his seventies. He was sitting at a corner table, next to the roaring fire, with Nightingale and another of the pub's regulars, a fifty-year-old former miner who gave his name only as Tommo. Nightingale had bought them several pints and had knocked back four Budweisers himself.

"I didn't know that," said Nightingale.

Willie nodded. "Loads of them. We were awash with witches in the sixteen hundreds. They had their own way of proving it. They'd stick needles in them and if they were innocent they bled and if they didn't bleed they were witches."

"That seems fair enough," said Nightingale.

Willie frowned. "Or was it the other way round?"

The three men laughed. "The thing is, though, witchcraft isn't always a bad thing," said Tommo. "My wife swears by crystals and pyramids, we've got dozens in the house. We even sleep under one."

"How does that work?" asked Nightingale.

"It's a paper lampshade, in the shape of a pyramid. And I have to say I've never had a bad night's sleep since she put it up." He rubbed his left knee. "She uses a crystal on my knee when it gives me grief and that works too." He shrugged. "Did it when I was down the mines. It's always worse in the winter but she rubs different crystals over it and the pain goes away."

"That's not really witchcraft," said Nightingale.

"If it works, it works," said Willie. "We've got haunted houses and spooky castles by the boat-load. You've heard about the Devil and Berwick, right?"

"The thumb thing? Yeah. Funny story, that. Makes you wonder why the Devil wanted the town."

"Must have had his reasons," said Willie. He drained his glass and looked at Nightingale expectantly. Nightingale grinned and headed over to the bar. The bill would be going on McBride's account, so he figured he might as well keep the locals happy.

He returned to the table with two pints and a bottle of Budweiser and sat down. "Speaking of the devil, did you ever come across Jimmy McBride?"

"The guy that shot the kids?" Willie sighed. "Aye that was a rum do, that was."

"You knew him?"

"Used to," said Willie. "There was a time when I used to give him a hand on the farm when he was busy, but he uses Polish gangs now."

"What was he like?"

"Quiet. Wouldn't say boo to a goose. Just got on with whatever needed doing."

"Never married?"

72

"He didn't seem to have much interest, if you ask me. But farming's like that. You work all hours, you tend not to have much of a social life."

Tommo chuckled. "How does that explain your six kids and fifteen grandkids, Willie?"

Willie smiled ruefully. "I met the right woman, early on," he said. "But it's a real problem for a lot of farmers. Days can pass when you don't leave the farm. Cows have to be milked, livestock has to be fed, there's the EU paperwork. You don't get much time for dating."

"And what was he like with kids?"

Willie frowned. "What do you mean?"

"He shot eight kids. Why would he do that?"

Willie shook his head. "God knows," he said.

"I wondered if kids had been vandalising the farm, giving him a hard time, something like that?"

"This isn't the big city," said Tommo. "We don't have gangs or vandals or even much graffiti."

"So why did he do what he did?" asked Nightingale.

The two men shook their heads. "Who knows?" said Tommo. "We've never had anything like that happen before."

"Happened in Scotland," said Willie. "Remember? Back in 1996. Dunblane. What was that guy's name now?"

"Thomas Hamilton," said Nightingale. "He shot sixteen children in a primary school."

"They never found out why he did it, did they?" said Willie. "Sometimes people just snap."

"Did he seem like the type who would snap?" asked Nightingale.

Willie shook his head. "He was rock steady," he said. "Never lost his temper, never a cross word."

"Did you hear about the Satanic stuff?"

"It was in the papers," said Tommo. "Didn't he have a black magic thing in his barn?"

"An altar," said Nightingale. "Yeah, that's what they said. Do you hear much about devil-worship up this way?"

"It's a bit cold to be dancing around naked in the open," said Willie. "That's what Satanists do, isn't it?"

"I think they can do it inside as well," said Nightingale.

"Does anyone really believe in that these days?" asked Tommo.

"Some people do," said Nightingale.

"What? A Devil with horns and a pitchfork?"

"Maybe not horns and a pitchfork, but the Devil, sure."

"And why would the Devil want him to go out and shoot kids?" asked Tommo.

"He does move in mysterious ways, doesn't he?" said Willie.

"I think that's God, but I take your point," said Nightingale.

"It's becoming a sick world," said Tommo. "Maybe there is a Devil and maybe he's behind a lot of what's going on." He gestured at the television behind the bar. "Did you hear about that young girl that got taken in

Southampton? That's the work of the Devil, it has to be. Why would anyone abduct a nine-year-old girl?"

"There's a lot of sick people in the world, that's for sure," said Nightingale.

"I just hope she's okay," said Willie.

CHAPTER
FOURTEEN

Bella Harper wasn't okay. She was far from okay. She was lying on a bed, curled up into a foetal ball and sobbing. Sitting next to her was Candice Matthews, Candy to her friends. Candy was 25 — her hair was blonde but unlike Bella's it was dyed, dry and slightly frizzy. Her cheeks were peppered with old acne scars and her nails were bitten to the quick. "Please don't cry, baby," she said, patting Bella on the shoulder.

"I want to go home," sniffed Bella.

"I know you do. But you can't just now."

"I want my mum and dad."

"I know you do."

"They'll tell the police and you'll get into trouble."

"We won't get into trouble, Bella. No one knows you're here."

Bella was wearing the clothes she'd had on at the mall. Skinny jeans and a Guess sweatshirt. That wasn't what Eric wanted her to wear. Eric wanted her in one of the dresses he liked best. It was a princess dress he'd bought from the Disney store, all soft and flouncy with puffy sleeves. The dress was lying on the end of the bed. Eric always liked the girls to wear the princess dress on the first night. It was one of his "things". Eric had a lot of "things", and what Eric wanted Eric got.

Candy stroked Bella's hair. "Just put the dress on, baby. It's like a game."

"I don't want to."

"Eric doesn't want to hurt you."

"So let me go."

"He will do. But first he just wants to show you how much he likes you."

"He can show how much he likes me by letting me go home."

"Baby, he will do." She stroked Bella's hair again. "He wouldn't want you to stay here for ever, would he?"

Bella didn't answer. She continued to sob softly.

"Baby, you have to stop crying. Eric doesn't like it if you cry. He'll get angry and he's not very nice when he's angry. Do you understand?"

"I want to go home."

"I know you do. And the quickest way for you to go home is to do what Eric wants. Just be nice to him."

"I don't want to be nice to him."

"Then think of it as a game. You've played games, haven't you? Fancy dress games. That's all it is. You put on the dress and then you can go home."

Bella rolled over and looked at Candy with tear-filled eyes. "Really?"

"Of course," lied Candy.

"If I put the dress on you'll let me go home?"

"Yes."

Bella sat up and rubbed her eyes. "Okay."

Candy smiled and patted the little girl on the arm. They always co-operated if you pressed the right buttons. Eric had taught her that. It was always easier if he stayed away during the first few hours. The girls always accepted the lies when they came from Candy. And by the time they realised that she was lying, it was too late.

Candy helped Bella remove her sweatshirt and jeans and put on the dress. "Wow, you look lovely, as lovely as a princess," said Candy. "Look in the mirror."

There was a mirror on the door of the wardrobe and Bella looked at her reflection. She nodded. "It's pretty." She turned to look at Candy. "Can I go home now?"

"Soon, baby," she said.

"You said I could."

"Yes, but you need to do something else. Okay? You need to comb your hair and make it look pretty."

"Why?"

"Because that's what Eric wants. You have to make yourself pretty for him." She picked up a comb from the dressing table and stood behind Bella, combing her hair as she looked at her reflection in the mirror. Tears began to run down Bella's face. "Now don't cry, baby. Eric doesn't like it when you cry. He wants pretty, pretty, pretty."

Bella sniffed. "And when I'm pretty, I can go home?"

"Of course," lied Candy. She smiled brightly. "Let's get you looking pretty, pretty, pretty and you'll soon be home with your mummy and daddy."

CHAPTER
FIFTEEN

Nightingale went up to his room just before midnight. He'd drunk eight bottles of Budweiser, and while he wasn't drunk he was slightly unsteady on his feet. There were only three bedrooms and no locks on the door. He sat down on the bed and reached for his cigarettes and lighter. He was just about to light one when he saw the "No Smoking" sign by the bathroom door. He sighed, grabbed his raincoat, and headed downstairs. The landlord was polishing glasses behind the bar. Nightingale held up his cigarette. "I'm heading outside for a smoke," he said.

"No problem," said the landlord. "I won't be locking up for a while, but if you're late back, there's a bell by the front door. Just give it a ring and I'll come down and let you in. How's the room, by the way?"

"Perfect," said Nightingale. "No lock on the door, though?"

"You're the only guest," said the landlord. "And you can trust me and the wife."

"I've nothing worth taking anyway," said Nightingale. He let himself out and lit his cigarette as he walked down to the beach. There were thick clouds overhead blocking out the moon and stars, but there was enough light spilling out of the pub windows for him to see. He walked onto the sand and stood watching the waves break onto the beach. A bitterly cold wind blew in from the sea and he shivered.

The sound of the waves was almost hypnotic and he found himself being lulled into a trance-like state, though that could have been a result of all the beer he'd drunk with his new-found Northumbrian friends. He finished his cigarette and flicked the butt towards the water, and was just considering lighting a second when something hard walloped against the back of his head. He fell to his knees and gasped, then something pounded between his shoulder blades and he fell forward. His face was pressing into the sand, and he coughed and spluttered and then something, probably a foot, slammed into the small of his back.

He twisted his head to the side and saw a pair of heavy mud-splattered workboots and frayed jeans. The foot was still in the middle of his back, so there were at least two of them. He tried to turn his head to the other side but as he did so the foot pressed down, pushing his face into the sand again.

"You don't want to be asking too many questions around here, Mister Private Detective," said one of the men. "You'd best be heading back to London." His accent was Scottish and didn't sound like any of the men that Nightingale had spoken to in the pub. "Be easy enough to knock you out and drop you in the sea. You wouldn't be the first southerner to fall foul of the North Sea."

Nightingale managed to turn his face to the side and he spat wet sand out of his mouth.

"Do you hear what I'm telling you, Mister Private Detective?"

Nightingale spat again, and grunted.

The foot between his shoulder blades gave a final push, and then he heard the two men jogging away across the sand. He rolled onto his back, gasping for breath, but by the time he'd got to his feet they had disappeared into the night.

He stood up and wiped his face on his sleeve. As he lit a cigarette with trembling hands he heard a car start up and drive away. "Bastards," he muttered under his breath.

CHAPTER
SIXTEEN

Candy slid back the bolts and opened the door to the bedroom. "Breakfast," she said, brightly. She picked up the tray and carried it into the room. Bella was in bed, the quilt pulled up around her neck. The princess dress was lying over the chair in front of the dressing table. Bella didn't react as Candy put the tray on the bed. "I made you Cocoa Krispies," she said. "And toast."

"I'm not hungry," Bella said.

"You have to be hungry."

"I feel sick." She curled up into a ball under the quilt. "I need to go to hospital."

"Don't be silly."

"What Eric did, it hurt me. Inside."

"It doesn't hurt. Every girl in the world does that. It's natural."

Bella sniffed. "He hurt me."

"And I'm telling you it doesn't hurt. That's what girlfriends do for their boyfriends."

"I'm not his girlfriend."

"Yes you are, baby."

"I want to go home."

"And you will go home. But you have to let Eric do what he wants."

"Please don't let him hurt me again, Candy."

Candy sat down on the edge of the bed and stroked the little girl's hair. "Eat your breakfast, baby."

Bella rolled over and looked up at Candy. "Please let me go home. I have to feed Floppy."

"Floppy?"

"My rabbit. I have to clean his cage. It's Saturday, and Saturday is the day I have to look after my rabbit. My dad says if I don't look after Floppy he'll send him back to the shop." Her eyes filled with tears.

"Now don't you start crying again, baby," said Candy. "You know Eric doesn't like that."

"Don't let him touch me again, Candy. Please."

"Now why do you say that, baby? You're his girlfriend now. His little princess."

"I'm not his girlfriend. I'm not."

"Yes you are, baby. And you have to accept that. You're his girlfriend until he says you're not. Now sit up and eat your breakfast."

"Then can I go home?"

"We'll see, baby. Eat your breakfast and then we'll talk about it."

CHAPTER
SEVENTEEN

Nightingale woke up at nine. He had a blinding headache, but he wasn't sure if it was the result of all the beer he'd drunk or the blow to the back of his head. He had a small mirror in his washbag and he used it and the mirror above the sink to check out his scalp, but he couldn't see any damage and there didn't appear to be any blood. He showered and shaved, then dressed and had a bacon sandwich in the bar before calling McBride. The call went straight through to voicemail. Nightingale didn't leave a message, waited fifteen minutes while he drank a second cup of coffee, then phoned McBride again. When he didn't answer the second time, Nightingale left a brief message saying that he was going out to the school.

He went back up to his room and packed his bag, then went downstairs and paid his bill. He threw his bag onto the back seat of his car and drove to the school. He parked some distance away before climbing out and lighting a cigarette. There was a lone policeman in a fluorescent jacket standing at the school gates, stamping his feet to keep the circulation going. Dozens of bunches of flowers had been laid along the pavement outside the school and the railings were dotted with handwritten notes, mainly from children. Nightingale walked over and nodded at the officer. "How's it going?" he asked.

"You press?" asked the policeman. "I'm not allowed to talk to journalists. You need to call the press office."

"I'm not press," said Nightingale. He blew smoke and saw the look in the officer's eyes. He took out his pack and offered him a Marlboro.

"Can't, I'm on duty," said the officer.

"I don't see any senior officers around, and this being Sunday morning I'm pretty sure that you won't. Most people are at the church service for the kids, so for the next hour or so I figure it'll just be me and you." He held out the pack.

The policeman looked around furtively, then took a cigarette. Nightingale lit it for him and the two men smoked for a while in silence.

"You were in the job, yeah?" said the policeman eventually.

"What gave it away?"

"You've got a copper's eyes," he said. "London?"

"Yeah. CO19."

"Armed cop, yeah? I thought it was SO19."

"They changed it. Around about the time it went from being a police force to a police service."

"Never wanted to carry a gun," said the policeman.

"They're an acquired taste," said Nightingale.

"You ever shoot anyone?"

"If you pull the trigger you've failed," said Nightingale. "It's all about containment and resolution. If bullets start flying then you've done it wrong."

"Funny that. You spend all your time training with guns but you never pull the trigger in anger."

"It's worse than that," said Nightingale. "You shoot someone and you're on immediate suspension until Professional Standards give you the all clear. And if you've not done everything by the book you can end up being charged with murder." He shrugged. "But at least you're part of a team."

The policeman looked up and down the empty street and chuckled. "Yeah, there is that," he said. "Why did you pack it in?"

"Pastures new," said Nightingale.

"You're not living up here now, are you?"

"Nah, I'm still in London. I'm a private eye now."

"Yeah, how's that working out for you?"

Nightingale wrinkled his nose. "I didn't realise I'd be doing so much divorce work, but it's okay. At least I'm my own boss."

"Money's good, is it?"

"I have good days and bad days," said Nightingale. "But there's no pension at the end of it."

"They're screwing us on pensions," said the policeman. "It's not the job it was." He inhaled and blew a decent smoke ring up at the sky. "So what brings you to Berwick?"

Nightingale nodded at the school. "That," he said.

The policeman frowned. "The shootings? Now why would that interest a private eye?"

"It's a funny one," said Nightingale. "You know the shooter has a brother?"

The policeman nodded. "Yeah. Daniel. He works in insurance or something."

"He's hired me."

The policeman snorted. "What the hell for? There's no doubt that he did what he did. None at all."

Nightingale shrugged. "He wants closure. He wants to know why."

"Why? Because he was a nutter, that's why." He grinned. "Does that mean we split the fee?"

"You heard about the black magic stuff they found in his barn and on his computer?"

The policeman nodded. "Yeah, the guys were talking about it."

"Well, the brother reckons he wasn't into that sort of thing. He went to church."

"Doesn't mean anything, does it, going to church?"

Nightingale nodded at the main school building. "Have you been inside?"

"I was in there on Wednesday. We did a sweep through to make sure no one was hiding."

"Must have been rough."

"They were still examining the bodies." The policeman shuddered. "I don't get killing kids, I really don't." He took a long pull on his cigarette and blew smoke. "You got kids?"

Nightingale shook his head.

"If you have kids, you know that they're the most important thing in your life. Nothing means more than your kids. You'd die for them, without even thinking about it. And once you're a father you'd never hurt another man's kids. You just wouldn't."

"McBride didn't have kids."

"That's right. So maybe that's why."

"That's hardly a motive," said Nightingale. "Anything known about him?"

"Seems not," said the policeman. "Couple of speeding tickets, but other than that he was a model citizen. Never married, which is a bit off, but then farmers tend not to date much. Too busy and not too many opportunities for dating."

"And no problems with kids? Vandalism on the farm, anything like that?"

"Nothing I heard of." He dropped his cigarette butt on the floor and stamped on it. "He was just a regular guy by all accounts."

"Someone said that maybe he was possessed."

"Possessed?" The policeman shook his head. "You were in the job," he said. "You know the score. Evil has nothing to do with the Devil or God or crap like that. It's people that are evil, pure and simple. People are nasty to each other. End of."

"But there's usually a tipping point," said Nightingale. "Something that makes them kick off."

"But not McBride, is that what you're saying?"

Nightingale finished his cigarette and flicked it into the gutter. "Doesn't seem to have been anything that set him off."

"But why kids?" asked the policeman. "That's what I don't get."

"Maybe he chose it at random?"

The policeman shook his head emphatically. "He walked from his farm to the school. Partly across the fields, but when he reached the village he walked past a garage where there are half a dozen people working, a haulage company, and the council offices. If it was some sort of grudge against authority he could have gone into the council and started shooting."

"I didn't realise that."

"Well, it's true. Walked right by the council to the school. But if it was about the school, why not shoot the teachers? He went into three classrooms and it was only kids that he shot."

"I thought he shot the deputy headmaster."

"Yeah, he did. Over there." The policeman pointed to the playground. "The deputy came out, probably to ask him what he was doing on school property. McBride shot him. But from that point on it was only kids that he shot. That's what I don't get. You open the classroom door and what's the first thing you see?"

"The teacher," said Nightingale.

"Exactly. The teacher, standing at the front of the class. But he didn't shoot any of the teachers. It was kids he wanted to shoot."

Nightingale nodded thoughtfully. "But if he just wanted to kill kids, why did he move from classroom to classroom?" It wasn't so much a question as Nightingale trying to get his thoughts in line.

"And he ended up in the gym," said the policeman. "And even there he didn't shoot the teacher. He shot two kids. That's when the armed police arrived and he killed himself."

"And he didn't shoot at the cops?"

"As soon as they arrived he turned his gun on himself. Blew his own head off. Probably best, because the way things are now a smart lawyer would have had him declared insane and sitting in some cushy hospital." Two pensioners wrapped in thick coats and headscarves were making their way down the street to the school. One of the ladies was holding a cellophane-wrapped bunch of flowers. The policeman straightened up and squared his shoulders. "Eight kids," he said quietly. "I hope he burns in Hell."

CHAPTER
EIGHTEEN

Nightingale was just getting back into his car when his phone rang. It was Robbie. "Hey, you wanted to talk to a cop on the McBride case?"

"I've already spoken to one but he was less than forthcoming."

"What was his name?"

"Stevenson. Colin Stevenson."

"Well, I've got a contact up there who says he'll talk to you, off the record and on the QT. He says he'll call you for a chat but all non-attributable."

"I've no problem with that. Who is he?"

"DI by the name of Simpson. He's the brother-in-law of a guy I know in Clubs and Vice. He's a bit jumpy but says he'll phone you if you want. He's worked on the case from Day One."

"That'd be great, Robbie. But can I meet him? I'm up here, might as well strike while the iron's hot."

"He says no to a meet. He's happy enough to brief you on the phone but he's a bit wary of a face to face, you being a private eye and all."

"I'll happily bung him a few quid."

"Oh yeah, a bribe will swing it."

"I didn't mean it that way, you daft bastard."

"Mate, the days of a cop accepting a drink are long gone. And I understand his reservations — I'd be the same if a private eye from up north wanted to pick my brains. These days you never know where that could end. So stop looking gift horses in the mouth and stay by the phone." Robbie ended the call.

Nightingale lit a cigarette and he was halfway through it when his mobile rang. The caller was withholding his number. "Jack Nightingale?"

"Yeah. Thanks for calling."

"Not sure there's much I can tell you, but what do you need?"

"Anything you can tell me about the McBride shootings would be helpful," said Nightingale.

"You're a PI, right?"

"For my sins, yeah."

"Who's the client?"

Nightingale had expected the question and had already decided that honesty was the best policy. If Simpson did show Nightingale the file he deserved the truth. "McBride's brother. Danny."

"I thought that might be it," said Simpson. "He's been in and out of our station every other day since it happened. He thinks there's some sort of conspiracy, right?"

"He just wants to understand, that's all. I think he's looking for closure and for that he has to know what happened."

"We know what happened. His brother shot dead eight kids and a teacher. Then he topped himself. It's as open and shut as it gets. Murder-suicide. And hand on

92

heart, everyone is happier it ended that way. A trial would have turned into a circus and some high-priced lawyer would have put in some insanity plea. You talk about closure, at least the parents have that. Their kids are dead but so is the man who killed them. That's probably easier to deal with than if he was in a cell with his PlayStation and choice of meals."

"I hear what you're saying," said Nightingale.

"You're not trying to prove that McBride didn't do it, are you?"

"Absolutely not," said Nightingale. "The brother knows that Jimmy did it. He knows what happened. It's the why he doesn't get."

"His brother went psycho. Who the hell knows what was going through his head? If he's hoping for an explanation he's going to be disappointed."

"You think that was it? He just snapped, for no reason?"

"It happens."

"But kids?"

"Who knows what sets a psycho off?" said the detective.

"There was no reason? No problems with the school or the staff? Kids throwing stones through his windows, that sort of thing?"

"His farm's in the middle of nowhere. We spoke to people in the nearby village and as far as they know he had no problems. He went to the local pub now and again, played dominos and cribbage, two pints and then he'd go home. Used the post office, shopped in the supermarket once a week. Nice enough guy by all accounts."

"A nice guy who just snapped?"

"Like I said, it happens. We weren't really interested in why. He did it, and he topped himself. Case closed. I understand that the brother wants more, but other than holding a séance I don't see that he's going to get that. The only person who knows why he did it is James McBride and he took the secret with him to the grave."

Nightingale tossed what was left of his cigarette out of the car window. "What can you tell me about the devil-worship thing?"

"There's an altar in the barn full of Satanic stuff."

"I saw that."

"When?"

"Yesterday. The brother took me around the farm. Other than the altar in the barn, what else did you find?"

"We've got his computer. We had the forensic computer boys go through his hard drive and they found all sorts of weird stuff on it."

"You saw it?"

"Sure. He'd visited hundreds of sites and posted on forums, asking about child sacrifice."

"I'm sorry to be a pain, but you saw this with your own eyes?"

"You don't believe me?"

"It's not that. I just have my own reasons for not believing the devil-worship thing."

"I saw the printouts."

"But not the computer itself?"

"The forensic boys have it. But we got printouts. I'm not making it up."

"Sorry mate, I didn't mean to offend you. I'm just trying to get my facts straight. You saw what you saw, I accept that, of course I do. What are the chances of me getting a look at the computer?"

"I doubt that'll happen. If you can make a request through the Met, then maybe. But they're not going to let a PI start messing around with evidence."

"Yeah, that's what I figured. So you think, what? He got caught up in some devil-worship thing? Voices in his head made him do it, that sort of thing?"

"Who knows? He didn't leave a note and there was nothing on the computer to explain why he did it."

"What about chatrooms? Was he talking to anyone specific?"

"Doesn't appear to have done," said Simpson. "It was more general appeals for information. Mostly he was guided to other sites. Some pretty sick ones, I have to say."

"Phone records?"

"Phone records?" repeated Simpson.

"Did he talk to anyone before the killings?"

"He was clearly acting alone," he said. "No one thought it necessary to start seeing who his contacts were. He picked up his shotgun, went to the school and started shooting."

"A lone nutter?"

"Obviously I'm not allowed to use phraseology like that. But he was clearly mentally unbalanced and he was acting alone."

"But you checked his computer? Whose idea was that?"

"That's pretty standard these days," said the detective. "No matter what the offence, we take a look at their computer. Same as we go through their house and car."

"Fishing expedition?"

"Drugs, terrorism, paedophile stuff. You were in the job, you know that if someone breaks one law they tend to break others."

"And the Satanic stuff was the only off thing you found?"

"That and the dead bodies, yeah." Simpson's voice was loaded with sarcasm.

"I mean, he didn't have money problems or he wasn't on anti-depressants. Nothing that might have set him off?"

"Nothing like that. You said it yourself, he was a nice guy who snapped."

"That's the thing, though. How does a nice guy get involved in black magic?"

"You'd need to ask a psychiatrist that question," he said. "Look, I think I've given you all the intel we have. Like I said, it's open and shut."

"Just one more question," said Nightingale. "I spoke with a DI called Stevenson."

"Colin? Yeah, it was him that gave me the printouts of the contents of the hard drive. He did the search of McBride's house."

"And the barn?"

"Yeah, he was straight out there. I was with the team at the school."

"He didn't seem very helpful, to be honest."

"Yeah, well, you can understand that, you being an outsider and all. And a PI to boot. He's not going to open up his files to you, is he? Be more than his job's worth. Even I've told you too much as it is."

"I get that. But they didn't pull any prints off the altar."

"Why would they need to do that? McBride lived there alone."

"To show that McBride was the one who set up the altar."

"Who else would have done it?"

"That's a very good question," said Nightingale. "If I come up with an answer, I'll let you know."

Immediately Nightingale ended the call his phone rang. It was McBride, apologising for not answering his phone earlier. "I was out with the kids and left the phone in the car," he said.

"I just wanted to let you know that I'm heading back to London. I've spoken to a few people and I'll get the stuff from the altar checked."

"Can we get the computer back?"

"Not yet," said Nightingale. "But let me work on that."

"I'm grateful for your help on this, Mr Nightingale. I know my brother wasn't crazy. And I know he didn't hate children."

CHAPTER
NINETEEN

Nightingale was about twenty minutes from Berwick, heading north to Edinburgh, when he saw the Land Rover behind him. It was a working vehicle, streaked with mud, and most of the number plate was obscured by dirt. It matched his speed, sticking about a hundred feet from his rear bumper, for the best part of a mile. A white Nissan came hurtling down the road, overtaking the Land Rover and staying in the wrong lane as it powered past Nightingale's Vauxhall.

Nightingale checked in his rear view mirror and saw the Land Rover was gaining on him. The hairs began to prickle on the back of his neck. There were two men inside, but all he could see was vague shapes. He squinted at the registration plate but could barely make out two of the numbers.

As he looked back at the road ahead he realised that the Nissan had slowed and was now only fifty feet or so ahead of him. He slowed, and as he glanced in his rear-view mirror he saw the Land Rover rapidly gaining on him.

He considered stamping on the accelerator and overtaking the Nissan, but the road ahead bent to the left and he couldn't get a clear view.

He heard the Land Rover's engine roar and it pulled out alongside him. Nightingale glanced over but the side window of the Land Rover was so streaked with dirt that he couldn't get a clear view of the man in the passenger seat.

Nightingale started to push down on the brake pedal but before he could make any difference to the Vauxhall's speed the Land Rover swung to the left and slammed into the side of him. Nightingale cursed and his fingers tightened on the steering wheel as he fought to keep control of the car. The Land Rover veered to the right and then immediately slammed back into the Vauxhall, much harder this time. The wheel wrenched itself out of Nightingale's hands and the car left the road, bucking over a grass verge and then crashing into a ditch. The airbag went off immediately and there was a scream of tortured metal.

The car came to a halt, nose down. Nightingale groaned, reached for the ignition key and switched off the engine. He didn't feel like moving, but there was a chance that his attackers would come back to finish off the job so he groped for the door handle and opened the door. It would only open a foot or so because of the side of the ditch, so he wound the window down as far as it would go and crawled out. He scrambled unsteadily out of the ditch and stood with his hands on his hips, looking down the road. There was no sign of the Nissan or the Land Rover.

He took out his pack of Marlboro and lighter from his raincoat pocket and lit one as he considered his options. Jenny had taken out full insurance when she'd made the booking for the rental car, so it wasn't going to cost him anything. He looked at his watch. If he waited for a tow truck to come out and pull the Vauxhall out of the ditch he'd miss his flight to London. He could phone a taxi from Berwick to come and pick him up, but he was starting to get a bad feeling about the citizens of the UK's northernmost town. He was still smoking and thinking when a Good Samaritan in a pick-up truck pulled up. "Are you okay?" asked the driver, a man in his fifties in a sheepskin jacket.

"Think a tyre burst," said Nightingale. "Spun off the road. Don't suppose you're going Edinburgh way, are you?"

"I am actually," said the man.

"You couldn't give me a lift to the airport, could you?"

"Sure," said the man. "But aren't you supposed to stay with the car?"

"No one's been hurt and it's a rental," said Nightingale. "Give me a minute to get my bag. I'll phone the rental company while we're on our way." He flicked the cigarette butt into the road. Finally he'd caught a lucky break. It was about time.

CHAPTER
TWENTY

Nightingale placed his overnight bag on the conveyor belt and undid his belt. He dropped the belt, his phone, watch, wallet and keys on top of his raincoat and walked through the metal detector arch. It remained silent and he smiled at the two shirt-sleeved security personnel, but they stared back stonily.

His coat and belongings came through first, and he put on his belt and coat. A bored woman chewing gum slouched in her chair as she stared at the screen in front of her. She waved her hand in the air and said something, and she was joined by an Asian man in a grey suit. He bent down to get a better look at the screen and nodded. As he straightened up, Nightingale had a sick feeling in the pit of his stomach as he realised that he'd forgotten about the knife.

The bag appeared from the scanner and the man in the suit picked it up and looked at Nightingale. Nightingale smiled apologetically. "I know, I know, I forgot all about it."

The woman picked up a phone and began talking into it.

"Is this your bag, sir?" asked the man.

"Of course it is. That's why I'm standing here." Nightingale could see from the look on the man's face that he'd chosen completely the wrong time to be sarcastic. "Yes," he said.

"Do you mind if I open it?"

Nightingale bit back a second sarcastic comment. "Sure. It's a ceremonial knife. I forgot it was there."

The man ignored his comment, moved the bag to a side table and unzipped it. He took out Nightingale's washbag, his laundry and travel alarm clock, then pulled out the evidence bag containing the crucible and frowned at it before putting it down next to the washbag. Then he pulled out the bag containing the knife. He held it up and looked at Nightingale, one eyebrow raised.

Nightingale shrugged. "I know, I know."

"Why were you trying to take this onto the plane?"

"I forgot it was there. I'm sorry."

"You forgot you were carrying a foot-long knife?"

"It's not really a foot long, is it? Nine inches, maybe." He smiled. "Not that size is everything, right?"

The man stared at him with cold eyes, still holding up the evidence bag. "You think this is funny?"

"We have a comedian, do we?" said a gruff voice behind him. Nightingale turned to see two uniformed officers standing either side of him. One was carrying a carbine in the ready position, the other had a Glock in a holster on his hip and his arms folded.

"It was an honest mistake," said Nightingale.

The uniformed cop with the folded arms shook his head. "No, sir. Forgetting to zip up your fly is an honest mistake, trying to take a knife onto a plane is a criminal offence."

CHAPTER
TWENTY-ONE

There were two of them and they could have been twins. Hard faces, receding hairlines, carrying more weight than was good for them and wearing cheap suits. They both had the weary faces of men who had been lied to for decades. Detectives. They looked the same the world over, and Nightingale figured that if he'd stayed in the job he'd probably have looked just like them by now.

Nightingale had been escorted to the room by the two armed policemen and left there until the two detectives had turned up.

One of the detectives was an inspector but he hadn't said anything. His colleague, a detective constable, had done the introductions and swung Nightingale's bag onto the table. Nightingale got the feeling that the constable was new to CID and the inspector was assessing his performance. The conversation wasn't being recorded and there didn't appear to be any CCTV cameras, which he took as a good sign, despite the hard stares. The constable's name was McKee and he had an accent so impenetrable that Nightingale had trouble understanding him. He held up the evidence bag containing the knife. "What is this?"

"A knife. A ceremonial knife. It's an antique."

McKee wrinkled his nose as he stared at the knife. "It looks old, I agree. But it doesn't look like an antique. And why were you taking it onto the plane?"

"I'm taking it to London."

"You know that you can't take knives onto planes?"

Nightingale held up his hands. "It was a mistake. An honest mistake. I'd forgotten it was in my bag, that's all."

"And why is it in an evidence bag?"

"I'm taking it to be analysed."

"Analysed?"

"I want to run it through a lab."

"A lab?"

Nightingale was about to make a joke about the detective repeating everything he said, but he doubted that he'd appreciate the attempt at humour. "I wanted to get the blood checked."

"You know there's blood on the knife, then?"

Nightingale nodded. "I'd noticed it."

"And can you explain how the blood got there?"

Nightingale took out his wallet. "I'm a detective, private," he said. He handed over a business card. "The knife and the crucible are a case. Evidence."

The detective studied the card and then passed it to the inspector. "Evidence or not, you can't take a knife onto a plane."

"Absolutely, I'm sorry. It was a genuine mistake. Look, I used to be in the job. I was a detective with the Met."

"Were you now?" He looked over at the inspector as if seeking his approval. The inspector nodded.

"CO19. And I was a negotiator. If you need a reference, I can give you the name of an inspector who'll vouch for me."

The detective held out his hand. "Do you have your passport?"

"Sure." Nightingale took his passport from his pocket and gave it to the detective.

The detective flicked through it, then studied the photo. He handed it to the inspector, who also flicked through the pages and checked the photograph. He checked the name in the passport with the name on the business card, then stood up. "I'll be back shortly," he said. His voice sounded more Northern Irish than Scottish.

Nightingale looked at his watch. "I'm going to miss my plane."

"We'll get you on the next one, Mr Nightingale," said the inspector. "Assuming that you check out." He went out of the room.

Nightingale smiled at the remaining detective. "Any chance of a coffee?"

"About as much chance of Hell freezing over," growled the detective.

"Good to know. Don't suppose I can smoke in here?"

The detective stared at Nightingale silently, his lips a thin bloodless line.

Nightingale folded his arms and sat back in his chair. Five minutes later the inspector reappeared and gave him back the passport. He sat down and interlinked his fingers. "Well, a police officer you were, Mr Nightingale. You left the Met under a cloud but at least you didn't kill anyone."

"That would be the silver lining," said Nightingale.

The inspector pointed at the knife. "You said that the knife was evidence in a case. Would that be a criminal case?"

Nightingale looked at the inspector and tried to smile as amiably as possible. Lying to police officers was never a good idea, especially detectives, but he didn't want to start a conversation about the murders in Berwick. "Divorce," he said.

The two detectives frowned in unison. "Divorce?" said the inspector.

Nightingale tried to keep the casual smile on his face as he nodded. "I'm acting for a woman who thinks that her husband is messing around with a coven of witches."

"Witches?" repeated McKee.

"Well, they claim they're a coven but the lady suspects that her husband is using it for casual sex. She found the knife and the crucible hidden in their house so she wanted me to get it checked to see if that's animal blood."

"Why does it matter what sort of blood it is?" asked the inspector.

That was a very good question, Nightingale realised. His mind raced, trying to come up with a believable answer. "It's more so that when she sues him for divorce she can say that she found a knife with chicken blood or whatever in his wardrobe. If she doesn't do the checks then he might just turn around and say it was a rusty knife he used in the garden. He's got a lot of money and he'll fight any divorce tooth and nail so she wants to get all her ducks in a row." He leaned forward and lowered his voice conspiratorially. "He's quite well connected, which is why she came to my firm. We're in London, so no one's going to tip him off."

The inspector nodded as if he was buying it.

"So can I go?" asked Nightingale.

"I don't think we need to keep you any longer. But you can't take the knife on the plane, not in your hand luggage anyway. I'd suggest you check it in with the airline. Put it in a box or a padded envelope and it can go in the baggage hold. Or use a courier service. It's Saturday, so you won't get next-day delivery, but it'll be in London Monday or Tuesday."

"Thanks," said Nightingale. He stood up and put the bagged knife into his kitbag.

CHAPTER
TWENTY-TWO

"Are you okay, is she making you happy?" asked Candy, watching Eric's face carefully for any sign of disapproval. Eric kept his feelings to himself most of the time. He never said if he was happy or sad, excited or worried, but sometimes, if she watched his eyes, she could get a clue to what he was thinking.

He smiled at her, but she knew from experience that a smile from Eric Lucas meant nothing. Smiling was his camouflage. He smiled to get his own way. He had several smiles, like an archer with a quiver of arrows, each one slightly different to the next.

"She's good," said Eric. "You made a good choice."

"I did, didn't I?" said Candy, nodding enthusiastically. "I knew she'd make a perfect princess for you."

Eric reached out and slowly stroked Candy's hair. "You did good, Candy. You did real good."

Candy smiled and felt her cheeks flush red. They were sitting at the kitchen table. She had made them cheese omelettes with toast and a pot of tea. The girl was asleep in the bedroom. Candy had given her a sleeping tablet to keep her quiet, but had tied her to the bed just in case the tablet wore off. Not that the girl could do anything even if she could move around the room. They had nailed boards over the bedroom window. The blinds were between the glass and the boards, so from outside no one could see that the window was boarded up, but there was no way that the girl could get out and no way that anyone would hear her screams. When they had first boarded up the window Candy had stood in the room and screamed her lungs out while Eric had paced around outside. He'd heard not a sound.

It was Sunday and they'd had the girl for two days. She knew that Eric enjoyed the first day the most and that his enjoyment decreased day by day until the fourth day, by which time it was over. Candy hated the fourth day, but she loved Eric so she helped him do what had to be done and then she helped him bury the bodies because without the bodies they would never get caught. That was what Eric always said and Eric was always right. Eric would never say how many girls he'd done it to over the years but Candy was sure there had been some. She was his only helper, that was what he said, and she didn't think that he was lying.

"You do love me, don't you, Eric?"

"Of course. More than anything."

"And the girls. They're just for fun."

"That's all it is. Fun. And you want me to be happy, don't you?"

Candy nodded. "More than anything."

"And you know that after I've had fun with the little princesses, things between us are so good, aren't they?"

"Yes."

"So it's a good thing we're doing. Anything that makes our relationship stronger is a good thing."

She reached over and held his hand. "No one loves you like I love you, you know that?"

"Of course I do." He squeezed her hand. "You're one in a million. A billion maybe."

"And we'll be together for ever?"

Eric grinned. "For ever and ever."

CHAPTER
TWENTY-THREE

First thing Monday morning Nightingale stopped off at Costa Coffee and brought two lattes before heading up the stairs to his office. "A coffee run, how lovely," said Jenny when she saw him. "What do you want?"

"I'm hurt," said Nightingale, placing one coffee in front of her and carrying the other through to his office. "I just wanted to show you how much you're appreciated." He had a carrier bag tucked under his arm.

"You needn't have got me a coffee, a pay rise would have been just as symbolic," she said.

Nightingale returned holding his raincoat. He handed her the carrier bag and hung up his raincoat. "I wanted a coffee, too," he said. "So it was killing two birds, really." He dropped down onto the chair opposite her desk.

"How did it go up in Berwick?"

"I got hit over the head with a blunt object and was almost killed when my car got forced off the road." He grinned at her and swung his feet up onto her desk.

"Ask a stupid question . . ."

"I'm serious," said Nightingale. "First night there I was cold-cocked and told to get out of town, and when I didn't a Land Rover side-swiped me into a ditch."

"Did you tell the police?"

"I didn't see the point. I couldn't identify anyone. And other than a sore head I'm fine." He gestured at the carrier bag and Jenny emptied the contents on to her desk. There were half a dozen Sunday newspapers and the evidence bags containing the crucible and the knife that Nightingale had taken from the barn.

"Can you send that off to the lab, get them to check the blood that's on these things."

She held them up. "Where did you get them from?"

"They were on a Satanic altar at McBride's farm. It looks like that's blood so I'm hoping the lab will confirm that and tell us what sort of blood it is."

"Lab work's not cheap," she said. "But I suppose we just add it to Mr McBride's bill."

Nightingale took out his mobile phone and handed it to her. "I took some pictures as well — can you print them so I can get a better look at them? There's a Satanic altar in the barn, or at least what passes for one. I'm going to make a few enquiries on that front, and the blood should go some way to either confirming or denying it's genuine. But there were upside-down crucifixes and goats with horns and pentangles . . ."

"But?"

"What do you mean?"

"I'm sensing a 'but' is on the way."

Nightingale looked pained. "It was almost too Satanic, if that's possible. It didn't seem organic, it was as if it had been put together so that it would press all the buttons."

"Like a film set?"

Nightingale nodded. "Exactly like a film set. And the brother was adamant he was in the barn two days before McBride kicked off. I don't see he'd lie about that. I mean, what'd be the point? There's no doubt McBride killed those kids. He said the Satanic stuff wasn't there and I believe him. So if it wasn't there two days before the killings, then either McBride put it all there or someone else did." He pulled out the sheaf of papers he'd taken from the altar. "And there's these." He gave them to her.

She frowned as she flicked through the photographs on his phone. "What are these?"

"They're printouts, as if McBride had been to Satanic websites and then made copies. But there's at least one wrong 'un in there."

"What do you mean?"

"There's a site belonging to the Order of the Nine Angels. They're a sect that's said to be involved with human sacrifice, mainly kids. But the thing is, it's actually called the Order of the Nine Angles. It's a common mistake that, people think it's about fallen angels but in fact it's nine angles and it refers to their insignia. The website there is a fraud, it's somebody messing about. And the real Nine Angles don't have a website."

"How come you know so much about them?"

Nightingale shrugged. "Something I worked on a while back. But if McBride was serious about Satanism and sacrifice he'd know that site was a fake. I think that stuff was planted in the barn along with the rest of the Satanic stuff."

114

"But who on earth would do that? And why?"

"I don't know," said Nightingale. "Yet. One of the cops. Or both. Or maybe they're covering for someone else."

"And what about the papers?" she said, gesturing at the carrier bag. "I usually only see you with the *Sun*."

"I didn't get much help from the cops I spoke to," said Nightingale. "But some of the journalists seem to have some half-decent sources. I need to work through exactly what happened. There's something not right about it."

"In what way?"

"It was something a cop said to me. A uniform who was standing outside the school. He said McBride was shooting kids but not teachers. And he didn't shoot at the cops. That doesn't make sense, does it?"

"It does if McBride hated kids."

"But there's no evidence of that. The opposite in fact. Shooters like McBride usually end up being shot by the police, but he didn't make a move against them. I want to take a closer look at what happened at the school."

"And the Sunday papers will help with that?"

"It's a start," he said.

CHAPTER
TWENTY-FOUR

The incident room for the hunt for Bella Harper was on the fifth floor of Southampton Police's Operational Command Unit, on the western approach to the city. The eight-storey limestone and glass building with its double-height canopy and public plaza was starkly modern, as were the thirty-six custody suites that were full to capacity most weekends. More than a hundred officers and another hundred civilian staff had been assigned to the case, and while the majority were out on the streets there were still more than fifty men and women answering phones and tapping away on computer terminals. It was just after eight o'clock in the morning and a lot of the people in the room had worked through the night.

The blinds were drawn and there was a line of whiteboards in front of the windows. There were photographs of Bella and a hand-drawn timeline and on one board a list of all the men on the Violent and Sex Offender Register who lived within fifty miles of the city. All the names on the list were being visited and their homes inspected.

On the opposite side of the corridor six offices had been taken over by the senior officers on the case. Word had come down from the Chief Constable that overtime wasn't an issue and that no expense was to be spared in the hunt for the missing girl.

One of the civilian staff, a man in his fifties with a greasy comb-over and sweat stains in the armpits of his shirt, was sipping coffee as he looked at the largest photograph of Bella. It was the one they were using on posters and on the TV appeals, a blow-up of her school photograph. Standing next to him was a young Asian police community service officer in a high-visibility fluorescent jacket that was a couple of sizes too big for her.

"It's true what they say, you know," said the man, gesturing at the photograph.

"Yeah, what's that?" said the PCSO.

"It's the ugly ones that come back," said the man. "Paedos keep the pretty ones." He shrugged. "It's a fact."

A massive hand grabbed the man by the back of the neck. "My office, now!" hissed Superintendent Rory Wilkinson. The superintendent frogmarched the man out of the room, across the corridor and into his office. He threw him inside and kicked the door shut.

The man put up his hands as if he feared the superintendent was going to assault him. "You can't do . . ."

"Shut the fuck up!" shouted the superintendent. "How fucking dare you make a cheap crack like that! A girl has been abducted and you think it's fucking funny?"

"I . . . I . . . I . . ." stammered the man.

The superintendent pointed a finger at the man. "You're a fucking civilian so I can't sack you but I want you out of this office now. Tell your fucking boss that you're off this investigation and if you've got anything like a brain behind that pig-ugly face you'll get transferred to another station because I am going to make your life a living fucking hell every time I see you. Now fuck off out of my sight."

The man turned, fumbled for the door handle and rushed out. The superintendent took a deep breath. His blood pressure had been borderline high at his last medical and dealing with civilian idiots wasn't helping. He closed his eyes and took another deep breath. He was fifty-four years old and hoped to retire in another year. His three children were all married with families of their own, and he and his wife had their retirement all mapped out — they had already bought a canal boat big enough to live aboard and they planned to spend six months of the year cruising the canal system and six months in their villa in southern Spain. Thinking of the canal boat always calmed him down — there was nothing more relaxing than pottering along at four miles an hour, the tiller in one hand and a mug of tea in the other.

"Sir?"

The superintendent opened his eyes. It was Aaron Fisher, a young detective who had only recently joined CID. "Yes, lad?"

"I've just had a call that sounded like the real thing." He mimed putting a phone to his head as if the superintendent might not understand what he meant. "Old couple out in Lyndhurst."

Lyndhurst was a small town close to the New Forest, half an hour's drive from Southampton. "Spit it out, lad."

"They say their neighbours turned up with a kid a couple of days ago. They didn't get a good look but they're pretty sure it was a young girl."

"A couple of days ago?" It was Tuesday morning. Bella Harper had been snatched on Friday.

"Sorry, sir. On Friday."

"They've seen the appeal pictures?"

"They know what Bella looks like, but they say the girl taken into the house was being carried so they didn't get a good look. They've not seen the girl since, so they think she might be in the house."

"Who lives there?"

"According to the electoral roll a guy called Eric Lucas. The caller doesn't know anything about them."

"Checked the Sex Offenders Register?"

Fisher nodded. "No Eric Lucas."

The superintendent rubbed his chin thoughtfully. The unit was getting several hundred calls a day, and the bulk of them were false sightings of Bella Harper. "What makes you think this is the real thing?"

"The timing, sir." Fisher looked at his notebook. "Mrs Pullman, she's the lady who rang in, said she's pretty sure she saw the girl at three o'clock in the afternoon on Saturday. She went missing at just before two-thirty."

"And this Eric Lucas doesn't have kids?"

"There's no wife on the electoral roll and Mrs Pullman says she's never seen a child there before, there are no toys in the garden."

"Today's a school day. She's sure the kid didn't leave for school today?"

"I asked that. Mrs Pullman was in her front garden all morning. She's not a great sleeper, she said, and she was doing some weeding. No one has come in or gone out."

"So this Eric Lucas doesn't work?"

"That's another thing that made me think she might have something. He usually leaves for work at seven-thirty in the morning. Today his car is still in the drive."

"Car? So no white van?"

Fisher shook his head. "Blue Mondeo," he said.

"What does he do?"

"Mrs Pullman doesn't know."

"Do they know who the woman is? Girlfriend? Sister?"

"She's been living there for the past year or so. But they keep themselves to themselves." He tapped his notebook against his leg. "Mrs Pullman isn't a timewaster. She kept saying she hoped she wasn't being a bother, but she had seen the TV appeals and she felt she had to let us know what she'd seen. Do you think I should go and check the Lucas house?"

The superintendent looked at his watch. It was just after mid-day.

"I keep getting this tingle on the back of my neck," said Fisher. "I know that sounds crazy."

120

"It doesn't sound crazy at all," said the superintendent. "A copper's hunch has helped me out more times than I can remember. You're right, the timing is bang on and the car still being there is a red flag. Get Dave Hopkins in here and we'll get something sorted."

CHAPTER
TWENTY-FIVE

Jenny McLean frowned when she opened the door and found Nightingale studying a large whiteboard on which he'd stuck photographs cut from the Sunday papers. She looked at her watch. It was ten to nine. "Early bird catching the worm?" she said as she took off her coat.

"Up with the lark indeed," said Nightingale. "Late rising is for the birds. Are we about done with the ornithological references?"

"I just mean it's not like you to beat me into the office." She walked over to him and looked at the information on the whiteboard. He'd drawn a map of the school and marked where the children had been killed with black crosses. He'd drawn red lines from the crosses to the relevant photographs. Eight of the crosses were of children. The ninth, in the playground, had a red line linking it to a balding man in his forties.

"What are you doing?"

"Trying to work out why McBride did what he did."
"He killed kids, we know that."

"Yeah, but if he just wanted to kill kids he could have just walked into one classroom and started blasting away. He had plenty of cartridges."

Jenny stared at the hand-drawn map of the school. "He walked down the corridor and into several classrooms?"

Nightingale nodded. "And then into the gym. That's where he shot his last two victims and where he killed himself."

"So the question is, why go to all that trouble?"

"Exactly. If the aim was just to kill kids then he'd have been a lot more productive if he'd just gone into one classroom and blasted away."

"Productive? That's a sick way of putting it."

"What I mean is if it was a body count he was after, he went about it in a bloody funny way. And if it wasn't about a body count, what was he doing?"

"Do you think the police are asking the same question?"

Nightingale grimaced. "Probably not," he said. "When the cops are on a murder investigation, they're looking at motive, means and opportunity. They construct a timeline and they investigate everyone who came into contact with the victim. But in this case they're not looking for a suspect. They know who the killer was, they caught him in the act. So they're not going to be worrying about a motive. So far as they're concerned, the case was closed when McBride killed himself. There'll be an inquest, but the verdict will be murder and suicide. It's not the coroner's job to say why McBride did what he did, though he might say something along the lines of the balance of his mind was disturbed."

"I don't think there's much doubt about that," said Jenny. "Well-balanced people don't usually ran amok with shotguns, do they?"

"No, but from the accounts in the papers, he didn't run amok. He was as cold as ice. Dead calm. And if you look at how he moved through the school, it was purposeful. It wasn't random."

"You think he was choosing his victims?"

She looked at the photographs one by one. They were all children aged between eight and ten, and most of the pictures had been taken at school. They were wearing uniforms and smiling happily at the camera, bright-eyed children with their lives ahead of them. Jenny pointed at one of the photographs, a dark-haired girl with a snub nose. "Manka?"

"Polish," said Nightingale. "Mum arrived in the UK ten years ago, the girl was born here. Mum's a single parent." He tapped another photograph. "Paul Tomkins. His mum's also a single parent."

"Coincidence?" asked Jenny.

Nightingale pointed at a third photograph. "Zach Atkins. His parents split up five years ago and he's being brought up by his dad."

Jenny frowned. "Are you serious?"

Nightingale moved his finger along the whiteboard to a photograph of a girl with curly red hair. "Ruth Glazebrook. Parents divorced. Lives with her mum." He looked at Jenny and shrugged. "Of the eight, those four are described by the papers as being in one-parent families. The parental status of the other three isn't

124

mentioned. Can you run checks on the rest? I figure the best way is to look at the electoral roll."

"Easily done," said Jenny. "But you can't seriously think he was killing kids from single-parent families."

"I don't know what to think at the moment. But if it wasn't random, we need to know why he killed the ones he did. If we can answer that question, we'll have a better idea of what was going on. But the more I look at it, the more I'm sure he wasn't a crazy devil-worshipper."

"What about the religious connection?"

"What religious connection?"

"The names. Paul. Ruth. Zach. And there's a Noah. All biblical."

"Zach? Since when is Zach biblical?"

"Zacharias. He was a prophet. Manka doesn't fit but maybe that's the exception that proves the rule."

"Manka is a Polish variant of Mary," said Nightingale.

"Is it now? But one of the girls was called Brianna. I'm pretty sure that's not in the Bible either. The point I'm making is you've got to be careful when you start looking for connections. Just because a few of them are from single-parent families doesn't mean that's why he killed them. You might just as well say they all have blue eyes or played the piano."

"How do you know they played the piano?"

Jenny sighed. "I didn't. I plucked that from the air."

"You noticed the date, by the way? And the time?"

Jenny frowned. "September the ninth, right? A couple of days after the kids went back to school."

"And the time?"

Jenny shrugged. "It was at the start of school."

"It was nine o'clock when he started shooting. On the dot."

"Am I missing something here, Jack?"

"Nine o'clock on September the ninth. The ninth month. Nine, nine, nine."

She frowned and shrugged again. "And?"

"Jenny, three nines. Nine, nine, nine. That's a Satanic number."

"It's also the emergency services number. Anyway, I thought six six six was the number of the Devil."

"The number of the beast," said Nightingale. "But Satan's number is nine nine nine. You can blame Hollywood for the whole six six six thing. And then there's the number of victims. Eight kids and one teacher. Nine."

"So what are you saying, now you think it was some devil-worship thing?"

"He picked up the shotgun and got to the school at nine o'clock," said Nightingale. "If he'd got there at ten we wouldn't be having this conversation, would we?"

"But his brother was definite, wasn't he? James McBride wasn't a Satanist."

"Yeah, but Satanists don't tend to advertise themselves, do they? If James was in league with the Devil there's a pretty good chance he wouldn't tell his brother."

"What do you want to do, Jack? He wants you to prove his brother wasn't a Satanist but everything in the papers says he was. And if you're right and the nine nine nine thing is significant . . ." She shrugged.

"He wants to know why his brother did what he did," said Nightingale. "I get paid whatever I find out. The altar was definitely wrong and I think the computer stuff is a definite red herring but the nine nine nine can't be a coincidence."

"Of course it can," she said. "Look at the conspiracy theories over the Twin Towers. September eleven. Nine one one. And that's the American emergency services number."

"It's not the same thing," said Nightingale.

"You've got to be careful reading something into random numbers, that's all I'm saying."

"What do you think then?"

"It doesn't matter what I think," said Jenny. "Mr McBride's going to want proof at the end of the day. And at the moment all we have is supposition." She pointed at the photograph of the adult. "That's the teacher who died, right?"

"Deputy headmaster," said Nightingale. "Simon Etchells."

"Single parent?"

"Married but no kids," said Nightingale. "You have to wonder why McBride shot this guy but none of the other teachers."

"Maybe he tried to stop him."

"Maybe. But I don't see him getting aggressive with a man with a shotgun. They tend to produce the opposite effect. That's why the shotgun is the weapon of choice for bank robbers and the like. It's all about

127

intimidation and a shotgun is just about the most intimidating gun there is."

"What are you saying?"

"I'm not sure, yet," said Nightingale. "But he went into four classrooms and there was a teacher in each one. The teacher would have been the first person he saw. Yet he didn't shoot them. He shot kids. The same in the gymnasium. There was a gym teacher there but McBride ignored him and shot two kids before the police arrived. According to the papers, the cops arrived when the shooting was going on. They heard a shot outside the school, and another when they went inside. Two shots. So that would be the two kids he killed in the gym." He tapped the photograph of Zach Atkins and another of a dark-haired boy with an impish grin. "Zach Atkins and Noah Woodhouse. But here's the thing. It took the cops a good three or four minutes to move through the school to the gym. And as soon as they got there, McBride took his own life. Here's the big question. Why did he stop shooting?"

"Ran out of cartridges?"

Nightingale shook his head. "There were several dozen in his knapsack. He could have shot more kids. And fired at the cops."

"What are you suggesting, Jack?"

Nightingale shrugged. "I don't know. But the way he behaved makes no sense to me. If he wanted to lash out at the world, why shoot kids? He could have gone into the council offices and shot dozens of people. Or the pub. Or the shops. He targeted the school."

"That happens," said Jenny. "Look at Dunblane. That bastard killed 16 children. And that Norwegian right-wing nutter, Breivik, he massacred seventy-seven people and most of them were kids."

Nightingale walked over to the window and then turned to face the board. He folded his arms as he studied his handiwork. "Okay, so let's suppose that for whatever reason McBride set out to kill children. Why shoot the deputy headmaster but then ignore the rest of the teachers? If he was just after kids he could just threaten to shoot the deputy and the guy would have shat himself."

"Lovely image."

"It's true, though. He chose to shoot the deputy, but he didn't shoot the teachers. And why move from classroom to classroom? If the aim was to kill kids, all he had to do was to walk into a single classroom and keep shooting. He had all the ammo he needed, he'd be standing at the only door, he could fire and reload to his heart's content. There were more than thirty kids in that first classroom, but he only shot one."

"Maybe he stepped out to reload."

"Maybe. But then he could have gone back into the same classroom. But he didn't. Plus, there's the fact he walked past two classrooms full of kids before he started shooting. Why would he do that? Why not just go into the first classroom in the corridor?"

Jenny shrugged and didn't say anything.

"When he does go into a classroom, he shoots a girl. Ignores the teacher. According to the teacher he walked into the room, fired once then turned and walked out.

He walks across the corridor into the second classroom where he shoots two more little girls. Ruth Glazebrook and Emily Smith. Again he doesn't shoot the teacher. Just blows the little girls away and then he's out. He walks along the corridor, reloads, and in the next classroom shoots a boy and a girl. Then across the corridor to shoot a girl. Then he crosses the corridor to shoot another kid. The Polish girl, Manka. Six children in four different classrooms.

"At that point he walks to the gymnasium. The teachers use that as an opportunity to get the kids out of the classrooms. That's about the time the police arrive. McBride reloads and walks into the gymnasium. The gym teacher manages to get the fire exit open and starts ushering the kids out. McBride shoots two of the kids, then stops. There's an interview with the gym teacher in the *Sunday Mirror*. He says he saw McBride standing in the middle of the gym after he'd fired the second shot. He didn't reload, he just stood there and watched as the kids ran out of the fire exit. Again, if he'd wanted to keep killing he could have done. He had all the ammo he needed. But he didn't. He stood there and waited until the cops arrived and then he sat down and blew his own head off."

Jenny nodded as she looked at the whiteboard. "He wasn't shooting at kids in general, that's what you mean." She frowned. "He was shooting specific children?"

"Maybe," said Nightingale.

130

"And you think he was shooting at children from one-parent families?" She turned to look at him. "That doesn't make any sense, does it?"

Nightingale shrugged. "That's why I need you to check the family circumstances of the rest of the children who died," he said. "But yeah, it doesn't make any sense."

They were interrupted by the phone ringing. Jenny hurried over to her desk to take the call and scribbled some notes on her pad. When she'd finished she replaced the receiver and looked up at Nightingale. "Pig's blood," she said. "That's what was in the crucible. And the knife."

"Interesting," said Nightingale.

"Is that significant?"

"I'm not sure," he said. "But I know someone who will be able to tell me."

CHAPTER
TWENTY-SIX

Joanna Pullman's doorbell rang and she looked up from her magazine. "Now who could that be?"

Her husband Melvin was sitting at the dining table, staring at a chess set. He belonged to the local chess club and they had a match coming up against their long-time rivals in nearby Cadham. "You could always answer it and find out," he said. He picked up a knight, tapped it against the side of his head, and then replaced it.

"I thought when you touched it you had to move it," said Mrs Pullman.

"I'm only practising," he said. The doorbell rang again. He sighed and pushed himself out of his chair. "I suppose I'd better get it."

"Well, you are nearest."

Mr Pullman chuckled. She was right, but there was only about three feet in it. He was still chuckling when he opened the door. Two men in British Gas overalls were standing there. There was a blue van parked outside their house. The younger of the two men, in his late twenties with short curly hair and piercing blue eyes, held out a black leather wallet with a silver badge on it. "Mr Pullman? I'm detective Aaron Fisher, I spoke to your wife on the phone." He was holding a dark blue plastic toolbox.

"You're not the gas man?" said Mr Pullman.

"I'm with Hampshire CID," said Fisher, putting his ID away. "This is my colleague, Inspector Hopkins." Inspector Hopkins nodded and held up a clipboard.

"Why are you dressed like gasmen?" asked Mr Pullman.

"Can we come in, please?" asked Fisher. "We really need a world with your wife."

"I suppose so," said Mr Pullman, holding the door open wide. "But do wipe your feet, she hates it when people walk mud over the carpets."

The two policemen took it in turns to wipe their shoes on a thick bristle mat on the doorstep before walking along the hallway and into the main room, where Mrs Pullman was still reading her gardening magazine.

Fisher put down his toolbox, introduced himself and showed her his warrant card. "You're a policeman but you're dressed like the gasman," she said, frowning.

"That's what I said," said Mr Pullman.

"We didn't want anyone to see that we were with the police," said Hopkins. He put his clipboard on the dining table next to Mr Pullman's chess set. "You called us about Mr Lucas."

Mrs Pullman's frown deepened. "Mr Lucas?" she repeated.

"Your next door neighbour. You did call us about him, didn't you? About seeing him with a young girl."

Mrs Pullman smiled. "I'm sorry, yes, I did. But I didn't know that was his name. He's not the sociable type and he's never introduced himself."

"Well, we think his name is Eric Lucas and he doesn't appear to be married, but you told my colleague you saw him with a woman on Saturday and they carried a young girl into the house."

Mrs Pullman nodded. "That's right."

"What time exactly?"

"It was three o'clock. On the dot. I know because I was in the garden and I had Radio Four on and I heard the time check."

Hopkins unclipped a photograph of Bella Harper from his clipboard. It was the school photograph they'd used for the public appeals, with Bella smiling brightly at the camera, her blonde curls pulled back from her face. "Was this the girl, Mrs Pullman?"

She took the photograph and looked at it for several seconds. "It could have been," she said. "I saw blonde hair. He had her in his arms, so I couldn't see her face. But we have a nine-year-old granddaughter and she's ten, and the girl he was carrying looked about the same size as Hannah."

"Hannah's your granddaughter?"

Mrs Pullman nodded.

"And they carried her from the car to the house. At three o'clock in the afternoon?"

"Not the car," said Mrs Pullman. "The car was in the drive. They drove up in a van."

"A white van?" asked the inspector.

"I suppose so. I mean, there was writing on the side. It was a company van. But I didn't pay it much attention."

"The woman drives a van sometimes," said Mr Pullman. "It's a plumbing company. Or a drain clearer. I've seen her in it in a few times."

"You didn't tell me that," said his wife.

"You never asked," said Mr Pullman.

"So this woman with Mr Lucas drives a white van?"

"Like my wife said, it's not really white. Greyish. With signs on the side."

"And where's the van now?"

Mr Pullman looked over at his wife and they both shrugged.

"Is it possible it's in the garage?" asked the inspector.

"I didn't see them put it away," said Mrs Pullman. "But I suppose it's possible."

"And you haven't seen the child since? Or heard anything?"

"Not a peep," said Mrs Pullman. "Do you think it's her? Do you think it's Bella?"

"We don't want to jump to any conclusions," said the inspector. "Is there an upstairs window that overlooks their house?"

"The spare bedroom," said Mr Pullman. "I'll show you."

The inspector followed Mr Pullman upstairs. Fisher knelt down next to his toolbox and opened it. He took out a pair of binoculars and a police radio and headed upstairs.

Mr Pullman was standing at the bedroom door while Inspector Hopkins peered around a dark green curtain. He held out his hand for the binoculars, then focused them on the house next door. There wasn't much to be seen. There was a window on the upper floor that was presumably a bedroom and the blinds were closed. He could see the blue Mondeo, but there was no window in the garage so he had no way of knowing if there was a van in there or not.

There were two green wheelie bins at the side of the house.

"When are the bins collected?" asked the inspector.

"Thursdays."

The inspector checked the rear garden through the binoculars. There were no toys, and no washing on the line. "And you haven't seen anyone coming or going since Saturday?"

"To be honest, we rarely see the neighbours on either side," said Mr Pullman. "We're all detached, and most people value their privacy."

The inspector put down his binoculars. He wasn't sure what to do. There wasn't enough hard evidence to call in an entry team, but if Bella was indeed next door then every second counted. He nodded at Fisher. "Take Mr Pullman downstairs while I make a call," he said.

He took out his mobile and phoned Superintendent Wilkinson.

CHAPTER
TWENTY-SEVEN

The Wicca Woman shop was tucked away in a Camden side street between a store selling exotic bongs and Bob Marley T-shirts, and another that sold garish hand-knitted sweaters. Nightingale pushed open the door and a bell tinkled. He stepped inside and his nose was assaulted by a dozen or more scents, including orange, cloves, lavender, lemon grass and jasmine. There was a dark-haired teenage girl with half a dozen facial piercings and web-like gloves on her hands standing at a display case full of crystal balls and pyramids.

"Is Mrs Steadman in?" asked Nightingale. A stick of incense was burning by the cash register, filling the shop with a sweet, almost sickly, scent.

"She's upstairs. She's got a headache." The girl scratched her arm as she studied Nightingale with cold green eyes.

"Can you do me a big favour and tell her that Jack Nightingale is here?"

"Like the bird?"

"Yeah. Like the bird."

"How do you get a name like Nightingale then?"

Nightingale frowned, wondering if she was joking, then realised that she probably wasn't. "It was my father's name," he said.

"Never heard of anyone called Nightingale before."

"There's a few of us around. So, can you see if Mrs Steadman has time for me?"

Before she could reply, a beaded curtain drew back and Mrs Steadman appeared. She smiled at Nightingale but he could see she wasn't well. Her eyes had lost their sparkle, and she had always been tiny but if anything she seemed even smaller, a bird-like little woman who looked as if she might break under the slightest pressure. "This is a pleasant surprise, Mr Nightingale."

"I'm sorry you're not feeling well, I just need some advice."

"Why don't we go for a walk?" she said. "Lori here can mind the shop and I think I could do with some fresh air. Wait while I get my coat." She disappeared back through the curtain and reappeared a couple of minutes later wrapped up in a thick black wool coat with a leather belt. "I won't be long, Lori," she said to her assistant.

They stepped out of the shop and Mrs Steadman slipped her arm through Nightingale's as they walked along the pavement. The heels of her boots clicked with every step, and Nightingale had to slow his pace so that she could keep up with him. "Are you okay, Mrs Steadman?" he asked.

She gave his arm a squeeze. "I've had a busy few days, my energy levels are a bit low, that's all."

"You're sure? You look tired."

"I am tired. But I'll be better soon. Really, you don't have to worry about me, I've been around a long time."

"How long exactly, Mrs Steadman?"

She laughed and it was a sound like birdsong. "A long, long time," she said. "Let's leave it at that, shall we?"

They walked through Camden market, weaving their way through the throngs of shoppers and tourists towards the canal. They followed the towpath for a few hundred yards and sat down on a wooden bench overlooking the water. They watched a brightly coloured barge go by, then Nightingale reached into his raincoat pocket and pulled out half a dozen of the photographs he'd taken at the McBride farm. He held them in his lap. "I need some guidance, Mrs Steadman. About black magic."

Mrs Steadman gasped slightly. "You know that's not my field of expertise," she said quietly.

"I remember you telling me once there was no black or white magic, it was all magic."

"That's true," she said. "Magic is power and can be drawn down for good or for evil. In the same way that electricity can be used to save a life, or take one."

"But you understand the mechanics of both?"

"I know messing around with the dark side is a very dangerous thing to do," she said. "As I've told you several times."

Nightingale nodded. A man walked by with two Jack Russell dogs and he waited until they were out of earshot before continuing. "I need to know if this is a real black magic altar or not," he said. He passed her the photographs.

Mrs Steadman looked through them in silence, spending several minutes staring at each one. When she had finished she looked up at Nightingale. "Where did you get these?"

"I took them," he said. "It was in a barn up in Berwick."

She nodded thoughtfully. "You've heard the story about the Devil and Berwick?"

"The Devil's thumb? Yes."

"It's a very strange place, Berwick. A lot of very unnatural things happen there." Realisation dawned and she sighed sadly. "The children?"

"I'm afraid so. That was what the police found in the man's barn."

"And you think something isn't right?"

Nightingale's eyes narrowed. "What makes you think that?"

Mrs Steadman patted him on the knee. "Why else would you be showing me these pictures?" She smiled at him over the top of her half-moon spectacles. "What do you think is wrong?"

He took the photographs from her and flicked through them, then pointed at the lead crucible that he'd had analysed by the lab. "I had this examined and the blood in it was pig's blood. That didn't seem right to me."

"Blood is used in black magic rites, but yes, pig's blood would be of no use. Chicken's blood if it was a voodoo ceremony of course, but otherwise it would

140

have to be human blood. And usually a particular type of human blood."

"From a virgin?"

"Not necessarily," said Mrs Steadman. "It would depend on the rite. But it would be human. Pig's blood, you say?"

"That's right. Do you mind if I smoke?"

Mrs Steadman looked pained. "I'd rather you didn't," she said. "I'm really not feeling well. You know, I could give you something that would help you give up smoking."

"Nicotine patches?"

She chuckled. "I was thinking of a spell," she said. "All it takes is a gemstone candle containing amethyst. I have some in the shop. It's so successful I offer a money-back guarantee."

Nightingale grinned. "I like smoking," he said. "I don't want to give up."

"Your one vice?" she said.

"Seriously, smoking makes me feel good."

"Even though you know the risks?"

"I think the risks are exaggerated," he said. "And let's face it, at the end of the day everyone dies whether they smoke or not." He shrugged. "I don't have too many vices. I figure I'm entitled to one."

"Just be careful, Mr Nightingale," she said. "Things that give you the greatest pleasure can sometimes cause you the greatest pain."

"I hear you, Mrs Steadman." He gestured at the photographs. "The fact that the blood is pig's blood means that it's not a real altar, right?"

"If it was a true black magic altar, it wouldn't be pig's blood, that's true."

"And what about the pictures?"

"You're right," she said. "Whoever made that altar didn't really know what they were doing. There are two inverted pentagrams, which are as they should be, but one of the pentagrams is the correct way up. That's how it is used in Wicca, and no Satanist would use it that way. The goat head is correct, it's the horned goat, the one they call Baphomet. Satanists use the goat to mock Jesus, who is the lamb of God. But the symbol is missing a burning candle on the head of the goat. Whoever put the altar together knows about the symbol but doesn't understand the significance of the candle." She sorted through the photographs, then pulled one out and showed it to him. "And here, do you see the star and crescent symbols here on the wall? The crescent represents Diana, the moon goddess. The star is Lucifer, the son of the morning. The way the symbol is drawn, with the star to the left of the crescent, is the way that it's used in Wicca. In a Satanic ritual, it would be reversed, the star would be to the right."

"So whoever constructed the altar made a mistake?"

"The symbols have to be correct in order to maintain their power," said Mrs Steadman. "It's all about channelling the energy. With the symbols mixed up as they are, any energy would be unfocused."

"It wouldn't work, is that what you're saying?"

"I don't see that it would function at all," she said. "Either as a Wicca altar or as a Satanic altar. Whoever constructed it really didn't know what they were doing.

142

Do you think that the man who killed the children did it?"

"I'm not sure," said Nightingale.

"If it was him, he's not a serious Satanist, I can tell you that for sure," she said.

"I'm starting to think that perhaps it wasn't his work," said Nightingale.

"Somebody wanted to make it look as if he was a Satanist?"

"I think so, yes. Somebody who didn't realise the significance of the symbols and the blood."

"But why would anyone want to do that, Mr Nightingale? He killed those children, didn't he?"

"I don't think there's any doubt about that," he said.

"So why was it so important to make him appear to be a devil-worshipper?"

"That, Mrs Steadman, is a very good question," said Nightingale.

CHAPTER
TWENTY-EIGHT

"So the time fits and there was a van?" said Superintendent Wilkinson. He'd been watching Sky News with the sound down as he'd listened to the inspector report on what he'd learned, which frankly wasn't much. Mr and Mrs Harper were due to make a live appeal within the hour, not that there was anything new for them to say. Just tears and scared faces and the same words over and over again. Please let us have our daughter back, please don't hurt her. Paedophiles didn't pay attention to appeals, Wilkinson knew that, but it was important to keep the missing girl in the public's thoughts.

"There's no sign of a van now, but there is a garage. Sir, we could try knocking at the door. We're overalled up as gasmen, we could say we're testing for leaks."

"You can't go in without a warrant or probable cause, you know that."

"We could do a walk around the outside. Try to get a look-see through the windows."

"Okay, but no knocking on the door and under no circumstances are you to go inside. But if they come out, you can speak to them. And watch young Fisher, he's still wet behind the ears."

"Understood, sir."

The superintendent ended the call. Mr and Mrs Harper were taking their places at a table, flanked by the deputy chief constable and a lady from the Press Office. He grabbed for the remote and turned the volume up.

CHAPTER
TWENTY-NINE

"Please don't let him do it to me again," sobbed Bella. "I want to go home. I want my mummy and daddy."

"Stop crying!" hissed Candy.

"You said you were my friend." Bella sniffed and wiped her nose with the back of her hand.

"I'm not your friend, you silly little cow! Now stop crying or I'll give you a slap." She raised her hand menacingly and Bella collapsed onto the bed.

"What's her problem?" asked Eric, coming into the bedroom.

"She's being a cry-baby," said Candy.

"It doesn't matter, we're almost done with her," said Eric.

"I want to go home," whispered Bella.

"You're never going home," said Candy. "Ever. You're never going to see your mum or your dad or your stupid rabbit. We're the last thing you're ever going to see, the last thing you're ever going to feel. You belong to us and when we're finished with you we're going to throw you away like the rubbish you are."

"No!" moaned Bella.

Eric pulled down his jeans and kicked them off. "Hold her down," he said. "And shut her up. I'm sick of her bloody voice."

CHAPTER
THIRTY

"Please keep away from the windows," said Inspector Hopkins. "We'll come back before we leave to let you know what's happening."

"Not a problem," said Mr Pullman. He opened the front door for them and closed it as they walked back to their van.

The two detectives walked back to the van. The inspector opened the door and tossed his clipboard onto the driver's seat. "Okay, we do a walk around the outside of the house. Do you have anything that looks like it'll detect a leak?"

"I've got a meter thing," said Fisher. He opened the toolbox and took out an electrical meter with an impressive-looking dial. The inspector nodded his approval. "Wave that around. If anyone comes out, leave the talking to me."

Fisher nodded. The inspector slammed the door shut. They walked towards the Lucas house. They walked either side of the Mondeo and then turned to the left to walk by the garage. Fisher waved his meter around and then tried the handle of the garage. To his surprise it opened. "Sir!" he said.

148

Hopkins hissed at him and threw him a dirty look. Then he motioned for him to pull up the door. Fisher stepped back and pulled the door up a couple of feet. Both men peered inside.

"Bloody hell," said Fisher. It was a white van with the name of a plumbing firm on the side.

Hopkins slipped inside. The signs were magnetic so that they could easily be removed. They had probably removed the signs during the abduction and replaced them when the car was in the garage. There was an internal door connecting the garage to the house. Hopkins tiptoed over to it. Fisher started to duck under the garage door but the inspector waved him back. He reached the connecting door, placed his hands against it and then gently pressed his ear to the wood.

CHAPTER
THIRTY-ONE

Eric rolled off the little girl and grinned at Candy. "That was good," he said. He wiped the sweat from his face with his hands. "That was really good."

Bella curled up into a ball and cried softly. There was blood on the sheets. Not that it mattered, because they always destroyed the bed linen and towels after it was over.

Candy put her hand around his neck and kissed him hard on the lips. Her tongue probed between his teeth and she moaned with pleasure. She groped between his legs and her heart leapt when she discovered that he was growing hard again. He wanted her. He always did after he'd had sex with the girls. "Do you want me, Eric?" she whispered.

"You know I do," he said.

"Do you love me?"

He reached for her and pulled off her shirt. He fumbled with her bra but he couldn't unhook it so she did it for him and threw the bra on the floor as her breasts fell free. He kissed her again, harder this time. Candy rolled onto her back, lifted her hips and slipped off her underwear. She could feel how wet she was. Eric tried to get on top of her but she pushed him off and rolled him onto his back. He grinned up at her as she straddled him. She grabbed his chin with her right hand, her fingers digging into his flesh. It was the one time that she had power over him. The only time.

"Say you love me," she said.

"I love you."

She lowered herself on to him, gasping as he entered her, then she began to ride him, faster and faster.

Candy stared down at the tearful little girl, her eyes burning with hatred. "Look at me, Bella. This is how a real woman fucks a man."

Bella put her hands over her face and continued to sob.

Candy pounded herself against Eric. "Come for me, baby," she shouted. "Come for me and then we'll kill the little bitch."

CHAPTER
THIRTY-TWO

Hopkins moved away from the door and over to Fisher. "I can hear voices, but it's muffled," he said.

"What do we do?"

"It's the Super's call," said the inspector. He took out his phone and called Superintendent Wilkinson.

"What do you think?" asked the superintendent after Hopkins had brought him up to speed.

"It's the same make as the van in the CCTV footage. This one has signs on the side but they're magnetic. And I can hear voices inside. I think this is it, sir."

"Where are you?"

"In the garage. The door was open."

"Well, get the hell out of the garage and wait for armed support. I don't want this turning into a hostage situation. Hang back and wait for the ARV. Hang on a minute." Hopkins heard the superintendent shout over to someone and then someone shouted back. "Fifteen minutes. Maybe twenty."

"We'll be in the van," said Hopkins.

"They'll radio you direct with an ETA," said the superintendent. "This had better be right or we're going to look bloody stupid." He ended the call.

The inspector nodded at Fisher. "Back to the van," he said. "Quietly does it."

That was when they heard the scream from inside the house.

CHAPTER
THIRTY-THREE

Eric clamped his hand over Bella's mouth. "Shut up or I'll snap your neck," he said. He'd dressed but hadn't put his shoes on. Candy had put on her clothes, too, and she stood at the foot of the bed, collecting up Bella's clothes. "All I'm doing is taking you upstairs to clean you. You need a bath. You have to be clean for when we take you back to your mummy and daddy. Do you understand me?"

Bella nodded fearfully.

"Good girl. Now I'm going to take my hand away from your mouth but if you scream I'll hurt you, I'll hurt you real bad. Okay?"

Bella nodded again and Eric slowly removed his hand. His palm was soaked with her tears and he wiped his hand on his jeans. "Candy said she was going to kill me," she whispered.

"She was joking," said Eric. He flashed Candy an angry glare. "We're going to get you clean and dressed and then we'll take you to see your mummy and daddy. Tonight you'll be tucked up safe and sound in your own bed."

"You swear?"

Eric nodded. "I swear."

"Cross your heart and swear to die?"

"Cross my heart and swear to die," said Eric. It was an easy lie to tell because he didn't believe in God. He didn't believe in anything much.

Candy laughed and Eric glared at her. He patted Bella on the shoulder. "You and me will go upstairs to the bathroom," he said. "Would you like a bubble bath?"

"I just want to go home," said Bella. She sniffed and wiped her nose with the back of her arm. "Please just let me go home."

"You are going home," he said. "Don't worry."

He took her by the hand and led her upstairs. First he would clean her, getting rid of any DNA evidence. Then he'd kill her. Then they'd drive her out to the New Forest and bury her near the others. And then the hunt would begin again.

CHAPTER
THIRTY-FOUR

Inspector Hopkins yanked at the door. It was locked. He stepped back and considered giving it a kick, but he could see immediately that it was strong enough to take a lot of punishment. He looked around and saw a garden fork and a spade hanging from hooks on the wall. He grabbed the spade and headed for the garage door. "Come on, lad," he said. "Grab that fork and follow me."

He ducked under the door and hurried around to the back of the house. The superintendent had said to stand by until the Armed Response Vehicle arrived, but the scream had changed all that. It was definitely a young girl and the sound had chilled his blood. It was a scream of a child in fear of her life.

He hurtled down the path to the back of the house. The kitchen door looked as solid as the one in the garage, but the window overlooking the rear garden was one large sheet of glass. Hopkins swung the spade back and brought it crashing through the window, turning his face to avoid any flying glass. Fisher joined him, and together they used their garden tools to hack away the remaining shards of glass.

Hopkins threw his spade through the window and crawled after it. He rolled over the windowsill, then wriggled across the sink and twisted so that he dropped feet first onto the kitchen floor. His shoes crunched on broken glass as he bent down to pick up the spade. Blood smeared across the handle and he realised that he'd cut his left hand. As he straightened up he saw Fisher struggling to crawl through the window. He leaned towards him, grabbed him by the scruff of the neck and dragged him through before running out of the kitchen.

There was a woman in the hallway, mid-twenties in a grubby sweatshirt and Adidas tracksuit bottoms. "Where's the girl?" shouted Hopkins.

The woman was in shock, her eyes were wide and her mouth open. She had an acne rash across her forehead and a tan that looked as if it had come from a bottle.

"The girl?" shouted Hopkins again, raising the spade with both hands.

The woman pointed up the stairs. "Bathroom," she said.

Hopkins walloped her left leg with the spade, just below the knee. As the leg buckled he pushed her face down on the floor, just as Fisher came running out of the kitchen. "Keep her down, and call the Super, fill him in," said Hopkins.

As he ran up the stairs, Fisher planted his foot in the middle of the sobbing woman's back and fumbled for his phone.

Hopkins took the stairs two at a time, the blade of the shovel scraping against the wall. He reached the landing and looked around. There was a door open to his left and he hurried towards it, raising the spade.

There was a man leaning over the bath. Hopkins saw a mop of greasy brown hair, a Chelsea football shirt and combat trousers. "Police!" he shouted. "Turn around."

Hopkins stepped into the bathroom and saw what the man was doing. "You bastard!" he screamed. The man had his hands around the throat of a girl, submerging her in the water.

Hopkins brought the spade crashing down on the back of the man's head. It made a dull thudding sound and the man slumped forward. Hopkins dropped the spade, shoved the man to the side and grabbed the girl under her arms. He hauled her out of the water and hugged her to his chest, then carried her out of the bathroom. He laid her on the carpet and scraped her wet hair away from her face. She wasn't breathing and he didn't waste time feeling for a pulse. It had been years since he had been on any sort of first aid course but he remembered enough to check that her airway was clear before tilting her head back and putting his lips over hers to blow air into her lungs. The second his mouth touched hers he knew that he was wasting his time.

CHAPTER
THIRTY-FIVE

The woman was begging Fisher to let her up and complaining that she couldn't breathe. Fisher had some plastic ties in one of the pockets of his overalls and he pulled one out to bind her wrists together. "You can't do this to me, I've got rights!" she shouted. "He hit me, he hit my leg with a bloody spade!"

Fisher stood up. As he took his phone out he looked down at the bloody gash on her leg. "You'll live," he said.

"I've got my rights!" she shouted again.

Fisher called the superintendent and told him what had happened.

"Do you have the girl?"

"I'm not sure," said Fisher.

"What the hell do you mean you're not sure? What are you playing at?"

"I'll check," said Fisher.

"Check? What do you mean, check?"

Fisher hurried to the stairs. "Sir, the Super wants to know if the girl's okay." There was no answer. "Sir?" He headed up the stairs. The inspector was kneeling next to the naked girl, blowing into her mouth, then he sat back on his heels and began a vigorous heart massage.

"Sir, is she okay? The Super wants to know if she's okay."

Fisher realised that there were tears streaming down the inspector's face and that little Bella Harper wasn't okay.

CHAPTER
THIRTY-SIX

Superintendent Wilkinson climbed out of the car and squared his shoulders. There were two police vans parked outside the house, a white SOCO van and three regular patrol cars. Two Police Community Support Officers were marking a perimeter with blue and white police tape.

Detective Sergeant Sean McKillop had driven from the station and he got out and looked over at the superintendent. "No ambulance?"

"There's one on the way." Wilkinson belched and rubbed his stomach. He'd had indigestion since he'd taken the call from Detective Fisher. He'd already chewed two Rennies but took them out of his pocket and popped another two in his mouth.

He walked towards the house, his hands in the pockets of his overcoat. Murder scenes weren't pleasant places at the best of times, but dealing with a murdered child was just about the worst scenario imaginable. He knew that he would be the ranking officer. The top brass would be giving the crime scene a wide berth. If Bella had turned up alive they'd be rushing over to take the credit, but no one wanted to be tainted with a dead child. That would be down to him, to stand in front of the cameras and give the bad news. His stomach lurched and he tasted vomit at the back of his throat.

As the superintendent ducked under the tape and headed for the front door, an ambulance arrived. There were no sirens or flashing lights, there was no need. Bella Harper was dead.

A uniformed constable was standing guard at the front door and he stepped aside to allow the detectives through. "Where's the girl?" asked the superintendent.

"Upstairs," said the officer.

"And the suspects?"

"Sitting room, first on the right."

The superintendent stepped into the hallway. There were two more uniformed officers there and a PCSO. They stopped talking as soon as they saw the superintendent and it was clear they hadn't been discussing work. Wilkinson jerked a thumb at the door behind him. "Out," he said.

There were four more uniformed officers standing in the kitchen. "Will you get the hell out of the house — this is a crime scene, not a bloody meeting hall!" shouted Wilkinson.

He went into the sitting room. There were another four uniformed officers there, one of them a sergeant that Wilkinson recognised. Denis Tyler, a twenty-year veteran of the Sussex police and an old school copper. Standing by the window was Aaron Fisher, white-faced and looking as if he was about to throw up. Sitting on an armchair by the TV was a woman in her twenties with an orange complexion and dyed blonde hair that looked as if it had been hacked with a breadknife.

162

There was a man on the sofa. He had greasy unkempt hair and a hooked nose over thin, bloodless lips. The man and the woman had their hands cuffed behind them.

"What's the story, Denis?" asked the superintendent.

"Eric Lucas and Candice Matthews. The girl's upstairs." He pointed at Lucas. "He strangled her."

"Have they been cautioned?"

The sergeant shook his head.

Lucas slumped forward and Wilkinson saw that the back of his head was bloody. "How did that happen?" he asked the sergeant.

"They were like that when we got here."

Wilkinson looked over at Fisher. "Inspector Hopkins hit him with a spade," said the detective.

"And he hit me, too!" shouted the woman. "Bloody animal, he is."

"Where is Inspector Hopkins?"

"The stairs," said Fisher.

"I want to go to the hospital," said the woman.

"That's not going to happen," said the superintendent. "We'll get you a doctor at the station."

"I'm bleeding to death here," said the woman. "Have you seen my leg? I know my rights. I want to see a doctor."

The superintendent nodded at Sergeant Tyler. "Get her out of here, Denis." He looked at Sergeant McKillop. "Put her in the car."

"He hit my Eric, too. Smashed his head in with a spade."

The two sergeants reached down and helped her to her feet. "Police brutality, that's what it is," she said. "Anyway, I can't walk." She let herself go limp and the sergeants had to let her fall back onto the sofa. "If you make me walk, I'll sue. I've got my human rights, I have."

"There's an ambulance just arrived, get the paramedics to look at her," Wilkinson said to Tyler. "But no hospital. She can be treated at the station."

"What about Eric?" said the woman. "He might have concussion. He needs a brain scan, that's what he needs."

The superintendent gritted his teeth. "Get them to look at him, then both of them to the station," he said.

As he walked back into the hallway, two paramedics appeared at the front door. One of them was holding a portable trolley. "Do me a favour, guys, and check out the two suspects in there," he said. "Do whatever first aid you need but I want them in the station ASAP."

"They said the girl's dead," said the elder of the two paramedics.

"Yeah. She's upstairs."

"To be honest, we'd rather take care of her first. If that's okay with you."

The superintendent was about to argue, but then he saw the haunted looks on the men's faces. Like everybody else they'd been following the case and hoping that the girl would be found and returned to her parents. He understood exactly how they felt. And if he had been in their place he wouldn't have rushed to treat her killers either. He nodded. "Sure."

He headed for the stairs and the two paramedics followed him. Inspector Hopkins was sitting on the stairs, his cheeks wet with tears. He looked up at the superintendent with unseeing eyes. There was an unlit cigarette in one hand.

"Are you okay?" asked the superintendent.

Hopkins shrugged. "Not really." The hand holding the cigarette was trembling.

Wilkinson gestured at the two paramedics. "They need to get upstairs to deal with Bella," he said. He put his hand on the inspector's shoulder. "You need to move. Come on, let's sit down in the kitchen. And put that cigarette away."

Hopkins stood up and followed the superintendent down the hallway to the kitchen. The paramedics tramped upstairs with the trolley.

The superintendent pulled a chair away from the kitchen table and motioned for the inspector to sit down. Hopkins slumped down and put his head in his hands.

"What happened to them?" asked the superintendent. "Lucas and the woman?"

"I hit them with a spade," said Hopkins.

"You did what?"

"There wasn't time to be nice about it," said Hopkins. "She was in my way and he was drowning the girl."

"But a bloody spade, Dave."

"Call it a shovel if that makes it easier," said Hopkins. He ran a hand through his hair. "He was drowning her."

"So you hit him over the head with a spade?"

Hopkins shrugged.

"You've got to pull yourself together, Dave," said the superintendent. "If they allege police brutality, Professional Standards will be all over you."

"Fuck them," said Hopkins. "They killed her."

"I hear you, but you need to get your story straight now. Professional Standards can be arseholes but they hate child-killers as much as you do. You have to give them the right story for them to give you a pass. And you have to have your story straight from the start. Okay?"

"Okay."

"Why were you holding the spade?"

"I used it to break open the window in the kitchen. I'd heard the girl scream."

"Fisher will back you up on that?"

Hopkins sat back in his chair and nodded. "We both heard it."

"And why did you hit the woman? Think carefully, Dave."

The inspector took a deep breath. "I came out of the kitchen and she was in the hallway. I identified myself as a police officer and asked her where Bella was. She came towards me in an aggressive manner and I used the spade to deflect her attack. I was then joined by PC Fisher who constrained her while I went upstairs."

"Excellent," said the superintendent, patting him on the shoulder. "What happened then!"

"She's breathing!" The voice came from upstairs. "She's okay!" The two detectives both jumped as if they'd been stung. They looked at each other in astonishment.

Hopkins shot up out of his chair and beat the superintendent to the kitchen door. They hurtled down the hallway, shoving a white-overalled SOCO out of the way.

The younger of the paramedics was standing at the stop of the stairs, beaming from ear to ear. He flashed the detectives two thumbs up. "She's okay!" he shouted. "She's bloody well okay!"

CHAPTER
THIRTY-SEVEN

A sky TV crew had arrived outside the house just as the paramedics were pushing Bella out on the trolley. They wanted to film her being taken to the ambulance, but by the time they had the camera out she was already inside. As the ambulance sped off, the reporter hurried over to Wilkinson with her crew in tow. Wilkinson knew her, she'd been covering the Bella Harper abduction from Day One. Her name was Carol Khan and she was one of the more professional reporters he'd dealt with, so he decided to give her a statement.

"Superintendent Wilkinson, can you tell us what's happened?" she asked, holding the microphone under his chin. The lanky cameraman had the lens aimed at Wilkinson's face and he automatically raised his chin, knowing from experience that with his head down he had several rolls of fat around his neck.

"I can tell you that Bella Harper is alive and well and will shortly be reunited with her parents," he said. "Two people are in custody and that's all I can say at the moment."

"Can you tell us if she has been sexually assaulted?" asked the reporter.

"Bella is on her way to hospital and she'll be examined there," said the superintendent.

"The people in custody, what can you tell us about them?"

"At the moment nothing, other than that we are not looking for anyone else in connection with this incident and that I am happy that Bella is safe. I'd like to take this opportunity to thank the public and the media for all their help. It was their assistance that helped us bring this investigation to a positive conclusion."

"Where are they now?" asked the reporter, but the superintendent shook his head.

"That's all for now," he said. "There will be a fuller statement later today."

The cameraman lowered his camera and the reporter flashed Wilkinson her most winning smile. "What about off the record, Rory? What's happening?"

"Off the record, the guy's name is Eric Lucas and that's his house. We'll be bringing him out in a bit. He was in the process of drowning Bella when two of our officers gained access to the house. Lucas seems to have been helped by his girlfriend, a woman called Candice Matthews. Nothing known on either of them. If you want to hang around we'll open up the garage door fully. The van they used is inside."

"We can film them when you bring them out?"

"Yeah, but we'll be covering their faces, you know that."

"Don't suppose I could persuade you not to," she said, and laughed.

169

"I've got to go," said Wilkinson. "I'm sure the DCC will have a full press conference at the Training HQ at Netley later today." The Netley HQ building was where Hampshire police's media team was based and it had a large auditorium that was tailor-made for major press conferences.

A second ambulance had arrived and two more paramedics were attending to Lucas and his girlfriend in the house. Wilkinson was still waiting for confirmation that they were fit to be taken straight to the station.

He ducked under the police tape and took out his mobile phone as he walked around to the rear of the house. He called the deputy chief constable's number and his secretary put him straight through. "Bella Harper's alive, sir," he said.

"She's what?"

"The call we got that she was dead turns out to have been a false alarm," said Wilkinson. "She's in an ambulance on her way to hospital as we speak. But she's fine. She's talking to the paramedics, all her vital signs are okay, they say she's in shock but other than that . . ."

"We were told she was dead. The press office is just about to put out a statement offering our condolences."

"Well, there's definitely no need for that, sir. Like I said, she's fine."

"How did that happen? How could they get it so wrong?"

"The men who went into the house found Bella being drowned in the bath. They got her out and did

170

CPR but thought that she'd stopped breathing. When the paramedics arrived, they checked and she was okay."

"That makes no sense to me, but I'm not about to start looking gift horses in the mouth," said the DCC. "What about the media?"

"Sky TV are here. That's it so far."

"And the suspects?"

"They're both a bit banged up but they should be okay to take straight to the station."

"And they're bang to rights?"

"Inspector Hopkins found Lucas with his hands around Bella's throat," he said.

"But no warrant, that's correct?"

"They heard her scream, sir. The lack of a warrant won't be an issue."

"You'll be handling the interrogation?"

"Yes, sir."

"Then I don't need to tell you to do it by the book, superintendent. No slip-ups."

"Understood, sir," said Wilkinson. He ended the call. He would be handling the interrogation but he was sure that the DCC would be leading the press conference, all smiles now that Bella was alive.

CHAPTER
THIRTY-EIGHT

Nightingale pushed open the office door and held up the two cups of Costa coffee. "For my favourite assistant," he said.

Jenny was standing in front of the television. She looked over at him and grinned. "My cup runneth over," she said. "Though I have to point out that I'm your only assistant."

Nightingale hung up his coat and went over to stand by her. The television was tuned to Sky News and a reporter was talking to camera in front of a suburban house. "What's happening?"

"They found that little girl. Bella Harper."

"Alive?"

"Yes, thank God."

"How many days was it? Four? That's really unusual. If they're not found within forty-eight hours . . ."

"Well, in this case it worked out for the best. I'm so happy for the parents. They must be so relieved." She went back to her desk and muted the sound. "So how did it go with the little old lady?"

"According to Mrs Steadman, that Satanic altar is just window dressing. Either McBride did it with next to no knowledge of what Satanism is about, or someone tried to frame him." He sat down opposite her.

"There's no doubt that he killed those children," said Jenny. "None at all."

"I meant frame him for the devil-worship thing. How are you getting on with the kids?"

"All good," she said. She stood up and took her coffee over to the whiteboard. "And you were right. All the children who were killed were from single-parent families."

Nightingale joined her. "That can't be a coincidence, can it?"

"More than half of all marriages end in divorce, but couples with children tend to stay together more than those who don't. So you'd expect half of the eight to be in single-parent families."

Nightingale frowned and rubbed his chin. "But why would he deliberately set out to kill kids with just one parent?"

"I don't know. But I don't see that it can be a coincidence. Having said that, it still doesn't explain why he only shot two girls in the first classroom. I haven't been able to check them all, but I did cross-check some of the pupils with the electoral roll and there must have been half a dozen or more kids from one-parent families in that first room that he didn't shoot."

"Okay, so all the children that he shot were from one-parent families, but there were children from one-parent families that he didn't shoot?"

"Exactly. But I'm not sure that helps us come up with a motive." She waved at the photographs. "Do you notice something else?"

Nightingale studied the photographs. "Five girls, three boys. Blonde hair, dark hair, one redhead. Eye colour?"

"Some have blue eyes, some have brown."

"Short hair, long hair. Straight hair, curly."

"It's more what you don't see," said Jenny.

Nightingale shook his head. "I don't get it." He stared at the photographs, then threw up his hands. "Got it. They're all Caucasian." He turned to look at Jenny. "He was targeting white kids? Is that what you think?"

"I though that might be significant until I checked the school roll. There are very few Asians or Afro-Caribbeans at the school. In fact Berwick is the most ethnically homogeneous district in the country. In the last census, 99.6 per cent of the population recorded themselves as white."

"So if it's not racial, what is it? What am I missing?"

"At the risk of being judgemental, how about the fact that they're all good-looking kids?"

"What?"

"The girls are pretty, the boys are good-looking, there isn't a fat, spotty or funny-looking one in the bunch."

"You're joking."

Jenny shook her head. "No, I'm deadly serious. You take any group of kids these days and probably a third are overweight. Another quarter are, shall we say, challenged in the looks department. I know that's cruel, but it's a fact of life. Some kids are good-looking, some aren't. I know that all parents think their kids are perfect, but when you take a step back you know that isn't true." She waved at the whiteboard. "These kids are all the sort you see in TV commercials."

Nightingale ran his hand through his hair. "So he was targeting good-looking kids from single-parent families?"

Jenny nodded. "You can see where I'm heading with this, right?"

"I'm not sure."

"Children from single-parent families are more likely to be abused. They're more vulnerable."

"So you think that McBride had been abusing these kids and decided to kill them?"

"I think that needs looking at, yes."

"His brother said he was great with kids."

"Yeah, well, just because he didn't abuse his own nephews doesn't mean he wasn't a child molester."

Nightingale sighed. "The brother isn't going to be happy about this. We prove that his brother wasn't a devil-worshipper by showing that he was a paedophile."

"He wants the truth," said Jenny.

"I'm not sure that he does. He might think he does but how's he going to react if we tell him that his brother was a paedophile?" He sipped his coffee as he looked at the photographs on the whiteboard. Jenny was right. They were all good-looking kids. He stared at the photograph of Grace Campbell. Long, curly chestnut hair. A snub nose. Smiling for the camera. Was it possible that she had been abused? She looked happy, as if she hadn't a care in the world. "We don't know for sure that these children were abused," said Nightingale. "We're going to have to be very careful here."

"What about the post-mortems?" asked Jenny. "They were all sudden deaths, so by law there has to be a post mortem, right?"

Nightingale nodded. "That's right."

"So talk to the coroner. If the kids were being abused, he'd know."

"It'll mean going back to Berwick. I doubt he's going to say anything over the phone."

Jenny smiled brightly. "I'll book you a ticket. And there's something else you might want to do while you're up there."

"I'm all ears."

"The lab still have the crucible and the knife. Why don't I get them to check them for fingerprints and DNA?"

"DNA's expensive," said Nightingale. "Don't forget that when the two grand has gone we're not going to be getting any refreshers."

"Just fingerprints, then. We can compare them to McBride's prints and we'll know if he set up the altar or not."

"You think he'd go to the trouble of setting up a fake black magic altar?"

"I don't know. But if it wasn't him, at least we'd have the prints of whoever did, and that might be a start."

Nightingale nodded thoughtfully. She was right.

"You touched them with your bare hands, right?"

"I wasn't thinking about prints, I was more concerned about the blood."

"Sure, but we'll need your prints to rule you out. And while you're up in Berwick you could get something with McBride's prints. Something that only he could have touched."

"Two birds with one stone?"

"Exactly."

CHAPTER
THIRTY-NINE

Sandra Harper held her husband's hand and squeezed it. "I can't believe it, I can't believe we got her back."

Will Harper looked over at their daughter, lying in the ICU bed connected to a machine that beeped softly, proof if they needed it that Bella was alive and well. The doctor looking after her, a bald Indian with a kindly face and an unpronounceable surname, had said Bella was in ICU purely as a precaution. Once the twenty-four-hour observation period was over she would be moved into a general ward, with every possibility of her going home before the end of the week. "If I get my hands on the bastard that . . ." He gritted his teeth and left the sentence unfinished.

His wife squeezed his hand. "We got her back, Will. That's all that matters. I don't know what I would have done if . . ." Tears pricked her eyes and she blinked them away.

"I just want one minute alone with him in a room, that's all," he said. "And that bitch with him. How can a woman help a man rape a child, Sandra? Can you answer me that?"

Sandra shook her head. "I don't know."

"I hope they throw away the key," Will muttered. "And I hope while they're in prison they get the shit kicked out of them. They hate nonces in prison."

Bella opened her eyes and Sandra jumped. "She's awake." She jumped up and hurried over to the bed. Bella smiled up at her. "Hi, Mummy."

Tears ran down Sandra's face. "Oh my God, my God, my God. Thank you."

"Where's Daddy?"

"I'm here, honey," said Will. He reached out and held her hand, careful not to disturb the drip.

"You look tired," said Bella.

"We haven't been sleeping much," said Will. "We were worried about you."

"I'm okay, Daddy. I want to go home."

"Soon, honey. The doctors want to check you're okay."

Sandra smoothed her daughter's forehead. She was cool to the touch, much cooler than usual. "How do you feel, Bella?"

"I feel fine, Mummy. I don't need to stay here."

"You'll be home soon, honey."

"Tell the doctor I'm okay."

"We will, honey, as soon as he gets back."

A male nurse popped his head around the door. "Everything okay?" he asked.

"She's awake," said Will.

"I'll get the doctor," said the nurse, and he hurried off.

"Can I have a drink of water, Daddy?" asked Bella.

"Of course you can."

"Or a Coke? Can I have a Coke?"

"You can have whatever you want, honey," said Will.

"There's a machine in the corridor," said Sandra. She carried on smoothing Bella's forehead as Will went off in search of her Coke.

"I love you, Mummy," whispered Bella.

Sandra felt tears run down her face but she didn't want to take her hand away from Bella's forehead, so she didn't wipe them away.

"Don't be sad, Mummy."

"I'm not sad, honey. I'm happy."

"Everything's going to be all right."

Sandra smiled down at her. "I know."

"I saw an angel, Mummy."

"When, darling?"

"When I was with those people. The bad people that hurt me."

"You saw an angel?"

Bella nodded. "When I went to sleep in the bath. I went to sleep and then I woke up and I saw an angel."

Sandra shook her head. "That wasn't an angel, honey. That was a paramedic. He came with an ambulance. He brought you back to us."

Bella smiled. "No, Mummy. It was a real angel. With wings and everything. He was nice to me and he said everything was going to be all right."

"Well, your angel was right, darling. Because now everything is all right."

"The angel said I didn't have to go to Heaven."

"He said that?"

Bella nodded earnestly. "He said it wasn't my time. But he said before I went back there were some people I had to see."

"Did he?"

"Yes, Mummy. He took me to see Grandpa Arthur. And Auntie Eadie."

Sandra frowned. "Who are they, honey?"

"You don't know? Grandpa Arthur is the father of Daddy's father. And Auntie Eadie was your sister." Bella giggled. "Did you forget?"

"I must have," said Sandra. She was genuinely confused at what her daughter was telling her, because while Sandra had three siblings, they were all boys. She didn't have a sister called Eadie, dead or alive.

"They talked to me and then they took me to see Jesus."

"Jesus?"

"Yes, Mummy. I went to see Jesus with the angel and Grandpa Arthur and Auntie Eadie. I spent ages talking to him. He is such a kind man. Like Father Christmas, but his beard was brown."

"That's nice, honey."

"Then Jesus said it was time to go back and the angel took me and I woke up and that's when I saw the paramedic. I know the paramedic wasn't the angel. The angel was Michael."

"Michael?"

"He's an archangel, Mummy. That's a really important angel. He said I was very special because Jesus only speaks to special people."

CHAPTER
FORTY

Nightingale phoned Danny McBride as he grabbed a coffee at Heathrow Terminal I and arranged to meet him at the farm later that day. He flew to Edinburgh, picked up a rental car and drove to the Northumberland coroner's office in Church Street. He managed to find a parking space close by and smoked a cigarette at the main entrance before going inside.

The coroner's officer who agreed to see him was a police sergeant by the name of Bernard Connolly. He gave him a business card and sat back and studied Nightingale with unblinking grey eyes. "Can I ask what your interest is in the case, Mr Nightingale?" he said.

"I'm representing a client who wants to know the background to the shootings."

"I don't suppose you'd tell me who that client is?"

Nightingale smiled thinly. "That would be covered by client confidentiality," he said.

"It would if you were a doctor or a lawyer, but gumshoes don't have that sort of protection."

"I don't think I've ever been called that before," said Nightingale.

The policeman smiled. "Gumshoe? I'm a big fan of Elmore Leonard. But I can assure you, Mr Nightingale, there's no mystery here. It's as open and shut a case as I've ever seen. Mr McBride took his shotgun, for which he had a licence, and used it to kill a teacher and eight children. Then he took his own life."

"There'll be an inquest, of course?"

"Of course. But there won't be any surprises, I can assure you of that." He tapped a gold fountain pen on an open notepad. "So assuming that client confidentiality doesn't apply, who are you working for?"

"I'd rather not say."

"I'm guessing a family member," said the policeman. "Probably someone who stands to gain from the will." He sat back in his chair and fixed Nightingale with a deceptively bored gaze. "Suicide, you see. That would negate any life insurance McBride had taken out."

"Only if it was a recent policy," said Nightingale.

"So it is a family member? The brother, I suppose."

Nightingale tried to keep his face impassive. "I really can't say."

"You're not a poker player, are you, Mr Nightingale?"

"Why do you say that?"

"Because you've got a tell, that's why."

"A tell?"

"A tell. It shows when you're bluffing."

Nightingale smiled amiably. The policeman was pulling one of the oldest tricks in the interrogator's handbook, trying to unsettle him. "I just need some information on the post mortems that have been carried out on the victims of the school shootings."

"Those details will be revealed at the inquest."

"I understand that," said Nightingale. "But can you at least tell me if there are any signs of sexual abuse?"

The policeman's eyes narrowed. "Sexual abuse?"

"It would be apparent enough in the post mortem. Did the pathologist mention it?"

The policeman tapped his pen on his notepad as he continued to stare at Nightingale.

"It's a reasonable question to ask," said Nightingale.

"I'm not sure that it is," said the policeman. "It's bad enough that eight children have died, why would you want to start a rumour like that? How do you think the parents would feel?"

"I think the parents deserve to know the truth," said Nightingale. "And really, isn't that the purpose of an inquest? To get the truth out there?"

"The purpose of an inquest is to determine the cause of death," said the policeman. "And that's pretty much a foregone conclusion."

"But what about motive? Why did McBride kill those children?"

"Because the balance of his mind was disturbed. Or as the tabloids will no doubt put it, he was as mad as a hatter. But again that's a matter for the inquest."

"He didn't behave like a madman," said Nightingale. "He seemed organised. Restrained even. He only killed eight when he could have killed a lot more."

"What are you saying, Mr Nightingale? Are you saying that you wish he'd killed more?"

"Of course not. But I'm not convinced he was mad."

"And if you were to prove that the children were abused, that would make him less of a madman?"

"It would help explain why he did what he did."

"And what has put this idea in your head, Mr Nightingale?"

"It's just a line of inquiry," said Nightingale. "You remember the Dunblane massacre back in 1996?"

"Of course. But what does that have to do with us here in Berwick?"

"The killer up in Dunblane was Thomas Hamilton. There were reports that he'd been involved in inappropriate behaviour with children. He was a Scout leader and worked in youth clubs and he lost his job after complaints that he had been taking semi-naked photographs of some of the boys. He made boys sleep with him in tents on camping trips, that sort of thing."

"I don't see where this is heading, frankly."

"The shootings came shortly after he failed to set up a new youth club. I was wondering if there was something similar driving Mr McBride."

The policeman frowned. "You have evidence that he was abusing children?"

"That's why I've come to see you. If any of the children had been abused, it would show up in the post mortem."

The policeman put down his pen and linked his fingers. "Well, I can assure you that the children were not sexually abused in any way."

"Can I see the pathologist's reports?"

The policeman stared at Nightingale for several seconds. "No," he said eventually. "I would be in breach of the Data Protection Act if I were to do that. The reports will be made public at the inquest and not before. But I can tell you, off the record and on a totally non-attributable basis, that none of the children had been abused."

Nightingale nodded slowly. "Okay," he said. He wondered if the coroner's officer was also a poker player and if the pulsing vein in his forehead was a sign that he was lying. Nightingale would have been prepared to bet that it was. But he didn't say anything, he just thanked the man, shook his hand and left the office.

He waited until he was outside before he called Jenny on her mobile and filled her in on what happened. "Now what?" she said.

"I'm going to go to the farm to get a sample of McBride's prints. I've arranged to meet the brother there."

"When you do see him, you might think about running some expenses by him," said Jenny. "Be nice if we could get some money for your travelling and the lab."

"Will do," said Nightingale.

"You'll still make the afternoon flight?"

"That's the plan," said Nightingale.

CHAPTER
FORTY-ONE

Nightingale went back to his rental car and phoned McBride, but he didn't pick up and the call went through to his answer service. Nightingale left a brief message saying that he was heading out to the farm, but then he realised he hadn't eaten all day so he popped into a local café for a coffee and a sandwich. He called again as he drove to the farm, but McBride still wasn't picking up.

When he arrived at the farm the five-bar gate was padlocked, so he left the car in the road. He climbed over the gate and walked down the dirt track. He made a final unsuccessful attempt to call McBride and then shoved his phone into the pocket of his raincoat.

As the track bent to the right he was able to see the farmyard and realised that McBride's car was parked there, its nose up against the side of the house. It began to rain as he got closer to the farmhouse, and he turned up the collar of his coat and jogged the last fifty yards. He rang the doorbell but there was no response. He rang again. The rain was getting heavier and he stood closer to the door to avoid the worst of it.

The front door remained resolutely closed. From where he was standing he could see that the barn door was ajar. He jogged over, his Hush Puppies splashing through puddles, and squeezed through the gap. Rain was beating a tattoo on the corrugated iron roof. "Mr McBride, are you in here?" he called.

Water dripped down the back of his neck and he shivered. As he looked to the left his breath caught in his throat. Danny McBride was hanging from the upper level, a thick rope around his neck.

Nightingale took a step back, his eyes open in horror. It didn't make any sense. McBride wasn't the type to kill himself. He was a husband and a father and there had been nothing about his behaviour that suggested he was depressed. He was upset about what his brother had done, but that was no reason for him to take his own life.

He'd been hanging there for a while, Nightingale realised. Hours, probably. His trousers were wet and there was a small pool of urine on the floor. The bladder always emptied itself on death. And so did the colon. Nightingale had attended several suicides when he was a police officer and the smell of death was always the same. Urine and faeces. The intestinal gases as they expanded and escaped, and finally rotting flesh. Nightingale shuddered. "Shit, shit, shit," he muttered under his breath. He took out a cigarette and lit it as he considered his options. He could get back into his car and drive to the airport without telling anyone about the body. Or he could be the dutiful citizen and phone the police. But if he did that he'd have to face Stevenson again and have to explain what he was doing on the farm. And he guessed that Stevenson would

188

relish any excuse to have Nightingale in a cell wearing a paper suit for a day or two.

Nightingale blew smoke up at the roof of the barn. If he drove away without reporting the death and the cops discovered that he'd been in the barn, he'd be in trouble. Not prison trouble, but helping the police with their enquiries trouble. And he'd probably need a lawyer.

But there'd be no evidence that he'd been in the barn and seen the body. There were the phone calls, of course. The call he'd made at Heathrow and the message on McBride's phone. He could get around that, though, and phone again saying that he wouldn't be able to meet McBride that afternoon. That might work. But he'd have to make the call well away from the farm.

Then there was his family. They deserved to be told. Somewhere there was a wife carrying on as normal, totally unaware that her husband was dead. And two boys who had to be told that their father was gone for ever.

He looked around the barn. Everything seemed exactly as it had been the last time he had been there. Except for the body, of course. He took a long drag on the cigarette and held the smoke for a good ten seconds before letting it out in a tight plume. He'd made up his mind.

CHAPTER
FORTY-TWO

John Fraser looked at his watch. It was six o'clock in the morning, which meant he had two hours to go before his shift ended and he could go home. The graveyard shift they called it, but that was actually a misnomer. It was quite rare for a patient to die in the ICU at night. Most died in the daytime, and the joke among the nursing staff was that the number of deaths rose in line with the number of doctors in attendance. Fraser knew that was a fallacy, too. Patients in the ICU were at their most stable when they slept, because then the body was able to get on with healing, or at least keeping itself stable. During the daytime, with all the lights and the noise, stress levels increased and with stress came an increased risk of death.

Fraser had asked for the transfer to the ICU but was starting to have second thoughts. He had assumed the medical staff there would be making life and death decisions and that those decisions would save lives, that they would make a difference. But in the six months he had been there, he had realised the medical care actually had very little to do with whether the patients lived or died. They came in, they were hooked up to machines that measured all their life signs, and they were monitored. Some patients got better and lived. Others got worse and died. But the medical staff tried equally hard with all the patients; they weren't the ones choosing who lived and who died. It wasn't a case of doing the right thing or the wrong thing — sometimes patients died no matter what the doctors did, and Fraser was finding it hard to come to terms with that. In almost any other job, the harder you worked the better the results. But not in the ICU. It didn't matter how hard they tried, patients still died.

The money was good, and the work was challenging, but Fraser was already thinking about asking for a transfer back to a general ward.

Fraser was doing a walk-around of the various units, checking that the equipment was functioning properly, drips hadn't been compromised and patients were as comfortable as they could be. He opened the door to Mrs Dawson's room. She was in her sixties and had been involved in a bad car accident that had burst her spleen, broken her back in three places and punctured her lung. She'd been lucky, she'd been wearing a seatbelt, and an airbag had cushioned her against the worst of the impact. Her husband hadn't been wearing his belt and the airbag in front of him had malfunctioned and he'd ended up under the rear wheels of the truck that had smashed into them. Her face was a black and blue mass of bruised tissue but she was breathing on her own, which was a good sign. Fraser checked her drip, then dabbed a paper towel at the dribble of saliva that was running from her open mouth to her pillow. She swallowed and then moaned softly. "Ron?"

Ron was her husband. Fraser tossed the paper towel into the bin and left the room. One of the unit's doctors was walking slowly down the corridor, texting on a BlackBerry. He looked up and smiled when he saw Fraser. His name was Joe MacDonald and he was newly qualified and still eager to please. "Fraser, how's everything?"

That was always the sign of a newly qualified doctor or an intern. They bothered to remember the names of the nurses because more often than not it was the nursing staff who pulled their nuts out of the fire. "All good, Doctor MacDonald."

"I'm going to have a lie-down. Give me a shout if you need me."

"No problem, Doctor MacDonald." MacDonald hurried down the corridor towards the windowless room that housed the camp bed where doctors could snatch a few hours' sleep when they needed it. It was one of the inequalities of the medical hierarchy. Doctors could nap, but a nurse would be sacked for sleeping on duty. Not that Fraser wanted to be a doctor. He didn't envy them their long hours, or the stress, or the decisions they had to make on an hourly basis. Fraser liked people, and he enjoyed helping them, and that's what nurses did. He'd always wanted to be a nurse, ever since he'd been in hospital as a child to have his tonsils removed. His classmates had teased him and his parents hadn't been keen on his choice of career, but Fraser had stuck with it and he couldn't have been happier.

He opened the door to Isabella Harper's room. The little girl was lying in her bed, looking up at the ceiling. She smiled when she saw him. She put her finger to her lips and went "shhhh", then pointed at the chair at the end of her bed where her father was sleeping, his head resting on a pillow jammed against the wall. Bella's parents took it in turns to stay overnight in her room. It was against the rules, but Bella was nine years old and after all she had been through it was generally agreed the parents could come and go as they pleased.

Fraser went over the bed. "Can't sleep?" he whispered.

"I'm not tired," she said.

"Are you okay? Do you need anything?"

Bella shook her head. "I just want to go home."

"Soon," said Fraser. "You're moving to a general ward tomorrow and I think you'll be home in a few days."

"I saw Jesus," said Bella solemnly.

"Really?"

Bella nodded. "He was very kind. And I saw the Archangel Michael. He was nice too."

"Good," said Fraser.

Bella's father snored and moved his legs, then went quiet again.

"Jesus gave me a message for you, John," said Bella.

"What?"

"There's something he wants you to know."

"Bella, come on now, it's time you were asleep."

Bella waved at him, urging him to move closer. "Come here, John, I'll tell you what he said. It's important."

Fraser frowned. He looked over at Mr Harper, but he was fast asleep.

"Really, John, it's important. But I have to whisper it, okay?"

"If I let you whisper it, you'll go to sleep?"

Bella nodded. "Sure."

"Okay," said Fraser. He bent over her and put his ear close to her mouth. He could smell her breath and he frowned. It was sour and he wrinkled his nose in disgust. Maybe the little girl hadn't been cleaning her teeth, or perhaps it was something she'd eaten. "What is it you want to tell me?" he asked.

CHAPTER
FORTY-THREE

Sally Fraser heard the front door open and she rolled over and squinted at the alarm clock on her bedside table. It was just after seven. She groaned. She had to be up at seven thirty and she doubted she'd be able to get back to sleep.

She heard slow, steady footsteps as John walked upstairs. Sally hated it when John worked nights. She was a teacher and had to be at school by eight, which meant they hardly saw each other — the best they could manage was a couple of hours after they'd put the kids to bed and before he headed off to the hospital. The only plus point was that he was able to drop the boys off at the childminder's in the morning.

She curled up and closed her eyes, desperately wishing she could slip back into sleep, and hoping John wouldn't slip into bed hoping for a quickie before she got up. She took a deep breath, and then frowned. It was just after seven, but John's shift didn't finish until eight. She opened her eyes again and blinked at the clock. Twenty past seven.

She sat up, rubbing her eyes. "John?" There was no answer. She got out of bed and padded across the carpet to the bedroom door. The first thing John usually did when he got in was shower, to get rid of the smell of the hospital. When he was on nights he used the guest bathroom, but there was no sound coming from it. "John?" she called but again there was no answer.

She walked down the hallway, past the bathroom towards the boys' room. The door was open and a shaft of yellowish light ran across the carpet and up the opposite wall.

"John, what's going on?" she said.

"Nothing, honey, go back to bed," said her husband. "I'll be with you in a minute."

"Don't wake them up yet, they were up late last night."

"Go back to bed, honey."

There was a tenseness to his voice and Sally realised something was wrong. She reached the door but froze when she saw three-year-old Darren lying on his back, his eyes wide and staring. She knew instinctively he was dead — there was an emptiness in his eyes and his tongue was protruding from his mouth. Sally gasped and she covered her mouth with her hands. Her whole body began to shake.

She reached out with her left hand and pushed the door open. It scraped on the carpet, and then she saw her husband, bent over Gary's crib. He had a pillow pressed over Gary and he was pushing it down hard. "Go back to bed, honey," he said.

"What are you doing?" she screamed, pushing the door wide open. "What the hell are you doing?"

John ignored her and continued to press on the pillow. She ran over to him and grabbed at his arm. "Get off him!" she screamed. She pulled hard and the pillow came away. Gary was as dead as his brother, his eyes open and lifeless, his mouth forming a perfect circle. Sally reached for him, tears pricking her eyes. "What have you done?"

Before she could pick up Gary, John seized her by the throat, his fingers digging into her trachea, cutting off her breath. "It's better like this," he said. "It's better they don't suffer."

Sally tried to speak, but his grip was too tight. There was a look in his eyes she'd never seen before. It wasn't anger, or hatred, it was something cold and hard, as if they had turned to glass in their sockets.

"It's going to be okay, honey. Jesus says so." He nodded earnestly. "Really, he says so." His left hand joined the right and he squeezed tighter. Her throat was burning and her chest was heaving but she couldn't get any air into her lungs. Sally didn't know enough human anatomy to realise it wasn't the lack of air that was killing her, it was the fact that her husband's hands had cut off the blood supply to her brain. She tried to beg him to let her go, but even if she could have formed the words she knew there was nothing she could say that would stop him. The last thought that went through her mind was that at least her boys hadn't suffered.

CHAPTER
FORTY-FOUR

Jenny was at her desk tapping away on her keyboard when Nightingale walked in. It was clear from the look on his face that something was wrong. He didn't take off his raincoat, just dropped down onto the chair opposite hers. "He's dead," he said.

"Who's dead?"

"Danny McBride. The client."

Jenny's jaw dropped. "Please tell me that's a sick attempt at humour."

Nightingale sat down. "I wish it was a joke."

"What happened?"

"He hanged himself, or someone hanged him. I had a quick look around and I didn't find a note. And the last time I saw him he didn't seem the suicidal type."

Jenny put her hand over her mouth. "That's awful."

"Tell me about it."

"Why are you only telling me this now? Why didn't you call me yesterday?"

"It wasn't something I wanted to share on the phone."

"I can't believe it. He seemed like such a nice man."

"He was."

"And his poor kids. And his wife."

"I know."

Jenny folded her arms. "I can't believe it. I just can't believe it."

"I'm as shocked as you are," said Nightingale.

"What did the police say?"

Nightingale looked pained. "I'm not sure if they know yet."

"What do you mean?"

He shrugged. "I couldn't call it in, could I? Then I'd be right in the middle of it. The cops are already pissed off at me, it'll only get worse if they think I had a hand in McBride's death."

"Jack! What, you found the body and you just left it there?"

"What else could I have done? The last time I made waves I got hit over the head and driven off the road. If I'd drawn attention to myself . . ." He shrugged. "Who knows what might have happened. So yes, I put my tail between my legs and skulked away. Discretion being the better part of valour and all that crap."

"And what about his family? Who's going to tell them?"

"Someone will find him eventually," said Nightingale. "His wife will report him missing and I'm pretty sure the cops will check the farm. It'd be the obvious place to look."

"But you said it was suicide. I don't understand why you couldn't just report it to the police."

Nightingale shook his head. "He was hanged but he wasn't suicidal. You met him. He was fine. And like I said, there was no note."

"So what are you saying? Someone killed him and made it look like suicide?"

"When McBride took me to the farm, he unlocked the gate and we drove down to the farm, leaving the gate open. When I found McBride his car was parked by the farmhouse but the gate was padlocked."

"So someone else padlocked the gate afterwards?"

Nightingale nodded. "Exactly."

"But who? Who would have done that?"

"That's the sixty-four thousand dollar question, isn't it? I'm guessing someone who realised that he had hired me, someone who wants to hide the truth about McBride's brother and what he did at the school."

"But that means it must be someone who knew you were on the case."

Nightingale rubbed his chin. "That thought had occurred to me," he said. "It could be the cop I spoke to, or the coroner's officer. Who was also a cop. Or the detective that Robbie put in touch."

Jenny's jaw dropped. "Are you saying the police are behind this?"

"I don't know, not for sure anyway. But I don't want to be sitting in a police cell waiting to find out." He shrugged. "But it might not be a cop. I chatted to the locals in the pub and we don't know who the cops spoke to."

Jenny ran her hands through her hair. "What are you going to do, Jack?"

"I'm not sure."

"But we don't have a client any more. That's it, right?"

200

"I don't see why. He paid us two grand in advance. What are we supposed to do? Give it back? We at least owe him two grand's worth of work. Besides, I want to know what's going on, because something is clearly rotten in the state of Berwick."

"Now you're misquoting Shakespeare?"

"I'm under a lot of stress," he said. He pulled an evidence bag from his pocket. Inside were a plastic-handled screwdriver and two spanners. Like the knife, they'd had to travel in the hold on the flight from Edinburgh to London. "I got these in the barn — it looked like he used them when he was working on his tractor."

Jenny took the bag from him. "What about your prints?"

Nightingale took a sheet of paper from her printer and pressed the fingers of both hands down onto it. He folded it and put it into another evidence bag. "There you go."

"You're such a professional."

"That's what they say. Coffee?"

"Are you asking or making?"

"I'm making."

"Then I'd love one."

CHAPTER
FORTY-FIVE

"Well, this is a nice surprise," said Sandra's mother, as Sandra kissed her on the cheek. "Dad'll be so sad to have missed you. He's fishing down at the canal."

"I'll be back, Mum. But I wanted a chat with you."

"Tea," said her mother. "The kettle's on. Come on through." She took Sandra down the hall and fussed around the tea things as Sandra sat down at the table and looked out over the back garden. It wasn't the house that she'd been brought up in; her parents had downsized ten years earlier when the last of her brothers had finally moved out. They'd sold their five-bedroom house, bought a small bungalow with a manageable garden and put the rest of the money into shares, providing them with a comfortable retirement.

"How's my lovely granddaughter?" asked Sandra's mother.

"She's fine. It's almost as if it never happened. She doesn't talk about it, and we don't ask her."

"When is she coming home?"

"Hopefully tomorrow. Friday at the latest. She wants to go now, but the doctors say they want to keep her in a while longer. But they have promised she'll be back home by the weekend."

"How is she . . . inside?" She rubbed her own stomach and winced as if she was in pain.

"The doctors say she's fine. They did all sorts of tests and she's all clear, you know, for HIV and things. And there's no damage, just bruising. They gave her a shot so that she won't get pregnant." Tears sprang to her eyes and she blinked them away. "Nine years old and they're worried she might be pregnant. How awful is that?" She took a deep breath. "She'll be fine. It's best we don't talk about it. It needs to be forgotten so that we can all move on with our lives."

"There isn't a day goes by when I don't say a prayer of thanks to God, you know that?" She poured boiling water into a earthenware teapot, complete with a red knitted tea cosy. Sandra had made the tea cosy at school almost twenty years ago and presented it to her mother on Mother's Day. "It was a miracle, a true miracle."

"It was," agreed Sandra.

"And Will? How is he?"

Sandra nodded. "He's okay. He's taken time off work, he doesn't want to let Bella out of his sight. He's in the hospital with her now. I get the feeling that he blames me. He doesn't say anything, of course, but I can see it in his eyes."

"I'm sure he doesn't. It wasn't your fault, it was those . . ." She shuddered. "Those animals. How could they do that to a little girl?"

Sandra shook her head. "The police say they think he's done it before. They're talking to the girl to see if she'll give evidence against him. Will gets so angry when he sees anything about them on television. He wants them dead. Says hanging's too good for them."

"Well, he'd be right about that," said her mother. "Killing's too good for them, though. They need to be made to suffer for every day they have left. They won't of course. It'll be Sky TV and PlayStations and probably conjugal visits. Prison today isn't really prison. They're like holiday camps."

"I don't think I can face a trial, Mum. The police say they hope that they will just plead guilty and then Bella won't have to give evidence. I couldn't bear the thought of her having to talk about what they did to her." She shook her head fiercely. "I don't want her going through that." She took a couple of deep breaths to calm herself down and then forced a smile. "Mum, I've got to ask you something and I know it's going to sound silly, but . . ." She threw up her hands. "I should just spit it out, shouldn't I? Did I ever have a sister? A sister called Eadie?"

Sandra could see from the look of horror on her mother's face that she'd struck a nerve. "Did your father say something?"

"No, Mum. I just need to know, did I have a sister?"

Tears filled her mother's eyes and she dabbed at them with a teacloth. "Why are you asking now?" she sniffed.

Sandra got up and walked over to her mother and hugged her. "It just came up, Mum. I need to know."

Sandra's mother trembled and Sandra found herself patting her on the back to reassure her. "It's okay, Mum." She flashed back to when she'd been a teenager and she'd been dumped by her first boyfriend. Her mum had hugged her and patted her back in exactly the same way and told her that everything was going to be all right, that there were plenty of fish in the sea and that one day she'd meet the man of her dreams. She'd been right. Will was the love of her life. "Come on, sit down, I'll make the tea."

Her mother sat down and kept dabbing at her eyes as Sandra poured tea into two mugs. She sat down and waited until her mum had sipped her tea before asking her again about Eadie.

"She lived for about an hour," said her mother. "Barely that." She sighed. "She was eight weeks premature and didn't stand a chance, really. I knew that as soon as I saw her." She held out her right hand. "The doctor held her like that, with one hand. She was so tiny. And she didn't even open her eyes. They put her in one of those incubator things, but I could see from the looks on the faces of the nurses that she wasn't long for the world. We'd already decided on the name. Eadie. Your dad's grandmum was Eadie. I know it's old-fashioned, but that's what he wanted and what your dad wants he usually gets." She dabbed at her eyes again. "She would have been our first." She shook her head. "No, she WAS our first. She was my first baby but I only got to hold her after she'd died. They wrapped her in a white cloth and said that I could hold her as long as I wanted. They meant it, too. I held her for hours and no one said a word."

"Why didn't you tell us?"

"Tell you what? That I had a baby and she died? What good would that have done? You all came along later."

"That's so sad." Sandra felt tears pricking her eyes.

"She didn't suffer. She just wasn't meant to be born. Your dad said she'd gone back to be with the angels."

"Did you bury her?"

"The hospital arranged a cremation and they had a vicar there." She wiped her eyes and smiled. "Not a day goes by when I don't think about her," she said. "In a way I'm glad you know. It wasn't a secret, it was just that your dad and I decided it was something we should keep to ourselves." She sipped her tea again. "What made you ask about Eadie now? After all these years?"

Sandra drank from her own mug as her mind raced. Telling her mum the truth would raise more questions than it would answer. How had Bella known about Eadie? She put down her mug. "It was a dream, Mum."

"A dream?"

Sandra nodded. "Just a dream."

CHAPTER
FORTY-SIX

Will was sitting next to Bella's bed when Sandra walked into the room. There was a tray on the cupboard on the other side of the bed, and Sandra lifted the plastic from the plate. There were two pale burgers, a spoonful of anaemic corn and three roast potatoes. Sandra could understand why Bella hadn't touched the food. She replaced the cover and smiled at her husband. "Everything okay?"

"We're good," said Will.

"I want to go home," said Bella.

"Soon, honey," said Sandra. "The doctors have to be sure that everything's okay."

"Everything IS okay," said Bella firmly. "I want to be able to sleep in my own bed."

"I'll talk to the doctors," said Sandra. She pointed at the tray. "How about I order you some fast food? A pizza? Or I can go and get you KFC or Burger King if you want."

Bella shook her head. "I'm not hungry."

"You have to eat, honey." Sandra looked across at her husband. "Do you want to get a coffee?"

Will stood up and looked down at Bella. "Are you okay if your mum and I go and get a coffee?"

Bella reached for the remote and began changing the channels on the wall-mounted TV. "Sure."

Will and Sandra walked down the corridor towards the lifts. "The police want us to do a press conference," he said.

"Why?"

"The woman from the press office said it was some quid pro quo thing they had with the media. They help us publicise the search for Bella and when she's found we give interviews."

"I suppose that's fair," said Sandra. "If it hadn't been for the publicity the neighbours wouldn't have phoned and . . ." She left the sentence unfinished.

"That's what I thought," said Will. He pressed the button to call the lift. "And at least it's good news, right? We just thank the police and the public. She said it might mean that they'll leave us alone then." The lift arrived and they got in. Will pressed the button for the ground floor.

"What did she mean? Leave us alone?"

"You know what the tabloids are like. They'd have paparazzi hanging outside our house, following her to school, all that nonsense. But if we have a press conference and everyone gets their photographs and our quotes then they won't bother us."

Sandra frowned and ran a hand through her hair. "Do you believe that?"

"I think we'll still have paparazzi around but what she says about the quid pro quo is fair. We do owe them, especially the TV people."

They arrived at the ground floor and walked to the canteen.

"What did she say, your mum?"

"You won't believe it," said Sandra. "Mum and Dad did have another daughter, but she died at birth. They'd never mentioned it. To anyone."

Will stopped and stared at her open-mouthed.

"I know. It's unbelievable, isn't it? She never said anything, all these years."

"And the baby was called Eadie?"

Sandra nodded. "It was a family name."

"How the hell did Bella know?"

"I wish I knew," she said. "Have you talked to your dad? About his father?"

"He's not answering his phone. You know what he's like. Let's get our coffee and I'll try again."

They joined the queue at the counter, picked up coffee and muffins, and took them to a free table. They sat down, and Will took out his mobile phone and phoned his father. This time his father answered. "Is everything okay?" asked his father immediately. "Is Bella okay?"

"She's fine, Dad."

"I'm coming to the hospital tomorrow."

"There's no need, Dad. She'll be home soon. Really, she's fine. Look, I have a quick question for you. What was your dad's name?" Will's grandfather had died not long after his father had been born, felled by a major stroke after twenty years of smoking two packs of unfiltered cigarettes a day.

"Arthur," said Will's father. "Why do you want to know?"

"Somebody was asking, that's all. Look, I've got to go, I'll let you know as soon as Bella's home." He ended the call and stared at his wife in astonishment. "Bella was right," he said. "Grandpa Arthur. How could she know?"

"Maybe your dad mentioned it sometime?"

"Why would he?"

"I don't know, Will. He spends a lot of time with her. Maybe they talked about him."

"I don't see why. Dad was just a kid when his dad passed away. And how do you explain the Eadie thing? Grandpa Arthur and Auntie Eadie, that's what Bella said."

"What are you saying, Will? That she went to Heaven and met dead relatives that we didn't know about?" She laughed and shook her head. "That's impossible."

"Is it?" said Will. "You believe in Heaven, don't you?"

"Of course. But Bella didn't die. She might have been unconscious for a few minutes but that's not the same as dead, is it?"

"I don't know. I'm just trying to understand what happened."

"Does it matter?" said Sandra. "We've got her back. That's all I care about. Nothing else matters."

Will smiled and nodded. "No arguments from me there," he said.

Sandra reached over and held his hand. "We should just count our blessings."

210

CHAPTER
FORTY-SEVEN

Nightingale was wondering whether to light a cigarette or head down to the pub for a lunchtime drink when Jenny opened the door to his office. He looked up from his copy of the *Sun*. "Don't you ever knock?"

"Why would I knock? You've got no secrets from me."

"I could be in an embarrassing situation."

"I don't consider struggling with the *Sun*'s Sudoku to be that embarrassing," she said. "Anyway, I knew you'd want to see this." She handed him a computer printout. "The lab's just got back to me. The only fingerprints on the knife and the crucible were yours and James McBride's."

Nightingale looked at the lab's report. "That's interesting."

"Well, it means that as you sure as hell didn't set up the altar, it can only have been McBride." She dropped down onto the chair opposite him. "What do you think?"

Nightingale ran a hand through his hair. "I think that Jimmy McBride framed himself as a Satanist. Or at least was party to it. But why would he do that?"

"Maybe he was disturbed. Schizophrenic, maybe. Perhaps he believed he was doing the work of the Devil."

"But nothing else about him points to that, does it? And while he might have set up the altar, he couldn't have downloaded the Satanic stuff onto his computer. He didn't have wi-fi."

"He could have taken the computer to somewhere that did have an internet connection."

Nightingale shook his head. "It wasn't a laptop," he said.

"Someone else must have loaded the stuff onto his hard drive."

"But it was the cops who took it from his farmhouse."

"Exactly."

"So the cops helped frame him as a devil-worshipper? Is that what you're saying?"

"The cops. Or a cop. But here's the thing, Jenny. He went out and killed eight kids and a teacher. Why does him being a Satanist make it more acceptable?"

"What do you mean?"

"The whole world will know that he's a child killer. Why bother to make it look like his motivation was tied in to devil-worship?"

Jenny shrugged. "I've no idea."

"There's only one reason to do that, and that's to distract from his real motivation. The Satanism thing is a distraction. He wanted us to think that's why he killed those children."

"So you think he had another reason?"

"I do. And I think that it all comes down to the children that he killed. There has to be some connection, some reason that he chose them. And whatever that reason was, he wanted to hide it. He didn't want anyone to know the real reason he was killing them."

"This is pretty heavy stuff, Jack."

"Tell me about it."

"What do you want to do?"

"To be honest, I don't know. I really don't know." He looked at his watch. "Maybe a drink will help me think."

"Yeah, because alcohol is known to increase your IQ exponentially, right?"

Nightingale's eyes narrowed. "Sarcasm?"

"Barely concealed contempt, actually."

"So you don't want to come to the pub with me?"

Jenny grinned. "I didn't say that."

CHAPTER
FORTY-EIGHT

Nightingale paid the barman and raised his bottle of Corona. Jenny clinked her glass of white wine against his bottle. "Here's to a clear head," she said.

Nightingale chuckled and drank. "So here's what I'm thinking," he said. "It started out looking as if McBride was a lone madman who was involved in black magic and Satanism. A nutter who just went crazy with a shotgun. But it's clear that he wasn't mad and he wasn't a Satanist. But he wanted people to think that he was. It wasn't that someone set him up; his fingerprints were on that fake altar, which means that he must have put it together. But a real Satanist would have had books on the occult in his house. And he would have fixed up an internet connection so that he could visit Satanic websites."

"That makes sense," said Jenny.

"So if he wasn't crazy and he wasn't a Satanist, we need to understand the logic of what he did. And that's what's making my head hurt."

"You're not alone there. But why couldn't he just be crazy? And faking the altar was part of his craziness?"

"Because the shooting wasn't the work of a madman. He chose his victims, moving from classroom to classroom. He shot one teacher and eight pupils and then he blew his head off. A madman would have just gone into one classroom and blasted away and not cared who he killed. And probably shot it out with the cops, too." He shook his head. "McBride wasn't mad, which means there was a logic to everything that he did."

"So we need to work out why he killed the kids that he did."

"And the deputy headmaster. I think he might be a clue to solving this." He sipped his lager. "Like I said before, he could have killed more teachers but didn't. We need to look at Mister . . . what was his name?"

"Etchells. Simon Etchells."

"We need to run a full check on him. And the kids."

"You still think that the kids are connected in some way?"

"They were all in single-parent families, which means they might have been more vulnerable."

"Vulnerable to what? Abuse?"

"Maybe. I didn't get anywhere with the coroner's officer, but I could talk to the parents."

"That's your plan? Walk up to complete strangers and ask if their children were being assaulted?"

Nightingale grimaced. "It doesn't sound too good when you put it like that."

"You have to be careful," she said. "They've already lost a child and you start asking questions like that. Your feet won't touch the ground."

"If this is about kids being abused, there has to be a reason why McBride decided to do what he did.

215

Something must have happened to kick him off." He took a long pull on his lager. "I need to talk to that cop that Robbie put me in touch with. He might have an idea what's going on up in Berwick."

"If he knew, surely he'd have done something already?"

"That depends on what it is. Maybe it's not common knowledge."

"Are you sure you want to do this, Jack?"

"What do you mean?"

"We don't have a client, remember. And we're coming up on two grand's worth already."

"Don't you want to know what happened?"

"We know what happened. You want to know why. There's a difference."

"I want to know why McBride killed those kids, yes. It's not about the money. If someone forced McBride to do what he did, I want to know."

"You think someone forced him to kill the children and then kill himself?"

"I don't know what to think. That's why I want to keep on the case, for a while longer at least."

Jenny looked at her watch. "Speaking of cases, you haven't forgotten you've got a job this evening?"

"Of course not." He grinned. "But remind me again what it is."

Jenny sighed. "Mrs Holiday. Her husband's knocking off his secretary at the Premier Inn every Thursday night."

"Ah yes, the old romantic."

"And she wants photographs to give to her lawyer."

"I'm on it," said Nightingale.

"The camera's in the office," she said. "I've charged it and there's a fresh memory card in it. Some video would be nice."

Nightingale saluted her sarcastically. "Aye, aye, ma'am."

CHAPTER
FORTY-NINE

Jeremy Barker checked himself in the mirror and smoothed down his hair. The white coat and the stethoscope draped casually around the neck gave him the look of a doctor, and providing he kept walking purposefully he doubted he would be challenged. People were used to deferring to men in white coats, and providing he didn't actually claim to be a doctor he didn't see he was breaking the law. He took a pair of horn-rimmed spectacles he'd borrowed from his aunt and put them on. Barker had just turned twenty-five but with his receding hairline and drinker's paunch he looked a few years older. He turned left and right, then nodded at his reflection. "Twenty milligrams of epinephrine and get the crash cart in here, stat!" he said, then he laughed. It would probably be best if he didn't say anything.

He took off the coat and glasses and put them into a backpack with a small digital voice recorder and a Casio digital camera. His car was parked a few yards from the building that housed his cramped rented flat and it took him just over an hour to drive from Clapham in south London to the hospital in Brighton. He parked some distance away, because the car park was covered by CCTV. He climbed out of the car, put on the white coat, and shoved the stethoscope into one pocket and the recorder and camera into the other.

It was nine o'clock in the evening. Barker had thought long and hard about the best time to visit the hospital. There would be more staff around during the day, so less chance of him being spotted, but in the evening more of the patients would be asleep and it was more likely the girl would be alone.

She was out of the ICU, which meant she would be on the children's ward. That was on the third floor and consisted of two dozen individual rooms. He'd been to the children's ward before and he knew there were windows looking into each of the rooms so that the nursing staff could check on the patients from the corridor.

As he reached the main entrance, he took the stethoscope out of his pocket and put it around his neck. The lifts were across the main reception area but there were stairs just beyond them. He put his mobile phone to his ear and kept saying yes, yes, and no until he was past the reception desk. He took the steps two at a time, keeping his phone in his hand.

He stopped when he reached the third floor and took a couple of minutes to steady his breathing. He knew there was almost nothing to worry about — the hospital was huge and doctors came and went, and on the off-chance anyone questioned him he planned to say he was a GP, there to check up on one of his own patients. He even had a fake business card in his wallet he could show if necessary.

He stepped into the corridor. To his right was a nursing station. For a moment he thought it was unoccupied, but then he spotted a nurse at a computer. He put the phone to his ear and began to walk. "Yes, I'll be here for an hour or so. Can you ask Derek if he can do it for me. I know, but he's on call." Barker kept the imaginary conversation going as he walked by the station, then slowed as he reached the patient rooms. There was a slot in each door containing a card with the name of the patient and any instructions for the nursing staff. The first room had a boy called Jake. The curtain to his room was closed. On the other side of the corridor the curtain was open and he could see a nurse talking to a girl swathed in bandages. Barker looked at the name on the card. Alison Cooper. Different girl.

There were boys in the next two rooms, and no nurses. The lights were off but there was always enough of a green glow from the monitoring equipment to see by. Double doors at the end of the corridor opened and a black doctor walked towards Barker, his long white coat flapping behind him. Barker took out his phone and began talking, but made eye contact with the black doctor and nodded as he walked by. He had to walk the full length of the corridor before he found Bella Harper's room. The curtain was half drawn and he checked the girl was alone before opening the door. As he stepped into the room he put his hand into the pocket of his coat and switched on the digital recorder. Bella was lying on her back, her blonde curls spread out over the pillow, giving her the look of a sleeping angel.

220

Barker closed the door softly and went over to the window to close the curtain. As he turned around his breath caught in his throat as he realised her eyes were open and she was staring at him. He swallowed. "Hello Bella, how are you this evening?"

"I'm fine," she said.

"I'm just going to put the light on," he said.

"Okay."

Barker flicked the light switch and two fluorescent tubes flicked on. "There we are." She brushed a lock of blonde hair away from her eyes. Her eyes were pale blue, Barker realised. He hadn't read that anywhere. Details like that helped to flesh out a story. "Have they told you when you'll be going home?"

"The day after tomorrow," she said.

"I bet you're looking forward to it." He sat down on the end of her bed, careful not to put any of his weight on the recorder.

Bella nodded. "I don't like hospitals," she said.

"Nobody does," said Barker. "I'll let you into a secret. Doctors don't really like hospitals either."

Bella giggled. "That's funny," she said.

"Bella, I need to take a photograph of you for our file, is that okay?"

"Sure," she said. "Can I comb my hair?"

Barker smiled reassuringly. "It's only for our file, no one will see it," he lied. He took out his camera and took a couple of shots. No photographs of Bella had been released, and while the UK papers would probably not publish them he was sure he'd be able to

221

sell them overseas. "How do you feel? Do you feel better?" He put the camera away.

"I feel a bit sore, still. The medicine helps me."

"Do you sleep okay? Do you have nightmares?" That would be a great storyline. Kidnapped girl plagued by nightmares.

"Not really nightmares," said Bella. "I don't really dream at all."

"What about when you get home? Is there something there you really miss? A pet?" Kidnapped girl reunited with her puppy. That would make a terrific picture.

"I miss my rabbit. Floppy. He has really long ears."

A rabbit wasn't such a great picture, but it would do. "And have Mum and Dad said they'll take you somewhere special? The seaside or Eurodisney or somewhere like that?"

Bella shook her head. "They just want me at home."

"I can understand that. They must have missed you so much when they were away."

Bella brushed hair away from her eyes again. "I think so."

"Can I ask you something, Bella?"

"Sure."

"When you were with the man and the woman who kept you prisoner. Can you tell me what they did to you?"

Bella swallowed but didn't say anything as she studied him with her pale blue eyes.

"We need to know so we can help other little girls that get taken away from their families." He nodded encouragingly. "You'll be helping us to help them."

222

Bella stared at him in silence and for a moment he was worried she was about to burst into tears. Then she slowly smiled. "You're not a doctor, are you?"

"Of course I am, sweetie." He took off his stethoscope and swung it around. "Why else would I have this?"

Bella smiled at him. "So people wouldn't realise you're a reporter," she said.

Barker's stomach lurched. "A reporter?"

"A freelance. You want to write a story about me that you can sell, but what you really want is a job on one of the big newspapers."

"How do you know that?"

Bella giggled. "I know everything, Jeremy."

Barker stared at her, his mind racing. How did she know his name? "Did somebody tell you I was coming to see you?"

Bella nodded.

"Who?"

"Jesus."

Barker screwed up his face. "Jesus?"

"I spoke to Jesus. An angel took me to see him."

"When was this?"

"When the bad man and the bad woman had me. But Jesus said everything would be all right. And he had a message for you, Jeremy."

"A message?"

"A message for you. Come closer, Jeremy, I have to whisper it to you." Barker stood up and looked down at her. She crooked her finger and beckoned him. "Come on. Before the nurse comes back. She'll be here soon."

Barker's left foot moved forward as if it had a life of his own.

"Closer, Jeremy." She smiled at him, showing perfect white teeth.

Barker took another step forward. The stethoscope slipped from his fingers and clattered to the floor.

"Good boy, Jeremy," said Bella.

CHAPTER
FIFTY

Nightingale got back to Bayswater just before eleven with several dozen photographs of the errant husband and his secretary in his camera, along with several minutes of video of them sitting in a bar, drinking champagne and getting in the mood. When he saw that Mrs Chan's Chinese restaurant on the ground floor was still open, he decided to pop in for a bowl of his favourite duck noodles. Mrs Chan served him herself and persuaded him to down another two Coronas, and after he'd finished eating she sat at his table and chatted about her son, who was running a very successful property company in Hong Kong. He had just had his second child, making Mrs Chan a grandmother six times over.

"When you marry, Mister Jack?" she asked him. She had been in London for almost thirty years but still spoke English as if it was her first day in the country.

"When I find the right woman, Mrs Chan," laughed Nightingale.

"What about that nice girl who works for you? Miss Jenny. She very pretty."

"She's too valuable as an assistant. And to be honest, I don't think I'm her type."

Mrs Chan laughed and patted his hand. "You wrong, Mister Jack. I see her when she look at you."

Nightingale threw up his hands. "Please, Mrs Chan, you've got to stop trying to marry me off. I'm happy being single."

"No, Mister Jack, you just think you happy."

Nightingale paid his bill and went upstairs to his flat. As soon as he opened the door and switched on the light he knew that something was wrong. The cushions weren't as he had left them on the sofa and the books on his coffee table had been rearranged. Nightingale didn't have a cleaner and Jenny had the only spare key, and he was pretty sure that she wouldn't have popped around to do some tidying up.

His mind raced. If someone had got into the flat then they'd done it without damaging the door, which meant they'd picked the lock or come through a window. The only vulnerable windows were in his bedroom and bathroom, and they were all locked. His flat wasn't an obvious one to burgle, as the street was usually busy outside and there were always people going in and out of Mrs Chan's restaurant. He took a long deep breath as he considered his options. There had been someone in his flat, he was sure of that. The question was, were they still there or not?

He whistled softly as he fumbled in his bag and pulled out his camera. He groped for the flash and fixed that to the top of the camera, then slipped the bag off his shoulder and tossed it across the room onto the sofa. Then he switched off the light and held his breath.

226

If he was wrong and he was alone in the flat then at least there'd be no one to see how stupid he was.

He cocked his head on one side, listening intently. He could hear cars driving by outside, and the buzz of conversation from the pavement down below. Then he heard a soft footfall, the sound of a leather sole brushing against carpet, and he knew that he wasn't imagining it.

He heard another footfall and then two shapes appeared in the bedroom doorway. He held up the camera and fired off a shot. In the flash of light he saw two men wearing ski masks. One was big, well over six feet, and carrying a hunting knife, the blade pressed against his trousers. The smaller man was holding a coil of rope.

Nightingale fired off a second shot. This time the men were standing open-mouthed, their hands up. Nightingale grabbed for the door and pulled it open. He stumbled downstairs, keeping the camera pressed to his side, taking the stairs two at a time. He fumbled for the lock on the downstairs door and ran out into the street. A black cab sounded its horn and he ran along the pavement and then darted across to the other side of the road, narrowly missing a courier on a bicycle who snarled and swore at him. Nightingale stood behind a parked car and looked up at his building. The light in the sitting room went on, and then a few seconds later went off. Then the light in the stairway came on and the two men emerged from the front door. They'd taken off their ski masks and there was no sign of the rope or the knife.

Nightingale tried to focus on the two men and snapped away, getting off a dozen shots as they stepped out of the doorway and headed down the road towards Hyde Park, keeping their heads down. He walked down the road after them but they turned right towards Queensway, and by the time he got there they were lost in the crowds.

He pulled out his mobile phone and called Jenny. She listened in silence as he explained what had happened.

"What are you going to do, Jack?" she asked when he'd finished. "Are you going to call the police?"

"And say what? Two men in ski masks attacked me? Without any way of identifying them I'd be wasting my time. Plus I've got a feeling that it's cops that are behind it."

"Why do you say that?"

"It was personal, Jenny. One of them had a knife and the other one was holding a piece of rope."

"Rope?"

"I think they were planning a lynching, making it look as if I'd killed myself. And the only case that I'm working on at the moment that would inspire that level of violence is up in Berwick. The cops I spoke to were clearly unhappy at the questions I was asking, and I'm pretty sure that Danny McBride was murdered. So at the moment I'm not convinced that going to the cops is a good idea." He ran a hand through his hair. "There is one cop I could talk to," he said. "But it means going back into the lion's den."

"Jack, will you stop talking in riddles."

228

"I need to go back to Berwick and talk to that cop that Robbie put me in touch with."

"Your diary is pretty much free tomorrow, and the day after is Saturday so it doesn't matter too much if you get back late. But I thought you said he'd only talk to you on the phone."

"Yeah, well, I'll get him to change his mind on that. After what's happened, he has to meet me. I'm not thrilled about another flight up to Edinburgh, though. Don't suppose you'll lend me the Audi, will you?"

"You suppose right. What about the train? It's probably only three or four hours."

"Sure. See if you can get me a seat to get there for lunch and a seat back in the late afternoon. I'll buy him lunch."

"I'm sure that'll work."

"Are you being sarcastic? I can never tell on the phone."

"Yes, Jack. I am." She ended the call before he could think of a witty comeback.

CHAPTER
FIFTY-ONE

Jimmy Patel looked up as the door opened and the bell tinkled. It was ten o'clock at night, which was about the time that the drunks started to turn up. The problem was that drunks were often the best customers — they wanted more booze or cigarettes or a snack and generally they didn't quibble about the prices. They didn't usually steal, though. Not like the schoolkids who came in during the day. Jimmy's father had Sellotaped a notice to the door saying that no more than two schoolkids were allowed in at the same time, but if Jimmy had his way he wouldn't let any in. They had the morals of sewer rats, and were just as cunning and quick. They'd shove a chocolate bar or a pack of sweets down their trousers and run out of the shop before he could do anything. Not that there was much he could do. He couldn't lay a hand on them, and they knew it. And the police weren't interested. The first few times he'd called nine nine nine but the operators had said that it wasn't an emergency and that he should call the local policing team. But they almost never answered their phone and when they did they said that shoplifting was very low on their priorities.

It might have been low on their priorities but it was important to Jimmy and his family. Margins were tight, and his rent and rates were all going up faster than inflation, and every pound that walked out of the door represented food off his plate. Jimmy worked twelve hours a day, every day, but he doubted that he ended up with more than if he was on the dole claiming benefits like most of his customers.

The man who walked into his shop wasn't on the dole, though. The stethoscope around his neck suggested he was a doctor, and by the look of it a man who'd had a hard day. Jimmy Patel smiled at the customer. There had been a time when Jimmy had thought about becoming a doctor, but his father had persuaded him that he was needed in the shop.

"All right?" said Jimmy.

The doctor grunted and walked down the centre aisle of the shop, looking left and right.

"Can I help you find something?" called Jimmy, but the doctor ignored him. Jimmy looked over at the curved mirror on the wall near the ceiling that gave him a view of the parts of the shop he couldn't see from behind the till. The doctor reached the end of the aisle and stood looking at the cleaning products. He bent down and took out an orange plastic bottle. He stared at the label for a few seconds, then turned and walked back to the till.

Jimmy looked at the bottle the doctor was holding. Mister Muscle drain cleaner. "Blocked drain?" asked Jimmy.

"How much?" The doctor's voice was hard and lacked any emotion. He sounded as if he'd just come off a long shift.

"You know what, you're better off with the bigger size," said Jimmy. "You get twice as much but it's only 20p more. We're getting a deal at the wholesaler." He gestured at the bottle in the doctor's hand. "That's old stock. You're better off with the bigger one, seriously."

The doctor looked at Jimmy blankly, nodded and then went back down the aisle. He reappeared a few seconds later holding the larger size.

"There you go, that's much better," said Jimmy.

The doctor tucked the bottle under his left arm and fumbled for his wallet. He handed over a ten-pound note.

"Do you want a bag for that?" asked Jimmy.

The doctor turned and headed for the door.

"Hey, your change!" The bell tinkled as the door opened and the doctor stepped out into the street. "Hey, mate, don't forget your change!" shouted Jimmy. The door banged shut and Jimmy cursed under his breath. He opened the till, put in the ten pounds and quickly counted out the change. He stepped out from behind the register and hurried over to the door. He pulled it open and looked down the street. The doctor was sitting on the pavement, his feet stretched out into the road. Jimmy opened his mouth but before he could say anything the doctor tilted back his head and began to drink from the orange bottle.

CHAPTER
FIFTY-TWO

Harry Simpson was younger than Nightingale had expected. The voice on the phone had sounded like a man in his forties but the DI was barely out of his twenties, fresh-faced and a heavy mop of hair that he was forever flicking out of his eyes. He agreed to meet in the Magna Tandoori restaurant in the centre of the town, a short walk from the railway station. He was already there when Nightingale arrived, tucked away in a corner table. He stood up to shake hands, then looked cautiously over Nightingale's shoulder. "If anyone sees us, you're an old mate from London, passing through."

"Understood," said Nightingale.

"I hope you do," said Simpson, sitting down. "I could get in real trouble talking to you."

"Trust me, I'm not that happy about having to schlep all the way up here on the train but I needed to talk to you." He had caught the 9 a.m. train from King's Cross station and had arrived in Berwick just over three and a half hours later. Nightingale took off his raincoat. A waiter reached to take it away but Nightingale shook his head and put it over the back of his chair.

"They'd put my balls in a vice if they found out I was talking to a private eye."

"I just want to run a few things by you," said Nightingale. "I'm not looking for confidential information or anything that'll breach the Data Protection Act."

"I'd have preferred to do it over the phone."

"What I've got to say, I thought you'd prefer it face to face. That way you know that nothing's being recorded."

"I still don't know that."

Nightingale held out his hands. "You're welcome to frisk me."

Simpson grinned. "Don't be bloody stupid. What is it you want to tell me?"

"I did a bit of work on the altar that you guys found in McBride's farm. I checked the prints on a couple of items and they match McBride's prints."

"That's hardly surprising, is it?"

Another waiter came over. "Okay if I order?" asked Simpson. "I'm a regular."

"Go ahead," said Nightingale. "I'm a big fan of Indian."

"The chef's from Bangladesh and he's a diamond," said Simpson. He ordered several dishes and rice and two Kingfisher beers.

"Here's the thing," said Nightingale once the waiter was out of earshot. "I'm pretty sure that McBride had zero interest in Satanism. But the fact that his prints were on the altar means he must have set it up. Why would he do that?"

"Because he was as mad as a hatter. The fact that he killed kids suggests that he wasn't right in the head, don't you think?"

"He didn't shoot like a madman," said Nightingale. "What he did was very cold and clinical."

"Sociopaths are cold and clinical." He frowned. "What do you mean, you checked the prints?"

"I took a couple of things from the altar and ran them through a lab. McBride's brother took me to the farm."

"You know he topped himself?"

"You think he committed suicide? There was no note."

"Suicides don't always leave notes," said Simpson. He stiffened. "How do you know there was no note?"

"You don't want to know," said Nightingale.

The detective leaned forward. "Actually I do," he said.

"Let's just leave it that I know," said Nightingale. "Are you on the case?"

"There is no case. It's a suicide."

"There'll be a post mortem?"

"I was there when they cut the body down," said Simpson. "There's no confusion about cause of death."

"He wasn't suicidal when I met him," said Nightingale. "Seemed happy enough, other than the fact that his brother had turned into a spree killer. Loved his family, and if he did have any money problems the death of his brother would have taken care of them. Plus he was driven to find out why his brother did what he did. None of that points to a man who would take his own life."

"Maybe insanity runs in the family."

Nightingale smiled thinly. "Now that's a glib statement if ever I heard one. I don't think Danny McBride was mentally ill and I've seen nothing to suggest that his brother was either."

"Other than his killing spree." Their lagers arrived. The waiter poured the contents into two glasses.

"You might want to take a closer look at McBride's hanging," said Nightingale, after the waiter had gone. "But if Bernard Connolly's on the case I'm guessing you won't get much from the post mortem."

Simpson frowned. "How do you know Connolly?"

"He's the coroner's officer I spoke to. Not very helpful, I have to say."

Simpson shook his head in amazement. "You haven't been here long but you've certainly put yourself about," he said.

"I wanted to ask about the post mortems of the kids who died at the school but he pretty much told me to mind my own beeswax."

"You can understand why," said Simpson. "It's not like you're in the job. But why were you asking questions about the post mortems?"

"I wanted to know if there were signs of sexual abuse."

Simpson's eyebrows shot skyward. "What? Where the hell did that come from?"

"The kids that he shot were all from single-parent families."

"So? Half of all marriages end in divorce these days."

"I know that, but all the kids that were shot were missing a parent. Not half. Not three-quarters. All."

"And you think McBride shot them because of that?"

"I don't think the killings were random. He moved from classroom to classroom. He only shot the one teacher. Simon Etchells, the deputy headmaster. He could have shot other teachers but he didn't. He could have shot at the cops, but he didn't. It looks to me that it was all planned and his targets were pre-selected."

"And having decided to shoot specific children, he set out to make it look as if he was doing it because he was some sort of devil-worshipper?"

"He was using that as a distraction, yes. And he must have had help because he didn't have internet access at his home, so someone else must have loaded the Satanic stuff onto his computer."

"This is making my head hurt, Nightingale. Just exactly what do you think is going on?"

"At the moment I'm not sure. That's why I'm here. I'm not sure what I've got into, but I was attacked last night."

"Attacked?"

"Two guys came at me in my flat. One of them was carrying a length of rope."

"Rope?"

"I think they were planning on hanging me."

"What happened?"

"I ran like the wind, that's what happened."

"And you think there's a connection with the waves you've been making up here?"

"I think the rope is the clue." He fumbled in his raincoat pocket and pulled out a handful of printouts of pictures he'd taken of the men leaving his building. He gave them to Simpson and the policeman studied them. He scratched his nose. "They're not very clear."

"Yeah, well I'm not a professional photographer and they were moving fast." The policeman held up two photographs, the first ones Nightingale had taken as the two men came out of the bedroom. "Ski masks?"

"Yeah."

"They were coming at you with a knife and you took their picture?"

"It was dark. I figured the flash would blind them, give me enough time to get out. It worked, as it happens."

"And you think they were from Berwick?"

He tried to hand the pictures back to Nightingale but Nightingale shook his head. "Keep them," he said. "You might recognise someone down the line. I don't know if they're from here or not. They might be from London but someone here could have paid them."

"To what? To kill you? That's one hell of a stretch, isn't it?"

"They were in my flat. They waited for me to come back. So it wasn't about robbery." He smiled ruefully. "Not that I had much to steal."

"So why do you think they turned over your flat?"

"Looking for the things I took from the altar, maybe. Or covering up for what they planned to do."

238

"What do you mean?"

"They brought some rope with them. I figure I was going to join the list of suicides." Nightingale shrugged. "I don't know, maybe I'm getting paranoid in my old age. But just because I'm paranoid doesn't mean they're not out to get me."

Two waiters arrived with their food and they spread it out across the table. Chicken tikka masala, prawn dansak, lamb jalfrezi, aloo gobi and saag bhaji. Simpson folded the printouts and slipped them into his jacket pocket. Nightingale helped himself to rice and waited until the waiters had gone before continuing.

"I need your help, Harry. The two cops I've spoken to up here haven't been helpful."

"Who else did you speak to?"

"The guy who has McBride's computer. Colin Stevenson."

Simpson nodded. "Yeah, I know him."

"Someone leaked the Satanic website thing to the press and I think it might have been him."

"You want to be careful throwing around allegations like that."

"I'm not throwing allegations around, I'm just mentioning it to you. Like I said, McBride didn't have an internet connection at his house, which means that he couldn't have visited those websites. Stevenson says that he did and the press got hold of the fact in double quick time. I'm happy to be proved wrong, but it looks to me like Stevenson might have another agenda."

"Like what?"

Nightingale shrugged. "I don't know."

"Seems to me there's a lot you don't know." Simpson tore off a chunk of naan bread and dipped it into the dansak.

"That's why I wanted to talk to you," said Nightingale. "Stevenson and Connolly might be more forthcoming with you."

"You want me to spy for you? That's not going to happen."

"You're on the case, right? Don't you want to know what really happened?"

"We know what happened. James McBride took his shotgun and killed eight children and a teacher, then he took his own life."

"But what if he was being used? What if there was someone behind him?"

"Behind him? What do you mean?"

"Someone put the Satanic stuff on his computer. I think they did that to hide the real reason for the killings. I'd have thought that you might want to know what that reason was."

"Why are you so interested? Your client is dead, right?"

"He paid in advance," said Nightingale. "But this isn't about money. It's about getting at the truth."

Simpson sipped his lager slowly as he thought about what Nightingale had said. "What specifically do you want from me?" he said, putting down his glass.

"I'd like to know if there was anything off about Etchells. The teacher that was killed."

"Off in what way?"

"McBride shot him point blank in the playground. He didn't have to. If he'd made any sort of threatening gesture with the shotgun, Etchells would have folded. All McBride had to do was point the gun at him. He didn't need to pull the trigger. And when he went to the classrooms, he didn't shoot the teachers. He chose to kill Etchells and I want to know why."

Simpson pulled a face. "I haven't heard anything."

"No, but you probably weren't looking. He was a victim. Same as the pupils. You don't look at victims in the same way as you look at the perpetrator."

"Okay, I can do that."

"And I'd really like to know why Colin Stevenson has been so uncooperative."

Simpson's eyes narrowed. "Are you suggesting he's bad? Because there's no way I'm getting dragged into a Professional Standards investigation."

"Someone put that Satanic stuff on McBride's hard drive and leaked it to the press. Whoever it was must have done it for a reason."

"And you think it was Stevenson?"

"He's the only name I've got."

Simpson put down his fork. "If I get caught sniffing around a fellow cop I could blow my career."

"What sort of cop is he?"

"Close to retirement. He'll be gone in a couple of years. He's like a lot of old school detectives, he's seen the job change and it's not changed for the better. You know what it's like, right? We get shafted by the politicians, our pay and pensions are attacked, the CPS and the courts let us down every day of the week and the public hates us." He shrugged. "Welcome to the new millennium."

"I know it isn't easy being a copper. It never has been. But eight kids died and I want to know why."

Simpson nodded slowly. "Okay. I'll put out a few feelers. But I'm not promising anything."

"That's cool."

"And we're splitting this bill, fifty-fifty."

"Which is also cool," said Nightingale. "Two more Kingfishers?"

CHAPTER
FIFTY-THREE

Sandra Harper ruffled her daughter's hair. "What do you want to eat, honey?" Bella was sitting in front of the television wearing her favourite Barbie pyjamas. The doctors had discharged her first thing in the morning and as soon as they'd got home she had retreated to the sofa. Bella shrugged and kept her eyes on the television. "I'm okay."

"Are you sure? Pizza Hut? KFC? Burger King? Your dad can drive and get you whatever you want."

"I'm not hungry, Mum."

"Tomorrow's Saturday, do you want to go to the pictures? It's been ages since we saw a film together. We could go with Grandma and Granddad. Make it a family day out?"

Bella shrugged but didn't say anything.

Sandra sat down next to her daughter. "Are you okay?"

"Don't worry. I'm fine." She continued to stare at the television.

"What are you watching?"

"A documentary on the Holocaust."

"The Holocaust? Why on earth are you watching that?"

"It's interesting."

"I'm not sure you should be watching that."

"Why not?"

Sandra picked up the remote and flicked through the channels until she found a cartoon show. "That's better."

"I hate cartoons," said Bella.

"You love cartoons." She brushed Bella's hair away from her eyes. "Are you sure you're okay?"

Bella sighed. "Really, I'm fine."

"The doctors said you might be in shock for a while."

"I'm not in shock."

"You don't have to go to school next week if you don't want to."

"No, I'll go. Really, I'm fine."

Sandra smelled something unpleasant and she frowned. "Did you clean your teeth this morning?"

"Sure."

Sandra leant forward to smell her daughter's breath but Bella turned her head away. "Mum, please . . ."

"Do you feel okay? Is your stomach bad?"

"My stomach's fine."

"So why aren't you hungry?"

"I'm just not," said Bella.

Again Sandra caught the smell of something bitter and acrid yet also sickly sweet. Like very old cheese. But before she could say anything, the doorbell rang. She frowned. "Now who's that at this time of night?" She went over to the window and pulled back the curtain. "Bloody Jehovah's Witnesses."

244

Will appeared at the sitting room door. "Who is it?"

"The God squad," she said. "Alisha said they were around yesterday."

The doorbell rang again. "I'll get rid of them," said Will.

Bella turned to look at her father. "What are Jehovah's Witnesses?" she asked.

"Nutters," said Will. "They want to come in and talk about God."

"Can I talk to them?"

Will frowned. "What? Why?"

"I'd like to talk to someone about Jesus."

"Honey, like Daddy says, they're nutters. They're a cult. If you want to talk to someone about Jesus we can go to a church, but these people are just a nuisance and they won't take no for an answer."

"Please, Daddy. I want to."

Will looked over at Sandra and she shrugged. "If that's what she wants . . ."

"Please, Daddy."

"Okay, but once we let them in we'll never be able to get rid of them."

Will went off to open the front door. A few seconds later he returned with a young man in a dark raincoat and a blonde woman on her thirties with dark hair pulled back into a ponytail. Both were carrying black briefcases.

"I'll leave you to it," Will said to his wife. "I've got to do some work on the car." He disappeared down the hallway before Sandra could say anything.

The woman held out her hand. "I'm Tina," she said. "Your husband said you'd be happy to talk to us. Have you heard the word of God?"

Sandra shook the woman's hand. "We go to church, yes," she said. "But it was my daughter who wanted to talk to you."

Bella smiled up at the two Jehovah's Witnesses. "I'm Bella," she said.

"Hello, Bella." She introduced her colleague. "This is David."

David was in his thirties, slightly tubby with thicklensed spectacles. He shook hands with Sandra and flashed Bella a beaming smile.

"Look, I have to say that I'm a little uncomfortable about this," said Sandra. "As I said, we go to church. I don't want you to start putting ideas into my daughter's head."

"I just want to talk to them, Mummy. It'll be fine." She patted the sofa next to her. "They can sit here."

The two Jehovah's Witnesses took off their coats and looked expectantly at Sandra. She took the coats from them and they sat down on the sofa, either side of Bella. "Why don't you get them some tea, Mummy?" asked Bella.

"Oh, I don't think they'll be here that long, honey," said Sandra.

"Actually a cup of tea would be lovely," said Tina, and David nodded.

Sandra sighed. "Right then, tea it is," she said. She walked out of the room, carrying the coats. Bella was looking at her, so Sandra mouthed "Ten minutes" and flashed her a warning look.

"So you are interested in God and how he can be a part of your life?" asked Tina.

Bella nodded. "Of course. God loves us and we are his children."

"That's right," said David. "But what is important is that we demonstrate our love for God. We must show that we are worthy of his love." He opened his briefcase and took out a handful of leaflets. He sorted through them and handed two to her. "These are especially for children," he said. "They will help you to understand what you must do to ensure your place in Heaven."

Bella smiled. "Oh, I don't think I'll be going to Heaven."

"Of course you will, if you do what God wants," said Tina. "Now, have you ever heard of a man called Charles Taze Russell?"

"He founded the Jehovah's Witnesses," said Bella. "He wrote the books *Studies in Scriptures*, which is what your theology is based on." She smiled sweetly.

Tina and David exchanged surprised looks. "Has someone from our Church talked to you already?"

Bella shook her head. "No, you're the first," she said. "But there is something I don't understand. You don't believe in the Father, the Son and the Holy Spirit, do you?"

"God is a single deity, there is only the one God," said Tina.

"Right, but you think that the Archangel Michael is Jesus, don't you?"

"It's not as simple as that," said David. "God created Michael and through him God created the universe, the earth, and all mankind."

"And that happened 42,000 years ago, you think."

David and Tina looked at each other. "Bella, who have you been talking to?" said Tina. "Have your parents put you up to this? Is this some sort of joke?"

"Because really it's not funny," said David. "God is not a laughing matter."

"I just worry about the dinosaurs, that's all," said Bella. "They were around millions of years ago so I don't see how that fits in with your 42,000-year theory." She clapped her hands. "But that's not what really worries me. It's the whole Archangel Michael thing."

Tina frowned at the little girl. "What do you mean?"

Bella sighed. "You believe that Michael became Jesus. And that God sent him down to be the saviour."

"That's right," said Tina. "He was without sin and he obeyed all of God's laws. He took on all the sins of mankind and then he died and was born again in spirit."

"And you believe that one day Jesus will return to earth to destroy Satan and establish God's kingdom on earth?"

"That's right," said Tina. "And only those who follow our path will be saved. That is why we come to people's houses, to give them the chance to choose their own salvation."

Bella nodded. "Here's what I don't understand," said Bella. "You say that Michael became Jesus Christ. But I've met them both. Michael took me to see Jesus."

Tina stood up. "I think I'll just go and see how your mother's getting on with the tea," she said.

As she left the room, David pushed his spectacles up his nose. "What was this, Bella, a dream?"

"I don't think it was a dream," said Bella. "I think I sort of died for a while and then Michael came to see me."

"Michael? The Archangel Michael?"

Bella nodded. "He was very kind."

"And you think he was an angel?"

"He had wings," said Bella.

"Wings?"

"Big wings. Like, huge."

"And he said he was Michael, the Archangel."

Bella nodded seriously. "Yes. And then he took me to see Jesus."

"Bella, you know this was a dream, don't you?"

Bella's face hardened. "No, it was Jesus. He spoke to me for a long time."

"Now come on, Bella, it's wrong to tell stories."

"I'm not telling stories. Jesus spoke to me. He told me lots of things. He told me about you, David."

David's jaw dropped. "What?"

"He told me about you and what you did to that little boy in Bristol."

David's eyes widened and the briefcase tumbled off his lap and fell to the floor, spilling dozens of brochures over the carpet. David ignored them and continued to stare open-mouthed at Bella.

"Jesus has a message for you, David."

"A message?" stuttered David. "For me?"

Bella crooked her finger. "Come closer, David," she said softly. "I have to whisper it to you."

CHAPTER
FIFTY-FOUR

Tina walked into the kitchen as Sandra was pouring hot water into two mugs. Sandra looked up and forced a smile. "Milk and sugar?" she asked.

"We both take it with milk and no sugar," said Tina. She folded her arms and leaned against the door frame as Sandra opened the fridge and took out a bottle of milk. "She's a very special little girl, Bella."

Sandra nodded. "She's our angel," she said.

"She's very bright. For her age."

"Really? You think so?"

Tina nodded. "She seems to know a lot about Jehovah's Witnesses."

Sandra looked up from the mugs. "Are you sure?"

"She knew about Charles Taze Russell."

"Who?"

"Exactly," said Tina. "His name isn't generally known by outsiders."

Sandra shrugged. "She must have seen it on TV. She's been watching a lot of strange stuff on TV recently." She poured milk into the two mugs and stirred.

"Or at school perhaps?"

"She hasn't been to school for a while. Not since . . ." She left the sentence unfinished.

"Since what?"

Sandra looked pained. "Bella was attacked. She was hurt quite badly. She's only just out of hospital."

"Oh my goodness, Bella Harper!" said Tina, putting her hands over her mouth. "I'm so sorry, you should have said. Oh my goodness."

"It's okay. She's fine now. She'll probably be back at school next week."

"Oh, the poor thing. It said in the papers that she'd been . . ." She saw the look of horror flash across Sandra's face and she immediately began apologising.

"It's okay," said Sandra, handing her one of the mugs of tea. "Like I said, she's okay. It was her idea to invite you in. She wanted to talk to you."

"A belief in God can help you through difficult times."

Sandra nodded. "She said an angel helped take care of her."

"That could be true," said Tina. "God loves children more than anything. Why wouldn't he use his angels to protect a child?"

"If that was the case, he was a bit late," said Sandra. "He should have sent an angel to keep the monsters away from her in the first place."

"You're angry," said Tina quietly.

Sandra's eyes flashed. "Of course I'm angry. Why would I not be angry?"

"You got your daughter back. For that alone you should be thanking God. So many missing children never come back."

Sandra forced a smile. "I suppose so."

"And she is such a lovely girl. A treasure."

Sandra took the mug of tea into the sitting room. David was on his hands and knees, gathering up the pamphlets, while Bella stared at the television. "Your tea," said Sandra.

David scooped the pamphlets into his briefcase then locked it and got to his feet. "We should go," he said to Tina.

"Our tea," said Tina, holding up her mug, but David was already walking out of the room.

"Bella, is everything okay?" asked Sandra.

"Everything's fine," said Bella, her eyes on the television. She'd changed the cartoon back to the Holocaust documentary.

"I'm sorry. I'm not sure what's wrong with David," said Tina. She handed her unfinished tea to Sandra, picked up her briefcase and hurried after David. She caught up with him down the street, heading for his car. "David, what's wrong?" she asked as she fell into step with him. He ignored her. He took his car keys from his raincoat pocket and unlocked the door of his Toyota, tossed the briefcase onto the back seat and climbed in. Tina hurried around to the passenger side. "David, what happened? What's wrong?" She got in and pulled the door shut. David had already started the engine.

Tina fastened her seat belt as David pulled away from the curb.

She tried to get him to speak several times but he ignored her. The seat belt warning beeper was going but David ignored that, too.

"Where are we going?" she asked. "We were supposed to be doing calls until nine."

As he turned onto the dual carriageway she realised that they were heading to London. She took out her mobile phone but she had no idea who to call. She was starting to get seriously concerned. David was usually talkative and she'd never seen him like this. There was a blankness in his eyes, as if his mind was elsewhere.

"David, please, you're scaring me. Just tell me what's wrong."

David said nothing. He accelerated and the speedometer moved past 40 to 50 and then 60 miles an hour. Something flashed and Tina realised that they'd driven past a speed camera.

"David, come on now. Slow down."

David never drove over the speed limit. He was one of the most careful drivers that Tina had ever come across, and he was proud of the fact that he had a totally clean driving licence.

"And you should put your seat belt on. Isn't that noise driving you crazy?"

"You know that God loves you, Tina?"

"What? Of course."

The speedometer reached 70 miles an hour and David twisted the steering wheel to the right. Tina screamed as she saw the petrol tanker heading directly towards them. She threw up her hands and closed her eyes and then the car slammed into the tanker and burst into flames. She was already dead by the time the petrol tanker exploded, killing another five people and injuring dozens more.

CHAPTER
FIFTY-FIVE

Nightingale's phone rang. The caller was withholding his number. It was Harry Simpson. "This is turning into a right can of worms, Nightingale." It was Sunday morning and Nightingale was lying on the sofa trying to work up the energy to make himself a bacon sandwich. He wasn't sure how to reply to that, so he said nothing.

"Simon Etchells was at the school for just over ten years. Before that he was at a comprehensive in Slough and before that he was at a girls' private school in Somerset. He left the girls' school under a bit of a cloud. Nothing official, but some parents had complained of inappropriate behaviour on his part."

"He's a paedophile?"

"You can't say that. The police were involved and they interviewed the girls but it wasn't thought serious enough for any charges. It was more texting and emails and being alone with them. The girls never said that he touched them. The school let him resign and that was the end of it."

"Sounds like he was grooming them and got stopped before it went too far."

"I can't argue with that. Anyway, as part of his resignation package he got a glowing reference and moved to Slough. When he was there two teachers were sent down for having sex with underage pupils. Statutory rape — the girls were willing enough but they plied them with booze and drugs. The girls were close to sixteen and the teachers were in their late twenties. They got three years apiece. One of them ended up marrying the girl he was sent to prison for."

"So all's well that ends well. How does Etchells fit in with that?"

"He left the school about a month before the other two were arrested. Could have been a coincidence . . ."

"Or he could have known that something was going to happen and decided to get out before he was implicated."

"You do like putting two and two together and getting five, don't you?"

"I'm assuming there's more, because nothing you've said so far could be considered a right can of worms."

"Three years ago there was a complaint from the parent of a girl in the Berwick school. A ten-year-old girl said Etchells had followed her into the toilets and said he wanted to check that her skirt wasn't too short."

"Nice."

"There was a file and Etchells and the girl were interviewed, but it was decided that the girl was just confused. The file wasn't even sent to the CPS, it just died. The girl left the school the following term. Case closed."

"That's more than enough red flags, isn't it?"

"That's not the can of worms, though. The inspector who closed the case was Colin Stevenson."

Nightingale felt as if he'd just been punched in the chest and he gasped. He put his hand against the wall to steady himself.

"You still there?" asked Simpson.

"I'm gob-smacked."

"Yeah, you and me both. I mean, it's by no means conclusive proof . . ."

"No, but it's one hell of a coincidence, isn't it?"

"Coincidences do happen," said Simpson. "The question is, what do you want to do next?"

"To be honest, we need to take a closer look at Stevenson. But I know you're not happy about that."

"I can hardly speak to him, can I? And I'm not going to Professional Standards."

"Is he a family man?"

"Divorced, I think. No kids."

"Can you get an address for him?"

"Probably. But why?"

"Best you don't know," said Nightingale.

CHAPTER
FIFTY-SIX

Nightingale pushed open the office door with his shoulder. He was holding two cups of Costa coffee and had a copy of the *Sun* under his arm. As he stepped into the office he realised that there was a man standing by Jenny's desk. He had a mane of grey hair combed back and was wearing a dark blue pinstripe suit. Even before the man turned around, Nightingale knew who it was. Marcus Fairchild. One of the coffee cups fell from his nerveless fingers and splattered over the floor.

"Jack!" said Jenny. She sprang from her chair and picked up the cup.

"Sorry," mumbled Nightingale.

Fairchild was grinning at him. He had a pug nose flecked with broken blood vessels, several tubular chins and a paunch that strained at his waistcoat and watch chain.

"It's all down your trousers," said Jenny, putting the cup on her desk. "I'll get you a paper towel." She hurried out, heading for the bathroom that was shared by the three offices on their floor.

Fairchild extended a pudgy hand with perfectly manicured nails. "Marcus Fairchild," he said. "We've never met, but Jenny talks about you all the time."

259

Nightingale shook. A large gold cufflink in the shape of a lion's head peeped out from under Fairchild's sleeve and he was wearing a chunky gold watch. "Ditto," he said. "Are you just passing by?"

"I wanted a word, actually. About your Berwick case."

Nightingale frowned. "How are you involved?"

Fairchild chuckled. "Good Lord, I'm not involved. I just thought I might be of some help, that's all. Jenny said that the case involves systematic child abuse and I've dealt with a number of such cases over the years."

"I thought you were mainly commercial law?"

"That's my bread and butter, of course, but I've covered the full range of legal work over the years. Jack of all trades."

"And master of none?"

He chuckled again. "Actually master of all of them." He adjusted the cuffs of his jacket.

Jenny returned with a handful of paper towels. She gave them to Nightingale and he dabbed at the wet patches.

"Sit down, Uncle Marcus," she said, waving him to a chair. She pulled up another chair and sat down next to him. "I was mentioning to Uncle Marcus about our case," she said.

"Yes, so he said."

"He's worked on a few similar cases and thought he might be able to help."

"I'm not sure that we need any help, to be honest," said Nightingale. He screwed up the paper towel and tossed it into the bin.

260

"It was the Satanic aspect that interested me," said Fairchild. "I was on a case a few years ago where a paedophile claimed that the Devil made him do it."

"You represented him?" asked Nightingale, sitting down on the chair behind Jenny's desk.

"Good lord no. I was working with the CPS. I know that everyone is entitled to the best possible defence but there are limits."

"I thought barristers worked like taxis and had to take the next case no matter what it is."

"That's the theory, but in practice there's some leeway. I certainly wouldn't want to represent a paedophile." Fairchild steepled his fingers under his chin and smiled at Nightingale. "So, you've been looking at this James McBride case?"

Nightingale shifted uncomfortably in his seat. He didn't want to discuss the case with Fairchild. In fact he didn't want to say anything to him, he just wanted the man out of the office. But with Jenny there, Nightingale's options were limited. "We've pretty much finished," he lied. "Jenny probably told you that our client killed himself."

"But we're still looking at it," said Jenny.

Nightingale forced himself to smile. "Well, not really . . ."

Jenny frowned in confusion.

"It wouldn't be the first time that a defendant has tried to use Satanic possession to avoid a guilty verdict," said Fairchild.

"McBride is dead," said Nightingale. "So the difference between guilty of murder or clinically insane is moot, really."

Fairchild smiled, but his eyes lacked warmth. "Jenny mentioned the Order of Nine Angles."

"Did she now?"

"The paedophile in the case I looked at claimed he was a member and we did a lot of research into it. It doesn't exist. Not as a credible organisation, anyway."

"That's good to know," said Nightingale. "Because aren't they involved in black magic and child sacrifice?"

Fairchild threw back his head and laughed, but it came out like a hollow death rattle. "Come now, Jack. You don't believe in black magic, do you?"

Nightingale shrugged but didn't reply.

"And child sacrifice? Do you think a group could kill children and get away with it?"

"A lot of children go missing every year and are never found," said Nightingale.

"It's a big jump from that to saying that there is a group of Satanic child-killers out there." Fairchild leaned forward. "I had researchers on it for several months and they came to the conclusion that the Order of Nine Angles doesn't exist. It's an urban legend."

"Good to know," said Nightingale.

"I just thought you might like to know, save you wasting your time."

"I appreciate that," said Nightingale. He looked at his watch. "To be honest, Marcus, I've got a busy morning."

"I understand," said Fairchild. "I have a meeting myself over at the Inns of Court. But if there's any guidance you need on the McBride case, don't hesitate to give me a call." He took out his wallet and gave Nightingale an embossed business card.

"Thanks, but like I said, we're pretty much done with it."

"Do you have any idea why he killed those children?"

"He just snapped," said Nightingale. "It happens." He stood up and held out his hand. "Thanks for dropping by."

Fairchild pushed himself up out of his chair and shook Nightingale's hand, then hugged Jenny and kissed her on both cheeks. She took him to the door, patted him on the back as he left, then closed the door and glared at Nightingale. "What the hell was that about?"

"What?"

"You were so rude. You practically kicked him out. And we're not finished with the case. Not by a long way."

"You didn't tell me you'd seen him."

"Didn't I? He was at Mummy and Daddy's at the weekend, doing some shooting."

"And you told him about the case? Why would you do that?"

"Is something wrong?"

Nightingale sighed. "It's just, you know, our business. Client confidentiality."

"Our client's dead."

"That's not the point. When people come to us for help they expect a modicum of privacy, don't they?"

"Well, yes, but Mr McBride's dead. And Uncle Marcus was really interested."

"I bet he was," muttered Nightingale.

"Jack, what's wrong? Why are you being like this?"

"Like what?"

"Like you've taken a real dislike to Uncle Marcus. He's a lovely man, he just wants to help."

"He's not a lovely man, Jenny."

She stiffened and looked at him with narrowed eyes. "What do you mean by that?"

Nightingale looked at her, a sick feeling in the pit of his stomach. "Nothing," he said. "I don't mean anything."

"What is your problem with him, Jack?"

He held up his hands. "Forget I said anything."

"He's never done you any harm. He just wanted to help."

Nightingale picked up his coffee and stood up. "Okay, let's just leave it."

"Jack!"

Nightingale ignored her and strode into his office before kicking the door shut behind him.

CHAPTER
FIFTY-SEVEN

The door opened and the headmistress looked up from her computer. "Here she is, Mrs Tomlinson," said Miss Rider, ushering in nine-year-old Bella Harper.

"Thank you, Miss Rider," said Mrs Tomlinson. She waved at a sofa in the corner of her office. "Why don't you sit there, Bella, and we can have a little chat." Bella did as she was told. "I'll bring her back when we've finished," the headmistress said to Miss Rider and the teacher closed the door behind her.

Mrs Tomlinson pulled up a chair and sat down opposite Bella. Bella had her head down and her hands were fidgeting in her lap.

"Bella, it's okay, you're not in trouble," said the headmistress. "Would you like a biscuit?" Mrs Tomlinson kept a pack of chocolate Hobnobs in her desk drawer to cheer up unhappy children.

Bella shook her head. "No, thank you," she whispered.

"Now, did Miss Rider tell you why I wanted to see you?"

"It's about Jesus," said Bella.

"Well, sort of," said the headmistress. Bella's curly blonde hair was hanging over her face, so she couldn't see if the girl was crying or not. She wanted to reach over and brush the hair away but she knew that touching children was never a good idea. "First of all let me say how happy we are to have you back at school. We all missed you a lot."

"Thank you, Mrs Tomlinson."

"And I know you've been through a lot. But we're all going to do what we can to make it easier for you, you know that, don't you?"

Bella nodded solemnly. "Yes, Mrs Tomlinson."

"Good. Now you've been telling the children about Jesus, haven't you?"

Bella sniffed and nodded. "Am I in trouble?"

"No, of course not," said the headmistress. "But you see, Bella, it's really not a good idea to be talking about Jesus in class. We explain about Jesus and other religious leaders in our religious education classes, so you should leave that sort of thing to Miss Rider. Do you understand?"

Bella nodded and clasped her hands together. "I'm sorry," she said quietly.

"You don't have to say you're sorry," said Mrs Tomlinson. "And I know that after everything you've been through, Jesus is probably a help to you."

"Yes. He is."

"And that's okay. That's good. But what you mustn't do is to talk about him in class. We are lucky to have children of many religions in our school and not everyone believes in Jesus. It might upset them to hear you talking about him. You must keep your faith to yourself. Do you understand that?"

266

Bella nodded again. "Yes, Mrs Tomlinson."

"That's a good girl. Have your parents been talking about Jesus at home, is that it?"

"Not really." Bella sniffed and rubbed the back of her nose with her hand.

"Talking about Jesus is fine at home," said the headmistress. "But at school, that's something for the teachers. Then we can learn about all the great religions of the world in a way that doesn't offend anyone. You understand that, don't you, Bella? It's important that people aren't offended."

"I understand," said Bella. She looked up and for the first time Mrs Tomlinson saw the little girl's face. Bella smiled brightly. "You believe in Jesus, don't you, Mrs Tomlinson?"

"That's a very personal question, Bella. And in school we don't like to ask personal questions because they can make people feel uncomfortable. A person's religious belief is their own business."

"But you believe in Jesus, don't you?"

"Bella, that's not a question that I'm prepared to answer. And it's not a question you should be asking your classmates."

"Jesus loves you, Mrs Tomlinson."

The headmistress stood up. "I'm sure that he does, Bella. Now come on, I'll take you back to your classroom."

Bella looked up at the headmistress and smiled. "Jesus has a message for you, Mrs Tomlinson."

"Now don't be silly," said the headmistress. She held her hand out. "Come on, let's go now."

"He's got a message for you about your dad."

Mrs Tomlinson's breath caught in her throat and her head swam. She sat down heavily.

"He knows what your dad did to you, Mrs Tomlinson. When you were little."

Mrs Tomlinson put her hand over her mouth.

"He has a message for you, Mrs Tomlinson. Jesus has a message for you." She beckoned the headmistress with her finger. "Come here, Mrs Tomlinson, and I'll whisper it to you."

CHAPTER
FIFTY-EIGHT

Nightingale stared at the Sudoku grid but couldn't concentrate. He knew that he had to go back into Jenny's office and apologise to her, but for the life of him he didn't know what to say. Marcus Fairchild was a predatory paedophile and the leading light of a group that thought human sacrifice was the route to Satanic power. But there was no way he could explain to Jenny how he knew that, and no way that Jenny would believe him. Any apology he made would be a lie, but he didn't see that he had any choice.

His mobile rang and he fished it out of his pocket, expecting it to be Jenny. It wasn't. The caller's number was withheld. He took the call. It was Harry Simpson. "I've got an address for Stevenson," he said.

"That's terrific, thanks."

"You're not planning to do anything stupid, are you?" asked Simpson.

"Like what?" said Nightingale.

"I don't know. I just worry how this is going to end up."

"But not worried enough to ignore me, right?"

There was a long silence. Nightingale didn't say anything. He figured that there was something Simpson wanted to tell him and he didn't want to spoil it by prompting.

"There've been some rumours, about cops and kids," Simpson said eventually.

Nightingale was about to say something, but he bit his lip.

Simpson sighed. "No names, and certainly no mention of Stevenson. But there's talk of a task force from London coming up here. Remember that list of paedophiles that was doing the rounds on the internet? Top Tory politicians and businessmen?"

"Yeah, I remember."

"Well, there's another list that hasn't been made public. And the rumour is that there are some very top people on it, a lot of Scottish bigwigs. Some serious names. The rumour is that the London cops are getting ready to blow the thing wide open."

"And the Northumbria cops have been left out of the loop?"

"Totally. Which suggests they don't trust us."

"But no rumours about Stevenson?"

"None that I've heard. So I'll give you his address, but then that's the end of it. And we never had the conversation."

"That's fine with me," said Nightingale. "Give me the address and then forget we ever spoke."

Simpson gave him the address and Nightingale scribbled it down on his newspaper. After he ended the call, Nightingale stood up and opened his office door. Jenny didn't look up as he walked in and continued to ignore him as he walked up to her desk. "I'm sorry," he said. "I don't know why I was being an arsehole."

She nodded but didn't look up at him.

"I over-reacted, I'm sorry."

"Okay."

"I know he's your godfather, and I realise he was only trying to help. I guess I just get possessive when it comes to cases. Tell him I'm sorry, will you?"

She looked up at him and smiled. "He's a really nice guy, Jack. You'd like him if you got to know him."

"I'm sure I would," lied Nightingale. "How about I make you a coffee, to make up?"

"Or you could buy me a Costa? And a chocolate muffin."

"I could do that," said Nightingale. "Oh, I'll be out of the office tomorrow. I'm back up to Berwick."

"Do you want me to book you a train?"

Nightingale shook his head. "I'm going up with Eddie Morris. We'll use his car."

"Eddie Morris housebreaker and burglar?"

"That's the one. But make that alleged housebreaker and burglar, he's never actually been convicted."

"What are you up to, Jack?"

Nightingale tapped the side of his nose. "Best you don't know," he said. "I wouldn't want to make you an accessory before the fact."

CHAPTER
FIFTY-NINE

Miss Rider looked up as the classroom door opened. It was Bella. Miss Rider expected the headmistress to pop her head around the door but Bella was alone. The heads of the three dozen children in the room swivelled to stare at Bella. "Sit down, Bella," said the teacher. "We're just talking about fractions."

Bella walked over to her table and sat down. Miss Rider went over to her whiteboard. She was trying to get the children to rank a series of fractions in order of size but it was proving to be an uphill struggle. She looked over at Bella. The girl had her hands clasped together on the table in front of her and her head down so that her hair was hanging over her face.

"So, Bella, which is bigger, a quarter, which is one over four, or a sixth, which is one over six?"

Bella didn't say anything.

"Bella, did you hear me?"

Two girls at the table by the window began to talk.

"Hush now," said Miss Rider. "Let's hear the answer from Bella."

Tommy Halpin stood up and pointed out of the window. "Tommy, come on now, sit down." Tommy had what his parents called Attention Deficit Disorder but

Miss Rider put down to a complete lack of discipline at home. The boy ignored her and continued to point.

"Tommy, please, we've spoken before about how your disrupting the class isn't fair to everyone else."

"It's Mrs Tomlinson," said Tommy excitedly. "On the roof." He turned to look at Miss Rider. "Why is she on the roof, Miss Rider?"

Miss Rider frowned and hurried over to the window. The children took it as a signal that they could go too and everyone rushed over to see what was going on.

The headmistress was on the roof of the administration block. Her hair and skirt were flapping in the wind and as Miss Rider watched, the headmistress slowly raised her arms to the side as if she was being crucified.

"What is she doing, Miss?" asked Tommy. "Is she playing at Superman?"

"She's a lady, she can't be Superman," said Kylie James, who was one of the most pedantic children Miss Rider had ever come across.

"Children, I need you to all sit down," said Miss Rider in her most authoritative voice. Her pupils ignored her.

Mrs Tomlinson took a deep breath, tilted her head back, and began to scream the Lord's Prayer. "Our Father, which art in Heaven, hallowed be they name." She fell forward as she shouted and the wind ripped the remaining words from her mouth as she fell, her arms still out to the side. It was a perfect swan dive, except that below wasn't a swimming pool, there was just the unyielding tarmac surface of the school playground.

"Oh my God!" screamed Miss Rider. She watched in horror as the headmistress plunged to the ground. Something snaked behind her and Miss Rider realised that it was a rope. The headmistress had tied one end of the rope around the neck and the other end to something on the roof.

"She's bungee jumping!" shouted Tommy, and at that exact moment the rope snapped tight and Mrs Tomlinson flipped head over heels and then the head parted from the body in a shower of blood and the two parts fell to the ground. The body hit first with a dull wet thud that they all heard through the classroom window and the head landed a fraction of a second later and rolled across the playground like a miskicked football.

Some of the children screamed and Kylie burst into tears. Miss Rider flinched and turned away, her stomach heaving. As she retched over the floor she realised that Bella was the only child still sitting at her table, her head down and her hands clasped in front of her.

CHAPTER
SIXTY

Eddie Morris opened one eye and looked at the speedometer. "You can put your foot down, you won't hurt it," he said. "German engineering."

It was Tuesday morning and the BMW was powering along the A1 at a steady seventy miles an hour. They had shared the driving since leaving London in Morris's brand new Series 5. "I don't want a speeding ticket," said Nightingale. "That's why we're driving and not flying, I don't want anyone to know that we're up here."

"It's one hell of a drive," said Morris, folding his arms and stretching out his legs.

"I'm paying you by the hour, aren't I? And by the look of this motor, the housebreaking business is booming."

Morris grinned. "Can't complain. I've been doing really well since I started targeting Russians and Arabs. They always have a lot of cash and jewellery in their houses, and as a lot of it is hooky they don't call the cops."

"Be careful with the Russians, mate."

"They're not all mafia, Jack. But most of them are dodgy."

Nightingale had insisted that they drive up to Berwick and had agreed to share the driving. They had to use the BMW because Nightingale's classic MGB wasn't up to a 700-mile round trip. Morris had picked Nightingale up in Bayswater at five o'clock in the morning. They had made good time, stopping only for fuel and coffee, and they reached Berwick at one o'clock in the afternoon. Nightingale had Morris call Stevenson from a phone box to check that he was in his office, then they drove around to the policeman's house on the outskirts of the town.

It was a terraced house of grey stone, with a white door that opened off the pavement. "I hate terraces," said Morris. "Front and back overlooked and the neighbours are right on top of you." He nodded at the burglar alarm box between the two upstairs windows. "See that?

"Alarms never worry you, Eddie. Not bog-standard ones like that. Are you going to go in the front or the back?"

"I'll have a walk by and check out the lock," said Morris. Nightingale took out his cigarettes. "Don't even think about lighting up," said Morris. "I don't want to lose the new-car smell."

"Your body odour has put paid to that," said Nightingale. "I'd be doing you a favour by fumigating it."

Morris pointed a warning finger at Nightingale's face. "I'm serious, Jack. You smoke in my motor and you're walking back to London."

Nightingale groaned and put the pack away as Morris climbed out of the car and pulled on a pair of black leather gloves. He crossed the road and walked by the house, glancing sideways at the front door, then continued down the pavement to a side road. He disappeared from view and Nightingale settled back in the comfortable leather seat. He'd known Morris for the best part of three years. They had been introduced by the solicitor who was representing Morris on a case of breaking and entering which, to almost everyone's surprise, Morris hadn't actually committed. Morris had been set up by a former girlfriend, who'd arranged for a pair of his gloves to be dropped at a crime scene. Nightingale had tracked down the real burglar and Morris had walked. Morris wasn't exactly a criminal with a heart of gold, but he never resorted to violence and usually stole from people who could afford to lose a few grand. Over the years he and Nightingale had become friends.

Morris returned after fifteen minutes and slid into the rear passenger seat behind Nightingale. "The front lock is a Yale, so that's not a problem, but the back is easier. There's an alley behind the houses and a small walled yard. There's a Yale on that door, too. I'll sort the alarm from the outside and go in the back."

"No breaking, just entering. I don't want anyone to know we've been there."

"No problem," said Morris.

There was a black kitbag on the back seat and Morris unzipped it. Inside was a pair of dark blue overalls and he took them out and unrolled them.

Under the overalls were several dozen Velcro-backed cloth badges, for most of the country's main burglar alarm and security companies and a few generic ones. He pulled out a badge that matched the logo on the alarm box and waved it at Nightingale. "It's all in the preparation," he said. He placed the badge on the Velcro pad on the back of the overalls, then slipped them on over his clothes. He zipped them up, then picked up a small toolbox up off the floor. "Pop the boot, will you?" said Morris, as he got out of the car. He walked around to the back of the BMW and took out a telescopic ladder that he pulled out to about eight feet. He walked over to the house, the ladder on one shoulder, whistling as if he didn't have a care in the world.

CHAPTER
SIXTY-ONE

Nightingale's mobile rang and he took the call. It was Morris. "You'd better not be smoking in there," said Morris.

Nightingale looked over at the house and kept his lit cigarette between his legs. He had the windows open and the air-conditioning on to blast the smoke out of the car. "Of course not," he said.

"I'm in," said Morris. "Come around to the back of the house and I'll let you in."

Nightingale locked up the BMW and walked down the road, around the corner and along the alley. He saw Morris standing at an open door and hurried to join him. He followed Morris across a concrete back yard and into the kitchen. Morris carefully closed the back door. "All good," said Morris. "Nothing broken and I can reset the alarm when we leave."

"Excellent," said Nightingale. He went through to the main sitting room and had a quick look around. A small flower-patterned sofa, a green leather armchair and a flat screen television above a Victorian fireplace. There was a desk by the window with a laptop and printer. Nightingale drew the wooden blinds closed and switched on the lights.

Morris was looking at a series of framed photographs on the wall. In several there was a man in a police uniform, and there was a framed commendation from the Chief Constable of Northumbria Police. "You didn't say anything about him being a cop," said Morris.

"Tinker, tailor, soldier, sailor, why does it matter what he does for a living?"

Morris put his hands on his hips. "Don't screw me around, Nightingale, you know why it matters."

"We're hundreds of miles from home and we're wearing gloves, no one's going to be putting your name in the frame," said Nightingale. "Relax."

"Relax? You're a bastard, really." He shook his head dismissively. "I can't believe you got me to break into a cop's house."

Nightingale patted him on the back. "That's Mister Bastard to you," he said. "Look, he's at work. He lives alone. We'll be away long before he gets back." He nodded at the computer. "I need you to have a look at his browsing history, emails, pictures, video, all that sort of stuff."

"Anything in particular?"

"Child abuse," said Nightingale. "Child pornography. That sort of thing."

Morris held up his hands. "This is giving me a really bad feeling," he said.

"It shouldn't. We're on the side of the angels on this one. I reckon that Stevenson is bad and I need proof. We're not here to rob, Eddie. In fact I don't want him knowing that anyone was here, okay?"

280

"That's fine by me," said Morris. "But next time we go breaking into a cop's house, at least have the decency to let me know first."

"Just check the laptop, I'll have a quick look around, and then we're out of here. Okay?"

Morris nodded reluctantly. "Okay." He sat down at the table and opened the laptop.

Nightingale headed upstairs. There were two bedrooms, either side of a bathroom. One was obviously where Stevenson slept. There was a dirty shirt thrown over a chair and the duvet was piled up in the middle of the bed. There was a mirrored sliding door over a built-in wardrobe but it contained nothing but clothes. There was nothing under the bed and he found only socks, underwear and T-shirts in a chest of drawers.

There was a pine wardrobe in the small bedroom, and on a shelf at the top was a small Samsonite shell suitcase. Nightingale took it out, swung it onto the bed and opened it. Inside was a collection of Masonic regalia, including robes, aprons, sleeve guards and shoes. Nightingale went through it piece by piece. He was by no means an expert on the Masons but from the clothing it looked as if Stevenson was fairly high up in the organisation. He closed the case and put it back on the shelf. There were several coats on hangers and he went through the pockets. Other than a couple of old receipts they were empty.

He stood by the bed and looked around the room. The floorboards were bare pine, polished and varnished, and there was a thick Turkish rug at the bottom of the bed. Nightingale pulled the rug to the side and smiled when he saw the scratches on two of the wooden boards. He knelt down and examined the scratches. They were either side of a board that moved slightly when he pressed it. He took a ten pence piece from his pocket and used it to pry up the end of the loose board until he was able to grip it with his fingers and pull it up. He placed the board on the floor and stuck his hand into the gap. His fingers touched a metal box and he carefully slid it through the gap. It was a Marks & Spencer biscuit tin.

Nightingale sat on the bed and opened the tin. Inside were more than a dozen pairs of underwear. Children's underwear. Each had a small label attached to it. Nightingale picked up a pair of purple pants. They looked as if they would fit a pre-teen. The name on the label read JULIE DAVIES. Nightingale felt a wave of revulsion wash over him. It was the man's trophy collection, souvenirs that would allow him to relive his abusive experiences. He put the underwear back in the tin, closed the lid, and replaced it in its hiding place. He put the board back and pulled the rug over it.

Morris looked up from the laptop as Nightingale walked back into the room. "You've got to see this," he said.

"What?" said Nightingale, looking over his shoulder.

"You were right. He's a bloody paedo all right." He clicked his mouse over a folder and dozens of thumbnail pictures appeared. He clicked on one and it expanded to fill the screen. Nightingale grimaced. A prepubescent girl was on her knees, her face pressed against a man's groin. The face of the man had been digitally blurred.

"This is a relatively minor one," said Morris. "There's a lot worse than this." He clicked on another thumbnail and a photograph of a fat middle-aged man having sex with a young boy appeared. Again the man's face was digitally obscured. "He's been sharing these pictures, on paedophile websites and through emails," said Morris.

"Can you print me out the list of email addresses?"

"No problem," said Morris. He clicked the mouse and the printer began to whirr.

"How many photographs?"

"Hundreds. Thousands maybe. Videos, too."

"Show me a video."

"Are you sure? It's pretty graphic."

Nightingale nodded.

Morris opened another file and clicked on a video. It was in HD, the camera focused on a young girl lying naked on a bed. A heavy-set man with a hairy back was lying on top of her. The man was wearing a black mask that covered his whole head. He was grunting as he pounded into the little girl. Whoever was holding the video camera moved around to get a better shot of the girl's face. Her eyes were glassy, as if she had been drugged.

Nightingale wasn't looking at the man, or the victim, he was concentrating on the room that the video had been shot in, and it didn't take him long to recognise it. It was one of the spare bedrooms in McBride's farmhouse.

"Show me another," he said,

Morris clicked the mouse a few times and a second video appeared. This one showed a tall thin man, also masked, sitting on a sofa with two young girls, neither of whom looked older than twelve. They were both naked. Nightingale recognised the sofa. It was in McBride's sitting room. A second man moved into shot. He was short and muscular, naked except for a ski mask.

"Okay, that's enough," he said.

Morris got rid of the video and clicked on another file. "Stevenson has been sending the pictures after he's blurred the faces, but he still has the originals. He's hidden them but they're still here." He clicked on a thumbnail and a photograph of a man abusing a young girl appeared. His face was clearly visible.

Nightingale's jaw dropped as he recognised the man.

"Is that who I think it is?" asked Morris.

"No question," said Nightingale. "He's on the TV every other night."

Morris clicked open more pictures. They were all of young girls and boys being abused by middle-aged and old men. Nightingale recognised several of the men, including two Members of Parliament, a Premier League football player and a television comedian. "This is sick," said Morris. "What were they doing, pimping the kids out?"

"I don't know, but it looks well organised," said Nightingale. The printer finished printing and he picked up the four sheets of paper containing the email addresses. "Here's what I need you to do, Eddie. I need you to email a dozen or so of those pictures and a couple of the videos to this email address." He pulled a sheet of paper from the printer and scribbled down an address. "And use Stevenson's email to send it."

Morris looked at the email address that Nightingale had written down. "That's a cop address."

"That's right. He works for the Met's paedophile unit."

"They'll trace it back to him straight away."

"That's what I want, Eddie. Once the Met take a look at the faces in the photographs and video they'll investigate Stevenson and they'll blow the whole thing sky high." He put the printed sheets into his raincoat pocket. "We'll be long gone by then." He handed Morris a thumb drive. "Just to be on the safe side, put as many of the pictures and videos on this as you can. Then delete all traces that we were here."

"Bloody hell, Nightingale, what have you got me involved in?"

"We're righting wrongs, Eddie. Just leave it at that. Get it done, we'll get back to London and you can forget you were ever here."

"I hate paedophiles," said Morris. "They should castrate them and kill them. End of."

"No argument here." He looked at his watch. "Come on, pull your finger out."

CHAPTER
SIXTY-TWO

Sandra put down a plate of fish fingers and chips in front of Bella, but she didn't react. She was watching a documentary on the Discovery channel. "Come on, Bella, you might at least say thank you. Those fish fingers didn't cook themselves."

Bella looked up, her face a blank mask. "Huh?"

Sandra pointed at the plate of food on the coffee table. "Your dinner."

Bella looked at the plate and wrinkled her nose. "I'm not hungry."

"What do you mean you're not hungry? What did you have at school?"

"I can't remember." Bella looked back at the television.

"Try," said Sandra, folding her arms.

Bella sighed. "I don't know. Spaghetti."

"You hate spaghetti."

Bella sighed again, louder this time.

"And stop that sighing, will you." Sandra sat on the sofa next to her daughter. "Bella, honey, you have to eat."

"I do eat," said Bella, her eyes still on the TV.

"You love fish fingers."

"I know."

"So try some. Please."

Bella sighed again, picked up a fish finger and nibbled it. "Honey, are you okay?"

Bella nodded.

"How was school?"

Bella shrugged. "Same as always. School's school."

"Are you still upset about what happened to Mrs Tomlinson?"

Bella frowned. "Of course not."

"You're sure?"

"She died, that's all," said Bella flatly. "People die. Everybody dies, right?" She put the fish finger back on the plate and stared at the television.

"What are you watching?" asked Sandra.

"Nothing."

Sandra squinted at the screen. She was fairly sure that she needed glasses because she was finding it harder to read newspapers and watch television. Her long-distance vision was fine and she could drive her car without any problems, but close up everything was blurry. It took her a minute or two to work out what the programme was about. Fred West, the serial killer.

"Bella, why are you watching this?"

"It's interesting."

"He killed lots of girls. Him and his wife. Why would you watch something like that?" She reached over and held Bella's hand. "Is it because of what happened to you, honey?" she asked quietly.

"Of course not."

"No one's going to hurt you again, honey. I swear."

"I know."

"Look at me, Bella."

"I want to watch this, Mum."

Sandra reached for her daughter and turned her head towards her. "Look at me, honey," she said. "You're safe now. Your daddy and I are never going to let anything happen to you again, I swear. You don't have to worry about serial killers or kidnappers or anything like that. You're safe."

"Mum, I know."

"So stop watching this nonsense. Watch cartoons or *Corrie* or that Ant and Dec show you like. Okay?"

Bella sighed. "Okay."

Sandra leant towards her daughter and sniffed at her mouth. Bella's breath was really foul. "Are you cleaning your teeth?"

"Of course." Bella twisted out of Sandra's grip and shuffled along the sofa.

"I'm serious, Bella. Your breath smells terrible."

Bella folded her arms. "Mum, please . . ."

"Do you floss?"

"Yes."

"Every night?"

"Yes."

"Okay. I'll buy some mouthwash. And it's about time you saw the dentist." Sandra heard a car pull up outside. "Daddy's home!" she said, but Bella didn't react. She continued to stare at the television, her eyes wide.

CHAPTER
SIXTY-THREE

Nightingale climbed out of the taxi, paid the driver, and turned up the collar of his raincoat. It was just starting to rain and he jogged towards Robbie Hoyle's neat semi-detached house, keeping a tight grip on the bottle of burgundy that he'd brought with him. Anna Hoyle opened the front door and air-kissed him. Anna was gorgeous, slim with shoulder-length blonde hair and amused green eyes. She looked a good decade younger than her true age and it was hard to believe that she was the mother of three daughters.

"He's in the front room playing with his Wii," said Anna.

"I thought he'd grown out of that," said Nightingale.

"I'm cooking, I'll be with you in a minute." She took the bottle of wine from him and nodded appreciatively at the label. "Fancy a glass of this?"

"I wouldn't mind a beer first."

"I got a pack of Corona in just for you," she said. "Though I've never understood why you drink Mexican beer."

"A girlfriend got me into it years ago," he said. "There was something sexy about the way she used her tongue to shove the lime down the neck of the bottle."

"More information than I needed," she laughed and headed off to the kitchen.

Robbie was playing virtual tennis against his eight-year-old daughter Sarah and she was trouncing him. "Fancy a game?" asked Robbie, as he tried and failed to return one of his daughter's serves.

"Tennis was never my game," said Nightingale, dropping down onto the sofa.

"Hello, Uncle Jack," said Sarah as she pounded another serve past her dad.

"Who's winning?"

Sarah laughed. "Who do you think?"

Anna brought Nightingale his lager, complete with slice of lemon in the neck. She grinned as he used his finger to push it down. "Dinner'll be ready in five minutes," she said.

Anna had cooked her signature beef and beer casserole with garlic mashed potatoes, and as always it was delicious. Robbie opened the bottle of wine that Nightingale had brought, and then a second bottle of red. Afterwards Anna took Sarah up to bed while Nightingale went out into the garden for a cigarette. Robbie kept him company and the two men stood looking up at the stars. High overhead an airliner headed towards Gatwick airport.

"You remember that Berwick thing?"

"The killings. Sure."

"It's all going to blow up soon. Big time." He reached into his pocket and took out the thumb drive that contained the pictures and videos Morris had taken from Stevenson's laptop. He handed it to Robbie.

290

"Have a look at that. You'll see some faces that you'll recognise."

Robbie frowned. "What do you mean?"

"McBride was part of a paedophile ring up in Berwick. They were abusing kids at his farmhouse. Serious abuse, Robbie. I don't know if they were drugging the kids or what, but they looked out of it."

"McBride was a paedophile?"

"I haven't seen him on any of the videos or pictures yet, but there are thousands of them. It's definitely his farmhouse, though. I recognise the rooms."

"And what am I supposed to do with this?" asked Robbie, holding up the thumb drive.

"It's a fallback position. I've sent the stuff to the Met's paedophile unit already, but I wanted another copy out there, just in case."

"Where did you get it from?"

"The computer of a cop up in Berwick."

"A cop? There's a cop involved in this?"

"Robbie, the cop's the least of it. There are some very, very important people involved. Showbiz, TV, politics. It's huge, mate. It's big and it's organised and I think Berwick is a very small part of it. It makes the Savile thing look like a tea party. In fact the Savile thing might even be part of it."

"Bloody hell, Jack. Are you sure about this?"

"Take a look at what's on that thumb drive. You'll see why I'm sure. Some of the names on the list are cops. I think that's why there was no real investigation of the school killings. No one up there seemed interested in why McBride killed the kids that he did, and now I know why."

"What about going to the papers?"

"The London cops need to move before the papers get involved. I don't want trial by media, I want the bastards behind bars. Once it's in the papers people are going to run."

Robbie put the thumb drive into his pocket. "So why did McBride shoot the kids?"

"Somehow the paedophiles found out that there was an investigation on the way, out of London. The London cops were going to talk to the teacher that was killed, the deputy headmaster. That was why McBride killed him. Then he shot the kids that were being abused. That's why he was moving from classroom to classroom. He was killing witnesses, Robbie. All those kids he killed were the ones that were being abused. He was covering his tracks. And then he killed himself."

"Are you sure about this?"

"I'm fairly sure. But the cops handling the investigation will find the proof, I'm sure of that."

"Why would he do that? Kill himself?"

"Maybe he knew that whatever happened he was finished. Maybe the others persuaded him to do it. Maybe they threatened him. Hypnotised him. I don't know, Robbie."

"And the Satanic stuff?"

"To throw the cops off the trail. If they thought it was the work of a lone madman then they wouldn't be looking for anyone else. It was sexual abuse, pure and simple. But organised and on a scale you can only imagine."

"And tell me again why you're giving this to me?"

"Insurance, I guess. Just in case the paedophile unit drops the ball."

"Why do you think that might happen?"

"Because this is big, Robbie. It's bloody huge. There are some bloody big names on that thumb drive. And some of them are in the photographs and video. I don't know who else is involved. There's already at least one cop in on it, but for all I know there could be senior officers in the Met involved. I need you to keep your ear to the ground and if nothing happens over the next few days then at least you've got the information there. You've got all the pictures, videos and the list of email addresses that were getting the doctored pictures."

"Doctored? What do you mean?"

"The guy who had them on his hard drive was taking the pictures and blurring the faces of the men involved and then emailing them. I've got the before and after pictures. Those pictures alone will send dozens of men to prison for a long, long time."

"And how did you get them?"

"Best you don't know, mate. But they're one hundred per cent kosher."

"Well, I hope you covered your tracks."

"I'm pretty sure I did." Nightingale tried to blow a smoke ring but the wind ripped it apart. "Can you sniff around, see if you can confirm that the Met was about to investigate the Berwick paedophile ring?"

"I'll give it a go."

"And I need you to do me a favour, Robbie."

"That's a first," said his friend sarcastically. He sipped his red wine.

"Have you heard of a lawyer by the name of Marcus Fairchild?"

"The QC?"

"Yeah. He's Jenny's godfather."

"Is he now? He's a big swinging dick, that much I know."

"I need you to check him out."

"In what way?"

"I need to know if there's anything known. That's all."

"Of course he's known. He's a multi-millionaire lawyer. He works for the CPS from time to time. What specifically are you looking for?"

Nightingale sighed. "You'll think I'm crazy."

"That horse bolted a long time ago," said Robbie. "Spit it out."

"He's a child molester. A paedophile."

Robbie was drinking his wine when Nightingale spoke and he almost choked. "What?"

"I want to know if he's ever been implicated in anything like that."

"Bloody hell, Jack. If he had, he'd hardly be working with the CPS, would he?"

"If it was hushed up, maybe."

"If it was hushed up, it won't be in the system."

"It might."

"What's going on, Jack? Is Fairchild on the thumb drive? Is he one of the guys in the photographs?"

294

"Not that I can see. And I don't see his name on the email list either. Could be a disguised email address of course, but no, I've no evidence that he's involved in the Berwick abuse. But he did tell me that he worked on a paedophile case a while back."

"So this is separate? Something else?"

"I think so, yes."

"And what exactly do you think he's been doing?

"Okay, what I'm going to tell you is going to sound crazy. Hell, it is crazy. But it's the absolute truth and you have to believe me."

"You're starting to worry me now, mate."

"Marcus Fairchild has been abusing Jenny since she was a kid. And he still is."

Robbie stared at him in amazement. "By abusing you mean what, exactly?"

"Sexual abuse."

"Jenny told you this?"

Nightingale shook his head. "She doesn't know."

"But you do?"

"Yes. I know it for an absolute fact."

"So report him."

"I can't prove it."

"You know it's a fact but you don't have any proof?"

"That's pretty much it, yes."

"You're right."

"I'm right?"

"You're right. It sounds crazy."

Nightingale drew smoke into his lungs and held it there.

"What's going on, Jack?" asked Robbie.

"I'm trying to protect Jenny."

"From abuse that she doesn't know about?"

"He's been doing it for years," said Nightingale.

"And she doesn't know? That's ridiculous."

"He uses hypnotism or suggestion or some drug or other. And he's part of a group called the Order of Nine Angles that carries out human sacrifice. They kill children."

"Now you're really starting to worry me, Jack. You're talking about one of the most respected lawyers in the country."

"It's true, Robbie. When Jenny told him that I was working the Berwick case he came rushing to my office to find out what I knew. There was stuff about the Order of Nine Angles in McBride's barn and Fairchild was desperate to pour scorn on it. Said it was an urban myth."

"He didn't want you looking at it?"

"That's what I figured. Look, I know he's got powerful connections. But there's a good chance that some of those connections are in it with him."

"And you think that a quick look at the Police National Computer is going to blow the whole thing wide open?"

"Of course not."

"So what do you expect me to do?"

"When you put it like that, I'm not sure." He took a final drag on his cigarette and flicked the butt away.

Robbie glared at him. "What are you doing?"

"What do you mean?"

"What's Anna going to say if she finds your old cigarette butts on the lawn? You pick it up, you soft bastard."

Nightingale laughed and went to retrieve the butt. He slipped it into his pocket.

"And even if by some miracle I do find something out, what then?" said Robbie. "Who do you go to with something like that? He's Establishment, through and through. It'll have to be at Commissioner level to stand any chance of moving forward."

"I can't just leave it, Robbie. I have to do something."

"And you can't tell me why you're so sure he's a paedophile and child-killer?"

Nightingale shook his head.

"It's something to do with all that spooky stuff you're always getting involved in?"

"Pretty much, yes. The only way I can think of to prove it to Jenny is to have her undergo hypnosis, hypnotic regression or something. But if I do that, it'll destroy her. She loves the guy. Trusts him totally. I don't think I can do that to her. But I can't let him continue to do what he's doing." He shrugged. "I guess I had this crazy idea that you could come up with something that would open the whole thing up."

"That's not going to happen," said Robbie. "I'm sorry. But if you want me to look at the PNC, I can do that. But I'll have to do it under someone else's log-in because there's a good chance it'll be red-flagged."

"No, you're right. There's no point. If I'm going to do something, it'll have to be more decisive."

Robbie turned to look at him. "What do you mean?"

"Best you don't know. Or at least best I don't say."

"Don't do anything stupid, Jack."

"Since when have I ever done anything stupid?" said Nightingale, straight-faced. He managed to hold it for a few seconds before both men burst into laughter.

Anna appeared at the back door. "What are you two laughing at?" she asked.

"Nothing," said Robbie.

"Well, come and get your coffee."

Robbie patted Nightingale on the back as they headed into the kitchen. "Whatever you decide to do, be careful," he said.

"Careful is my middle name."

"I thought danger was your middle name."

Nightingale grinned. "Changed it by deed poll."

Anna appeared at the kitchen door. "Do you two guys want to stay out there all night or are you going to come in for coffee?"

"Coffee sounds good," said Robbie. He patted Nightingale on the back. "Seriously, mate, you be careful." They walked back to the house together. Nightingale knew that his friend was right. He had to be careful. But he had to do something about Marcus Fairchild. Something drastic.

CHAPTER
SIXTY-FOUR

The telephone rang and Sandra Harper went to answer it. Bella was sitting next to her father on the sofa watching television. Will Harper was eating Kentucky Fried Chicken but Bella's lay untouched on her plate.

Sandra picked up the phone, listened to whoever called and then said: "No, we're not interested. And please don't call again." She replaced the receiver and scowled at her husband. "Bloody journalists. That was the *Mirror*. They just won't give up."

"I don't know why you answer the phone," said her husband. "They're just about the only people who call on the landline. I told you we should have gone ex-directory."

"We did go ex-directory, last week," said Sandra. She squeezed onto the sofa next to Bella. "Are you not hungry?"

Bella shook her head. "I had a big lunch at school."

"Yeah? What did you have?"

"Pizza."

"Do you want pizza now? I can order one for you."

"Mum, I'm fine." Sandra leaned closer to her daughter and sniffed. Bella turned away. "Mum, don't fuss."

"Are you cleaning your teeth?"

"Of course."

"Your breath smells bad. Really bad."

"I'm cleaning my teeth, Mum."

"If your breath isn't better in a day or two I'm going to take you to the dentist."

"Okay, okay."

Sandra leaned over and took a drumstick off her husband's plate and bit into it.

"Mum, why don't you want me to talk to the journalists?"

"Because they want to talk about what happened to you and it's best that we forget about it. We have to move on." She put her arm around her daughter and gave her a hug. "It's in the past. You're home now and we're just going to enjoy that."

"But they said they'd pay, didn't they?"

"How do you know that?"

"I heard you and Dad yesterday. You said that one of the papers had offered you ten thousand pounds for an interview and more if you'd agree to a photograph."

"You heard me say that? I thought you were upstairs." She shook her head, trying to clear her thoughts. She was tired and finding it hard to think. "Your dad and I just decided it was best not to say anything to anybody."

"Your mum's right," said Will, reaching for a piece of chicken. "You can't trust journalists, everybody knows that."

"And we don't want everyone knowing our business," said Sandra. "We don't want to tell the world what you went through, honey." She gave her daughter another squeeze. "We just need to put it behind us, like it never happened."

"But I could tell them that I saw Michael. And Jesus."

"I'm not sure that's a good idea, honey," said Will. He bit into his chicken and chewed noisily.

"But I could talk about that, and you and Mummy would get ten thousand pounds. Maybe more."

"We don't need the money that badly, Bella," said Sandra.

"You could put it towards my university fees," said Bella. "Put it in the bank to pay my tuition fees."

"University?" said Sandra. "You want to go to university?' She exchanged a surprised look with her husband. He shrugged.

"Of course," said Bella. "What harm could it do, Mum? I could tell them about Jesus and everything."

"What do you think?" Sandra asked her husband.

Will swallowed and shrugged again. "She's got a point. University's expensive, we could put the money in an ISA or something. Save it for when she needs it. How many papers have asked for interviews?"

"All of them," said Sandra. "And the magazines."

"Why don't you talk to them, see how much they'd pay?"

"You think?"

Will picked up another piece of chicken. "What harm could it do?" he asked.

CHAPTER
SIXTY-FIVE

Nightingale took a black cab to Clapham and had it drop him a hundred yards or so from Smith's house. It was late Saturday evening and the sky was threatening rain but he hadn't wanted to risk driving in his MGB. Smith was a nasty piece of work and wouldn't think twice about riddling the car — or Nightingale — with bullets if the conversation didn't go well. Smith's house was in a terrace, two storeys tall and fronted with black railings around steps that led down to the basement level. Most of the houses had been converted into flats and bedsitters but Perry had kept his house as a single unit. There were two large black men standing outside the front door, wearing matching Puffa jackets over tracksuits. Nightingale recognised one of the men. He lit a cigarette before walking over to talk to then.

There were deep booming vibrations coming from inside the house — rap music being played through an expensive sound system. Nightingale doubted that the neighbours would complain. Not more than once, anyway.

The heavy that Nightingale knew was big, close to seven feet tall. He had wraparound Oakley sunglasses pushed on to the top of his head. "Hi T-Bone, how's it going?"

The heavy's eyes narrowed. "I know you?"

"In another life, maybe."

"Yeah? Well, I sure as hell don't know you in this one, so keep on moving."

"I need to talk to Perry."

"He know you?"

Nightingale shrugged. "We're back to that another life thing."

"You Five-0?"

Nightingale shook his head. "I'm a private dick, as they say."

"Well, if you don't want your private dick shoved between your private lips, you'd better walk away right now."

Nightingale put up his hands. "Look, I didn't mean to get off on the wrong foot. I just want a word with Perry. You don't know me, but I do know you. I know how you got your nickname, for a start."

"Everyone knows that," said T-Bone.

"Do they all know that he was coming at you with a machete when you shoved the stake in him? And I know about the lock-up in Streatham where you keep the guns."

T-Bone's eyes narrowed. "You sure you're not Five-0?"

"Cross my heart and hope to die."

"Yeah, well, if you're lying that could well happen."

"If I was Five-0, or if I wanted to screw you over, one phone call is all it'd take for that lock-up to be busted and you along with it."

T-Bone's forehead creased into deep furrows as he struggled to follow Nightingale's logic.

"Look, I want to put some business Perry's way. To be honest I'd be happier just talking to you but I know how important the hierarchical thing is."

"What's he talking about?" asked T-Bone's companion.

"Stay there," said T-Bone. He opened the front door and disappeared into the house. Nightingale held out his pack of cigarettes to the second heavy but he shook his head.

"Cigarettes kill you," he growled.

"I think the jury's still out on that."

"Evidence seems pretty compelling to me."

"I've met people who've smoked for thirty-odd years and they've never had a problem. And thousand of non-smokers die of cancer every year." Nightingale shrugged. "Each to his own, I guess."

"Makes your teeth go yellow," said the heavy.

"Yeah, I was wondering about that. Do you think I should get them whitened?" He bared his teeth at the heavy, but before the man could reply the door opened and T-Bone reappeared.

"In," said T-Bone. "But lose the cigarette."

Nightingale took a final drag on the cigarette and then flicked it into the gutter. He followed T-Bone into the hallway. It ran the full length of the house, with a kitchen at the far end. There were purple doors leading off to the right and a flight of stairs leading upstairs that had been painted purple. The hallway was throbbing with rap music that vibrated up through the floorboards and into the soles of his feet.

T-Bone turned and without saying a word pushed Nightingale up against the wall and professionally frisked him. "I'm not carrying, in fact that's why I'm here," said Nightingale.

"Yeah, well, forgive me for not taking your word for that," said T-Bone. He jerked his thumb at the door to Nightingale's right. "In there."

Nightingale opened the door. His ears were immediately assaulted by a sound system being played at full blast, so loud that it made him wince. The walls of the room were painted a pale purple and there was a huge white spherical lampshade hanging in the centre. There were three large leather sofas around a glass coffee table that was loaded with all sorts of drugs paraphernalia, including several multi-coloured bongs and a crystal bowl filled with white powder. There were half a dozen lines of the powder at one side of the table, along with two teaspoons and a cigarette lighter. There was a flat screen TV dominating the wall opposite the sofas, showing an episode of *Family Guy*. Nightingale couldn't tell if the sound was muted or if it was just being drowned out by the sound system.

Perry Smith was sitting in the middle sofa with his feet up on the coffee table. He had a remote in his left hand and a gun in his right. He waved the remote at the sound system and the volume decreased markedly.

"Who the fuck are you and how do you know about the Streatham lock-up?" snarled Smith.

"Name's Nightingale. Jack Nightingale."

"Like the bird?"

"Yeah. Like the bird."

"Well, you need to start singing, Bird-man." He stood up and dropped the remote, but kept the gun pointing at Nightingale's chest. "You hear me?" Smith was wearing a silver tracksuit and gold Nikes and had several heavy gold chains on both wrists.

"I hear you," said Nightingale. "I just want to do some business, that's all."

"Business?"

There were two teenage girls sitting together on one of the sofas. One of them rolled a fifty-pound note into a cylinder and leaned forward to sniff up one of the lines of white powder.

"I want to buy a gun."

"Do this look like a gunshop?"

"I need someone I can trust, and strangely enough I know that I can trust you." He moved his hand slowly inside his raincoat. Smith aimed the gun at Nightingale's face. "Don't try anything funny," he said.

"T-Bone frisked me already," said Nightingale. His hand reappeared holding a brown envelope. He tossed it onto the sofa next to Smith. "There's a monkey in there. I know you're a fan of the MAC-10, but I want something simpler. A revolver will do it so that I don't leave any cases behind. And six rounds will be more than enough. I'm not a big fan of spray and pray."

"What you mean by that?" said Smith, frowning.

"By what?"

"I'm a fan of the MAC-10, you said."

"It's your weapon of choice, right?"

"How did you know that, Bird-man? You got a file on me?"

"Like I told T-Bone, if I was a cop I'd have had your Streatham lock-up busted and you in a cell." He nodded at the bowl of white powder. "There's enough coke there to have you put away for a ten-stretch, and the gun in your hand's worth another ten. But I'm not a cop. I just want to buy a gun. Ideally something that can be traced back to someone else."

"Say what?"

"A gun that was used in a gang thing, maybe. So that when I've used it, the cops will be off on the wrong scent."

"And what are you gonna do with this gun that I might or might not sell you?"

The second girl took the rolled-up banknote and sniffed a line of white powder, then collapsed into giggles. The first girl hugged her and they lay back on the sofa.

"I'm going to shoot someone."

Smith grinned. "Are you now?"

"In the head," said Nightingale.

"And why would you want to do something like that?"

"Because he's evil. He abuses kids. He kills them, too."

Smith frowned. "Why would he do that?"

"I said. He's evil. He thinks he gets power by killing them."

"And you know this how?"

"Same way I know about your lock-up and your choice of weapon. Same way I know how T-Bone got his nickname. I know things."

Smith frowned and cocked his head on one side as he looked at Nightingale. "Do I know you, Bird-man? We met before?"

"Not in this life, Perry."

"I feel like I know you."

"In a way, you do," said Nightingale. "But no, we've never met. But I know that I can trust you. I know that you're a gangster and that you've got blood on your hands. I know you deal drugs and you do all sorts of other shit that turns my stomach. But I need a gun and I know that you can sell me one. So how about it?"

Smith put the gun down on the coffee table next to the remaining lines of white powder and picked up the envelope. He opened it and flicked through the fifty-pound notes with his thumbnail. "A paedo, yeah?"

Nightingale nodded. "Dyed in the wool."

"I fucking hate nonces," said Smith. "Fucking scum." He tossed the envelope back to Nightingale. It hit him in the chest but he managed to catch it with fumbling hands. "You can have this on the house," he said.

"Thanks."

Smith grinned. "Yeah, you can owe me one."

Nightingale held out the envelope. "I'm happy to pay."

"Yeah, well, I'm happy not to take your fucking money. You can owe me one. Okay?"

Nightingale nodded, wondering for a moment if Smith was going to ask for his soul as well. "Okay," he said.

Smith waved his hand at T-Bone. "You get Bird-man sorted," he said.

"Whatever you say, boss." T-Bone patted Nightingale's shoulder with a massive hand. "Let's roll."

CHAPTER
SIXTY-SIX

Barbara McEvoy was lying on a yoga mat trying to get her left leg behind her head when her doorbell rang. She was in her late twenties, with dark green eyes and freckles peppered across her nose and cheeks. She sighed, untangled herself, and padded barefoot to the front door. She grinned when she saw Jenny McLean. "This is a nice surprise," she said.

"Just passing by," said Jenny. She nodded at Barbara's lilac tracksuit. "Pilates?"

"I was doing a few relaxation exercises, but now you're here I might as well switch to alcohol. Wine?"

"Go on then, twist my arm."

Jenny went into Barbara's sitting room and dropped down onto the sofa while Barbara went into the kitchen, returning a short time later with a bottle of pink champagne and two glasses. Barbara's two-bedroom flat was close to Portobello Road in Notting Hill, and street parking was almost impossible when the market was in full flow on a Saturday, so Jenny had taken a taxi to see her friend. The flat doubled as an office, and Barbara had converted her spare bedroom to a consulting room where she saw patients on the days when she wasn't based at one of the many hospitals where she worked.

"Are we celebrating?" asked Jenny.

"It's Saturday. Best day of the week for champagne, right?"

Barbara sat down on the sofa next to Jenny and looked at her over the top of her glass as she sipped her champagne. "What's wrong?"

Jenny raised her eyebrows. "What on earth makes you think there's something wrong?" she asked.

"Darling, I'm a clinical psychiatrist. It's my job to read people. And you're as tense as a kitten in a cage of Rottweilers."

Jenny laughed, but there was a nervous edge to it.

"And it's Saturday and we almost never get together on a weekend unless I'm in the country with you." She frowned. "Weren't you going to Norfolk today to see the folks?"

"I decided not to," said Jenny.

"And you came to see me instead," said Barbara. "Is that significant?"

Jenny leaned back and drew up her legs. "You're good."

"I'm damned good," said Barbara. "But unless you tell me what's wrong I won't be able to help."

Jenny sipped her champagne. "This is going to sound crazy," she said.

This time it was Barbara who laughed. "You wouldn't believe how many of my patients start off by saying that," she said. "The thing is, most of them ARE crazy."

"I might be, too," said Jenny. She sighed and then took a deep breath. "Okay, this is it. Jack is being really weird about Uncle Marcus. He keeps asking me if I'm seeing him and he went very strange when Uncle Marcus turned up at our office unannounced."

"Marcus? He's a sweetie. He's a bit pompous but he wouldn't harm a fly."

"That's what I keep telling Jack. I've known him since before I could walk. He's one of Daddy's oldest friends."

"And what's Jack's problem with him?"

"Jack won't say. He does that Jack thing of just changing the subject or making a joke. But here's the thing, Barbara. Now I've been having . . . I don't know what they are. Flashbacks? Déjà vu? Just a feeling that there's something wrong."

"In what way?"

Jenny sighed in exasperation. "That's the crazy thing. I don't know. It's a feeling of . . . I don't know . . . dread, I guess. Uncle Marcus is in Norfolk today doing some shooting with Daddy and his friends and I was supposed to be there."

"And you changed your mind?"

"I keep getting these feelings, Barbara. A sense that something is wrong."

"Dread, you said."

"I know, it sounds silly. And really, I can't put my finger on it." She sipped her champagne and sighed. "Maybe it's just Jack's silliness rubbing off on me. Like you said, Uncle Marcus is a sweetie."

"Jack has never said anything concrete about Marcus?"

"Never."

"And you don't feel uncomfortable when you're around Marcus?"

"Uncle Marcus? Of course not. He's my godfather, Barbara."

"But the fact that you're here suggests that subconsciously at least there is something wrong."

Jenny shrugged. "I guess." She sighed again. "I thought that maybe you could do that regression thing of yours. Put me under and see if you can find out what's causing this."

"Are you sure?"

"You do it with your patients all the time."

"Not all the time," said Barbara. "It's not helpful in all cases."

"But if there is something worrying me then it would be one way of getting to the bottom of it, wouldn't it?"

Barbara nodded and put her champagne down on the coffee table. She went into her consulting room and returned with a small digital recorder.

"What's that for?" asked Jenny.

"When you come out of it you won't remember anything," said Barbara, sitting down in the armchair facing the sofa. "I'll be able to play the recording back to you."

"We're going to do it now?" asked Jenny.

"Strike while the iron's hot," said Barbara. "Kick off your shoes, lie back and let's see how we go."

CHAPTER
SIXTY-SEVEN

Jack Nightingale was eating a bacon sandwich and watching football on Sky Sports when his mobile rang. He didn't recognise the number but he took the call anyway. "Jack? It's Barbara."

It took Nightingale a couple of seconds to pull the name from his memory — Barbara McEvoy, one of Jenny's oldest friends. "Barbara, how the hell are you? Long time no hear."

"I need to see you, Jack. Now."

"What's wrong?"

"I'll tell you when I see you."

"Is it about Jenny?"

"Just get yourself over here now, Jack. Now."

Nightingale left his half-eaten sandwich on the coffee table, grabbed his raincoat and hurried downstairs. He flagged down a black cab in Inverness Terrace and fifteen minutes later it dropped him close to the Portobello Road. It was market day, and the street was packed with tourists and locals milling around the stalls selling antiques, bric-a-brac and cheap clothing. He threaded his way through the crowds and down the side street where Barbara lived.

She buzzed him in and had the door open for him when he reached her second-floor flat. "Is everything okay?" asked Nightingale. "You sounded a bit panicky on the phone."

"Go through to the sitting room," she said, closing the door behind him.

"Is Jenny here?"

"She left just before I phoned you," said Barbara.

"Is she okay?"

"She's fine. Or at least she thinks she's fine."

"Barbara, you're talking in riddles."

He turned to look at her but she put her hand on his shoulder and pushed him into the sitting room. "Sit," she said, pointing at the sofa.

Nightingale did as he was told, but then stood up again to take off his raincoat. Barbara dropped down onto the armchair. "What do you know about Marcus Fairchild?" she asked.

"What do you mean?" He put his coat on the arm of the sofa and sat down.

"Marcus Fairchild. Uncle Marcus. Jenny's godfather. She said you had a thing about him, you thought he wasn't to be trusted."

"Is that what this is about? Jenny's asked you to give me a bollocking?"

Barbara shook her head and looked at a small digital recorder on the coffee table. "That's not it, Jack. Jenny doesn't know you're here."

"What's happening, Barbara?" asked Nightingale. He frowned as he looked at the small metal recorder.

Barbara sighed and sat back in the armchair, crossing her arms. Nightingale didn't have to be an expert in body language to know that something was troubling her.

Barbara sighed again and slowly shook her head. "I can't believe it, Jack. I don't want to believe it."

"You regressed her," said Nightingale.

Barbara's jaw dropped. "How do you know that?"

"You regressed her and she remembered what Fairchild has been doing to her."

Barbara shook her head in amazement. "Have you suddenly become psychic?" she asked. She leaned forward and picked up the recorder. "You need to listen to this." She held out the recorder to him but Nightingale didn't take it. "I don't," he said, "I know what's on it. You regressed Jenny and she remembered Fairchild abusing her. He's been doing it since she was a child. She doesn't remember because he does something to her. Hypnosis or drugs."

"You knew about this and you didn't say anything?"

"Did you tell her?"

Barbara didn't reply and avoided looking at him.

"The fact that I'm here on my own suggests that you haven't told her. Why?"

"I wanted to talk to you first."

"Because you know that if you tell her it'll destroy her, right?" Barbara nodded. "So you regressed her, then what? Doesn't she remember?"

"I took her back to the last time she met Fairchild at her parents' house in Norfolk. Fairchild went into her

316

bedroom late at night." She winced. "The things he did to her, Jack. He's an evil bastard."

"Tell me about it."

"Then I regressed her back to when she was a teenager. And younger. Fairchild is always there, Jack. Abusing her. I don't understand how he manages to get away with it."

"He uses hypnotism. Or drugs. Or a combination of the two."

"When I brought Jenny back, she didn't remember anything. And I kept it that way."

"You lied to her?"

"I can't tell her what happened. Jack. Not without a lot of preparation. When she finds out, it could destroy her."

"So why regress her in the first place?"

"She asked me to. She's starting to get a feeling that something isn't right. Maybe because of the comments that you've been making. But I lied. I said she remembered nothing of any significance." She gestured at the recorder. "I told her that I'd switched off the recorder because there was nothing of interest on it."

"And she believed you?"

"I'm her friend, Jack. Of course she believed me." She forced a smile. "What are we going to do?"

"You're not going to do anything, Barbara. You're going to destroy that recording and try to forget what you heard."

"How long have you known?"

"Not long. And like you, I don't know what to do about it. The cops won't take a regression session as evidence, and even if you play that tape to her she still won't remember. There's no forensic evidence, no physical signs of abuse. And he's Marcus Fairchild, a top QC with a lot of very influential friends."

"You're going to do something though, right?"

Nightingale nodded slowly. "It's in hand."

"What? What are you going to do?"

"Best you don't know, Barbara. Best you forget about it. But trust me, I'll take care of it."

CHAPTER
SIXTY-EIGHT

Kathy Gibson pointed at the semi-detached house ahead of them. "There you go, number twenty-six, park anywhere near here," she said.

The photographer's name was Dave McEwan, a dour Scot. He was a freelance but pretty much worked full-time for the *Express*. Kathy was staff and had been for six years, but she was considering an offer to move to the *Mail on Sunday*. The Bella Harper interview was just what she needed to get the *Mail* to increase their offer.

McEwan found a parking spot and reversed into it. Kathy checked her make-up in the overhead mirror while McEwan pulled his camera bag out of the boot.

"Let's get the family shots done right off," said Kathy. "It'll give me the chance to get them talking. Then we'll do the interview, then maybe hit the park."

"Sounds like a plan," said McEwan. "You got an angle?"

"Pretty much writes itself," said Kathy. "Kidnap girl back in the bosom of her family, hopes and plans for the future. Great Sunday for Monday feature. We're pretty much guaranteed a good show. Piece on the front and a centre spread."

"How much are they getting paid?"

"You're such a cynic."

"Just asking."

"Twenty-five grand is what I heard."

McEwan grimaced. "Not much for what she went through," said Kathy.

"That's the thing. No one knows for sure what he did to her."

"They said raped, right? That was the charge, wasn't it? Rape and abduction."

"One of my cop contacts says she was dead. Says that when they got into the house she was dead but the paramedic bought her round."

"Bastards," said McEwan. "It's the woman I don't get. Why would she help a paedophile?"

"You're asking the wrong person," said Kathy. "I'd hang the two of them without a moment's thought. Have you got kids?"

"In theory," said McEwan. "The wife has them now and I get to see them every second weekend. You?"

"No, but I've got nieces that are Bella's age and if anything happened to them . . ." She shuddered. They reached the front door and Kathy pressed the bell.

Bella's mother answered the door. Kathy remembered her from the numerous television appearances she'd made with her husband when her daughter was missing. She'd looked drawn and haggard back then, dark patches under her eyes from lack of sleep, her skin blotchy, her hair greasy and unkempt. But now she looked ten years younger, her hair was glossy, and she smiled brightly as Kathy introduced herself and the photographer.

Sandra shook hands with them both and showed them into her neat semi-detached home. Her husband was sitting on the sofa next to Bella. He'd put on weight since Bella had been found, and looked a lot happier. Like most of the viewing population, at the time Kathy had suspected that Will Harper had been involved in his daughter's disappearance. It was almost a cliché that the male family member who appeared most often on television when a child had been killed turned out to be the murderer. Bella's case had been unusual in two respects — she had come back and her kidnappers had been total strangers.

Will stood up and shook hands with them both. He was good-looking, tall with an unruly mop of chestnut hair that kept falling over his eyes, and Kathy knew that he'd photograph well.

"And this is Bella," said Sandra.

Bella smiled up at them. "Pleased to meet you," she said.

Sandra offered them tea but Kathy said that they'd rather get on with the photographs first. She handed them over to McEwan and he ran through what he wanted. A family shot on the sofa, Bella playing with her toys, perhaps a walk to the park later.

"What about Floppy?" said Bella. "What about a photograph of me and Floppy?"

"Floppy's a rabbit?" Bella nodded. McEwan said that was a great idea, and he spent the next hour taking the photographs as Kathy gently teased out the quotes that she wanted. How their prayers had been answered, how Bella's abductors should be given the death penalty, how grateful they were to the police. It was all stock stuff but Kathy knew that it would be a good read. So many abducted children stories ended badly, and it was a pleasant change to write about a success story. Kathy intended to skip over what had happened to Bella during the hours she'd been held captive. She could only imagine the horrors that the nine-year-old had gone through, and her news editor had made it clear that she wasn't to spell out the details.

McEwan took them out into the back garden to get pictures of Bella cuddling her rabbit. As Bella brushed her cheek against the animal's soft white fur, she smiled over at Kathy. "I saw an angel," said Bella.

"That's nice," said Kathy.

"Really. An angel came to see me."

Kathy looked over at Bella's mother. The mother smiled uncomfortably. "A real angel, with wings and a halo?"

"No halo, but wings, yes. Really long wings with white feathers. Michael is an archangel, one of the top angels."

"And this was in a dream, was it?"

Bella shook her head. "It was real. But in my head. Do you understand?"

"I'm not sure," said Kathy.

"Michael said that I was dead. But that I wasn't to be scared. He said Jesus wanted to talk to me."

"Jesus?"

Bella nodded excitedly. "Yes, Jesus Christ. He wanted to talk to me."

"And Michael took you to see him?"

"We went to this huge white house. More like a palace. Everything was white and so clean and there were other angels there. And my Grandpa Arthur. And Auntie Eadie."

Kathy looked over at Sandra, frowning.

"Grandpa Arthur is my husband's grandfather. Auntie Eadie was . . ." She shrugged, wondering how she was going to explain it. "My mother had a baby before me. A girl. Eadie. She died very young. Bella never knew her." She shrugged again. "I can't explain it, but that what she says happened."

McEwan finished taking pictures of Bella and the rabbit. "How about the park now?" he asked.

"You know what, I'm parched," said Kathy. She smiled at Sandra. "Don't suppose there's a chance of a cup of tea now?"

"Of course," said Sandra. "I'll put the kettle on."

McEwan flashed Kathy an annoyed look but she smiled sweetly and touched him gently on the arm. "I want to keep them talking," she said. "Give me a few minutes, then we'll head to the park."

"I'm worried about the light," he said, looking up at the grey clouds that were gathering overhead. "And it might rain."

"Half an hour, tops," said Kathy.

They followed Sandra and Bella into the kitchen. Bella sat down at the table and Kathy sat next to her. "Surely someone must have told Bella about this

Grandpa Arthur and Auntie Eadie?" she said to Sandra.

Sandra shook her head. "Never. Even I didn't know that my mum had had another baby. And Will didn't know the name of his grandfather. But we checked and yes, his paternal grandfather was Arthur Harper. He died long before Will was born." She turned on the kettle.

"They were really nice to me," said Bella. "They said they would look after me when it was time for me to stay there but it wasn't time yet."

"Bella, are you saying you were in Heaven?"

"I don't know where I was. It was a palace, I guess. But I don't know where the palace was."

Kathy frowned and ran a hand through her hair. What had started out as a simple family reunion story was becoming much more complex, and she wasn't sure how the features editor was going to react if the story took a religious turn.

"Perhaps we should talk about what you're going to do this year," said Kathy. "What about Disneyland? Is that somewhere you'd like to go?"

"Don't you want to talk about Jesus?" asked Bella.

"We can talk about anything you want," said Kathy. "What about when you're a grown-up, what do you want to do?"

"I want to be a good person, like Jesus," said Kathy. "Jesus loves you, Kathy." She looked over at the photographer. "He loves you too, Dave."

"Good to know," said the photographer.

Bella smiled at him, then turned back to Kathy. "Jesus wants us all to be happy."

"I'm sure he does."

"He thinks there are lots of things wrong with the world and that we need to fix them."

"That's interesting, Bella. Really. But let's talk about you and what your plans are."

"Do you want to know what Jesus told me?" asked Bella.

Kathy forced a smile. It was the last thing she wanted to know, but she needed to keep the little girl talking. "Sure," she said.

Bella crooked her little finger and beckoned her to move closer. "I have to whisper it," she said.

CHAPTER
SIXTY-NINE

Bernie Fowles screwed up his face. "She said what?"

Fowles was the *Express*'s features editor. He was in his fifties and was an old school journalist, known to keep a bottle of Bell's in the bottom drawer of his desk even though alcohol was banned on the premises. His liking for whisky was written on his face — his cheeks were perpetually flushed and his nose was flecked with broken veins.

Kathy sat down. "She says she has messages for the Prime Minister and the Archbishop of Canterbury and Prince William, from Jesus."

Fowles rubbed his eyes and cursed under his breath. "Is she crazy? Or have her parents put her up to it?"

"She's a nine-year-old girl, Bernie."

"Nine-year-old girls can be manipulated, and manipulative," said Bernie. "Remember that kid in the States, wrote that bestseller about going to Heaven. He was only four."

"I don't think they're planning to write a book, Bernie."

"Maybe not now, but if we run a piece saying that she spoke to Jesus then all the big publishers are going to be knocking on their door." He stood up and began to pace up and down behind his desk. "The pictures are good, right?"

"Brilliant," said Kathy. "Lots of stuff around the house and a really great shot of the three of them walking through the park. Sitting next to her dad on the swings, that sort of thing. And some very pretty ones with her rabbit."

"Kids and cuddly animals, you can't go wrong with that," said Fowles. "And she wants to talk to the PM? Face to face?"

"She said Jesus gave her messages for the PM, the Archbishop and the Prince."

"And you don't know what those messages are?"

Kathy shook her head. "She says the messages are personal."

Fowles sat down again. "So you don't think the parents put her up to it?"

"Mum and Dad aren't particularly religious. They go to church sometimes and they prayed when she was missing, but they're not religious fanatics. If anything, the mum seemed embarrassed at what Bella was saying."

"And the girl's not deluded?"

"I'm not a psychiatrist, Bernie. She seems okay, but you've got to remember what she's been through. Kidnapped. Raped. She was pretty much dead when they found her."

Fowles leaned back in his chair and steepled his fingers under his nose. "Tell me about that."

"I don't know much, but one of my police contacts told me that when they first went in they thought she was dead. One of the cops felt for a pulse and couldn't find one. Then a while later a paramedic realised she was breathing."

"So was she dead or not?"

"Cops aren't medically trained."

"They're trained enough to spot a corpse," said Fowles. "Is this maybe some sort of out-of-body experience? Lack of oxygen to the brain bringing on hallucinations?"

"Sure. That's possible. Anything's possible."

Fowles grimaced. "See, I'm worried that we give her coverage on this whole Jesus thing and then it turns out it's down to brain damage. That'd make us look pretty stupid, wouldn't it?"

"She's a bright kid. Very articulate. Doing well at school, her parents said." She leaned forward. "You know, she's at the school where the headmistress killed herself. Threw herself off the roof."

"Are you serious?"

Kathy nodded. "Bella didn't see it, but a lot of kids were traumatised. The school was closed for a couple of days. Do I mention that in the story?"

"It's an angle, isn't it? Kidnap girl sees teacher suicide."

"She didn't actually see it."

"You don't want to spoil a good story with the facts. Already in shock from abduction, little Bella faced more heartbreak . . . hell, you don't need me to write it."

"And what about the intro? Do I go with messages from Jesus or abduction girl back with her family?"

Fowles took a deep breath and exhaled slowly, his brow furrowed. It was Sunday and it had been a quiet weekend, news-wise. The story of a child who had come back from the dead would put some energy into what threatened to be a very dull Monday paper. "What the hell," he said. "Who dares, wins. Let's go with the Jesus angle. Who knows, maybe we can get the PM to drop by to pick up his message."

CHAPTER
SEVENTY

Nightingale was walking down a long corridor. There were doors to the left and right, heavy doors, the wood aged and cracked. There were bare floorboards running the length of the corridor, worn smooth by generations of feet, and they creaked like old bones as he walked over them. There was a single light bulb hanging from a frayed wire in the middle of the corridor, flickering and hissing. A handful of small moths fluttered around it.

Nightingale found himself being drawn to one of the doors. There was a brass handle, mottled with age, and it was warm to the touch when he grasped it and turned it. The room inside was pure white, a glossy white floor and white walls and a white ceiling. Nightingale stepped inside the room and warm breeze ran across his face. He could smell herbs. Rosemary. And tarragon. And mint.

"Mr Nightingale?"

It was Mrs Steadman. She was standing in the middle of the room, wearing a long black dress and with a black wool scarf wrapped around her neck. On her right hand was a ring with a large black stone in it.

"Hello, Mrs Steadman. Am I asleep?"

"Yes, Mr Nightingale."

"And you wanted to talk to me?"

"That's right."

"So why not just phone me?"

"I don't have your number, Mr Nightingale."

"I'm in the phone book. Under Nightingale."

Mrs Steadman giggled girlishly. "I didn't think of that."

"Do you do this a lot, Mrs Steadman?"

"Not a lot, no."

"It's a bit confusing. I'm dreaming, so how can I tell what's real and what isn't?"

"You could try pinching yourself."

Nightingale pinched himself but didn't feel anything. "That's interesting," he said. He raised his arms to the side and took a deep breath. As he exhaled he rose slowly up into the air. He hovered about six inches above the floorboards. "I'm flying," he said.

"It's more levitating," she said. "But you can fly. You can do anything you want. It's your dream."

Nightingale lay back and his feet rose up so that he was parallel to the floor, staring up at the white ceiling. "This is so cool."

"Dreams can be fun," said Mrs Steadman. "You just have to be careful that they don't turn into nightmares."

Nightingale slowly returned to an upright position and then lowered himself to the floor. Mrs Steadman watched him with amused eyes.

"So what is it that you want, Mrs Steadman? Why are you here?"

"I need to talk to you," she said.

"I'm all ears," said Nightingale.

"Not here," said Mrs Steadman. "In the real world."

"Shall I come to your shop?"

"Outside would be better," said Mrs Steadman. "There's a park about half a mile from the shop. Close to the Tube station. I'm sure you can find it. Shall we say eleven o'clock in the morning?"

"I'll be there," said Nightingale. He rose up off the ground again and turned around slowly, the toes of his Hush Puppies pointing down at the floor. By the time he had done a complete turn, Mrs Steadman had vanished.

"Mrs Steadman?"

His feet brushed the floor and then the floorboards squeaked as they took his full weight. He looked down. The white floor had gone and in its place were thick oak floorboards. He looked around. Furniture had appeared and now there was red flock wallpaper on the walls. There was a heavy four-poster bed, a chunky dressing table and a shabby armchair. There was a mirror over the bed and he stared at his reflection. There were dark patches under his eyes and his hair looked as if it hadn't been combed in days. He ran his hand through it. "If it's a dream, why do I still look like shit?" he asked his reflection.

He flinched as something slammed against the door. He whirled around, his hands up defensively. His heart pounded as he stared at the door, his hands clenched into tight fists. Something scratched slowly at the wood, and then suddenly stopped. The only sound was that of Nightingale's breathing.

He walked towards the door and slowly reached for the door handle. But before he could touch it the handle began to turn on its own. "Who is it?" he asked.

There was no answer. The handle clicked to the fully open position and then the door began to slowly creak open.

"Mrs Steadman?"

His nose wrinkled as it was assaulted by a foul smell, a mixture of sulphur and acid and faeces. His stomach lurched. He grabbed the handle and pulled the door open, and that was when he woke up, bathed in sweat, his chest heaving as if he'd just run a marathon. Realising he was safe in his own bed, he smiled up at the ceiling. "Next time, Mrs Steadman, just use the phone," he muttered to himself.

CHAPTER
SEVENTY-ONE

Nightingale took the Tube to Camden and walked to the park. He got there at a quarter to eleven but Mrs Steadman was already there, sitting on a bench overlooking a group of children playing on a slide under the watchful eyes of their mothers. She was wearing a thick coat and the same scarf that she'd had on in the dream. She smiled up at him as he sat down next to her. "I hope you don't mind me contacting you like that," she said.

"Can anyone do it?" he asked.

"With practice," she said. "I can lend you a book that will teach you the techniques."

He nodded. "I'd like that."

"It's a lot less useful than it used to be," she said. "These days we have Skype and email and mobile phones. But when I was younger it was often the quickest way of contacting someone."

One of the children yelled as he sped down the slide but he fell awkwardly and burst into tears. His mother rushed over and scooped him up, smothering his cries against her chest.

"Do you have any children, Mrs Steadman?" Nightingale asked.

She shook her head and smiled wistfully. "No," she said.

"I'm not sure if I want them or not," said Nightingale. "I don't think I'd make the best of fathers."

"I don't think anyone really knows what sort of parent they'll be until the day that the baby arrives," said Mrs Steadman. "They have a way of bringing out the best in people." She sighed. "And the worst."

Two little girls sat down behind the swings and began to play pat-a-cake. "Why did you want to see me, Mrs Steadman?" asked Nightingale.

Mrs Steadman watched the little girls play their game. "You heard about the girl who was taken in Southampton? Isabella Harper? The paedophile and his girlfriend, remember? They took her to a house outside Southampton and abused her."

Nightingale nodded. "They deserve to be strung up," he said. "But the way the world works, she'll walk and he'll do ten years." He shuddered. "They almost killed her, didn't they? If the cops hadn't got there in time she'd be dead."

"I'm afraid it's not as simple as that," said Mrs Steadman.

"She's all right now, isn't she? She's back with her parents."

"As I said, it's difficult to explain," said Mrs Steadman. She sighed again and lowered her eyes. "What I'm about to tell you is going to sound so fantastic that you simply won't believe me. But I can assure you that it's the absolute truth."

"You're starting to worry me now, Mrs Steadman."

She looked up and her coal-black eyes bored into Nightingale's. "You have every reason to be worried," she said. "We all do. What has happened is so awful, so terrible, that it puts everything at risk. Everything."

"Just tell me what's happened," said Nightingale. "How bad can it be?"

"Very bad," said Mrs Steadman. She took a deep breath and exhaled slowly. "The police didn't arrive in time, Mr Nightingale. Little Isabella was dead. She came back to life, but it's not Isabella. Something came back but it wasn't her."

Nightingale felt the hairs stand up on the back of his neck. And he turned up the collar of his raincoat. "She's possessed? Is that what you mean?"

"There is no she," said Mrs Steadman. "Isabella is dead. But something has taken the place of her soul, something evil, something that is determined to cause havoc and misery."

"But I've seen her on television. She's a happy, smiley little girl. Wouldn't her parents have seen something?"

"Whatever it is has learned to hide its true identity. They see what they want to see, their dear darling daughter. They don't see what lies within."

Nightingale pulled his cigarettes out of his pocket but when he saw a look of disdain flash across Mrs Steadman's face he put them away hastily. "So what is it you want from me?" he asked. "Please don't tell me you want me to organise some sort of exorcism."

Mrs Steadman shook her head. "An exorcism wouldn't help," she said. "An exorcism is called for when a demon takes temporary possession of a body. Once the demon is exorcised, the person can go about their life again. That's not what's happened in this case. Isabella is dead. Nothing we do will bring her back. She has been possessed by a Shade. And Shades cannot be exorcised."

"Shade? Is that what it's called?"

"I'm not a great one for labels," said Mrs Steadman. "But they have been called that and it's as good a label as any."

"So what is it you want me to do with this Shade?" asked Nightingale.

Mrs Steadman smiled thinly. "Let's walk, shall we?" she said. She stood up and they walked down the path together. "You trust me, don't you, Mr Nightingale?"

"Of course."

"And you know that I'm a good person."

"One of the best, Mrs Steadman. What's wrong? There's something you don't want to tell me, isn't there?"

"I have to tell you," she said. "What's worrying me is how you'll react." She stopped and looked up at him. She really was tiny, Nightingale realised. She barely reached the middle of his chest. Her jet-black eyes bored into his. "The Shade is using Isabella's body as a vessel. A container. If you kill the vessel then the Shade will die with it. Providing you do it in a particular way."

Nightingale frowned. "What are you saying, Mrs Steadman?"

"You have to kill the demon, and the way to do that is to kill the body it's inhabiting."

"You're asking me to kill a nine-year-old girl?"

Mrs Steadman shook her head. "Isabella is dead already. Nothing will change that. But the empty shell that is left has to be destroyed. That is the only way to stop the Shade."

"And I do this how?"

"You have to use knives that have been blessed by a priest. Knives made from pure copper. Three of them. In the heart and in both eyes."

Nightingale took a step back. "Are you insane?"

Mrs Steadman shook her head sadly. "I almost wish that I was," she said.

"You're asking me to shove knives into the eyes and heart of a nine-year-old girl?"

"No, I'm asking you to kill a Shade. The girl is already dead. The Shade does not exist outside the girl. It is only when the Shade is in possession of the girl that it can be killed. Do you understand what I'm saying?"

"I understand, but that doesn't mean I can do it."

"Somebody has to, Mr Nightingale."

"Have you ever killed a Shade?"

"That I can't do," she said. "It has to be . . ." She paused and then grimaced. "It has to be someone like you."

"But before, you found someone to do it?"

She nodded slowly. "Yes. It was difficult, but yes."

Nightingale rubbed his face with both hands.

"I realise it puts you in a terrible position," she said.

Nightingale lowered his hands and looked at her. "How can you ask me to do something like this?"

"I have no choice," she said. She reached over and gently touched him on the arm. "I am sorry, Mr Nightingale. Truly."

CHAPTER
SEVENTY-TWO

Nightingale waved at the barman, pointed at his empty bottle of Corona and mouthed "One more". The barman nodded and went off to get a bottle from the fridge. Nightingale's phone rang. He fished it out of his raincoat pocket and looked at the screen. It was Jenny.

"Where are you?" she asked.

"The pub?"

"Doing what?"

"Well, gosh, Jenny, what do people usually do in the pub?"

"Are you working?"

"Not as such." The barman put a Corona down in front of Nightingale, a slice of lime sticking out of the neck.

"You said you were going to see Mrs Steadman."

"I did."

"And you said you'd be right back."

"There's been a change of plan."

"What's going on, Jack?"

"Hell, Jenny, can't I have a beer in peace?"

"You know that Mrs Hawthorne is here? About her husband."

340

Nightingale swore under his breath. Mrs Hawthorne was a housewife with four children who suspected that her husband was playing fast and loose with his secretary. Nightingale's initial enquiries suggested that she was probably right, but to prove it she was going to have pay another couple of grand. He'd forgotten that he'd arranged for her to come into the office.

"Jack, are you there?"

"I'm sorry, it slipped my mind. Can you tell her I'm on a case and that I'll call her this evening?"

"She's not going to be happy, Jack. She's come in all the way from Gravesend."

"What do you want me to do, Jenny? Open a vein? I fucked up. I'm sorry."

"Where are you?"

"I told you. The pub."

"Which pub?"

"The Swan."

"Bayswater Road?"

"That's the one."

"Don't go anywhere."

"I wasn't planning to," said Nightingale.

"I'm serious, Jack. Stay put." She ended the call.

The barman was watching him with a sly smile on his face. "Wife giving you grief?" he said.

"As good as," said Nightingale, pushing the slice of lime down into the bottle with his thumb.

"Women, hey? Can't live with them, can't strap them into a car and send them over a cliff."

Nightingale looked at the barman. He was in his fifties, with receding grey hair drawn back into a ponytail, and a beer gut that strained at his dandruff-flecked shirt. "You married?"

The barman grinned. "Three times. Got my fourth off the internet. Latvian."

"Nice," said Nightingale. "How's that working out?"

"So far, so good."

Nightingale raised his bottle in salute. "I'll drink to that."

Nightingale was on his fourth Corona when Jenny slid onto the stool next to him. "What's wrong with you today?" she asked.

"I'm just blowing off some steam," said Nightingale. "I'm the boss. I'm allowed."

Jenny slid a cheque across the bar. "Mrs Hawthorne paid up."

"Good to know."

Jenny put the cheque into her handbag, a beige Prada. The barman came over and winked at Nightingale. "The wife?" he said.

Jenny glared at him. "His assistant," she said, "Get me a glass of Chardonnay and a pair of scissors."

The barman frowned. "Scissors?"

"Someone needs to put that rat on your head out of its misery," she said.

"I'd get her the wine, because she probably means it," said Nightingale. The barman scowled and moved away.

"How many have you had?" asked Jenny.

"Now you're my mother?"

"I'm not your wife or your mother, Jack. I'm your assistant and your friend."

342

"I know," he said. "I was trying to lighten the moment."

"What's wrong, Jack?"

Nightingale shrugged. There was no way that he could tell Jenny what Mrs Steadman has asked him to do. "I just felt like a beer."

"Where did you go today?"

Nightingale took a long pull on his Corona and shrugged. "I went for a walk," he said. That was partly true, at least.

"This isn't fair," she said.

"What isn't?"

"You keeping stuff from me like this." The barman placed a glass of wine in front of her and then waddled over to the far end of the bar. "Don't you trust me?"

Nightingale looked across at her. "Of course I trust you. More than anyone. You know that."

"So why won't you tell me what's going on?" Nightingale drained his bottle. He was about to wave for another when Jenny put a hand on his arm. "Please don't," she said.

"You won't believe me," he said. "And if you do believe me you'll think I'm crazy for even considering it. And if I do what she wants, and I tell you, then you'll be an accessory . . ." He tailed off, shook his head and stared at the bar.

Jenny tightened her grip on his arm. "She? Who are you talking about?"

Nightingale turned to look at her. "Trust me, you don't want to know. Just leave it be."

343

She shook her head fiercely. "Tell me."

Nightingale closed his eyes and sighed, then nodded slowly. "Okay, but don't say I didn't warn you."

CHAPTER
SEVENTY-THREE

Jenny sat back, a look of horror on her face. "You are kidding me," she said. They had moved to a corner table, away from the barman's baleful stare. There he'd told her everything that Mrs Steadman had said to him.

"I wish I was," said Nightingale.

"She wants you to kill a nine-year-old girl?"

Nightingale nodded.

"With knives? In her eyes and heart?"

"That's pretty much it."

"What are you going to do, Jack?"

Nightingale flashed her a tight smile. "Oh, I thought I'd pop around this evening and do the dirty deed. Like you do."

"I'm serious." Her face had gone pale and there was a small vein throbbing in her left temple.

"I can see that."

"You should call the police."

Nightingale shrugged. "The police wouldn't get it. They're not geared up to dealing with demons and stuff."

"I mean the stupid old woman, Jack. She's clearly deranged. Mad as a bloody hatter and dangerous with it. She might find someone stupid enough to do what she says. She should be sectioned."

"What?"

"Sectioned. She needs to be in a place where she can't hurt anybody."

Nightingale swirled his beer around and watched the slice of lime bob up and down. "Mrs Steadman isn't crazy," he said.

"How can you say that? You think it's rational behaviour to go around talking about sticking knives into kids?" She drained her glass and pushed it across the table to him. "Get me another, will you? If I go anywhere near that barman I won't be able to stop myself grabbing his pony tail."

"He's just bought a mail order bride," said Nightingale, getting to his feet. "A Latvian."

"God help the poor girl," said Jenny.

Nightingale went over to the bar and ordered a glass of wine and a Corona. "She's a bit of a ball-breaker, isn't she?" asked the barman, nodding at Jenny.

"She's okay," said Nightingale.

"I prefer Eastern European women. Easier to handle."

"Nah, she's fine," said Nightingale. "She likes you."

"Like fuck she does."

"Seriously. She only acts like that when there's attraction. It's what she does when she's flirting."

"Seriously?"

"On my life," said Nightingale. The barman gave him his drinks, Nightingale paid and carried them over to Jenny. "Mrs Steadman knows what she's talking about," he said as he sat down. "Up until now she's always made a lot of sense."

"You think it's sensible to even talk about killing a child? Jack, the woman is off her rocker. If she told you then she's probably telling other people and there are plenty of sickos out there who might take her at her word. What did she say it was? A Shade, did she call it?"

"It's an evil entity without form. It can only act when it's taken possession of something else." He saw the look of contempt on her face and held up his hands. "I know how crazy it sounds."

"Do you? Are you sure about that, because if you really knew I think you'd have turned her over to the authorities already."

"She isn't like that," said Nightingale.

Jenny sipped her wine. The barman was grinning at her, and as she put down her glass he winked at her and gave her a thumbs-up. "What the bloody hell is he grinning at?" she asked.

Nightingale twisted around in his seat. The barman moved down the bar, collecting empties. "I dunno," he said. "Probably just wanted to know if the wine was okay." He swirled his bottle again. "Look, I know everything I've said sounds totally mad, but Mrs Steadman has always steered me right in the past."

"I've never understood the attraction you have for that woman," said Jenny.

"Attraction?"

"You know what I'm saying. Whenever she calls you drop everything to go and see her. And it's Mrs

Steadman this and Mrs Steadman that. She's a witch, you said."

"A white witch."

"A white witch who sells crystals and spells and voodoo dolls?"

"Not so much voodoo. But Wicca stuff, yes. Spells and charms."

"Well, that right there is the sign of a disturbed mind. She's best avoided, Jack."

Nightingale lowered his head and moved closer to her. "But what if she's right?"

"Can you hear yourself?"

"I'm just saying, what if? What if there is such a thing as a Shade and what if it has taken over the little girl?"

"Then it's not our problem. Let them get a priest or a vicar or whoever it is that the church uses for exorcisms."

Nightingale shook his head. "An exorcism won't work. That's what she said."

"But shoving knives into her eyes and heart will?"

"Special knives. Any old knife won't do."

"Of course not. It probably has to be knives blessed by a vestal virgin or some such nonsense."

"She said she'll give me the knives when I'm ready."

"Ready? When will you be ready?"

"She said she didn't expect me to believe her, not right away. She said I should find out for myself what's going on."

"What does that mean?"

Nightingale shrugged. "The Shade has an agenda. Something really bad, she said. The Shade can get people to do things, things they wouldn't normally do. She says that I should find out who the little girl has spoken to, and see what happens to them."

"That's just ridiculous," she said.

Nightingale grimaced, then reached for a copy of the *Evening Standard* that was sticking out of his raincoat pocket. He spread the paper out on the table and opened it at page five. The main headline read — "FATHER SLAYS FAMILY THEN KILLS HIMSELF". Nightingale tapped the headline with his finger. "The inquest was today. Murder-suicide."

Jenny frowned as she read the story. "He was a nurse," she said.

"That's right."

"Please don't tell me that he worked at the little girl's hospital."

Nightingale nodded. "In the ICU, where she was first taken."

Jenny stared at the article in horror. "That doesn't make any sense, Jack."

"It does if Mrs Steadman is telling the truth," he said.

"What are you going to do?"

"I'm a detective. I'm going to detect. That's the easy part. But if she's right and something has taken over the little girl, then God only knows what I'm going to do."

"What do you mean by detect?"

"I'm going to head down to Southampton and ask some questions."

"Of whom, exactly?"

"I want to find out why the nurse killed himself, for a start." He grinned across at her. "Fancy a drive?"

"I'm not a taxi service, Jack."

"I was thinking more of your role as my sidekick."

"Sidekick?"

"Robin to my Batman. Lewis to my Morse. That pretty red-haired bird to my Doctor Who."

"Gromit to your Wallace?"

"See, you do get it. Seriously, it'll be useful to have a feminine face by my side, especially when I start asking awkward questions."

Jenny sighed. "Okay, you've talked me into it."

Nightingale grinned. "Excellent. And can we take your car?"

"Jack . . ."

He held up his bottle. "I've been drinking."

"So have I."

"Nah, wine doesn't count. And you've barely touched yours."

CHAPTER
SEVENTY-FOUR

"That's it," said Nightingale, nodding at a detached house with a tiny garden in front of it. Jenny pulled up at the side of the road.

"I think the police tape all over the front door is a clue," said Jenny. They were in a small road on the outskirts of Southampton. The front door of the house was criss-crossed with blue and white crime scene tape and there was a yellow seal over the lock. "You weren't planning on breaking in, were you?"

"I doubt that there'll be much to see," said Nightingale. "The cops'll have taken away anything interesting."

"And you haven't got any cop friends who can tell you what happened?"

"It's Hampshire police and I don't have any contacts there. I rang Robbie and he doesn't either."

"So what's the plan?"

"We'll talk to the neighbours. See what they have to say."

"They're not going to be able to tell you if Bella Harper is possessed."

"Oh ye of little faith," he said. They climbed out of the car and Nightingale turned up the collar of his raincoat. The sky overhead was gunmetal grey and there was a cold wind blowing down the street. According to the newspaper, the bodies had been discovered by a neighbour, and while the reporter hadn't identified the neighbour, Nightingale figured that it was a fair bet that it would be the occupant of the house next door.

Jenny followed him as he pushed open the wooden gate and walked down the path to the front door. He'd already checked the electoral register and there were two people living in the house — Ronald Edwards and Ruth Edwards. He rang the doorbell and practised his smile as he waited for the door to be opened. He heard footsteps and then the rattle of a bolt drawn back. The door opened on a security chain. It was a grey-haired woman in her sixties. "Mrs Edwards?"

"Yes," said the woman, squinting up at him with narrowed eyes.

"My name's Jack, Jack Nightingale." He took out his wallet and gave her his business card. "I'm a detective. This is my assistant. Can we talk to you about what happened next door?"

"I need my glasses," she said.

"I'll wait while . . ." She closed the door on him before he could finish the sentence. Nightingale and Jenny waited and after a couple of minutes Mrs Edwards opened the door. This time she was wearing spectacles. She waved the card at him. "You're not a real detective," she said accusingly.

"I'm a private detective," he said. "I don't work for the police. But I do have some questions for you."

"Why? I told the police everything."

"I'm trying to understand what happened. That's all."

"I keep getting journalists knocking on my door but I won't talk to them. They just want the gory details so they can sell their newspapers."

"I'm not a journalist, Mrs Edwards."

"I know that. But why does a private detective want to know what happened?"

"I used to be a policeman. Part of my job was to deal with people in crisis, especially people who wanted to hurt themselves. I want to know why Mr Fraser did what he did, that's all."

"Really, we won't take up much of your time, Mrs Edwards," said Jenny. "We just need to know what happened, and you probably know more than anyone, don't you?"

She looked Nightingale up and down, then nodded. "Come on in, but wipe your feet, I've just had the carpet cleaned." She unhooked the chain and opened the door.

Nightingale carefully wiped his Hush Puppies on a mat as the woman watched, then Jenny did the same. She closed the door, replaced the security chain and took them along to the kitchen at the far end of the house. "I've just made tea," she said. She waved them to chairs next to a Formica table. "I'll just take my husband his tea and then we'll talk." She picked up a mug of tea and went up the stairs.

Nightingale looked around the kitchen. It was neat and tidy, with an old gas cooker that had been polished until it shone and a fridge that was just as clean but must have been made in the fifties. Something moved under the table and Nightingale flinched, but then relaxed when he realised it was a tortoiseshell cat. The cat stared at him, its tail twitching, and then it walked stiff-legged out of the kitchen.

"You're jumping at shadows, Jack," laughed Jenny.

"It wasn't a shadow, it was a cat."

Mrs Edwards returned. "My husband isn't well," she said.

"I'm sorry," said Nightingale.

"Cancer," she said, patting her chest with the flat of her hand. "He needs oxygen to breathe properly. You're not a smoker, are you?"

"No," lied Nightingale. "Disgusting habit." Jenny looked away, suppressing a smile.

"Ronnie smoked forty a day. I told him, those things will kill you, but he wouldn't listen."

Nightingale shifted uncomfortably on his chair as Mrs Edwards poured tea into three cups.

"So what did you want to ask me?"

"It's about what happened next door," he said.

"I assumed that, young man," said Mrs Edwards.

"Did you discover the bodies?"

She nodded and grimaced. "It was horrible. Horrible."

"Can I ask you why you went into the house?"

"I hadn't seen the children. But his car was parked outside. He always took the boys to the childminder when he was at home during the day. I don't sleep much, so I'm awake when he takes them out and he

354

didn't. And I didn't see Sally come back from work. She works at an estate agents in the city centre. She gets the bus in and I'm usually in the front room reading when she gets home. And I had a package for her."

"A package?"

"Nothing important, just some clothes she'd ordered for the boys. From a catalogue. I always took in parcels for her. I don't go out much." She sipped her tea.

"So you went around with the parcel?"

"Not that day. I thought perhaps the boys were poorly or something, so I waited. And the next day I didn't see them, so that evening I went round and knocked on the door. Nobody answered. So I went round to the back just to be sure, and the back door wasn't locked. I opened the door and called for Sally but there was no answer and that's when I realised something must be wrong." She shuddered. "I wish I'd called the police then and there because what I saw . . ." She shuddered again. The cat walked back into the kitchen and Mrs Edwards scooped it up and began to stroke it. The cat mewed and Mrs Edwards kissed it gently on the top of its head.

"Can you tell me what you saw, Mrs Edwards?" asked Nightingale.

"It was horrible," she said. She shivered and kissed the cat again. "He'd used a knife, on his wrists and his throat. He was sitting in the lounge, in the seat that he always sat in. He watched TV there and Sally would be on the sofa. When I went round I'd sit next to her. The chair was his, even the kids couldn't sit there." She closed her eyes and shook her head slowly. "There are some things that you see that you wish you'd never seen. Does that make sense to you?"

"Perfect sense," said Nightingale.

Mrs Edwards opened her eyes. They were misty with tears and she blinked them away. "The knife was still in his hand, even though he'd been dead for more than a day. The blood had soaked everywhere, over his clothes and the sofa and the carpet. It had congealed, like jelly, and it was swarming with flies. I couldn't understand the flies. It's September. There shouldn't be flies but they were everywhere. On his face, on his neck, all over the blood. Every time I see a fly now I wonder if it was one of the flies from the house." The cat looked up at her and mewed. "Yes, darling, I know," she whispered.

"And the family?"

"He'd killed them," said Mrs Edwards quietly. "The children he'd suffocated with pillows as they slept, so at least they hadn't suffered." Tears rolled down her cheek and she lowered her face so that she could use the cat's fur to brush them away. "They were little angels, those boys. I should never have gone upstairs, should I, Mr Nightingale?"

Nightingale shrugged, not sure what to say. He needed her to continue talking and he didn't want to say anything that would stem the flow. He looked across at Jenny and she grimaced.

"Seeing something like that, it's like having a photograph that you can't erase. It's been years since I could remember what my father looked like. These days he's just a big man with a moustache, I can't remember his face. But those children, their faces will stay with me until the day I die."

"And Mrs Fraser?"

"Sally? He'd strangled her. And banged her head against the wall. It had smeared down the wall in the boys' bedroom. The flies were in the bedroom, too. Buzzing and crawling over their faces."

"Then you called the police?"

Mrs Edwards nodded. "They were here almost immediately. You hear stories about how slow the police are, but I phoned nine nine nine and I was still talking to the operator when the first police car came."

"It must have been terrible for you."

"I was in shock, I think. A very nice policewoman took me into my house and made me tea and put far too much sugar in it. She said sugar helps you when you're in shock."

"It does."

She smiled. "It didn't help me, I can tell you that. A doctor came over and he gave me an injection and that made me feel a bit better, so at least I got some sleep that night."

"The thing is, Mrs Edwards, do you have any idea why he would have done what he did?"

She shook her head. "He loved those boys. Loved them with all his heart. And Sally was the apple of his eye. Once a week I'd babysit so that they could have an evening out. And he was always bringing her flowers and chocolates."

Jenny leaned forward and smiled encouragingly. "How long had they been married?"

"Five years, I think." She frowned as she stroked the cat. "Their anniversary was in July. He took her out for a slap-up meal with champagne and everything and he bought her a gold bracelet." She shook her head sadly. "I don't understand why he did what he did."

"Was he a drinker?" asked Jenny. "Or drugs?"

Mrs Edwards laughed harshly. "Good grief, no. I mean, he'd have a beer sometimes and wine with meals but he didn't have a drink problem." She nodded at the ceiling. "Now him upstairs, he went through a phase a few years ago when he was drinking way too much but his diabetes put paid to that. But John was as good as gold. He was a lovely man, Mr Nightingale. He was great with the kids and Sally loved him with all her heart."

"They didn't argue?" asked Nightingale.

"Of course they argued. What sort of marriage would it be without arguments? And raising boys is never easy. But he never lifted his hand to the boys and barely even raised his voice to them."

"So no shouting matches, no outbursts?"

"Nothing. He wasn't the type. And Sally was a lovely girl. A slip of a thing. John was always so protective of her."

"So why do you think he did it, Mrs Edwards?" said Nightingale. "What do you think made him snap?"

Mrs Edwards tried to rub her face against the cat's back but the animal slipped from her grasp and jumped down to the floor. Mrs Edwards looked over at Nightingale. "You know what I think? I think he was possessed. I think something made him do it."

CHAPTER
SEVENTY-FIVE

Nightingale lit a cigarette as they walked towards Jenny's Audi. "You're not getting into my car smoking that," she said.

"Come on, the new car smell went ages ago," said Nightingale.

"It's not about the smell, it's about secondary smoking being a killer."

"I'm not sure that's true," said Nightingale. He took a lungful of smoke, held it deep in his lungs, and let it out, careful to blow it away from the car. "There's a lot of anti-smoking hysteria these days."

Jenny shook her head, unwilling to get into a discussion about the rights and wrongs of smoking with Nightingale. "So what do you think?" she said.

"About what?"

"About what she said? Possession? Do you believe that?"

Nightingale shrugged and took another drag on his cigarette. "If he was possessed then maybe whatever it was moved from the girl to the nurse."

"So where is it now?"

"I'm no expert on this, kid," he said. "Maybe it just moved on. I don't know." He dropped the remains of his cigarette onto the pavement and ground it out.

"There is another possibility, of course," she said.

"Yeah? What's that?"

"Mrs Steadman might just be stark raving mad."

Nightingale smiled thinly. "To be honest, I hope you're right," he said. "Because if she isn't, I've no idea what the hell I'm going to do."

Jenny's phone rang. She smiled apologetically at Nightingale and took the call. "Uncle Marcus!" she said, and Nightingale winced at the enthusiasm in her voice. "Sure. Dinner would be great. Excellent."

She ended the call and put the phone away. "Uncle Marcus?" said Nightingale.

"He's in London on Friday and wants to take me for dinner." She unlocked the Audi and climbed in.

Nightingale forced a smile. "You can't turn down a free dinner." He got into the front passenger seat.

"Not at the Ivy, anyway," said Jenny. "Do you want to come? It'd give you a chance to get to know him."

"I'd love to," lied Nightingale. "I've got nothing on."

"Jack, I promise not to mention work," she said.

"The thought hadn't even entered my mind," said Nightingale.

CHAPTER
SEVENTY-SIX

"Come on, Bella, open wide." The dentist smiled down at her but Bella steadfastly refused to do as she was told.

"I don't want to."

Malcolm Walton had been a dentist for almost twenty years and he'd never liked working with children, but they represented a big chunk of his six-figure income so he'd learned to just grin and bear it. "I'm not going to do anything that will hurt you," he said. "This is just a check-up. And afterwards you can choose a toy from my toy jar."

His assistant Debbie picked up the big glass jar of cheap plastic toys and shook it as she smiled encouragingly.

"I don't want a toy."

Debbie put down the jar. "Would you like to watch a DVD?" she said. "We have some great cartoons. *Ben 10*? Do you like *Ben 10*? Or we have some great *Barbie* DVDs."

There was a flat screen TV up near the ceiling that they used to distract patients. It worked well. Cartoons kept the kids occupied, men could be distracted by rock videos with scantily dressed dancers, and Walton had most of the soaps recorded to keep the housewives quiet.

"I don't want a cartoon," said Bella. "I want to go home."

"Well, you know that's not going to happen until I've had a look at your teeth," said Walton. "I'm sure your mummy won't be happy if you don't let me at least do that. I'm not going to drill or anything, we just need to check that everything is okay." He flashed her his most sincere smile. "A few minutes is all it'll take, Bella."

The girl looked like she was going to argue but then she sighed, leant back, and opened her mouth.

"That's a good girl," he said. He adjusted the overhead light, picked up his mirror and a probe and leaned over her. He gasped when the smell from her mouth hit him. "My God!" he said in disgust. He leaned back. "That's . . ." He realised that Debbie was watching him and he forced a smile. "That's quite some halitosis you've got there, Bella. Are you cleaning your teeth?"

"Every morning and every night."

"And how long do you spend cleaning them?"

"Mummy says two minutes so I do two minutes."

"And do you floss?"

Bella nodded solemnly.

Watson scratched his chin with the back of his hand. "What about food? Do you eat a lot of spicy food? Takeaway curries, things like that?"

She shook her head. "I had beef burgers and chips at school today."

"And for breakfast?"

362

"Coco Pops."

Watson frowned. Beefburgers and Coco Pops wouldn't account for the foul smell coming from the little girl's mouth. At first glance her teeth seemed clean enough, and she was far too young to smoke or drink, which were the two major causes of bad breath.

"Do you use a mouthwash?"

Bella shook her head. "Mummy said that she would buy some for me."

"Well, I'll give you some anti-bacterial mouth rinse to take away with you," he said. "But you have to make sure that you clean your teeth carefully. In a few years you'll be having braces and then you'll really have to be careful, so it's best to get in the habit of doing it properly now." He looked over at Debbie. "Can you get my face mask?" he asked her.

Debbie went over to the cupboard where he kept his protective masks and pulled out his full-face plastic visor. He used it when he was carrying out invasive dental surgery but he figured it would cut down on the smell from Bella's mouth. She gave it to him and he clipped it onto his head and snapped down the clear visor. "Anyway, let me have a closer look and I'll give them a quick clean and polish."

Walton sat down and bent over the little girl. The mask cut down on some of the smell but it was still bad enough to make him gag. Wherever the stench was coming from, it wasn't her teeth that were the problem. She was cavity-free, there was little to no plaque on her teeth or furring on her tongue. He checked the gaps between all her teeth and there was no trapped food, and no pockets in the gums. It was as healthy a mouth as he'd ever seen. He sat back, frowning. The smell was appalling, worse then he'd ever come across and he'd had some terrible mouths in his chair over the years. There were a number of diseases that could cause bad breath, including respiratory tract infections like bronchitis or pneumonia, diabetes, acid reflux and malfunctioning kidneys. But Bella seemed fit and healthy.

"Well, your teeth actually look quite good," he said. He lifted up the plastic visor. "They are a little uneven but we'll fix that with braces when you're older. And I'll give you some mouthwash to take home with you."

The phone in reception rang and Debbie hurried out to answer it. The regular receptionist was off sick and Debbie had been juggling two jobs all day.

Walton put his tools down and took off his mask. "So I'll see you again in six months," he said.

"Do you believe in Jesus, Dr Walton?"

Walton frowned, not sure if he'd heard her correctly. "Do I what?"

"Do you believe in Jesus?"

"I'm Jewish, Bella. We believe in God but we don't believe that Jesus was his son."

Bella smiled. "Your people killed Jesus. But he forgives them."

"What are you talking about, Bella?"

Her smile widened. "Jesus has a message for you, Dr Walton. About your wife."

"My wife?"

"Jesus wants you to know what your wife is doing, Dr Walton. But I have to whisper it to you." She beckoned him to move closer. "Come here, and I'll tell you what Jesus says."

CHAPTER
SEVENTY-SEVEN

Nightingale grunted as he saw the thick-set man in his thirties holding a black Met kitbag walk out of the Southampton police station and head to a nearby car park. Jenny had parked the Audi where they could get a clear view of the main entrance and they had been there for the best part of two hours. "That's him, isn't it?"

Jenny took another look at the newspaper cutting that had a photograph of Hopkins, identifying him as the hero police officer who had rescued Bella Harper. "Yes, I think so," she said.

Nightingale peered over at the photograph and back to the man with the kitbag. He nodded. It was definitely him. "Do you mind staying here? I want to talk to him man to man."

"Sexist as always."

"All right, cop to cop."

"How about former cop to cop?"

"I knew you'd understand." He climbed out of the Audi and hurried after the policeman. "Dave Hopkins!" he called and the policeman stopped and turned to look at him.

"Inspector Hopkins?" said Nightingale.

The inspector narrowed his eyes suspiciously. "Who wants to know?"

Nightingale handed him a business card. "Jack Nightingale," he said. "I used to be in the job but I'm private now."

"The Met?"

"How did you know?"

"You look like the Met," said Hopkins. "Look, the days of cops being able to talk to you guys are long gone. The fact that you've even spoken to me means I've got to enter it into the log."

"I just need a chat," said Nightingale. "Actually, I just need one question answering. And you're the only one who can answer it."

"I can't. Seriously. It's more than my job's worth."

"It's important."

"Yeah? What are you on? A couple of hundred a day plus expenses?"

Nightingale shook his head. "This isn't about money. I'm just . . ." He shrugged. "I'm doing a favour for a friend. But it's not a case I'm interested in. It's a victim."

The inspector frowned. "A victim?"

"Bella Harper."

CHAPTER
SEVENTY-EIGHT

Nightingale paid the barmaid and handed Hopkins his gin and tonic. "Thanks," said the detective. They were in a quiet pub a short walk from the police station.

Nightingale raised his bottle in salute. "You're not a smoker, are you?"

"Bloody right, and I'm gasping."

They went outside and Nightingale offered him a Marlboro. Hopkins shook his head. "Can't stand them," he said. "I'm a Rothmans man, always have been." He took out his own pack and they lit their own cigarettes and blew smoke. "So. Bella Harper."

"Must have been rough," said Nightingale.

"I was sure she was dead." He shivered and took a long drag on his cigarette. "You know, I was almost up on charges. I hit the bastard over the head with a spade. And that bitch of a girlfriend. They killed her and I was the one being threatened with charges."

"Nothing came of it, though?"

"My Federation rep stepped in. It went away. But it shows you what it's like these days. The criminals get the breaks and the victims are treated like shit." He sipped his gin and tonic.

"You'll be at the trial?"

"That's months away. They're pleading not guilty. She says she didn't know what he was doing, he says Bella slipped and fell in the bath."

"Bastards."

"Yeah. Tell me about it."

"Should have hit him harder with the spade."

Hopkins laughed harshly. "Yeah, I wish I had now. I could have claimed that he'd slipped and fallen."

"He'll get life."

"You think? Child abduction doesn't always mean life. The woman will get away with a few years if they can get her to give evidence. He might get ten. Fifteen. Could be out in five."

Nightingale took a drink of his Corona. "Still, Bella's okay, that's the important thing. Could have been a lot worse."

"Tell me about it."

"You said you thought he'd killed her."

"I was sure of it," said the inspector. "She was under the water when I pulled her out. He'd had his hands around her throat. There were no bubbles, she wasn't moving. I put her down and gave her the kiss of life but she was gone, I could tell. She wasn't breathing, she was just . . ." He shrugged. "Gone. You've seen dead people, right?"

Nightingale nodded. "More times than I care to remember."

"So you know. The life goes. You can see it in the eyes. It's not about body temperature or brain activity or any of that crap. You're either dead or you're alive and Bella was dead. I gave her the kiss of life and I did heart massage but looking back I wasn't doing it for her, I was doing it for me. I thought that so long as I kept trying it wouldn't be true. But nothing I did made any difference. She was dead." He took another long pull on his cigarette, held the smoke deep in his lungs, and then exhaled slowly. "So then the cavalry arrive and my Super takes me in the kitchen and the paramedics go up and then the next thing is they're shouting that she's alive."

"That's strange, all right," said Nightingale.

"Yeah. Except she wasn't, Jack. I know dead. And she was dead. She might be alive and well now but that day, when I was working on her on the landing, she was dead."

"You might have missed something. Drowning victims can be resuscitated."

"That's what I was doing, but it didn't do any good. She wasn't coughing up water. He strangled her. That's what killed her. She didn't inhale the water."

"Like a coma, then. Signs of life suppressed. Then she woke up when the paramedics arrived."

"Yeah, maybe that was it," said the inspector, but there was no conviction in his voice. "I'm just glad that it turned out the way it did. She's back with her parents and at the end of the day that's all that matters."

"Have you seen her, since?"

The detective shook his head. "Nah. The press office were talking about a reunion thing, you know? A photograph of little Bella and the hero cop that saved her life. But I said no."

"Because?"

370

"Because I didn't save her life. The girl I dragged out of the bath was dead. I did everything I could but she was still dead. I'd given up, I was in bits, and that's when they found out she was alive. Whatever happened, it was nothing to do with me." He drained his glass. "So what was the question?" he asked. "What did you want to know?"

"You've already answered it for me," said Nightingale. He drained his bottle and put it down on the trestle table. "I'm good." He turned up the collar of his raincoat and walked away. He took his phone out and called Jenny. "All done," he said. "Where are you?"

"Back in London, I figured you could get the train back."

"You're joking!"

"Of course I'm joking, you daft sod. Let me know where you are, I'll come and get you."

CHAPTER
SEVENTY-NINE

Malcolm Walton poured himself a glass of red wine and sipped it. "Can I have some?" asked his wife. Walton nodded and sloshed some into a second glass on the kitchen counter, then walked into the dining room. The dining table was set for two. He sat down at the head of the table and took another sip of wine.

His wife joined him, carrying two plates. Steak, mashed potatoes and asparagus. She put down the plates and then went back to the kitchen to retrieve her wine glass.

"Where are the kids?" he asked as she sat down.

"They went to see a film. They had a pizza before they went." She smiled. "They won't be back until ten. I thought it'd be nice to have the house to ourselves." She picked up her wine. "Anyway, cheers."

Walton looked at her glass and frowned. His wife waited expectantly but then realised he had no intention of clinking his glass against hers. She put her own glass down. "Malc, are you okay?" asked his wife.

Walton shrugged.

"Bad day at the surgery?"

He shrugged again. He couldn't be bothered saying anything to her. She picked up her knife and fork and cut herself a small piece of steak. She was always a delicate eater, pecking at her food like a small bird. She popped the morsel into her mouth and chewed slowly.

Walton picked up the knife with his right hand and ran his left thumb slowly down the serrated edge of the blade.

"Is something wrong?" asked his wife. She put down her knife and fork. "Are you not feeling well?"

Walton stood up slowly.

"Malc, what's the matter?" she asked, but then she seemed to sense what he was planning to do and stood up suddenly. Her chair fell back and hit the floor with a loud bang.

Walton moved quickly around the table. She turned and ran for the door but he lashed out with the knife and cut her across the shoulder. She shrieked in pain and stumbled against the wall, but then regained her balance as Walton struck her again, this time a stabbing motion that thrust the knife several inches into her back. She screamed but Walton knew that no one would be coming to help her. Their house was detached and their nearest neighbour was in her seventies and virtually deaf. His wife scrambled through the door as blood soaked into her shirt. Walton ran after her and stabbed her in the back again. "Help me!" screamed his wife and Walton grinned savagely. She could scream all she wanted, it wouldn't help.

She ran into the hall, towards the front door. He was hard on her heels and he knew that she wouldn't have time to unlock the door, so he anticipated her move to the right to head up the stairs. He slashed out with the knife and cut her just below the knee, the serrated blade slicing through her flesh as if it were paper. Blood spurted down her leg.

She fell and only just managed to get her hands up to break her fall, then scrabbled up the stairs on all fours. Walton changed the grip on the steak knife and brought it down into the calf of her right leg, burying it up to the handle. He felt the blade scrape the bone as it went in and again when he pulled it out savagely.

His wife reached the top of the stairs, where she pushed herself to her feet and ran down the landing to their bedroom, blood pouring down her leg. She got there a fraction of a second before him and tried to slam the door in his face, but he hit the door hard and she staggered backwards and fell onto the bed. She tried to roll to the side, but Walton was too quick for her and he stabbed her four times in the chest, hard and fast, grunting with each blow. Blood blossomed over her breasts and Walton snarled and stabbed her again, this time closer to her throat. She finally stopped screaming as her windpipe filled with blood. He could see the panic in her eyes as bloody foam spewed between her lips. "Die, you stupid bitch!" he hissed, and virtually on cue the life faded from her eyes and she went still.

Walton climbed off the bed and stood grinning down at his dead wife for almost a minute as her blood soaked into the duvet. Then he looked at his watch and smiled to himself. There was plenty of time to finish his steak and drink some wine before his kids came home.

CHAPTER
EIGHTY

Nightingale pushed open the door to his office. Before he could take off his coat Jenny rushed over to him holding a newspaper. "Did you see the *Express* yesterday?" she asked.

"I'm more of a *Sun* man, as you know."

"Well, you need to take a look at the *Express*," she said, thrusting the paper at him.

Nightingale went through to his office and sat down behind his desk, still wearing his raincoat as he scanned the *Express*. There was a news story on the front page and a feature article across the two centre pages of the paper, a couple of thousand words, with photographs of Bella Harper and her family. There were also photographs of the Prime Minister, the Archbishop of Canterbury, and Prince William. The headline read: "BELLA'S MESSAGES FROM BEYOND THE GRAVE".

"It's a world exclusive," said Jenny. "But it'll be syndicated around the world tomorrow."

"This is bad," said Nightingale, gesturing at the newspaper.

"Do you think?"

"The Prime Minister? She wants to talk to the PM? And Prince William?"

"Not so worried about the Archbishop then?"

"I figure he can take care of himself," said Nightingale.

"You think it's a joke, Jack?"

Nightingale threw up his hands. "I don't know what to think."

"We can't let the PM talk to her. We can't let anyone talk to her."

"I know that. You think I don't know that?"

Jenny folded her arms. "So what are you going to do? What are WE going to do?"

"I don't know. I'm thinking."

"Oh, that's all right then. The great Jack Nightingale has his thinking cap on so it's all going to turn out for the best."

"Sarcasm doesn't suit you, Jenny."

Nightingale pointed at the headline. "She wants to see three of the most important people in the country. She wants to talk to them. And we know what happens to people that she talks to. That nurse killed himself and his family.

"I don't see any of them turning up at her front door."

"You don't? Then you underestimate the power of public relations. They got the Queen to jump out of a helicopter at the Olympics opening ceremony. You think they wouldn't persuade the Prince to pop around for a photo opportunity with a girl who came back from the dead? And you think the PM's PR won't be telling him that this would be a great way of connecting with voters?"

Nightingale grinned. "You know that wasn't actually the Queen that leapt out of the helicopter, right?"

Jenny didn't smile. "This isn't funny, Jack. We have to do something."

"Let me talk to Robbie."

"Robbie? You think the police can help?"

"I'll ask Robbie to see if anyone else connected with Bella has . . ." He shrugged. "Let me talk to Robbie, then we'll work out what we should do."

Jenny nodded and walked out of the office. Nightingale reached for his phone. He'd call Robbie all right. But there was someone else he needed to talk to, and for that he'd need more than a mobile phone.

CHAPTER
EIGHTY-ONE

Nightingale dropped the two black plastic rubbish bags on the ground and bent down to unlock the padlock that was what passed for security for his lock-up. He pulled up the metal shutter and flicked on the light switch. A fluorescent light flickered into life. The lock-up was empty — he'd already moved his MGB to a multistorey car park close to his office. He opened one of the bags and took out a red plastic bucket and a scrubbing brush. At the end of the line of garages was a tap set into the wall and Nightingale used it to fill the bucket. He spent the next fifteen minutes scrubbing the concrete floor clean. When he was satisfied he used paper towels to pat the floor dry, then stood up and admired his handwork.

He'd worked up a sweat, and he knew that he had to be spotlessly clean because any impurities would weaken the protective circle. He secured the lock-up and walked back to his flat. He showered twice, using a new bar of coal tar soap, taking care to use a plastic nail brush to clean under his fingernails and toenails. He shampooed his hair twice, then rinsed himself off and used a brand new towel to dry himself.

He had already laid out clean clothes on his bed and he put them on. The shoes were a new pair of brown suede Hush Puppies that he'd bought a month earlier but hadn't broken in yet. He pulled on his raincoat and walked back to the lock-up, his hair still damp.

He took off his raincoat and hung it on a nail by the light switch, then pulled down the shutter. He stood for a while in the middle of the garage, steadying his breath, then got to work. He took a large cardboard box from one of the bags and opened it. Inside was a box of chalk. The lock-up was about fifteen feet long and ten feet wide. The protective circle had to be just that, a circle, so he carefully drew one six feet in diameter. In the second bag he had a birch branch that he'd ripped from a tree on Hampstead Heath, and he slowly ran it around the perimeter of the chalk circle. When he'd finished he put the branch back in the bag and with the chalk drew a pentagram inside the circle. He'd already worked out that the front of the garage faced north, so he drew two of the five points of the pentagram facing that direction.

He carefully drew a triangle around the circle, with the apex pointing north, and then wrote the letters MI, CH and AEL at the three points of the triangle. Michael. The archangel.

Nightingale placed the two rubbish bags close to the shutter and put the cardboard box in the centre of the circle. He put the chalk back in the cardboard box, took out a small bottle of consecrated salt water, removed the glass stopper and carefully sprinkled water around the circle. He took five large white church candles and placed them at the five points of the pentagram, then used his lighter to light them one at a time in a clockwise direction.

He stood in the centre of the circle and checked that everything was as it should be, then he bent down over the cardboard box and retrieved a plastic bag full of herbs. He opened the bag, took out a handful of herbs and sprinkled them over the candles one by one, moving clockwise around the circle. The herbs sizzled as they burned, filling the air with cloying fumes, and for the first time Nightingale wondered if it had been such a smart move to be playing with fire in a garage with the door down.

He bent down, fished a lead crucible from the cardboard box and poured the rest of the herbs into it. He used his fingers to form a neat pile and then set fire to it with his lighter. He straightened up, his eyes watering from the pungent fumes, and pulled a folded piece of paper from his back pocket. On it were the words that he needed to say, written in Latin.

He took a deep breath but immediately began coughing. His eyes were watering and he wiped away the tears with the back of his hand. He managed to stop coughing and began to read the Latin words, slowly and precisely. When he reached the final three words he said them loudly, almost shouting. "Bagahi laca bacabe!"

The fumes from the burning herbs began to swirl in a slow, lazy circle and then behind him was a flash of lightning and the smell of a burning electrical circuit. The concrete floor began to vibrate and the cloying fog grew thicker. He forced himself to breathe shallowly through his nose, trying to minimise the damage to his lungs.

The fog swirled around him, faster and faster. It was now so thick that he could barely see the brick walls of the garage and the fluorescent light was just a dull bright patch above his head. There was another flash of lightning, then another, the cracks so loud that they hurt his ears.

He stared ahead, tears streaming from his eyes. Then space folded in on itself and there were a series of bright flashes and she was there, dressed in black as usual, her black and white collie dog at her side. Proserpine. A devil from Hell. One of many, but one of the few that Nightingale knew by name. Her face was corpse-pale, her hair jet-black and cut short, her eyelashes loaded with mascara and her lipstick as black as coal, emphasising the whiteness of her small, even teeth. She was wearing a long black leather coat that almost brushed the floor over a black T-shirt cropped so short that it showed the small silver crucifix that pierced her navel. Her tight black jeans were ripped at the knees and she wore short black boots with stiletto heels.

She stared at him with her cold black eyes, her upper lip curled back in a sneer. "Jack Nightingale," she said. The dog growled as its hackles rose. She had it on a steel chain and she pulled on it to get its attention. "Hush, we won't be here long," she said. The dog sat down and stared at Nightingale with eyes as cold and black as those of its mistress. "I told you last time, I'm not to be summoned on a whim."

"This isn't a whim," said Nightingale. "I need your help."

"We're not friends, Nightingale. We never were and we never will be." She looked around the garage and smiled. "Salubrious," she said. "Looks like you've fallen on hard times."

"It's private, that's all that matters," said Nightingale. "It doesn't matter where the pentagram is, all that matters is that you have to stay between the triangle and the circle until I say you can go."

"That's one way of looking at it," said Proserpine. "The other way is that so long as I'm here you're trapped inside that puny little circle with nowhere to go. I could easily just stand here until you die of old age and your bones crumble to dust."

"So it's a Mexican stand-off. Let's keep it as short as we can, shall we?"

"What do you want, Nightingale?"

"I need some questions answering. About Shades."

"Try Wikipedia."

"I don't believe anything I read in Wikipedia."

"But you believe me?"

"Sounds crazy I know, but yes. So will you help me?"

"No," she said flatly.

"No?"

Proserpine shrugged carelessly. "Why should I?"

"What if I did a deal?"

"You're offering me your soul?"

Nightingale laughed, but it sounded like a harsh bark and the dog pricked up its ears. "I only need information," he said. "My soul's worth more than that. But I can offer you something else."

"I'm listening."

"Help."

Proserpine tilted her head to the side. "Help?"

"I'm starting to understand how things work," said Nightingale. "You and your kind move in and out of this world but there are things you can't do yourselves."

"That's your great insight, is it?"

"I know, we're ants compared to you, but we're still here and you're still dealing for souls and not just taking them. That's always had me thinking. You're all-powerful devils from Hell, why don't you just take our souls, harvest them like a farmer culling cattle?"

Proserpine said nothing.

"I'll tell you why. Because there are some things that you just can't do. Either because there are rules that you have to follow, or because there are physical constraints on what you can do. Either way, sometimes you need help. You need us to do things that you can't. So here's the deal. Answer my questions about Shades and I'll owe you one. If you need something doing, something you can't do yourself, you can ask me."

"That's very open-ended."

"I'll risk that," said Nightingale. "You've always played fair with me."

"Plus I'm assuming you're reserving the right to refuse?"

"Like I said, I think you'll respect the deal."

"And not ask you to kill a child?"

Nightingale stiffened, wondering if Proserpine was toying with him. Did she know about Bella Harper already? Did she know what Mrs Steadman had asked him to do?

Proserpine laughed and the garage walls shook. "If I do a deal with you, how do I know you'll stick to it?"

"Because I always keep my word."

She laughed again and this time dust showered down from the ceiling and a jagged crack appeared in the concrete floor. "I'll need more than that," she said. "I tell you what, if you refuse to do whatever I ask in return, then I get your soul." She watched him with unblinking black eyes.

Nightingale took a long breath and exhaled slowly as he considered his options. He needed Proserpine's help but he didn't want to put his soul at risk, not after he'd gone to so much trouble to make it his own. "What will you ask me to do?" he said.

Proserpine smiled coyly. "Now if I told you that, it would spoil all the fun, wouldn't it?"

"I'm not prepared to kill for you."

"Fine."

"Or to do something that would result in someone dying."

"Fine."

"And it's a one-off deal. You ask me to do something for you and I do it. Then we're good."

"And if you refuse to do what I ask, you forfeit your soul."

Nightingale nodded slowly. "Agreed."

"Okay, it's a deal," she said. She held out her hand. "Let's shake on it, shall we?" Nightingale instinctively reached out to shake her hand, but pulled it back when he realised what he was doing. She laughed. "Almost got you."

Nightingale stared at her hand, just outside the protective circle. The pentagram only kept Proserpine from him so long as he didn't breach it.

"So, ask away," she said.

"You know about Shades?"

"Of course I know about Shades. Nasty pieces of work, but nasty for nasty's sake."

"As opposed to your lot, you mean?"

"My lot, as you call it, serve the Lord Lucifer. Shades serve no one."

"So they're not devils? Or demons?"

"You are forever using terms that you don't understand, Nightingale. But no, Shades are not demons or devils, or angels or spirits. They never have been nor will they ever be. Shades are Shades." She narrowed her eyes. "You have come across one?"

"You don't know?"

"Nightingale, you seem to think I take a personal interest in your comings and goings. That is so typical of your kind, thinking that the universe revolves around you. You are nothing to me. You are less than a speck of nothingness on nothing. I have not given you a single thought since the last time we met and immediately I have left this place you will be gone from my mind."

"So I should take you off my Christmas card list, then?"

She laughed and the sound seemed to come from the bowels of Hell itself, a deep throbbing roar that he felt in the pit of his stomach. The ceiling shook and plumes of dust scattered down through the fog.

"You're a very funny man, Nightingale. But if you are planning to interact with a Shade, be very careful."

"They're dangerous?"

"Lethal. Do not get too close."

"They bite, is that it?"

Proserpine shook her head. "They are more insidious than that. They get inside your head. They plant thoughts, thoughts that you wouldn't normally have. They bend you to their will."

"By talking?"

"That's what they do. That is their power. They don't stab or shoot or bludgeon, they suggest. They manipulate. They charm."

"And they are always evil? There are no good Shades?"

She threw back her head and laughed again, louder this time. The shutter pulsed back and forth with the sound of tearing metal and Nightingale felt a hot blast of wind across his face that made him gasp.

"No, Nightingale, there are no good Shades."

"Then answer me this. What do they want? What is their purpose?"

"Their purpose? They want to cause chaos. They want to cause pain. But it's instinct, nothing else. There's no plan, no rhyme, no reason."

386

"So they won't stop? Once they've started?"

"There is nothing to stop them. They're not working to a plan or a timetable. They just keep on doing what they do."

"And what stops them? Say they move into a body and take it over. How long can they stay?"

"That depends," said Proserpine.

"On what?"

"On the strength of the Shade. On the condition of the host. The host will decay. Slowly, but it will decay. And eventually it will die and the Shade will die with it."

"And how do you kill a Shade?"

"That's what you want to do, Nightingale?" She wrinkled her nose. "You try that and I'll never be able to hold you to your end of the deal. How can you kill something that can change your every thought? Point a gun at a Shade and you'll shoot yourself in the head. Try to stab a Shade and you'll put the blade through your own heart."

"Assuming that's true, assuming that you could get close to one, how do you kill it?"

"I have heard that there are knives, blessed knives, and you have to drive them through the eyes and the heart of the host. But seriously, Nightingale, the best thing to do is to run and to keep on running."

Nightingale nodded. At least Proserpine had confirmed what Mrs Steadman had told him.

"Who told you about the Shades?" asked Proserpine.

"Why do you think anyone told me?"

"Shades pass unnoticed in your world," said Proserpine. "They inhabit the recently dead and are rarely discovered. Was it Mrs Steadman?"

"I'm going to pass on that," said Nightingale. "No comment."

Proserpine laughed and Nightingale felt the vibrations through his feet. "You need to be careful of that one," she said.

"She's on the side of the angels," said Nightingale.

"Are you asking me, or telling me?"

"She's never steered me wrong yet," said Nightingale. "I trust her."

"Well, good luck with that," said Proserpine. "Don't come crying to me when it goes bad. And it will."

"What do you mean?"

Proserpine smiled. "For the answer to that question, I'd need your soul," she said. "Give me your soul and I'll answer any questions you want."

"My soul's not for sale."

"So you say," said Proserpine. "But you can call me when you change your mind. In the meantime we're done here. Let me go." The dog growled menacingly at Nightingale. Proserpine flicked its chain. "It's all right, we're going now." She looked up at Nightingale. "Time to say the words, Nightingale. I've got people to see, places to go."

Nightingale nodded, looked at the piece of paper he was holding, and said the words to release her. Space folded in on itself, there was a flash of light and she and the dog were gone.

Nightingale's phone rang and he took it out of his pocket. It was Robbie Hoyle. "Where are you?" asked Robbie.

"The lock-up," said Nightingale.

"That bloody car of yours is a money pit," laughed Robbie.

"It's a classic."

"It's an old banger. I need to see you, mate."

"The Swan?"

"You read my mind. I'll be about an hour. Mine's a pint."

CHAPTER
EIGHTY-TWO

Nightingale saw Robbie walk into the pub and ordered his lager before turning to shake his hand. "This is turning into a right can of worms, you know?" asked Robbie.

"I'm fine thanks, all good," said Nightingale. "Whatever happened to the social niceties?"

"You want small talk or do you want to talk about what's going on?"

"I don't know what's going on, that's why I called you."

The lager arrived and Nightingale paid the barman. He gestured at a table by the fireplace. "Bit quieter over there," he said.

Robbie took off his overcoat and draped it over the back of a chair before sitting down. Nightingale sat opposite him and sipped his Corona. "You should drink that in a glass," said Robbie.

"Tastes better out of the bottle."

"Rat piss," said Robbie.

"Nah, I'm serious."

"I mean rat piss. Rats run across the crates and pee on the bottles. Mate of mine runs a pub and he says never drink from a bottle, always use a glass."

Nightingale shrugged. "Maybe that's what makes it taste so good."

Robbie laughed and shook his head. "You're mad," he said.

"Yeah, they do say." He put down his bottle. "So you've got something for me, yeah?"

"You wanted to know if anyone connected with Bella Harper had died recently. Apart from the nurse who killed his family?"

"Yeah."

"Do you want to tell me why?"

"It's a case, sort of."

"Sort of?"

"I'm just making some enquiries, Robbie." He took a drink from his bottle. "Have you found something?"

Robbie nodded. "I did, yeah. A suicide. Freelance journalist killed himself in Clapham."

"What's the Bella Harper connection?"

"He talked to her about three hours before he died."

He saw the look of astonishment on Nightingale's face and raised his glass. "That good enough for you?"

"Are you serious?"

"As cancer, mate. He went into a corner shop, bought a bottle of drain cleaner and drank the lot. How do you do that? How do you drink a bottle of it? It's as corrosive as hell."

"I heard of a guy who killed himself by drinking a bottle of furniture polish."

"A lovely finish?"

Nightingale grinned. "It's an old joke. So what's the story?"

Robbie leaned closer as if he was worried about being overheard. "Guy's name was Jeremy Barker. He was a freelance reporter but he wasn't averse to taking photographs of celebrities behaving badly. He sold titbits to the tabloids and the overseas press. Living hand to mouth, pretty much. His death was suicide, no question of that, but in his jacket was a digital camera and a voice recorder. There were two photographs of Bella Harper on the camera."

"Shit. How did he get to her?"

"Did I say he was wearing a white coat and carrying a stethoscope? Bastard pretended to be a doctor and walked right in. The Sussex cops have checked the hospital's CCTV and there's footage of him going in and out."

"And the digital recorder?"

Robbie nodded. "I thought you'd pick up on that," he said. He took an iPhone from his pocket. "I couldn't take the recorder but they were okay with me making a copy. He was only with her a few minutes." Robbie tapped on the screen of his phone, then held it out. Nightingale took it and held it to his ear. He frowned as he listened. The end of the conversation was impossible to hear. He switched it off and gave it back to Robbie.

"So she whispered to him? Something about Jesus?"

"The whole conversation is weird, Jack. How did she know he was a reporter? How did she know his name?"

"Had she met him before?"

"Doesn't sound like that. The thing is, there's no doubt that it's suicide. The shopkeeper saw him drink the drain cleaner. So it's not as if it's a murder investigation. The detective who caught the case listened to the recorder thinking it might be a verbal suicide note, but then realised it was Bella. So he's passed it on to the detectives on that case. But they're not really interested because Barker wasn't involved in the abduction."

"Never wrote about it?"

Robbie shook his head and put the phone back in his pocket. "Nope. Not a word. Looks like he was after an exclusive, he'd be able to sell the story and pictures for a lot of cash, maybe not in the UK but the foreign papers would have bitten his arm off."

"Like you said, the big question is how did she know who he was. He was dressed like a doctor, right?"

"I haven't seen the CCTV footage but I spoke to the detective who did and yes, you can see him walking through the hospital in his white coat with his stethoscope around his neck. Looked like any other doctor and no one paid him any attention."

"But she knew he was a reporter."

"And she knew his name, Jack."

"Did he have a badge on? With his name on it?"

Robbie shook his head. "I asked that. No."

Nightingale sat back in his chair and swirled his lager around in the bottle. "So somehow she knew his name and that he was lying about being a doctor, and then she wants to whisper something about Jesus to him?"

"Do you have any idea what's going on here, Jack?"

Nightingale shrugged. "I'm as bemused as you are."

"I'm not bemused, I'm fucking gob-smacked. Who the hell drinks drain cleaner? And why? He was short of cash and owed a few grand on his credit cards but who doesn't these days?"

"Woman trouble?"

"He was gay, and gays don't tend to top themselves over a love affair gone wrong."

"Do the cops have a theory?"

"To be honest, mate, it's a suicide plain and simple. They're not going to bust a gut trying to find out why."

"Case closed?"

"It's not even a case. The Bella Harper thing made them prick up their ears but that's all." Robbie sipped his lager. "You heard about the headmistress, right?"

"Bella's headmistress?"

"Yeah. She hanged herself. Her bloody head came right off, Jack. She tied a rope around her neck and jumped off the school building. You won't have heard about the dentist yet, though. The cops are keeping that under wraps until all the relatives have been informed."

"What happened to the dentist? This is Bella's dentist, right?"

Robbie nodded. "Guy called Malcolm Walton. Goes home and stabs his wife to death. Sits down and finishes his dinner. When his two teenage kids come home he butchers them. Then he goes into the kitchen and starts smashing wine glasses. Half a dozen of them. Uses a rolling pin to crush the glass and then swallows it. All of it. Not a nice way to die, Jack."

Nightingale stared at his friend in horror.

"So I'm guessing this isn't a series of coincidences," said Robbie. "You ask me to see if anyone close to Bella

Harper has died in strange circumstances and I find them piling up like a serial killer's convention. Do you want to tell me what's going on?"

"You won't believe me, Robbie."

"Try me."

Nightingale sat back in his seat, ran his hands through his hair and groaned. "If I tell you, you'll think I'm crazy."

"That ship sailed some time ago. Who is your client?"

"There's no client."

"Pro bono? You're helping someone out for free?"

"Sort of." He picked up his Corona again. "Okay, I'll tell you what I've been told. That doesn't mean I believe it, okay?"

"Okay."

Nightingale groaned again. "This is going to sound stupid, I know." He took a deep breath. "A friend of mine, someone I've known for a while, someone I trust, told me that Bella Harper has been possessed."

"Possessed? By what? A ghost? A devil?"

"By something. Something bad. And this friend said that whatever it is wants to do . . . Bad things."

"Bad things?"

"She wasn't specific. In fact she wasn't specific about much, just that something had possessed Bella. I wanted to see if she was right or not."

"The girl's with her parents, Jack. If there was something wrong, they'd have seen it."

"Maybe, maybe not."

"I don't believe in ghosts and that nonsense but surely, if there was a demon or something there'd be signs."

"I know as much about possession as you do. I was just asking around to see if it was possible."

"Several people who came into contact with her have killed themselves, that's true enough. But how does a nine-year-old girl come to be responsible for that?"

Nightingale shrugged. "I've no idea. The nurse was definitely murder-suicide."

"You spoke to the Sussex cops?"

"I did a bit of detecting on my own."

"Bloody hell, Jack, be careful. They throw away the key for impersonating a cop these days."

"I played it by the book, more or less," said Nightingale. "I went to see the neighbour. She told me that the nurse suffocated his family and then slashed his wrists. But before that he was a loving father and husband."

"People snap. Happens all the time. And most murders are domestic, that's a fact of life."

Nightingale nodded. "I know. But something must have kicked him off. Same with this guy Barker. You don't just one evening decide to drink drain fluid."

"And you're suggesting that Bella Harper was involved." He shook his head. "Both times she was tucked up in her hospital bed when it happened."

"I get that," said Nightingale.

"So what's your friend claiming, that a little girl somehow forced them to kill themselves?"

"Maybe that's what the whispering was about. You can't hear what she says at the end."

Robbie's eyes widened and he put down his lager. "What, you're saying she hypnotised him? A nine-year-old girl hypnotised Barker to go away and drink drain cleaner?"

"She whispered something to him. About Jesus. So what the hell was that about?"

Robbie threw up his hands. "Mate, what could she possibly have said that would have led him to kill himself two hours later? She's a kid."

"I said you'd think I was crazy."

"If you're actually considering this then yeah, you are out of your mind." He leaned forward again. "Look, people snap and kill themselves. Sometimes they take out their anger on someone else before they do it. Shit happens. You were in the job, you know that."

"So what's the connection with the girl?"

"Maybe there is no connection," said Robbie. "Maybe it's a coincidence. A nasty little coincidence."

"I hope so."

They both drank in silence for a while.

"It's not a coincidence, is it?" said Robbie eventually.

"I don't think so, no."

"Shit."

"Yeah. And some."

"We can't tell anyone, can we?" said Robbie. "No one's going to believe us. And it would pretty much kill my career dead."

"Even if they did believe it, and that would be one hell of an if, what could they do? Arrest a nine-year-old-girl? And charge her with what?"

"You know about this spooky stuff? Can't a priest do an exorcism or something?"

"I'm told not. Whatever is inside her isn't a spirit as such. It'll take more than a few Hail Marys and some Holy Water."

"Like what?"

Nightingale picked up his Corona and drank as his mind raced. He didn't want to lie to his friend, but there were some things better not said. Killing a child was definitely high up on that list, even if the child was already dead. He put down his bottle. "I'm not sure," he said. "But before we get to the stage of doing something we need to be one hundred per cent sure."

"What are you thinking?"

"If there are two, there could be more. If there are more . . ."

"Then we'll know for sure. But that doesn't take us any further forward, does it? Even if we have absolute proof that a nine-year-old girl can make grown men kill themselves, what do we do?"

Nightingale nodded but didn't say anything. Robbie wouldn't have to do anything. It would be down to Nightingale. Mrs Steadman had made it painfully clear what he was supposed to do — thrust knives into the eyes and heart of Bella Harper.

"Is this connected to what's going on up in Berwick?" asked Robbie.

"I don't think so."

"What about Marcus Fairchild?"

Nightingale shook his head.

"Your life is bloody complicated, Jack."

"Tell me about it," said Nightingale. "I need a cigarette."

They went outside to the terrace overlooking Kensington Gardens and sat near a propane heater. "You know the history of this place?" Nightingale asked Robbie.

Robbie shook his head.

"It's been around for ever," said Nightingale, lighting a cigarette. "The sixteen hundreds anyway. They used to bring prisoners here for a drink before taking them over to Marble Arch to the hanging tree."

"Nice," said Robbie.

"That was back in the day when they hanged you for stealing a loaf of bread or looking at the squire wrong." He shrugged. "The good old days." He took another long pull at his cigarette. "Did you turn up anything about Fairchild?"

"I looked, mate. But there's nothing known, certainly nothing along the lines of what you were talking about."

"Okay."

"I did see if he'd worked on any paedophile cases, like you said, but couldn't find any cases at all, not for the prosecution or the defence. He specialises in company law — I doubt that he would have been involved in anything involving paedophiles."

"Yeah, I think he was lying about that."

"Jack, are you sure he's what you say he is?"

"No question."

"So what are you going to do?"

Nightingale smiled ruefully. "Best you don't know," he said.

CHAPTER
EIGHTY-THREE

Nightingale sat staring down at the gun on his coffee table. It was a matt black Taurus .45, small enough to conceal in a pocket. It would make a loud noise, but Fairchild's Sussex house was a good half mile from his nearest neighbour. It was Wednesday, and on Friday Fairchild was due to take Jenny for dinner. Nightingale was sure that Fairchild had more than dinner in mind, so if he was going to stop the man it had to be done that night or the next.

He took a deep breath, put the loaded gun into his raincoat pocket and went downstairs to the street. His car was back in the lock-up and he headed towards it. He looked left and right and then jogged across the road. A bus heading his way seemed to accelerate towards him but it still missed him by yards. The driver glared at him as the bus went by and Nightingale realised that the acceleration had been deliberate. He turned up his collar against the wind as he walked by a Halal butchers. Two women swathed from head to foot in black niqab went by and they also seemed to be glaring at him through the slits in their headcoverings.

A traffic warden in a fluorescent jacket looked up from the car he was checking and his upper lip curled back into a snarl. Nightingale hurried on his way. A group of three young men in hoodies and low-slung jeans turned to stare at him with undisguised hostility.

He stopped at an intersection and looked both ways before crossing over. Two middle-aged housewives in cheap cloth coats stopped talking and frowned at him as he passed. He scratched his head, wondering if he was imagining all the hostile looks.

"Got any spare change, mister?"

He turned to see Proserpine, sitting on the pavement with her legs drawn up to her chest. Her dog was sitting next to her, its tongue lolling out of the side of its mouth, Proserpine was holding a cardboard sign with "ANY SPARE CHANGE MUCH APPRECIATED" scrawled in capital letters.

Nightingale stopped and looked down at her. She smiled up at him. Her hair was spikier than the last time he'd seen her, and she was wearing more black mascara than before, making her face appear even paler. She was wearing a black leather motorcycle jacket with silver studs in the form of small crosses and there was a heavy silver inverted cross hanging from a thick chain around her neck.

"Penny for your soul, mister," she said, and winked.

"Are you here for me or is this just one of those awkward coincidences?"

"It's all about you, Nightingale," she said. "It always is. So is that a gun in your pocket or are you just pleased to see me?"

"What do you want, Proserpine?"

"I sense hostility in your voice, Nightingale. Aren't we friends any more?" The dog growled and she rubbed it behind the ear and made a shushing sound.

Nightingale took out his pack of cigarettes and tapped one out.

"Those things will kill you," said Proserpine.

"Everybody dies," said Nightingale. He lit the cigarette and took a long pull on it.

"That's not strictly speaking true," said Proserpine. "But there are different ways of dying, and lung cancer isn't a pleasant way to go."

"Death is death," said Nightingale.

"True, but there's a big difference between death and dying. Wouldn't you rather die happily in your sleep, dreaming of fluffy clouds and puppy dog tails or whatever floats your boat?"

"What do you want, Proserpine?"

"A cigarette for a start."

"Not scared of cancer, then?"

"Not much scares me." She reached out her hand. There were thick silver rings on her fingers, studded with what looked like runes.

Nightingale gave her a cigarette. He was about to take his lighter out of his pocket but she smiled up at him. "No need," she said. She glanced at the cigarette and the end glowed redly and began to smoke.

"Nice trick," said Nightingale.

"It's not a trick," she said. "You sound stressed. In a rush? Somewhere to be? And you still haven't answered my first question. That is a gun in your pocket, isn't it?"

"You know it is, don't you?" he said, putting the cigarette pack back into his coat pocket.

She smiled. "Not much gets by me, Nightingale."

"So you know where I'm going and what I'm going to do."

"You're going to kill Marcus Fairchild." It was a flat statement and not a question.

"He deserves it."

"People don't always get what they deserve, do they?"

Nightingale kept his eyes on Proserpine as he took another long pull on his cigarette and held the smoke deep in his lungs.

"Cat got your tongue?"

Nightingale blew smoke up into the air. "I'm waiting for you to tell me what it is you want."

"We have a deal, remember?"

"Of course."

"Well, now it's time for you to pay the piper. You're not to go near Marcus Fairchild."

"What?"

"You heard me. You're not to go near him. You're not to speak to him, you're not to contact him in any way. And you're most definitely not to kill him."

Nightingale's eyes hardened. "He's one of yours." It wasn't a question.

"That's nothing to do with you. The deal we have is that I ask you to do something and you do it. Or you forfeit your soul."

"He's an evil bastard."

404

Proserpine smiled and shrugged. "And?" She smoked her cigarette as she stared at him.

"Ask me for something else," said Nightingale eventually.

She shook her head. "I don't want anything else."

"You set me up," said Nightingale.

"You contacted me, remember? You opened the door."

"But you knew I'd be after Fairchild. And you wanted to stop me."

"Again, you offered me the deal. I didn't twist your arm. You wanted information about the Shades, and I gave it to you. Now you need to keep your end of the bargain. Or give me your soul. It's your choice."

"He kills children. He sacrifices them."

"Yes, I know. But you make it sound as if that's a bad thing."

Nightingale took another long pull on his cigarette as his mind raced. She was right, he'd entered into the deal willingly and yes, it had been his idea. And complaining that it wasn't fair wasn't going to change the mind of a demon from the bowels of Hell. The choice was his and his alone. He could agree to leave Marcus Fairchild alone, or he could kill Fairchild and hand his soul over to Proserpine. He blew smoke at the pavement and nodded slowly. "You win," he said.

"I usually do," said Proserpine.

Nightingale flicked his cigarette into the gutter, turned and walked away.

"Hey, Nightingale." Nightingale turned to look at her. "Word to the wise," she said. "Beware of men in white vans."

Nightingale flashed her a cold smile and walked away.

"Be lucky!" Proserpine called after him.

CHAPTER
EIGHTY-FOUR

Nightingale's head was whirling as he walked slowly back to his Bayswater flat. Proserpine had tricked him, he was sure of that, but that didn't matter. What mattered was that he couldn't stop Marcus Fairchild and within the next twenty-four hours he'd be in London with Jenny. He had to do something to stop the man, but what? If he interfered, he would forfeit his soul. But if he did nothing, Fairchild would continue to abuse Jenny in ways that Nightingale could only imagine.

The rear doors of a white Transit van ahead of him opened and two men climbed out. They were already walking towards him when Nightingale realised who they were. They were the two men who had broken into his house. This time they weren't wearing ski masks and both were holding knives.

Their faces were set hard as they walked purposefully towards Nightingale. They were in a quiet side street, and while Nightingale could hear traffic off in the distance, the road they were in was quiet and the pavements were empty.

The smaller of the two men was also holding a sack. Nightingale could see how this was supposed to go down. The bag over his head, into the van, and off. There was another man in the back of the van, looking at him. Waiting.

Nightingale waited until the men were two paces away from him before pulling out the gun. The two men stopped immediately and looked at each other and then back to Nightingale. "Surprise!" said Nightingale.

The man with the sack put up his hands. "There's no need to do anything stupid," he said. He had a Scottish accent.

"Doesn't feel that stupid to me," said Nightingale. "Now sod off back to your van before I put a bullet in your nuts."

Both men turned to go but Nightingale waggled the gun at the big man. "Not you," he said. "You can stay for a chat."

The smaller man hurried away and climbed into the back of the Transit van.

"Who sent you?" hissed Nightingale.

"Fuck you," replied the man.

"Turn around," said Nightingale.

The man didn't move and continued to glare at Nightingale, breathing heavily like a bull at stud.

Nightingale lowered the gun so that it was pointing at the man's groin. "I'll shoot you in the nuts and walk away," he said. "No skin off my nose."

The man slowly turned around. The rear doors of the van slammed shut and the van pulled away from the kerb with a squeal.

"Looks like your friends have left you in the lurch," said Nightingale. "I guess they weren't expecting me to bring a gun to a knife fight."

Nightingale transferred the gun to his left hand and jabbed the barrel at the base of the man's spine. He slid his right hand into the man's trouser pocket and pulled out his wallet. He flicked it open and saw that there was a driving licence among the credit cards. Nightingale slid the wallet into the pocket of his raincoat. "Now I know who you are and where you live," said Nightingale. "If you or anyone else comes near me again, I'll hold you responsible, you hear me?"

"I hear you."

Nightingale jabbed the gun into the man's back again. "You wouldn't be the first person I'd shot, either. Loud noises don't scare me."

"I said I hear you," said the man.

"And first thing tomorrow morning the cops get your details and your name goes in the frame for the murder of Danny McBride. So if I were you I'd run far and I'd run fast." He jabbed the man again. "Now walk away before I change my mind and put a bullet in your leg for the sheer hell of it."

The man did as he was told, running down the road as if the hounds of Hell were on his heels. Nightingale slid the gun back into his pocket, glad that he hadn't had to fire the weapon. At least now Perry Smith would take it back.

CHAPTER
EIGHTY-FIVE

Nightingale parked his MGB on the second floor of a multi-storey car park close to Camden market. He walked around the market for a while, smoking and thinking before making his way to the Wicca Woman shop. Mrs Steadman was standing behind an old-fashioned cash register and she smiled when she saw it was him. "Mr Nightingale, so nice to see you," she said. "Tea?"

"Tea would be good, Mrs Steadman. Thank you."

Mrs Steadman pulled back a beaded curtain behind the counter and called upstairs for her assistant. There was a rapid footfall and a teenage girl appeared, dressed in black with green streaks in her hair. Mrs Steadman patted the girl on the arm. "I'm making a cup of tea for Mr Nightingale — would you be a dear and mind the shop?"

"Of course," said the girl.

Mrs Steadman patted her arm again, then took Nightingale through the curtain into the back room. There was a gas fire burning against one wall and the overhead Tiffany lamp was throwing multicoloured blocks of light over the floor. Mrs Steadman waved him to a circular wooden table and busied herself with the kettle and teapot. "Is everything okay — you look worried?" she asked.

Nightingale took off his raincoat and sat down. He pulled the *Express* from his pocket and put it on the table. "Did you see the *Express* on Monday?" he asked.

Mrs Steadman laughed. "I don't read any newspapers," she said. "They're far too depressing." She turned to face him and folded her arms. "It's about the Shade, isn't it?"

"She says she wants to speak to the Prime Minister. And the Archbishop of Canterbury. And Prince William."

"Of course. It wants to create havoc. That's what Shades do."

"People have died already. A nurse, a teacher, and a journalist. They all spoke to her and then they killed themselves."

"It was practising," said Mrs Steadman. "Testing itself."

The kettle boiled and she poured water into a teapot. She opened a green fridge and took out a blue and white striped mug and put it onto a tray, then carried it over to the table. Nightingale moved the paper out of the way.

"At least now you believe me," said Mrs Steadman as she sat down.

"It was never a question of believing you," said Nightingale. "I just needed to prove it to myself."

"And now you have done?"

Nightingale nodded. "Is there nothing else that can be done? No other way of handling it?"

Mrs Steadman reached over and put her hand on his arm. It was tiny, not much bigger than a small child's. "I wish there was," she said. "But there is only one way of dealing with a Shade."

"Can't you find someone else to do it?"

"It has to be someone of this world," said Mrs Steadman. "And it has to be someone who has a good heart and who believes. Men like you are few and far between, Mr Nightingale."

Nightingale laughed harshly. "A good heart? Is that what you think?"

"It's what I know," said Mrs Steadman. She poured tea for the two of them and passed him a mug. "I realise how difficult this is for you. It's a terrible thing to ask someone to do, I know that. But if it isn't done, Mr Nightingale, if the Shade continues on its path, the whole world will suffer in ways that you can only imagine."

"What about putting the girl in a place where she can't speak to anyone?" said Nightingale, but even as the words left his mouth he realised that he was suggesting the impossible. Put the girl in a dungeon somewhere and throw away the key? They didn't even do that to terrorists — there was no way it could be done to a nine-year-old girl.

Mrs Steadman didn't reply, she simply shook her head sadly.

"Can this Shade thing move around, Mrs Steadman? Say someone talks to Bella, could it move over to that person?"

412

"No," she said, putting her hands around her mug of tea. "A Shade comes from outside and moves into a body at the moment of death. That's where it stays."

"Can it go back to where it came from?"

She nodded. "That's why the eyes must be dealt with first. The Shade enters and leaves through the eyes. Once that avenue is blocked, the Shade dies with the host."

Nightingale shivered, even though the room was uncomfortably hot. A gas fire hissed and spluttered against one wall.

Mrs Steadman watched him carefully as she sipped her tea. He could feel her weighing up, wondering if he was prepared to do as she asked.

"I don't know if I can do it," he whispered.

"Somebody has to," she said. "And there is no one else."

Nightingale closed his eyes and shivered again.

"If you don't, a lot of people will die. Many of them children. Remember the nurse? He smothered his own sons."

Nightingale opened his eyes. "I thought you said you didn't read the papers?"

"Just because I don't read newspapers doesn't mean I'm not aware of what's going on," she said. "And what has happened so far will pale into insignificance once the Shade hits its stride."

"She's a child," whispered Nightingale.

Mrs Steadman shook her head. "She was a child, but that child has gone. Her shell is now inhabited by an entity that is pure evil. You will be killing the evil, not the child. Bella Harper is already dead, her soul is no longer in the body."

"So where is her soul? Heaven?"

Mrs Steadman looked uncomfortable. "So long as the Shade remains in the body, Bella's soul remains trapped in the Nowhen. She cannot move on."

"Can she come back? If I kill the Shade, can her soul come back?"

"That's not possible, I'm afraid. Bella Harper is dead."

"But in limbo?"

"Until this is resolved, yes."

"Then I know what I need to do," said Nightingale. "I need to talk to her."

Mrs Steadman's eyes widened. "Mr Nightingale, talking to the dead is never a good idea."

Nightingale flashed her a thin smile. "It's all right, Mrs Steadman. I've done it before."

CHAPTER
EIGHTY-SIX

Colin Stevenson's hand tightened on the receiver, gripping it so tightly that his knuckles turned white. "Did you hear what I said, Colin?" The caller was a detective sergeant in the Met, a long-time friend of Stevenson's who worked in the Paedophile Unit.

"Yeah, I heard you," said Stevenson. "Basically I'm fucked."

"With a capital F," said the sergeant. "Look, the investigation is going into overdrive, the shit is well and truly going to hit the fan."

"I understand. Is there any way out?"

"You can run, but there's already a stop on you at the ports and airports and they're coming for you first thing tomorrow morning. They don't trust the locals."

"What about a deal? Can I cut a deal?"

"They've got stuff off your hard drive, Colin. It got emailed to them. That's all they need."

"Who the hell did that?"

"I don't know. But it came from your computer. That's what I'm told."

"That's impossible."

"Impossible or not, it happened. Look, I don't see there's anything you can do. They've got you bang to rights and they've got your mailing list. The only reason I'm tipping you off is that my name isn't on that bloody list."

"Shit." Stevenson banged the receiver against his head.

"I need to know you haven't got my name anywhere they can find it."

"You're okay," said Stevenson.

"No number on your mobile? Nothing written down?"

"You're fine."

"For fuck's sake keep it that way, Colin."

"I said, you're fine," said Stevenson.

"I fucking hope so," said the sergeant. "This is huge, Colin. You know the names that are on the list."

"Yeah, I know."

"What the hell were you doing keeping them on your computer?"

"It's a bit late to be crying about spilt milk," said Stevenson. "Do you have any idea who screwed me over?"

"It came out of the blue, I'm told. And like I said, it came from your computer."

"I don't see how that can have happened," said Stevenson. "No one else has access to my place."

"Yeah, well, seriously, I'm sorry it's worked out this way," said the sergeant. "What are you going to do?"

Stevenson didn't say anything.

"Colin? Are you okay?"

Stevenson laughed harshly. "No, I'm not bloody okay. But I'll sort it. And don't worry. Your secret's safe with me."

CHAPTER
EIGHTY-SEVEN

"You are stark raving mad," said Robbie, staring down at the Ouija board that Nightingale had placed on the table. "That's for kids."

"It's more than a kids' game," said Nightingale, lighting three white candles on the mantelpiece. He went over to the window and pulled the blinds down.

"If you wanted a romantic evening in, you should have had Jenny round," said Robbie.

"First of all I don't fool around with the staff, and second of all I wouldn't want her near this."

"But I'm okay, right? What's going on, Jack? I can see why you wouldn't tell me over the phone, because I wouldn't have come round if I'd known you were going to be messing around with spooky stuff."

Robbie bent over the table and examined the Ouija board. It was made of cardboard that had frayed at the edges. The words YES and NO were printed in old-fashioned letters in the top corners, and below them were the letters of the alphabet in two rows, and below them the numbers zero to nine.

At the bottom of the board, in capital letters, was the word GOODBYE.

"Where did you get this from?" asked Robbie.

"A junk shop in Portobello Road. It's from the sixties."

"What's the plan? Chat with Jim Morrison?"

Nightingale walked around the room lighting another half a dozen candles.

"Bella Harper."

Robbie's jaw dropped. "Tell me that's a sick joke."

"If she's dead then there's a chance I can communicate with her."

Robbie picked up the grubby white planchette. "With a piece of cheap plastic? You don't believe in this nonsense, do you?"

"The Ouija board works," said Nightingale. "Plastic, wood or twenty-four-carat gold, none of that makes any difference. It's about channelling. And believing."

"But I don't believe, Jack."

"No, but I do. You're here for balance."

"Balance?"

"There have to be at least two people on the planchette. It won't work with one." He finished lighting the candles and went through to the kitchen, returning with a crystal vase of fresh flowers and a crystal glass of distilled water. He put them on the coffee table, above the board. Then he went over to his bookcase and picked up a Hamleys carrier bag. He took out a small Paddington bear and placed it between the flowers and the glass of water. He grinned at the look of confusion on Robbie's face. "Spirits generally like fresh flowers, and I figured that as Bella's a kid she might like the bear."

Robbie sat down on the sofa, shaking his head. "You're mad," he said.

"Sit down at the table, mate," said Nightingale, gesturing at one of the two wooden chairs he'd put there. He went back to the kitchen and came back with a tray on which were three small brass bowls containing sage, lavender and consecrated salt, courtesy of Mrs Steadman.

Robbie was sitting at the table, toying with the planchette. Nightingale put the bowls on the table, then lit five large white church candles and placed them around the board. He took the planchette from Robbie and put it on the board, between YES and NO.

"Right," he said. "Let's get started." He sprinkled liberal amounts of sage over the burning candles. The herb flared and sizzled and gave off a sweet aroma. Then he rubbed some of the herb over the planchette and around the edge of the board.

"You're a right Jamie Oliver, aren't you?" joked Robbie, but Nightingale flashed him a warning look. He sprinkled salt and lavender over the board, then put the brass bowls on a bookshelf.

He sat down next to Robbie. "Seriously mate, don't screw around. I realise you don't believe in it, but any negative energy will spoil it. So only think positive thoughts."

Robbie nodded. "Okay."

Nightingale held out his hands. "Hold my hands and close your eyes."

Robbie opened his mouth to say something but then changed his mind and did as he'd been told. Nightingale squeezed Robbie's hands, closed his eyes and began to speak in a loud, authoritative voice. "In the name of God, of Jesus Christ, of the Great Brotherhood of Light, of the Archangels Michael, Raphael, Gabriel, Uriel and Ariel, please protect us from the forces of evil during this session. Let there be nothing but light surrounding this board and its participants and let us only communicate with powers and entities of the light. Protect us, protect this house, the people in this house, and let there only be light and nothing but light, amen."

He waited for Robbie to say "Amen" but when he didn't he squeezed his hands.

Robbie got the message. "Amen," he said.

"Okay, you can open your eyes now," said Nightingale. Robbie did as he was told. "Okay, now you have to imagine that the table is protected with a bright white light. First you imagine it coming down through the top of your head and completely surrounding your body. Then push it out as far as you can go. Do you understand?"

"A white light?"

"As bright as you can imagine. Like a white fluorescent light. Try to picture it coming from the ceiling, down through the top of your head and then dispersing through your body. And as you do that, we both put our right hands on the planchette."

"Okay," said Robbie, but Nightingale could hear the uncertainty in his friend's voice.

"One thing. If anything goes wrong we slide the planchette to GOODBYE and we both say 'Goodbye' in a loud, firm voice and then I'll say a closing prayer."

"Do you want to spell out what you mean by 'go wrong' or shall I just leave that to my imagination?"

"The Ouija board is a conduit to the other side," said Nightingale. "Just because I'm asking to talk with Bella doesn't mean that she'll come through. And there are evil and mischievous spirits out there. But don't worry, they can't do any harm through the board."

"That's good to know."

Nightingale nodded. "Okay, so start to visualize the light and put your hand on the planchette."

The two men concentrated and reached out to touch the plastic planchette.

Nightingale took a deep breath and looked up at the ceiling. "We're here to talk to Bella Harper," he said. "Bella Harper, please come forward. We are here in the light, safe from the dark."

The candle flames flickered, casting shadows on the walls.

"Bella, my name is Jack Nightingale. I need to talk to you. Please come forward."

A car alarm went off outside and both men jumped. Robbie grinned and shook his head.

"Bella, this is a safe place, a place protected by the purest of lights," said Nightingale. "Please come forward."

The alarm stopped as abruptly as it had begun.

"Bella, Bella Harper, please come into the light."

The planchette began to vibrate and Nightingale looked over at Robbie. It was clear from the look of surprise on his friend's face that he wasn't responsible for it.

"Bella, is that you?"

The vibrations intensified and then the planchette began to move. It slid slowly across the board, the pointed end towards the word YES.

"Bloody hell," muttered Robbie.

Nightingale flashed him a warning look.

The planchette stopped, a couple of inches from YES.

"Bella, this is a safe place. My name is Jack Nightingale, I just want to talk to you. Please let me know that you can hear me."

The planchette began to vibrate again, then resumed its slide across the board. It came to a halt with the tip just over the letter E.

"That's a good girl, Bella. I won't keep you long. Hello."

The planchette backed away from YES and then moved slowly towards HELLO. It stopped over the H.

Robbie's mouth was wide open as he stared at the planchette.

"Bella, where are you?"

The planchette twitched back and forth as if it wasn't sure which way to go, then it scraped slowly across the board and stopped at the letter D. Then it moved down to O. Then left to N.

"D-O-N," whispered Robbie. He spelled out the letters as the planchette moved to them. "T-K-N-O-W. Don't know."

"But you're not at home, are you? You're not with your mum and dad?"

422

The planchette scraped across the board and pointed at NO.

"Are you okay, Bella?"

The planchette moved away from YES and headed to NO. It stopped with the tip nudging the O.

Nightingale opened his mouth to ask another question but Robbie spoke first. "Is it really her?" he asked Nightingale. "It is really Bella Harper?"

The planchette moved over to "YES".

Robbie stared at the planchette with wide eyes.

"I'm sorry you're not okay, Bella," said Nightingale. "Is there anything I can do to help?"

The planchette backed away from "YES", trembled, and then returned to "YES".

Nightingale leaned over the board. "What, Bella? What do you want me to do?"

The planchette scraped slowly across the board. "K-I-L-L-M-E." The planchette stopped and Robbie looked up at Nightingale in horror. "Kill me? What the hell's going on, Jack?"

CHAPTER
EIGHTY-EIGHT

Colin Stevenson popped two of the tablets in his mouth and washed them down with malt whisky. He was halfway through the bottle, a twenty-year-old single malt that was as smooth a whisky as he'd ever drunk. He sat back in his chair and stared at the computer screen. He'd thought about deleting everything on his hard drive, but from what the Met sergeant had told him there'd be no point. The Met investigators had everything already.

Running was pointless, Stevenson knew that. Even if he could get out of the country there would be nowhere to hide. Wherever he went they'd find him and they'd drag him back and he'd get life. Except that life as a convicted sex offender wouldn't be any sort of life. And then there were the dead kids, too. McBride was dead, but they'd find some way of linking him to the deaths and then they'd throw away the key.

He picked up another two tablets off the desk, swallowed them and drank more whisky before refilling the glass. There had been just over fifty tablets in the vial and he was sure that they would be more than enough to do the job. They'd been prescribed a year earlier when he'd been having trouble sleeping. His GP had given him all the usual warnings about not taking too many and about the dangers of becoming addicted, but Stevenson was a decorated police inspector in a stressful job, so the doctor had signed several repeat prescriptions without a second thought.

Stevenson couldn't do prison. Not as a sex offender. It would be hell on earth. He swallowed two more tablets and took another mouthful of whisky. He opened the file of videos and watched a short clip that he'd taken a couple of years earlier. It was a ten-year-old boy. Jason. Stevenson smiled and drank more whisky as he watched the video of himself stroking the boy's soft skin. There was nothing that came close to the feeling of young flesh. Stevenson shuddered and felt himself growing hard. He switched off the video and opened a Word file. They said that confession was good for the soul, but Stevenson didn't believe in souls, any more than he believed in God or Heaven. But he did want people to know why he was doing what he was doing. He wasn't taking the coward's way out, it was important to Stevenson that people knew that. It took courage to end your life on your own terms. The coward's way would have been to let justice take its course and to die behind bars a sad, old man. Stevenson wouldn't die behind bars, nor would he run and hide. He'd do what had to be done and he'd do it without any fuss. He'd had a good run. And hand on heart he had no regrets. In a perfect world he'd have gone to his grave with no one any the wiser, but the world wasn't perfect. He swallowed two more tablets and gulped down more whisky. He could feel them starting to work but he knew he had enough time to get a few things off his chest. He began to type.

CHAPTER
EIGHTY-NINE

"What did she mean, Jack? She wants you to kill her?"

They were in the Swan pub in Bayswater Road, around the corner from Nightingale's flat.

"You heard her," said Nightingale. They were sitting at a table outside so that Nightingale could smoke. He had his regular bottle of Corona and Robbie a double brandy. A propane heater hissed behind them.

"I didn't hear anything," said Robbie. "That plastic thing spelled out the message."

"The planchette."

"Whatever. Jack, I need you to swear that you weren't pushing it."

"What?"

"Swear to me on anything you believe that you weren't pushing it."

"Are you insane? Why would I do that?"

"I don't know," said Robbie. He took a gulp of brandy. "I don't know what to think at the moment."

"I didn't push it. I swear to God, cross my heart and hope to die, but I'm amazed that you would even think that."

"What's the alternative? That we were talking to a young girl who isn't dead? And she's asking you to kill her?" He shook his head. "That's fucked up, Jack. That's fucked up big time."

Nightingale blew smoke across the street. It was just after eight o'clock in the evening but the pavements were still busy. As always it was a cosmopolitan mix, and in the few minutes they'd been sitting there Nightingale had heard half a dozen languages being spoken.

"She's already dead," said Nightingale. "Bella Harper died in that house in Lyndhurst."

"Oh, I forgot to tell you. There's news on that front. The woman has started to talk. She and Lucas have killed before, they're taking her out to the New Forest next week to look for graves."

Nightingale shuddered. "I hope she didn't cut too good a deal," he said.

"She'll go down for a long time. No doubt about that."

"Yeah, well, Bella was one of their victims. They killed her, Robbie. When the cops moved into the house she was already dead."

"So why the message that she wants you to kill her?"

"Not her. Her body. She's already dead, but there's a Shade in her body. She can't move on until the Shade is killed."

"And you know how to do that?"

Nightingale nodded. "It's been explained to me, yes."

"And are you going to do it?"

"I think I have to."

"What do you have to do?"

Nightingale shook his head. "Seriously, mate, you don't want to know." He took a wallet from his raincoat pocket and tossed it over to Robbie. Robbie caught it and opened it. "What's this?"

"The guy that belongs to tried to get me into a van yesterday."

"What?"

"He was one of two guys that broke into my flat a while back. I think they were planning to kill me. Murder by suicide."

Robbie slid the driving licence out and looked at it. "Lives in Berwick."

"Might have been a cop," said Nightingale. "I'm pretty sure they were the ones who killed my client."

"Why do you say that?"

"Come on Robbie. Don't you think it's one hell of a coincidence? Danny McBride is found hanging in his brother's barn and the guys who broke into my flat brought rope with them? I don't think they were planning to go skipping with me, do you?"

"And you fought them off? Since when did you turn into Chuck Norris?"

"There wasn't much fighting, truth be told," said Nightingale. "But if they've got any sense they'll be on the lam already. Any news on that front?"

Robbie nodded. "There is a Met team looking at abuse in Berwick and north of the border. Operation Springboard. Half of the Operation Yewtree team have been moved over now that the Savile thing is coming to an end. They're going to be moving in next week."

"And the stuff I sent?"

"The paedophile unit handed it over to the Operation Springboard team. One of my mates has been seconded to the unit. They can't work out how the email came from Stevenson's computer but they're not looking in the mouths of any gift horses. It's going to be huge, Jack. Bloody huge. Some very big names are in the frame."

"They deserve everything they've got coming to them," said Nightingale.

"Pity you won't get any credit for it."

Nightingale shrugged. "There's no credit for anyone in all this," said Nightingale. "There's something wrong with a society that allows this to happen. A lot of people have to turn a blind eye for organised abuse like that to take place. The world can be a sick place at times."

"You did a good thing, Jack," said Robbie. He leaned over and clinked his glass against Nightingale's bottle.

Nightingale forced a smile. "Yeah," he said. "I guess I did at that."

CHAPTER
NINETY

Marcus Fairchild lit a cigar and blew a cloud of bluish smoke across the back seat of the Jaguar. His driver didn't complain; he was a heavy smoker, one of the reasons that Fairchild had hired him ten years earlier. They were driving into central London. Fairchild had three meetings fixed up at his City office, high-powered clients who paid seven-figure retainers for his legal expertise, and later he was going to take Jenny McLean for dinner. And after dinner he would do to her what he'd been doing to her ever since she was a child. He felt himself grow hard as he pictured himself on top of her, entering her. She never remembered, of course, A combination of drugs and hypnotic suggestion mean that she had no idea of what they did during their time together.

He opened his copy of the *Financial Times* and turned to the editorial comment page. It always amused him to see what journalists thought was important in the world. Most of them had next to no idea what really went on behind the scenes, which is how it was supposed to be. The true rulers of the world preferred to stay hidden from view and they would certainly never let journalists know what they were up to. And on the very rare occasions that a journalist did discover the truth, well, there were ways of dealing with them.

The Jaguar slowed and Fairchild looked up to see a red light ahead of them. He sighed. London traffic seemed to be getting worse year by year, which was why he tended to avoid the city centre whenever possible.

There was nothing on the editorial page to hold his attention so he flicked through the paper to the share prices. The traffic light changed to green and three cars moved forward, but the black BMW in front of the Jaguar stayed where it was. Fairchild's driver waited a couple of seconds and then beeped his horn, a quick blip to alert the driver. Road rage was something else that was on the increase in London and a mistimed horn could easily result in a violent confrontation. The BMW stayed put and the driver blipped the horn again.

"Why the hell isn't he moving?" said Fairchild.

"Engine trouble, maybe," said his driver. "The road ahead's clear."

"Well, pull around him, we can't sit here all day."

The driver turned on his indicator, but before he could turn the wheel a powerful motorcycle roared up next to them and came to a halt next to the rear passenger door.

"Now what?" said Fairchild.

The motorcycle rider was a big man dressed from head to foot in black leather. He was wearing a red full-face helmet with a tinted visor. He gunned the engine and turned to look at Fairchild.

"Tell him to get out of the way," said Fairchild. He looked at his watch and tutted in annoyance.

As the driver began to wind down his window, the motorcyclist reached inside his jacket and pulled out a squarish gun with a snub barrel. Fairchild knew enough about weapons to recognise it. A MAC-10. It wasn't the most accurate of weapons but at such a close range accuracy wasn't an issue.

Fairchild opened his mouth to roar with rage, but before he could make a sound the motorcyclist had pulled the trigger with a gloved finger and the gun spat bullets at a rate of more than a thousand a minute. The clip emptied in a fraction of a second and more than half of the thirty-two bullets slammed into Fairchild's face and chest. He was dead before he pitched across the seat and the motorcyclist sped off down the road, followed by the black BMW.

CHAPTER
NINETY-ONE

Nightingale turned into the alley and saw the church ahead of him. He looked at his watch. He was ten minutes early. He took his cigarettes out of his pocket and lit one, then walked back to the main street and window-shopped as he smoked. When he'd finished he tossed the butt into the gutter and headed back to the church. It was built of grey stone and appeared to be several hundred years old. It was hemmed in by much taller steel and glass office blocks that had been built around it over the years.

There was an arched oak door and next to it a noticeboard covered with plastic sheeting detailing the service times and announcing that there was a coffee morning every Saturday to which everyone was invited. There were black metal studs set into the door and heavy hinges and a large metal keyhole. Nightingale half expected the door to be locked but it swung open easily.

He stepped inside. The floor was large granite slabs and the walls rough stone. There was a Virgin Mary set into the stone to his left and to his right were wooden plaques containing the names of parishioners who had fallen during the two world wars. There were two lines of oak pews facing a small altar on which there was a brass cross, and to the left of the altar a wooden podium with a large Bible open on a lectern. Behind the altar was a huge arched stained-glass window, with Jesus putting his hand on the head of a young child.

The church was empty. Nightingale looked at his watch again. It was three-thirty. He looked back at the door.

"Mr Nightingale?"

Nightingale whirled around. Mrs Steadman was sitting in the front pew on the right. He frowned. How had he missed her? She was wearing a black coat with the collar turned up and a black beret. She motioned for him to join her. He walked down the centre aisle, towards the altar. He wasn't religious but he had a sudden urge to bow his head and make the sign of the cross on his chest. He shuffled along to join Mrs Steadman and sat down next to her. "I wasn't sure that you would come," she said.

"I said I would."

"Do you always do what you say you'll do?"

"I try," said Nightingale. He looked up at the stained-glass window. It was impossible to tell if the child that Jesus was blessing was a boy or a girl. "Why here, Mrs Steadman? Why a church?"

Mrs Steadman reached into a shapeless black leather shoulder bag by her side and took out a small leather roll, fastened with a braided leather strap. "These have to be handed over on hallowed ground," she said. "They must be returned the same way." Nightingale put out his hand to take the roll but Mrs Steadman moved it out of his reach. "Once taken, there is no going back, Mr Nightingale," she said. "You must understand that."

"I'm not sure that I do."

"The knives in the roll have an energy that needs to be controlled. That is why they have to be given on hallowed ground. Once they are in your possession that energy will start to wane. If you do not do what has to be done within a day, the knives will be rendered useless for ever. That must not be allowed to happen, Mr Nightingale."

"So it has to be done today?"

"Within twenty-four hours. And the clock starts ticking from the moment the knives are in your possession." She undid the braided strap and unrolled the sheet of oiled leather. She lifted a flap to reveal the metal hilts of three knives. The two outer knives were about four inches long. The hilts were ornate spheres made up of a mesh of dozens of small crosses. The knife in the centre was about twice as long, and its handle was a crucifix with a figure of Christ on it. All three knives were pitted and blackened with age.

"They've been used before?"

"Several times," said Mrs Steadman.

"I assumed that they would be left in the body," said Nightingale.

Mrs Steadman shook her head. "Oh no, Mr Nightingale. These are the only knives of their type. They have existed in this form for more than a thousand years." She took out one of the shorter knives. "These are for the eyes," she said. "They should be

436

plunged in at the same time if that's possible. If they have to be done one at a time then it needs to be done quickly. They have to be thrust in right up to the hilt."

Nightingale nodded, trying not to think what it would look like to see the knives piercing a child's eyes.

Mrs Steadman slid the knife back into its slot and took out the longer knife. It was made of copper, dull and mottled with age. She held it delicately, just under the crucifix, her fingers just touching the feet of the Christ figure. "This has to go into the heart," she said. "It must pierce the heart and go right through it. The blade must stay in the heart until the Shade dies."

"How will I know that the Shade is dead?" asked Nightingale.

"The Shade will die with the host," said Mrs Steadman. "Once the host is dead, you are to remove the knives and return them to me. Do not clean them, just return them as they are. I will do what has to be done. Now, this is important, Mr Nightingale. There are words you must say at the moment you insert the third knife."

"Words?"

"An incantation. In Latin. Do you speak Latin, Mr Nightingale?"

Nightingale smiled. "Sadly, no. I went to a comprehensive."

"You must say the incantation perfectly," said Mrs Steadman. "And it cannot be written down. It must be said from the heart."

"Okay," said Nightingale.

"You have to memorise it," she said. "Word for word. Now listen to me carefully." Mrs Steadman spoke for almost a full minute. "Do you think you can repeat that?"

"There's more chance of me growing wings and flying around this church," he said.

"Then I'll break it down into smaller sections," she said, ignoring his attempt at humour. "But this is important. As important as the placing of the knives. Without the incantation, the knives will not work."

Nightingale nodded. "I understand."

For the next fifteen minutes Mrs Steadman went through the incantation with Nightingale until he was able to repeat it faultlessly, even though he had no idea of the meaning of the words. Mrs Steadman said that it didn't matter whether he understood it or not, the words themselves held the power. When she was satisfied, Mrs Steadman asked him if he was ready to accept the knives.

Nightingale felt suddenly light-headed and he took a deep breath and exhaled through pursed lips. "I guess so."

"I need you to be more positive than that," she said. She replaced the knife, flipped the flap back and carefully fastened the strap around the roll. "Now, are you ready, Mr Nightingale?"

Nightingale forced a smile. "As I'll ever be," he said. He could see from the admonishing look on her face that his answer wasn't positive enough so he nodded earnestly. "Yes," he said, more confidently. "Yes, I am."

She nodded and handed the roll to him. "God bless you, Mr Nightingale."

CHAPTER
NINETY-TWO

Nightingale parked his car a couple of hundred yards away from Bella Harper's house and smoked a Marlboro before climbing out. He locked the door and walked slowly along the pavement. He'd driven down the street a couple of times during the day to get a feel for the place. It was a neat semi-detached house with a small wall and a wrought iron gate that opened onto a path leading to the front door. There was no garage, but half of the front lawn had been paved over as a parking space for the family's five-year-old Hyundai.

He eased open the gate, slipped inside and closed it behind him, then walked carefully down the path, squeezed by the car and walked around the side of the house. He stopped and peered through the kitchen window until he was sure that there was no one there, then walked to the kitchen door. He tried the handle and wasn't surprised to find that it was locked. He looked up at the back of the house. The curtains on the bedroom window had Hello Kittys on them, so he figured that was where Bella slept. There was a small window open in what was probably a bathroom and at a pinch he reckoned he could reach it by climbing the drainpipe. He squinted up at the window and tried to work out if he'd be able to slip through. He made his mind up that the window was out of the question when he tapped the drainpipe and discovered that it was plastic. He moved past the kitchen door. There was a large glass sliding door that led into the sitting room. The curtains were drawn but there was enough of a gap to see that the room was in darkness. He pulled on a pair of grey surgical gloves and took a screwdriver from his pocket. It took him only seconds to force the screwdriver into the gap between the door and the wall and pop the lock. He gently slid the door open, pushed the curtain aside and stepped into the sitting room. He stopped and listened for a full minute, then tiptoed across the sitting room and into the hallway, listened again, and then headed up the stairs, keeping close to the wall to minimise any squeaking boards.

When he reached the landing he stopped and listened again. There were four doors. There was one to the rear of the house, which he assumed was Bella's bedroom. The door immediately to his left was open. The bathroom. He guessed that the bedroom facing the street would be the master bedroom, where Mr and Mrs Harper were sleeping. The door was open slightly and Nightingale tiptoed over to it, breathing shallowly.

He pushed it open. Mrs Harper was closest to him, sleeping on her side. Her husband was on his back, snoring softly. Nightingale took a handkerchief and a can of diethyl ether from his pocket, twisted the top off the can of ether and soaked the material with the fluid. He tiptoed across the carpet and held the ether-soaked handkerchief under the woman's nose for the best part of a minute, then draped it over her face.

He prepared a second handkerchief and did the same to the husband.

When he was satisfied that they were both unconscious, he tiptoed out of the room and pulled the door closed behind him. His heart was racing and he stood where he was a for a full minute, composing himself, before soaking a third handkerchief with ether and pushing open the door to Bella's bedroom.

She was lying on her back, breathing slowly and evenly. Her eyes were closed and her blonde hair was spread across her pillow. Her skin was as pale as porcelain, unlined and unblemished the way only a nine-year-old's could be. Her hands were clasped together on top of the duvet as if she was praying. Nightingale closed the door quietly, wincing as the wood brushed against the carpet. When he turned back to the bed, Bella's eyes were wide open and she was staring right at him.

"You're Jack Nightingale, aren't you?" she said.

Nightingale said nothing.

"You've come to kill me, haven't you?"

Nightingale stared at her in silence.

The girl smiled at him. "I've been expecting you." She slowly raised her hand and beckoned him to come closer. "I've a message for you," she said. "From Jesus."

CHAPTER
NINETY-THREE

Nightingale took a step towards the bed. He had the ether-soaked handkerchief in his right hand. The girl continued to beckon him with her finger. Nightingale felt light-headed but wasn't sure if it was the fumes or if the Shade was somehow making it hard for him to concentrate.

She was smiling angelically, her blonde hair glinting in the glow of the streetlight that shafted in through a break in the curtains. Her finger continued to beckon him forwards. Nightingale's feet shuffled towards the bed as if they had a life on their own.

He worked the handkerchief in his hand, rolling it around his palm until it formed a tight ball.

He took another step. And another. He was at the side of the bed, looking down at the girl. Her smile widened and he wrinkled his nose at the foul stench that seemed to be coming from her mouth. "Come closer, Jack," she said. Her voice had grown deeper and more masculine and her eyes were no longer the eyes of a little girl, they were black and as hard as glass. "There's a good boy. I have something to tell you."

Nightingale sneered at her. "You can say anything you want, I can't hear," he said.

"You can hear me, Jack," she said. "And you going to do exactly as I say. Now lean forward and let me whisper to you."

Nightingale stared at her as he moved his face closer to hers. She grinned in triumph and opened her mouth to speak. Nightingale moved quickly, jumping onto the bed and grabbing her wrists. He forced her arms down by her sides and then knelt over her, trapping her with his legs, his knees digging into the side of her chest. She took a deep breath, but just before she screamed he thrust the balled handkerchief between her teeth. He used his left hand to clamp her jaw shut as he pulled a roll of duct tape from his raincoat pocket. He used his teeth to pull a few inches of tape from the roll and then slapped it down over her mouth. She thrashed about, but he quickly wound tape around her head several times. The tape and handkerchief reduced her screams to muffled grunts and her eyes burned with hatred.

Nightingale wiped his forehead with the sleeve of his coat. He sat back on his heels and stared at her. "I'd like to say that this is going to hurt me more than you, but that's probably not true," he said. He reached up with his hands and gently pulled out the yellow foam rubber earplugs that had stopped him hearing anything that the Shade had said to him.

The girl stopped thrashing around and her eyes narrowed. They were less human now, totally black and featureless.

Nightingale put the earplugs into his pocket and took out the leather roll that Mrs Steadman had given him. The girl began to thrash around as she realised what was happening. Nightingale ignored her and concentrated on undoing the braided strap. He flipped open the flap and pulled out the two shorter knives, one in each hand. He deftly swivelled them around so that the mesh spheres were in the palms of his hands and the blades were pointing down.

His heart was racing and his breath was coming in ragged gasps. He took a deep breath to steady himself, then raised his hands above his head. His felt a searing pain at the back of his head, as if someone had stuck a burning needle into his skull. He could hear words, not through his ears but from somewhere inside his head. "No, no, no, no!"

He ignored the voice in his head, steeled himself for a second, and then drove the knives down into the girl's eyes. The blades had to be forced through and there were simultaneous loud pops as the eyeballs burst. Grey fluid squirted out and dribbled around the blades and down the girl's cheeks. The body went into convulsions beneath him and he gripped tightly with his knees so that she couldn't throw him off. He leaned forward and pushed down, wincing at the tearing sound that the knives made as they pushed through the skull behind the eyes and on into the brain.

Blood gushed out of the wounds as Nightingale used his full weight to drive the knives all the way in. He stopped when the mesh spheres were flush against the eyeballs and sat back, wiping his bloody hands on the duvet.

The Shade wasn't screaming any more, it was making a whimpering moan muffled by the gag.

Nightingale tried not to think about what he was doing. He fumbled for the third knife. The big one. He took it in both hands, the small figure of Christ protruding from the V formed by his crossed thumbs.

He looked down, trying to work out where the heart was. The angle was wrong, so he shuffled back, keeping his knees tight against her legs.

The moaning intensified and Nightingale wished that he'd left the earplugs in because the sound was painful, but it was too late to remedy that now. The headache had intensified and his brain felt as if it was expanding and pressing against his skull. He took a deep breath, steeling himself for the killing thrust.

The girl began to lift herself up, then she fell back, still moaning. She did it again and again, as if she was doing abdominal crunches, up and down, faster and faster. Her hair was sticky with blood and the grey stuff that had oozed from her ruptured eyeballs, and the gooey mess trickled down her face and over the duct tape. Nightingale forced himself to ignore the fact that it was a girl he was about to kill. Bella Harper was already dead. The being below him wasn't a nine-year-old girl, it was an evil entity bent on destruction.

He raised the knife above his head, mentally rehearsed the Latin phrase that Mrs Steadman had given him, then brought the knife down, hard and fast. It pierced her skin and slid easily between the second and third rib, and then he felt resistance as it touched the heart. He spat out the words as he pushed the knife down, and he felt it pop through the heart muscle and blood squirted around the blade and soaked into the Hello Kitty nightdress. He pushed harder, still repeating the Latin incantation, then changed his grip and pushed down with the palms of his hands, driving the knife down as far as it would go.

As he finished the incantation, the girl went suddenly still. As Nightingale watched, her hands unclenched and an audible sigh escaped from between her lips. He took a deep breath and exhaled slowly. It was done. The Shade was dead. And so, finally, was Bella Harper.

CHAPTER
NINETY-FOUR

Nightingale let himself into his flat and hurried down the hallway to the kitchen. He knew that the best thing for stress was hot sweet tea, but what he wanted was alcohol to dull the pain, the purer the better. He had several bottles of Corona in his fridge but that wasn't strong enough for what he wanted. There was a bottle of Russian vodka in the icebox and he took it out, unscrewed the top and drank from it. He took three gulps before it began to burn his throat and he gasped.

He half filled a tumbler with vodka then popped the tab of a can of Coke and poured that in. He took the tumbler, the Coke can and the vodka bottle into his sitting room and put them on the table by the window. The Ouija board was still there, surrounded by the five candles.

He took a long drink of vodka and Coke and began pacing around the room. His mind was whirling and he found it impossible to concentrate. All he could think about was the knives going into Bella's eyes and the way her body had gone into convulsions when he'd thrust the final knife into her heart.

He wiped his forehead with his sleeve and then took another gulp of vodka and Coke. He wanted to get drunk, so drunk that he wouldn't remember what he'd done. His stomach lurched and he fought the urge to vomit.

He pulled his mobile phone from his raincoat pocket. He wanted to talk to somebody. Jenny maybe. Or Robbie. But what he could tell them? And if he told them the truth, what would they say? He tossed the phone onto the sofa, then took off his raincoat and draped it over the back of a chair. He drained his glass and grabbed the vodka bottle for a refill.

As he sloshed vodka into the glass he noticed movement on the Ouija board. He frowned and stared down at the planchette. It was vibrating. He shook his head, wondering if his eyes were playing tricks on him. But there was no doubt, the planchette was juddering. As he watched it began to move slowly across the board. Nightingale held his breath, the vodka bottle and glass forgotten. The planchette moved slowly but surely in a smooth motion until it reached the word GOODBYE. Then it stopped dead. Nightingale felt a cold breeze on the back of his neck and he shivered. "Goodbye, Bella," he whispered, then drained his glass in one.

CHAPTER
NINETY-FIVE

Nightingale came awake instantly from a dreamless sleep. He lay on his back, staring up at the ceiling, listening to the sound of his own breathing. He heard a police siren far off in the distance, but that wasn't what had woken him. Then he realised he wasn't alone in the room.

He sat up and peered into the dark corner furthest away from the window. Proserpine was standing there, her black and white collie at her side. She was wearing a long black leather coat that almost brushed the carpet and knee-length black boots with stiletto heels. Her hair was loose around her face and she had a fringe that almost covered her eyes. She glared at Nightingale malevolently. "You lied to me, Nightingale," she said, her voice a low rasping whisper.

"Not really," he said.

The dog growled menacingly and Proserpine jerked the chain to silence it. "I told you that you weren't to go near Fairchild."

"I didn't."

"I told you that you weren't to kill him."

"And I didn't."

There was a deep growling sound and Nightingale couldn't tell if it was her or the dog. "You think you can play games with me, Nightingale?"

Nightingale reached for his cigarettes and lit one before answering. "I think you choose your words carefully," he said. "And so did I. I didn't go near Fairchild. I didn't talk to him. And I didn't kill him."

"You had him killed," she said quietly.

"And that right there is why the choice of words is so darn important," he said. He tried to blow a smoke ring but failed miserably. "I had him killed. That's not the same as killing him. So all bets are off."

Proserpine glared at him. "You paid to have him killed, that's the same as killing him."

Nightingale shook his head. "I didn't pay a penny. In fact I didn't even ask for it to be done. I just talked to someone who hates nonces even more than I do."

"Perry Smith?"

"Gangster of this parish. He gave me the gun that I was carrying that night you stopped me. I gave him the gun back and he asked why. I told him that I couldn't kill Fairchild. Perry said that he'd do it in a heartbeat. His kid sister was abused when she was in a care home, so he's got personal reasons for hating paedophiles."

"You told Smith that Fairchild was a paedophile?"

"Which he was," said Nightingale. "I didn't tell him about the Order of Nine Angles, of course. Or the whole devil-worship thing. That would have muddied the water, I figured. But like I said, he offered to kill Fairchild and I didn't try to dissuade him. So it doesn't affect our deal and I get to keep my soul."

Proserpine and her dog stared at Nightingale for several seconds. "You think you've beaten me, do you?" she said eventually.

"I don't think there are any winners or losers in this," said Nightingale. "The whole thing is a mess. But Fairchild can rot in Hell for all I care."

"He'll be in Hell, but he won't be rotting," said Proserpine. "He has earned his place in Hades."

"Fine," said Nightingale. "I hope you'll all live happily ever after. Now can I get back to sleep, I've got a busy day ahead of me?"

"You're very sharp, Nightingale. You want to be careful you don't end up cutting yourself."

"I'll do that."

Her eyes narrowed. "You think you can trust Mrs Steadman, don't you?"

"I don't know who I can trust these days," he said.

"Well, don't say I didn't warn you," she said. She looked down at her dog and smiled. "Come on, let's go play catch." She jerked his chain and then the room folded in on itself and there was a deafening cracking sound and the smell of burned leather and she was gone. Nightingale stubbed out what was left of his cigarette and lay down. He stared up at the ceiling for the rest of the night, unable to sleep.

CHAPTER
NINETY-SIX

Nightingale was in the shower when his mobile rang. He wrapped a towel around himself and padded into the bedroom. It was Robbie. "Bloody hell, mate, the bodies are piling up."

"What do you mean?"

"Colin Stevenson has topped himself and Marcus Fairchild was killed yesterday."

Nightingale sat down on the bed. The roll of knives was on his dressing table. He looked at his watch. He was supposed to return them to Mrs Steadman before noon. "You're sure Stevenson killed himself?"

"Tablets and whisky and he left a note. He typed it, but as they found him dead on the keyboard they're pretty sure it was him."

"Bastard," said Nightingale. "I won't be shedding any tears over him."

"Yeah. According to what he wrote, he was just misunderstood. No one understands the love between a man and a child is the purest kind of love, all the crap that paedophiles spout to justify what they do. But there was some hard info in there. For a start, Stevenson says he was the one who got McBride to kill the kids."

"How did he manage that?"

"McBride's farmhouse is where a lot of the abuse took place, so McBride's life would be pretty much over however it went. But Stevenson threatened him, too, said that he'd kill McBride's nephews if he didn't do it. Stevenson says that McBride was talking about killing himself anyway once he knew that the cops were onto them. It just took a bit of manipulation to get him to shoot the kids first."

"How did they know the cops were on to them?"

"There's a leak in the Paedophile Unit. Stevenson got a call from a phone box not far from the unit's London base a few hours before he topped himself. They reckon the same mole tipped Stevenson off about the first investigation. All they had at the time was the name of one of the kids, but they were coming up to do interviews across the school. Stevenson and the rest figured if they could make it look like the kids had been killed by a lone disturbed gunman, the abuse investigation would die with it. And with the number of cops who seem to be involved, they might have been right. This goes right across the UK, Jack. It's bloody huge. And by the look of it, it's been going on for years."

"And what about Danny McBride? Did Stevenson say anything about that so-called suicide?"

"Nope. Like I said, most of it was rambling self-justification. And it wasn't helped by the fact that he'd washed the sleeping tablets down with a bottle of whisky."

"Yeah, well, like I said, good riddance to bad rubbish."

"And I'm assuming that sentiment goes for Marcus Fairchild too?"

"I couldn't possibly comment," said Nightingale, running a hand through his wet hair.

"It's been put down as a gangland killing," said Robbie.

"Yeah, well, there's a lot of that about."

"You don't mess about, do you, Jack?"

"He had it coming, Robbie. Let's just leave it at that, shall we?"

"Jack?"

"Yeah?"

"How did the Bella Harper thing go?"

Nightingale didn't say anything for a while. "What have you heard?" he asked eventually.

"There's a news clampdown until the press office gets its act together. SOCO are in the house as we speak. She's dead, right?"

"She died three weeks ago," said Nightingale flatly.

"Are you okay?"

"Not really," said Nightingale. "It wasn't pleasant."

"And what happened? When you did it?"

"It died. End of."

"And Bella died too?"

"I keep telling you, she was dead already. She died in that bath and she was never coming back, no matter what I did. Robbie, you need to forget about it. Seriously."

"I'm not sure that I can do that."

454

"Well, you're going to have to. I don't want to talk about it again. Ever."

"You are sure, right?"

"About what?"

"About the whole business. That whole Ouija board thing. Bella asking you to kill her. That was real, wasn't it?"

"It was real, Robbie. Now please, just forget about it. Like it never happened."

"I'll try, mate."

Nightingale ended the call and reached for his cigarettes. Forgetting what had happened was going to be a lot easier said than done.

CHAPTER
NINETY-SEVEN

Nightingale shivered as he walked into the church. Mrs Steadman was in the front pew, her head bent forward. As he sat down next to her he realised that her eyes were closed and her hands were clasped together in her lap. He sat with her in silence, looking up at the figure of Jesus in the stained-glass window. He'd smoked a cigarette in the alley outside the church but he already craved another. He tried to remember how many Marlboro he'd smoked during the night as he'd finished drinking the bottle of vodka. Ten? Twenty? He'd gone out just after midnight and bought two packs from an all-night supermarket in Queensway.

Mrs Steadman sat back and opened her eyes. "It is done," she said, and it sounded more like a statement than a question.

"Yes," he said.

"Thank you," she said.

"I'm not sure it's something that deserves to be thanked." He slid his hand into his raincoat pocket and pulled out the leather roll. He weighed it in his hand, then passed it to her.

"You did a good thing, Mr Nightingale. You saved a lot of lives."

Nightingale shivered again. "I need to know something, Mrs Steadman. When the Shade died, would Bella's soul still be around?"

"I'm not sure I understand you," she said. She slid the roll of knives into a shapeless black bag on the floor between her legs.

"I was in my flat, afterwards. There was an Ouija board on the table and the planchette moved. It went to GOODBYE. I wondered . . ." He shrugged, not wanting to finish the sentence. His head ached. It had been a long time since he'd suffered from a hangover, but then it had been a long time since he'd last demolished a whole bottle of vodka.

Mrs Steadman smiled and patted him on the arm. "She would be moving on from the Nowhen. She must have stopped by to let you know that everything was okay. You helped her, Mr Nightingale. And she would have been grateful for that."

Nightingale sighed. He ran a hand through his hair and stared at the altar. "I'm not sure that I can live with what I've done, Mrs Steadman."

"You did the right thing, Mr Nightingale."

"Even so." Nightingale shrugged.

"I might be able to help."

"Help?"

"I could make you forget. It would be as if it never happened."

"But it did happen."

Mrs Steadman nodded. "Yes, it did. And because it happened the world is a better place. But I can take away the memory."

457

Nightingale forced a smile. "You can do that?"

"I can do pretty much anything I want," she said. "Providing my motives are pure."

"And my friend Robbie. Robbie Hoyle. He's a detective. He knows what I did and he's a cop so it puts him in a very difficult position. And Jenny. I think it's best that she doesn't remember, either."

Mrs Steadman nodded. "I can do that, too. I can remove the memory of what happened for you and for your friends."

"Then I think I'd like you to do that," he said.

She tilted her head on one side. "It's done," she said.

"You're an angel, Mrs Steadman."

"So they say, Mr Nightingale. So they say."

ISIS publish a wide range of books in large print, from fiction to biography. Any suggestions for books you would like to see in large print or audio are always welcome. Please send to the Editorial Department at:

ISIS Publishing Limited
7 Centremead
Osney Mead
Oxford OX2 0ES

A full list of titles is available free of charge from:

Ulverscroft Large Print Books Limited

(UK)
The Green
Bradgate Road, Anstey
Leicester LE7 7FU
Tel: (0116) 236 4325

(Australia)
P.O. Box 314
St Leonards
NSW 1590
Tel: (02) 9436 2622

(USA)
P.O. Box 1230
West Seneca
N.Y. 14224-1230
Tel: (716) 674 4270

(Canada)
P.O. Box 80038
Burlington
Ontario L7L 6B1
Tel: (905) 637 8734

(New Zealand)
P.O. Box 456
Feilding
Tel: (06) 323 6828

Details of ISIS complete and unabridged audio books are also available from these offices. Alternatively, contact your local library for details of their collection of ISIS large print and unabridged audio books.